# JEFFREY WHITTAM

# SONS of AFRICA

COCOPAN

First published by Jeffrey Whittam as an eBook in 2011
ISBN: 978-0-9573665-0-3

This edition published by Cocopan Publishing in 2013
ISBN: 978-0-9573665-2-7

A CIP catalogue record for this book is available from
the British Library

Cover design by Pentacor Book Design, High Wycombe

Additional artwork by Lon Chan Design & Illustration,
Brighton

# Sons of Africa

Jeffrey Whittam was born in Lancashire, England in 1947. His formative years in Southern Rhodesia were spent fishing, hunting and exploring the wilderness. Still in his early twenties, Jeffrey became a prospector of note and sold his first gold claims in 1973. For the best part of the bush war, he fought with the Rhodesia Regiment's 10th Battalion. He now lives in the wilder reaches of Lancashire's fell country with his wife, children and three dogs. Sons of Africa is his first novel.

Available soon in paperback:

Empress Gold

*This book is for*

## VICTORIA

*She is the wind upon which I soar*

# I
# RHODESIA, 1978

Lee Goddard sprung the Land Rover door with his knee and stepped out into the sunlight. He scowled at the vehicle's broken wing mirror and recalled from memory just how easy it had once been to find a replacement before belligerent western superpowers had dropped their trade embargo across Rhodesia's borders. A tall Matabele sat in the passenger seat, his head turned for the latest broadcasted account of the country's armed forces run-in with ZANLA insurgents on the north-eastern border. Like his employer, he was still in his late twenties and when he adjusted the radio's volume the muscles of his upper forearm stood out black and hard as rope beneath his skin.

'You go on ahead,' he called to Lee. 'I'll catch up.'

Lee angled his way between parked cars and pick-up trucks. He took the Mines Office steps two at a time. At twenty nine, the first indelible lines were already set to the outer corners of his eyes. His hair was thick and black as a midnight sea – behind the smile lurked the deep indomitable mind of the risk-taker. He made straight for the Government Mining Engineer's open door and waded in with his query.

'So where's my funding, Peter? All four boreholes picked up payable reef at six hundred feet.'

'Values?' cut back Peter McKenzie. 'Average values and proven tonnage? You know the story, Lee.' McKenzie frowned over the top of his glasses. The department needed hard, mathematical certainties before parting with government funding – a full, factual collation of the exploration's viability.

As MD of the largest, privately owned gold mine in the Victoria province, decision making was solely Lee's responsibility. The bureaucratic value of company paperwork ran as a poor second to hands-on development of the Empress Deep's recently discovered basal reef. The thrill of mining new ore bodies lay for him in the exploration and bringing to surface that first skip load of precious gold-bearing ore, not in collating what he saw as nonsensical piles of printed dross for armies of bean counters to cluck over.

'The bank's assay department has had our latest core samples for almost six weeks.' His focus slid to a collection of old photographs on the wall behind McKenzie's desk. 'Our shaft-sinking crews are already two hundred feet below the last level. With or without the development grant, we cross-cut to pick up the reef two weeks from now.'

Most were of street scenes. First Street – where he had parked his company Land Rover, but as it was a hundred years ago, filled with adventure and the smells of unspoilt wilderness. Dirt roads, Kimberley brick and corrugated tin roofs, bearded men in calico breeches and sweated shirts. All of them portrayed that stoic countenance of early picture taking. Hardly a smile, just hooded eyes, gaunt cheeks, a few weather-worn bowler hats and scuffed boots. Metfords and Martini-Henry rifles leant against wagon wheels; and horses – lots of horses – standing lop-eared from the heat to the frontage of some seedy thatch-and-pole hotel veranda. 'Rogues, the lot of them,' Lee guessed, though found himself spellbound by the photographs.

McKenzie swivelled away from his paperwork. He singled out one of the pictures.

'Read the caption at the bottom.'

Lee stepped past McKenzie's desk. The writing was typically old fashioned and swept flamboyantly across the base of the photograph. He read aloud. 'Victoria's Wild West – entertaining stuff.'

Now it was Peter McKenzie's turn to smile.

'Must be a family quirk, your great-grandpappy wrote it. Fiery old buzzard, apparently. Never went anywhere without an American Colt six-shooter shoved inside his belt; wasn't afraid to use it either.' He pointed out another photograph. 'That's him on the right – leaning against the ten-stamp Sandycroft, a dollar in your pocket if you can work out who's standing next to him.'

Apart from Mathew Goddard, only one other man in the picture conveyed that same, resolute aura – stockily built, and though partly covered by shadows, his stare was that of the dominant lion, that commanding glare of the insatiable imperialist.

'Got to be Cecil Rhodes. Who's the man to the right of him?'

'Old man Morrish. Managed the Cotapaxi Mine, that's where the picture was taken. Tough guy to work for by all accounts, taught your great-grandfather most of the mining skills needed for his first crack at your Empress Deep.'

'And the black guy carrying the axe?'

'Mathew's right-hand man. Came up with him from Kimberley, where Mathew went the black guy followed. The story goes they were inseparable.'

Lee made a mental note to find out more. His grandmother had often touched on the subject though never in detail. Since the tragic death of his parents, only rarely had the Goddard family lineage been spoken about, mere whisperings across the dinner table.

'What happened to the Cotapaxi Mine?'

'The gold values dropped off, started to lose money so they shut her down. Office records suggest our Mister Rhodes showed more than a healthy interest in your Empress Deep.' McKenzie swung the conversation back to the present. 'How's your graduate mining engineer coming along?'

'Top man, wouldn't be doing without him.'

McKenzie fidgeted his paperwork into a neat pile. 'You could have employed a white man?'

'I could have,' said Lee, 'though choosing someone

merely because he's white didn't come into it. He got the job on merit. Best man for the job.'

'There's a war on,' McKenzie reminded, 'how can you trust him?'

'Why don't you ask him, yourself, he's standing behind you?'

Rex's eyes glittered. Like those of a crocodile watching its victim from just beneath the waterline.

'Perhaps, I should have used the servant's entrance, Mister McKenzie?' He held out his hand. 'Washed it this morning; black, but clean.' Rex purposely prolonged their handshake.

McKenzie's face coloured. He felt his fingers creak in the grip.

'Didn't know you were there.'

'Obviously not.'

'Rex, isn't it?'

'Rex Khumalo – at least that's what it says on my passport, though nowadays I'm not so sure that being black and from Matabeleland are attributes worth mentioning.' He let go of McKenzie's hand.

Annoyed by McKenzie's bigotry, Lee did his best to change the subject.

'Tell that beautiful daughter of yours I'll be over to pick her up for the weekend.'

McKenzie winced, he had given up on his daughter setting her sights more in favour of the academic; Karen had dug in her heels. He swung back to Rex.

'How long were you out of the country for?'

'Seven years. Did Europe after finishing 'varsity and followed on with a year in the Far East.'

McKenzie's eyes widened – suspicious and hawk-like behind his glasses. Rhodesia was at war and communism was the beast howling at her borders.

Rex picked up on McKenzie's political paranoia and gleefully fanned the flames.

'China, in particular. Great eye-opener; we could do well

6

to learn from their patriotism.'

'Time to move,' said Lee and herded Rex for the door. 'Promised my Gran we wouldn't be late – memory like a bull buffalo, not a good idea to keep her waiting.' He mustered a smile for McKenzie. 'I'll check with the bank and hurry them up with those assay results. Don't forget to tell Karen about the weekend.'

They left McKenzie in the doorway, massaging the ache from his crushed fingers. Lee watched him disappear from the Land Rover's mirror.

'You were bating him, Khumalo. Surprised he didn't get the police in to search your pockets for Chairman Mau's little red book.'

'The man's totally paranoid, had me earmarked for ethnic cleansing as soon as I walked through the door.'

They both laughed and with fading interest discarded Rex's run-in with McKenzie. Lee geared down and swung the Land Rover onto a gravel side road.

'My Gran's dying to see you again – gave strict instructions for me to bring you back to the homestead. Must warn you though, besides putting on lunch for us I suspect an ulterior motive so prepare to be mentally dissected, the old girl's still pretty relentless when it comes to wheedling out family gossip.'

-2-

Isabella Goddard took her expected place at the table's head. Cut from the mountainous slopes of the Chirinda forest, the dining table had been fashioned from raw, blood-red Teak, each piece a foot across and a full six inches in depth. The strength of two grown men would be needed to lift away any of its five separate, twenty foot lengths – invisibly butted together so that the table's top, hard as any iron glowed as a single, polished slab of ancient hardwood. For five weeks, Robert James Goddard had encamped at the forest's edge with a cart and span of eight, waiting for six Shangaan carpenters to cut and shape the seasoned timber ready for transportation.

'The finishing and polishing he did himself,' Bella recalled, and for a moment forgot that she wasn't alone at the table.

'Would that be soup for everyone, madam?'

'Yes. Yes, of course, Philip.' She looked around at the others. 'Am I right in saying so? And of course I will take a little wine with mine and the boys I should imagine would like a cold beer?' She waved her spoon at Lee. 'Sit next to me then I can see you properly.' She turned to Rex, affording him a warm smile as if he were part of her own family. 'And you, young man? Lee has been telling me all about your skills as a mining engineer. Would that be of similar work to that of a geologist or are the two totally different? I'm a little out of touch with what you have been up to.'

'A bit of both,' said Rex, but his concentration had been side-tracked. Bella's servant was obviously ill at ease with him being there. Bella picked up on Rex's agitation.

'Are you going to bring the soup, Philip? Or are our guests to be left in a permanent state of being without?'

'I am going, madam.' Philip dropped his eyes and like some disgruntled marabou stork, strode for the kitchen; as he passed the in front of the window, sunlight found the silver in his hair. With fond affection, Bella watched him trundle out of the room.

'Too damned old for the job, I suppose. Forgets where he is at times, but then again, so do I. Two of a kind, you might say.'

Her eyes, though small were fixingly bright like those of a northern rook – cut from that deep, ice blue of an arctic ocean. Through her abhorrence of midday heat, her skin had been generously spared the effects of ageing. Fair as that of an English rose though not pallid, slightly creased, but not indelibly scoured by those unforgiving claws of African sunlight. Her hair, the colour of ground steel was swept back from her forehead and fastened at her nape with a simple clasp of native gold and mother-of-pearl.

'There is so much that I have to tell you – so much to show you, but first you must eat and build up your strength.' Her voice was clear, vibrant, that of a younger woman.

The soup had been made from wild mushrooms, thickened with cream from the homestead's own small, but adequate dairy and finished with sprinklings of fresh herbs from Bella's kitchen garden, followed by grilled fillets of red-breasted *tilapia*. For the main course, Bella's home-trained chef brought out glistening racks of spring lamb, along with roast potatoes, peas, and carrots, complimented with emerald-green mint sauce freshly made that morning.

'Cheesecake? Coffee? Both if you like?' Bella suggested, but Lee and his guest shook their heads in unison.

'Not another crumb,' pleaded Lee, 'just coffee or I'll explode all over your carpet.'

'Likewise,' said Rex and clasped his hands over a burgeoning stomach.

Philip navigated his way round the table and filled their cups with dark, steaming coffee.

'Better in the living room, comfy chairs and more light,' decided Bella. She stood up from the table. 'Bring your coffee through. Cigars and matches on the mantle above the fire.'

'I suspect there is more to our being here than at first meets the eye, my darling grandmother?'

'Then you have suspected correctly,' Bella admitted. Her eyes twinkled from the success of her gathering in. 'Two birds with one stone, so to speak.' She went straight to the reason for them being there.

'There are certain things, happenings, call them what you

9

will, facts relevant to your lives that you have a right to know about.' She let their curiosity hang – then, like a startled bird, sprung back from behind her woolly veil of old age. 'How little or how much either of you know about your lineage has perhaps, until today been wildly speculative. I made a promise to your parents – on both your accounts. Promises that I intend to keep whilst I still have a reasonable grasp of what is real and what is not.'

She turned to Rex and gave the young Matabele her total attention.

'Part of what I tell you might well have been heard before so bear with me, young man. What you hear now are not just the ramblings of an old woman; at least not all of them.' She took a deep breath. 'Your surname, what does it mean to you?'

Rex shrugged his shoulders.

'Haven't bothered with it. Never thought of it as that important.'

Bella smiled, his disinterest had been expected. She struggled to rise and gestured to Lee.

'Help your Grandmother up from this blasted chair. There are things I have guarded for years and now have chance to be rid of.' She pointed to a door, rendered inconspicuous by its placement at the far corner of the room. 'The key if you would. Top shelf of my bookcase; left hand side, behind that ridiculous stone hippopotamus.'

Rex found it.

'Open the door, young man. The light switch is to the left as you walk in. Mind the dust and keep an eye out for resident creepy-crawlies.'

Rex pushed back the door and immediately the smell of stale air rolled over him. He found the light switch and from the far wall, a single incandescent lamp glowed dull yellow through its covering of dust.

'No windows?'

'Had them bricked up at the start of the war,' Bella explained. 'Just air vents; couldn't do with undesirables breaking in for a rummage.'

To Lee, the storeroom was a veritable treasure chest. The room in its entirety had been hung almost to its high ceiling with hunting trophies and vibrant paintings. A hundred other treasures had been arranged in orderly rows and draped with protective cotton sheets. A single, narrow strip of floor space had been left open for access to the room's furthest parts and it was along this that Bella urged the men in front of her.

'Halfway down, that tall, pointy thing on the right, take off the dust cover. There's a standard lamp underneath with a chord switch. Turn the damn thing on before I fall over something.'

Lee cast an appreciative eye over the contents of the storeroom. He would need weeks, not days to sift through it all. Rex pulled off the dust sheet and turned on the lamp.

'Better,' sounded Bella. 'Now at least we stand half a chance of seeing what's what in this dust hole, though I sometimes curse your grandfather for leaving me all this blasted family paraphernalia.'

She moved towards the light. 'Your father's roll-top desk,' said Bella. She found the recessed handle; pine slats rumbled away from a cubby of pigeon holes and inlaid leather. Each of the fine oak boxes and conjoining shelves were filled with used stationery. 'Your father was a stickler for an orderly existence, every written reference to the family heritage is here, all the way back to your great-great-grandparents' time in Kimberley.'

There were brown manila envelopes, packed in bundles and tied with ribbon or simple twine and all of them, to Lee, cried out to be opened.

'Most of them I have looked at,' said Bella, 'but be warned, some of the writing will tear out your heart – especially this one.'

Reverently, she touched just the tip of one finger to a faded calico wallet, as though afraid its contents might crumble and be lost to the four winds.

'Your great-great-grandfather's. You would be well advised to be alone when you open it.'

Bella steered them both towards the west wall. 'The ladder.' She pointed it out for Lee. 'Up you go, young man. Let's see what we have here.' She smiled at Rex. 'I hope you're ready for this?'

'As ready as I'll ever be,' said Rex and steeled himself for the unexpected.

Bella nodded her head at Lee and the dust sheet fell to the floor.

The portrait had been richly done in oils, copied from an early photographic likeness of a Matabele warrior barely into his prime.

'Guardian of the Royal bloodline,' Bella accredited. 'Without the man you are looking at, the chances are that you would not be here today.'

'The Mines Office.' Lee realised. He looked to Rex for an inkling of recognition. 'Damn it man, the picture on McKenzie's wall? Standing behind my great-grandfather – the guy with the axe?'

'Before I came in,' Rex countered. 'So who exactly is our mystery axe-wielder?'

It was thick with the colours of Africa, as a portrait laced with infinite detail it ranked highly amongst Bella's favourites. The Induna stood with both hands laid palm down to the haft of a great battleaxe. Behind him, a hundred times the mass of Saint Peter's Basilica's domed roof rose a gargantuan batholith of living rock. About the warrior's neck hung the claws of a bateleur eagle and those of a king leopard. His waist was tied about with tails of civet and blue monkey and at his ankles were the threaded rattles of war.

'A man who raised your father as his own,' said Bella. 'His name was Mhlangana, the king's favourite. Your father was the firstborn son of Thabisa, the king's youngest wife.'

Her focus shifted to Rex. 'By my reckoning, Rex Jando

Khumalo, that makes you a direct descendent of Lobengula, The Black Elephant, Shaker of Mountains your people called him. You are in fact the last link with the royal house of Khumalo, the only true voice of the Matabele.'

Rex, still mesmerised by the portrait shivered at the revelation.

'Not sure that I want to know all this.'

'Just keeping my promise,' said Bella.

Lee playfully exploited Rex's uneasy acceptance of royal lineage.

'So, your Highness, what does it feel like to have an empire at your feet?'

'A simple tugging of one's forelock will suffice. Though doubling your king's salary would be more appreciated.'

'In your wildest dreams,' Lee countered. 'Unearth your family fortune and then we'll talk about it.'

'If only it were true,' said Rex. 'All that stuff about Lobengula's treasure?' He shook his head. 'Pure fantasy, straight from a child's story book.'

'That's where you're wrong. The treasure's real enough. Finding where the old man hid it, that's the clever bit.'

Rex grinned at him. 'So you're a believer? How much is this treasure supposed to be worth?'

'You don't want to know. A one hundredth part of it would be enough to make your head spin.'

'How much?' Rex pushed him for an answer.

'In American dollars? About forty million, give or take a fortune or two.'

'You were right.' Rex whistled softly, 'that amount of money is just too much to get your head around, even for a king.' They followed Bella out of the storeroom

Lee tossed him the keys to the company's standby pick-up. 'Take the Mazda. I'll be staying over.'

'Your Gran's storeroom?' Rex smiled. 'Can't wait to get back in there?'

'My old man's desk.' Lee nodded. 'First inklings of

Matabele treasure maps and I'll give you a shout.'

He watched Rex out through the homestead's heavily meshed security gates before going back inside. Bella was seated at the dining room table, chasing a lemon pip from the rim of her second gin and tonic with her fingertip.

'Must be some sort of record or has that insatiable curiosity of yours sparked the urge for another rummage?'

'Your sense of humour, Gran is what keeps me here.'

'Liar.' Bella admonished, but could not disguise her delight at her grandson staying over. 'You'll be spending the night?'

Lee nodded his head; 'I'll kip down in your storeroom. Save old Philip from kitting out the guest room.'

'The guest room has been made up permanently since you and Karen were here at Christmas. Speaking of whom, I thought you two were off for a weekend's shenanigans?'

'Cancelled,' said Lee. 'Right now my cup runneth over with things important, the old Goddard curiosity has gotten the better of me.'

-3-

There would be rain that night, and until sleep overtook her, Bella watched armies of insidious black thunderheads march in close to the hills. The smell of wet earth and ironstone came down to her from the high ridge above the Empress Deep. Above the treeline, aircraft warning lights blinked as tiny eyes from the topmost part of the shaft head gear and if the breeze blew from the right direction, the clatter of iron tubs being wheeled into the shaft conveyance, or the sound of miners' ribald laughter would carry unhindered, all the way down to her open window.

Lee closed the storeroom door behind him, then quietly made his way to his father's roll-top desk and threw off the dust sheet. For hours he sat hunched over, sifting through letters, bullion transactions and sketches of the first proposed layout of the Empress Deep's vertical shaft and underground workings. Faded assay reports were read, entries scrutinised for similarities with present day production figures. Letters signed by Cecil Rhodes, Leander Starr Jameson and addressed personally to Lee's great-grandfather were carefully opened, their contents devoured and returned to where he had found them – then, no longer able to distance himself from that fateful moment, he drew out the bound calico wallet from its pigeon hole.

Yellow candle wax still adhered to the stitching. Lee hesitated; Bella's poignant warning still fresh in his mind. With unforced solemnity he untied the simple binding and held his breath.

The note had been hurriedly written – almost faded from the paper, compelling him to hold it closer to the lamplight. *December, 1893* had been scrawled as the letter's heading, then his eyes flooded and he was forced to set it down.

Thunder echoed through the homestead – on the red tin roof the rain drummed as impatient fingertips and for a long time, Lee listened to it. Only when his morbidity subsided totally did he dare to reach again for the scrap of folded paper.

There was a sad potency in the writing – given of a man lost to those final moments of his life on earth.

*My dearest Catherine. Your reading this will confirm Mathew's safe reaching of the Fort at Victoria. My thoughts are with you both. Be strong, my sweet. Wherever you go, my love and my memory will always be with you.*

*Yours for all eternity,*

*Nathan.*

A locket slid from the wallet, strung to a chain of fine gold and at its centre, a single half carat diamond winked from a bed of silver. Lee sprung the lid with his thumbnail.

Both halves were precisely fitted with tiny portraits, cut from old photographs – one of a man, his slouch hat set at a rakish angle, his jaw covered with the coal-black beard of the wild frontiersman. The other was that of a woman.

'You have to be Catherine.' Lee smiled, though the pain from what he had found still simmered just below the surface.

The living room clock chimed midnight just as he found the pocket book pushed to the back of a bottom drawer. A binding of blue ribbon stopped it from falling apart.

*

The phone rang for a full two minutes before Rex answered. 'It's one in the morning, or hadn't you noticed?'

'Something's come up,' said Lee. 'I need you to meet me at the mine first thing tomorrow morning.'

'Tomorrow's Saturday?'

'So I'll owe you. Take a couple of days in lieu.'

'What's wrong with Monday?'

'No good,' Lee countered. 'I need access to the upper levels. Humour me or I'll put you to work with McKenzie at the Mines Office.'

'What time?'

'Six would be good.' He heard Rex grumble into the mouthpiece. 'I'll throw in dinner and free beer so bring a change of clothes.'

He replaced the phone. Six o'clock would be perfect, the last of Friday's night shift would be clocking out for the weekend. He buttoned the pocket book inside his shirt pocket and closed his father's desk before leaving the storeroom.

16

Rex waited for Lee at the shaft collar. Behind him, like a serpent from its lair beneath the ground, a non-spin steel rope, thick as a girl's wrist hissed at almost eight metres per second for its sheave wheel spinning high above in the shaft headgear. The powerful winding engine growled to 'creep speed' and within that same minute, a steel conveyance, large enough to carry a load of thirty men edged its lower sill in line with the surface bank. Shaft signal bells crashed out twice and the banksman freed up the conveyance's heavy roller door. Men poured out – thankful of the natural light.

Rex moved to one side and while Lee parked up beside the head gear, watched the final throng of nightshift miners make their way to the change house shower rooms. The sky was a mantle of blue and lemon-yellow.

'Beginning to think you had stayed in bed.' Rex smiled at his employer and signalled to the banksman to hold the cage on surface. Lee hooked his lamp battery to the metal tangs on his belt.

'Couple of hours at the most and we'll be out of here.' He gave instructions to the shaft onsetter. 'Take us down to 267 Level. Anyone else still underground?'

'Just maintenance crews on the incline hoist on 690.' The managing director's choice of levels perturbed him. 'If you don't mind me asking, Mister Goddard – why the *madala-side*?'

Lee smiled at the onsetter's jargon. *Madala-side* was the Shona colloquialism for 'old workings'. Haphazard mining techniques had been used to strip out gold-bearing reef from the uppermost levels, some had already collapsed. Others left as cavernous stopes, abandoned to a world of permanent darkness and miners' superstitions.

'Routine inspection,' he lied. 'If we're not back at the main shaft in a couple of hours, call out the cavalry.'

Lighting on the uppermost level was limited to the station's immediate area. Fifty metres from the shaft gates there was total darkness. Lee unfolded a layout of the old workings and with his cap lamp, lit up the drawing.

'We're here – on the east haulage. Another hundred yards or so and there should be a short cross-cut.' He turned his lamp to the front. Narrow gauge cocopan rails snaked away beneath a fifty year covering of dust.

'Where exactly are we going?' asked Rex.

'I found this,' said Lee and reached inside his overalls for the pocket book. 'Shoved to the back of a drawer in my old man's desk.'

Rex flicked through several ruined pages – all of them water stained, the text scribbled, almost unreadable.

'You've lost me. What am I looking for?'

'Turn to the back.'

Rex went straight to the last page. 'Weird drawings and something about ancient workings?'

'Spent half the night deciphering my great-grandfather's handwriting. Somewhere on this level the old man walled up the entrance to an old stope.'

Rex's eyes glittered. 'Lobengula's treasure?'

'You wish,' Lee countered. They carried on walking, then, as a black hole, the cross-cut they were looking for opened up in the sidewall.

Both men stood at the cross-cut entrance; silently they contemplated the foolhardiness of exploring the Empress Deep's abandoned workings.

'There could be gas?' Rex warned.

Deadly pockets of poisoned air often hung undetected in old workings. A few minutes breathing in oxygen-robbing methane and carbon monoxide was all it would take.

Lee shook his head. 'The air's clean I can feel the ventilation.'

Rex turned his lamp on the hanging wall – a roof of

living rock, barely a metre above his head.

'I pray the roof's still good. Being buried alive is pretty much near the bottom of my Christmas list.'

The dark swallowed them. Grey dust shrouded the floor and sidewalls. Total quiet enveloped the lamplight – compressed to a solid world of silence by a million tons of hanging rock. Rex touched Lee's shoulder. Both lamps focused on a waist-high breach in the rock where the cross-cut ended.

'Don't like the look of it,' said Rex. Superstition breathed inside his collar. 'I have bad feelings about going in there.'

Lee felt his own concerns rise up at him. There were no records of anyone having set foot inside the Deep's abandoned workings. For all he knew, the entire stope could be ready to cave in.

'The first signs of bad ground and we're out of there.' He crouched at the entrance, like a young boy contemptuous of his father's advice he disappeared inside the stope.

'Come on through.' He signalled to Rex with his cap lamp. 'It opens on to a tipping platform for the old ore pass.'

Reluctantly, Rex clipped his lamp to his hard hat and dipped inside the entrance. Within seconds he was through. A six-foot diameter hole yawned at him from the gully footwall, partially covered by a steel grizzly – old tramming rails, cut and welded together as boxed sections to limit the size of rock being tipped inside the ore pass.

'Two hundred metres straight down to the first draw point,' said Lee. 'Fall in there and they'll have to scrape you off the floor with a teaspoon.'

Lee skirted the ore pass and went at the gully's upward gradient. Again the passage narrowed, enough to almost bar the way ahead. He stopped, mid-stride.

'Can you hear that?'

'Leaking air line?'

Lee shook his head. 'Don't ask me how, but the ventilation fans are pulling in air from a dead end.' He turned his lamp on the wall. Crack lines showed through a barricade of old brick – some were wide enough to take the thickness of his little finger. Lee held the palm of his hand to the structure. 'Coming through breaks in the brickwork.' He gauged the wall's extent with the beam from his lamp. 'Got to be fifteen, maybe twenty metres of walling. Wait here for me.'

He was back within minutes, laden with abandoned barring tools. A rock breaker's fourteen-pound sledge hammer and six-foot, steel pinch bar.

'Miners always stash heavy gear close to their workplace.'

Rex took up the sledge hammer.

'Stand upwind of me. Give me some room.'

At first the blows were tentative and exploratory, then, engaging the full weight of his shoulders, Rex sent fragments of brick spinning through the lamplight. Dust came off as grey sheets and billowed ghostlike for the ore pass.

'It's starting to give!' Lee went at the cracks with his pinch bar. Steel bit through brick and old mortar. He made room for Rex and together they threw their combined weight at the lever.

The bar flexed – like a bow, bent by the full draw of a powerful archer. Without warning, a wide portion of the wall came away from the rock. Half as tall again as the men alongside it, wide enough for half a dozen more to pass through walking shoulder to shoulder. Like some hidden door the man-made wall swung outwards and crashed to the gulley floor.

Both men stood in silence, upwind of the dust cloud. Powerful ventilation fans drew the airborne debris away. Where once had stood a wall of Kimberley brick, now there gaped a black and infinite emptiness.

'I take it all back,' said Rex, 'if the national antiquities people get wind of this they'll be all over the Empress Deep like starving rats on a cheesecake.' He illuminated the highest part of the cavern's roof. Roots from mountain acacia and strangler fig hung like matted ropes, some to the cavern floor.

Lee followed his lead and swept the hanging with his lamp.

'The reef must have been rotten with gold, or they wouldn't have risked getting up there.'

Holes had been bored in the ironstone sidewall.

'More than likely to support some kind of rudimentary scaffolding,' Rex hazarded. Crude, overhead stoping methods had taken out most of the upper pay shoot. 'We can't be more than a hundred feet from surface.'

Lee traced the reef with his lamp and where it dipped towards the cavern floor the abandoned workings still showed signs of adze scrapes and fire soot.

Rex lowered his lamp for the opposite wall. The opening to a horizontal shaft had been blocked by a fall of ground.

'That would have been their way in.'

There was the musty smell of rotting detritus and from fissures in the hanging, the damp of that last night's storm. But the smells of some long-gone time were more apparent, insidiously real – those of a thousand fires forced to unholy temperatures by the incessant rush and hiss of ancient bellows. Dust, fine as talc, had in places drifted inches deep to the sidewalls. Overall, the workings stank of man's fear – of being trapped beneath the earth, of pain manifested by heat and steam from the quenching fires and wherein the deepest parts of miners' lungs, quartz dust, barbed and razor sharp had been quick to take a hold. Almost a thousand years had passed since those last pieces of rich ore were roasted free of the reef, but to Rex, that infinite span of time seemed little more than just a single day. Where his arm had brushed against the sidewall, now the ironstone glowed with living colour. Through its covering of dust an iconic window had opened up to another time.

'Take a look at this,' Rex whispered. For long minutes, both men stared in awe of what Rex had uncovered. Both

21

were held enraptured by a sudden profusion of artwork.

With each fresh sweep of Rex's hand, more of the ancient splendour was stripped of dust – given life by the lamplight. Countless brush strokes, greens and vivid blues refined of Malachite and Azurite – ores of natural copper. For their blends of yellow and burnt sienna, the ancient artists had searched out oxides of raw iron, decomposing limonite, leached as tawny rust-like powders from weathered breaks in the ironstone.

'First thing Monday morning,' said Lee, 'get a crew inside the stope gully and have them re-seal the entrance. Put a steel door in the wall and bring me the key.'

Rex went on with clearing dust from the sidewall. Only after the entire frieze had been laid bare did he stop working.

The raw stone was covered with ancient artworks. Not the stick-like re-enactments of the Bushman's hunt, portrayed in basic reds and charcoals; these were vibrant and realistic – the colours skilfully intermingled, lapped one upon the other where the artist demanded subtlety of shadow or that deep vermilion light for the windward edge of his storm sky.

Ranks of warrior tribesmen, some black as fire-setters' charcoal were poised to overrun the stone ramparts of an ancient city. Rex imagined the chaos – the slaughter and the screams of hundreds, slashed, crushed and disembowelled. He touched the stone canvas, his fingers inexplicably drawn to it. Like the chapters of a book, scene by scene and with horrific splendour the ancient mysteries surrounding the ruined city of Zimbabwe were revealed to him.

'Too much to take in,' Rex whispered. 'Too much detail.' His eyes skittered, unable to settle. It would take a dozen top archaeologists weeks to decipher it all.

With the beam of his lamp still focused directly on the final part of the frieze, Lee reached inside his overalls for his trouser pocket.

'Something else I found in the old man's desk.'

The talisman was no bigger than Rex's little finger, though the weight and colour of it left him without any doubts as to its origin. He turned it over in the lamplight – part bird, part reptile; sculpted from solid gold – a stylised avatar. Its sightless eyes stared up at him.

-5-

Four men dressed in denim jeans and camo shirts looked down from the hillside. Other than Kalashnikov rifles and small, military style haversacks they carried little else. Below them, the homestead security gate opened momentarily and a shadow-like figure slipped unseen into the forest. By the time Philip reached the pre-arranged rendezvous, his lungs burned with fatigue.

'Why do you hide like baboons so high up on the mountain? The climb will be the death of me.'

'And you may well get your wish, comrade.'

Philip dismissed the remark. The youth's threat disturbed him little more than the bite of a blanket louse. A high African sun brought out sweat from his forehead.

'He will be there until tomorrow morning. I will leave the gates unlocked.' He looked directly at the cadre leader. 'On your father's memory, no one will be harmed. Nothing will be taken or destroyed.'

'You have my word, old man. No one will be harmed.'

## 6

Philip had laid the table with a covering of fine white linen. Vibrant Stuart Crystal showed off servings of Sauvignon Blanc from the Cape Winelands. The setting was brought to life by sterling silver candelabra, filling the room with glittering points of shattered candlelight.

Karen McKenzie stared across the table at the man she had fallen in love with, glad that she had driven out unannounced to the homestead. Sometimes, Lee's antics in front of guests could appear boyish and unforgivably asinine – conversely, he was the most loving person she had ever met. Their first meeting came spinning back to her; standing at the edge of a deep and verdant valley, her life until that moment had been totally immersed in the ruined city of Zimbabwe where she worked as first assistant to a doctor of archaeology from the University of the Witwatersrand in South Africa. Lee had made some ribald comment about her choice of trenching locations. After that, several arguments and a reparatory dinner at the Great Zimbabwe Ruins hotel they had become inseparable.

As though he had sensed her mood, Lee stood up from his chair and raised his glass. He waited for the chatter to ease then swung the conversation in Karen's favour.

'I give you the girl of my dreams, my incredible, unselfish, uncomplaining companion. Besides being first lady of my life, Karen McKenzie, ladies and gentlemen, is now a fully qualified Doctor of Archaeology.' Karen openly blushed. 'A fossicker of all things ancient, which would of course account for her fortuitous finding of yours truly.'

'Wonderful news!' piped Bella. 'Will you be continuing your work at the ruins or moving on to greater things?'

'I'll be staying on,' Karen admitted. 'The Department of Antiquities will be funding the project. They want me to open up the hill fortress and part of the inner temple.'

From diagonally opposite, Rex Khumalo screwed up his eyes at Lee, urging him to disclose their find.

Lee reached inside his trouser pocket.

'If that is the case, my darling official fossicker of ancient ruins, then you may well find this an interesting start to your career.' He laid the gold talisman in front of her. The yellow metal drew soul from the candlelight.

Nothing of such exquisite beauty had yet been recovered from the ruins of Great Zimbabwe, nothing she had ever seen could compare with this precious artefact – a casting of pure sunlight.

'Pick it up,' Lee encouraged, 'it won't bite you.' But Karen hesitated, seemingly intimidated by the stylised golden creature that lay before her.

'It's almost too beautiful to touch, there's something spooky about it.'

Tentatively, she held it at eye level, surrounded it with candlelight. From memory, she compared the metal raptor to its larger, stone replicas housed inside the museum at Great Zimbabwe. The same cruel eyes stared back at her and below them, the raptor's beak curved to its chest, a wicked scimitar of almost pure gold. The wings, though folded back seemed tensed for flight and with golden talons it clutched to a perch of that same precious metal – alert as a living eagle, ready to spring for the eyes of those now gazing down upon it.

'Where did you find it?'

'Truthfully? In my father's desk,' Lee admitted, and then looked to his grandmother for her to pick up the thread.

'It belonged to Lee's great-grandfather,' said Bella. 'Quite the man for collecting all things unusual, my own darling mother-in-law being one of them – Elizabeth Anne.' Bella went off at a wistful tangent. 'She was quite something – someone out of the ordinary.' She paused for a sip of wine. 'Mathew's first sighting of his bride-to-be was from outside the old hotel on First Street. Doel Zeederberg was bringing his coach in.' As recounted by her father-in-law, she poured out recollections of that fateful day; the artefact in Karen's hand already forgotten. 'The driver with his hat curled back from the wind; the crack of his whip. Elizabeth was leaning out of the window – that's when he saw her. Hair streaming... *the colour of a midnight sea ripping the tide off Cape Agulhas* is how he described her. I shall never forget it.'

Again, Karen found herself staring at Lee. The old woman's memories had stirred the romance in her, to the point of imagining herself alighting from that same, Western style Zeederberg stagecoach.

Bella leant over and touched her shoulder, 'You're good for him, you know. Lee needs the stability of someone like yourself – keeps his feet on the ground or he'll be up to all sorts of fanciful things.' She waved her empty glass at Philip. 'A lot like his grandfather, I'm afraid. Has to be something brimming with excitement to hold his interest.'

Philip came back with a second bottle, his usual attentiveness not there. As before, Rex picked up on the old man's restless mood and commented lightly. He spoke Ndebele, the language of the Matabele people, and softly enough for others not to hear him.

'You seem troubled, old man?'

'Perhaps you are mistaken,' Philip countered. He hovered to Rex's right elbow. 'Should I fill your glass? I have much to do in the kitchen.'

Outside, the driveway security gates had been left unlocked. The moon, already above the trees gave light to secret pathways through the forest. A breeze came in from an open veranda door, forcing a shiver from Karen when it brushed across her shoulders.

Philip sensed that same, slight ingress of cool air; in with it was the smell of feral, human odour and wood smoke. His hands trembled and he was forced to set the bottle down. As the strange incantations of some tribal seer, Philip's voice rose up spirit-like from his throat.

'Thousands will perish at the hand of their own kind and the kings of all nations will not take up the spear against them – not until the descendants of Lobengula and the Rozwi empire are united and rise up as single nation!'

'What in God's name are you babbling on about, Philip?' Bella put down her glass. 'Someone help him back to the kitchen. The old fool's been at the brandy again.'

Rex felt an almost irrepressible urge to protect himself. From the corner of his eye he picked up on the silhouette of a man crossing from the patio doors of Bella's sitting room. Within seconds, four heavily armed insurgents were inside the dining room.

'Stay seated!' Philip warned. 'Or they will kill us all.' He turned to the cadre leader and met his eyes unflinchingly. 'You gave your word.'

Rex swung round in his chair. 'You let them in – what in God's name for?'

'Had I refused, by now we would all be dead and this room would be our pyre.'

'Get out!' Bella stood up from her chair. Her disgust was immediate, it writhed in her stomach. Now she turned to the local dialect of the Karanga people to emphasize that revulsion. With the eyes of a leopard she glared at the cadre leader.

'You are nothing but killers and thieves. Like dogs you stand at the white man's table with big eyes and empty bellies. You are nothing but jackal, *hungubwe*, unable to hunt your own food.'

She turned her anger on Philip and her frail body seemed as though it might implode from the violence of her tirade. There was no fear in her eyes for what was happening, only bitterness.

'I gave your family all that it ever needed, and this is how you repay me? Your son's schooling, his university and all the damned extras that went with it.' She looked at Rex. 'Yes,' she added, 'I paid for every book, lesson, tutor and God knows what else you needed for your education; ever

27

since you were old enough to hold a pencil.' She slumped back into her chair and swung her gaze back to Philip. 'Or more's the truth, old enough to hold a gun.'

The cadre leader stood over her, his breath a rank curtain enveloping her face – the barrel of his Kalashnikov hard against Bella's cheek.

'Were it not for him, old woman, I would already have cut out your tongue.'

Bella pushed the rifle away, her stare defiant – ice cold in the candlelight.

'Were I a man, comrade. You would already be dead. Is this what it means to free a country of its colonists? Destroy everything your kind fails so miserably to create?'

He lifted a succulent slice of roast chicken from Bella's plate and sucked the sliver of white flesh from between his fingers. His attention swung to Lee. He had sensed the white man's aggravation.

'Your rifle hangs by the door, Captain Goddard. Trying to reach it will bring only death. I suggest you let it alone.' He saw the look of surprise on Lee's face. 'There is little about you that I do not know Captain. You are a soldier with Smith's colonial army. Many were the times that I could have killed you.' He turned to Karen, encompassing the back of her neck between his thumb and forefinger. 'I could have killed you both.' He looked at his men, inviting them with a sly narrowing of his eyes. 'Perhaps I will let my comrades have your woman. It might well prove interesting.' He relaxed his grip on Karen, 'but that is not what we came for.'

Like a lion to its prey he turned to Rex. 'We came for you my friend. *Pamba*! We march!' he ordered his men. 'Take what food you can carry and then we leave.'

## 7

For the first mile they moved quickly th
eastwards along a network of ancient
trails. The path the cadre had chosen sto
arterial line in the moonlight, linking forest to forest,
grassland to valleys, striking for the heart of what was now
a lost and ruined empire.

'The old man tires, Comrade Commissar – he will not
last the hour.'

They halted in deep shadow. Like a bird beaten to
ground by storm winds, Philip lay on his side, totally
exhausted. The old man's breathing was shallow and
laboured.

'In God's name,' whispered Rex, 'Why did you do this?
Why, my father?'

With desperate fingers Philip clutched at the centre of his
sternum, for now the pain was a spiteful living beast inside
his chest.

'Listen to them, my son – do what they ask of you.' He
opened his hand to the moonlight. 'Take it, keep the bird
with you.' Rex took up the ancient talisman. In the
moonlight, the metal shone as bright silver. 'The eyes of
the people are upon you. Go with them. Leave me where I
lie, my son, my life is over.'

'I will not leave you.' In a final act of desperation, Rex
lifted his father's sparrow-like form from the ground.
'March!' he shouted along the line of men. 'We are ready
to go on.'

But as a moth would fly from an opened window, already
the life had flown from the old man's heart.

*

Rex searched out a natural cleft in the granite; with only
moonlight to guide him he interred his father's corpse. He

e grave with rocks to ward off scavengers, for
ly they would have picked the scent of death from the
eeze. Words stuck fast in his throat, but now was not the
time. The others were restless. To them, death was merely
a brief happening – a small matter.

'*Mhanyisa*!' The cadre leader urged them forwards. He
took the rifle from the man behind him and thrust the
weapon at Rex. 'Make your choice, comrade. Take the
lead. Keep the moon to your left shoulder and the pace
steady.' He sensed the rising up of Rex's anger. 'Heed your
father's words, Khumalo – believe in the people's struggle
for freedom or die where you stand.'

Briefly, Rex held back – then, for reasons he did not fully
understand he took the weapon and started into the night.
The men who ran behind him were veterans, committed to
the armed struggle. With each new stride his own
commitment grew, for the first time in his life the
unremitting heartbeat of Africa ran with its hand on his
shoulder, as though his father's death had proved the
catalyst and because of it his own life was changing. The
Kalashnikov rifle instilled in him an almost mystical
strength, for like the rhino and the bull buffalo, now he
carried with him the heavy curse of terrible weaponry.

For what seemed an eternity, Rex led the cadre steadily
south-eastwards, then through a break in the forest a single
pinprick of tungsten light stopped him dead and he
beckoned to the cadre leader.

'Perimeter fence lights?'

'What we want lies beyond them. We will have to move
further away to the east or their security people will hear
us. I will take the lead from here, comrade. You have done
well.'

He took them in a wide arc and far enough for their
movements not to be detected by military reservists
manning the security fence. Then Rex caught sight of The
Great Zimbabwe's ruined enclosure, ghostly grey in the
moonlight.

For hundreds of years the great walls had stood all-powerful, a stone bastion until the ancient city's final overrunning by ravaging Bantu hordes from the north. The temple wall was twelve feet thick at its base, high enough to take the reach of five men stood one upon the shoulders of the other. The elliptical sweep of its circumference was large enough to encompass an army of five hundred. The ruined enclave still exuded that sinister atmosphere of some lost and ancient empire, so that when Rex passed close to its walls he walked with his finger curled inside the trigger guard.

He was made to stand in the leeward shadow of a small hill and where moonlight drenched the hillside, he made out more of those same stone walls perched precariously on granite overhangs. Dark eyelets, open passageways stared down at him, linked together with hidden walls of the hilltop fortress. An owl called out from the trees. He saw it take to the air – a momentary glimpse of outstretched silver wings and then it was gone.

'Come with me.' A hand touched his shoulder and guided him further along the granite face. 'Tread carefully. If you fall, there will be no way of reaching you.'

He was led beneath the earth; the last, faint glimmer of moonlight disappeared.

'Prepare yourself. On your life, do not use your rifle. What you see will be beyond your understanding, but no harm will come to you, Rex Khumalo.'

Alone in total darkness, a faint orb of wavering light rose up to him from deep in the hillside, then movement, as dry leaves over a wooden porch.

'I see you, Rex Khumalo.'

It was not the voice of the man who had led him there. This was stricken with age, emanating from lungs that were filled with viscid fluid from the breathing in of foul air. Rex waited for the wraithlike figure to materialise in front of him; when the creature turned about in the narrow passageway the full horror of the harridan's

31

affliction flung him back against the sidewall.

About her shrivelled waist was tied a simple belt of leather. Hung from it, on sinew stripped from the limbs of the Vervet monkey were the sickening tools of her wizardry: slivered body parts, bone and teeth from venomous forest vipers, charms and ancient powders searched from a hundred secret places. Ashen body hair stood out from the juncture of her legs, the skin about her groin and upper thighs transparent enough for Rex to see the veins and arteries that for more than a hundred years had kept her living. Above the darkened pits that were her eyes, verminous colonies scurried to hide from the lamplight.

'Follow me, Rex Khumalo, there are many things for you to see.' Without warning she raised her lamp to the granite sidewall. 'Behold the mothers of Kagubi and Muroyiwa, the bewitched ones, messengers from beyond the wall of death. Eaters of genitals and lovers to dogs.' Like steel on glass her voice keened inside his head; her eyes glittered and threads of silver spittle drooled from her lower lip. Rex suppressed a sudden urge to dash out her brains on the sidewall.

'Touch them, Rex Khumalo – touch the ancient guardians of this fallen city of stone.'

Ghostly insects skittered inside his shirt. Alcoves had been fashioned into the living granite, the grisly remains of what once were living beings were held in place by hand-forged iron pegs. Dry air and the skilful hands of their embalmer had held off putrefaction – the victims' jaws set in that final grinning rictus of an agonising death.

'And my own child...' Perverse pleasure thickened her voice, willing him to gaze upon the handiwork. Shrouded in swirling dust she appeared wraithlike and seemed to float above the ground. 'My own mother drew off the child's blood and stuffed its belly with balm to hold off the maggots.'

Rex's eyes bulged in their sockets. He felt trapped by the

ancient rituals and superstitions of his own race. The harridan's strength of mind held his feet to the earth.

'How did the child die?'

'From the bite of the *mubobo*, the black mamba,' she told him, her voice sibilant. With a skeletal hand she reached out and caressed the tiny, shrivelled neck. Then her lips parted and for a brief moment Rex caught the reptilian flick of her tongue. 'Here, where the child's blood was hot and close to the heart.'

The powerful neurotoxins in the snake's venom had caused the child's spine to arch backwards. The head had been drawn with it, forcing the mouth wide open. Rex turned away and fought to hold his voice steady.

'What of these things, old woman? Why do you show them to me?'

Mutiswa held the lamp to his face.

'As this flame takes life from the oil on which it feeds, so will the sons and daughters of the new order take life from the strength they find in you, Rex Khumalo.' Her eyes narrowed. For a hundred years, this was the moment she had lived for – the resurrection of a people whose voice once held sway over an entire land. Again the bull bellow of the Matabele would be heard above the whine of their Shona underlings.

'Was it not the power of the past that brought you here?' Again, she shuffled forwards and raised the lamp to the sidewall.

'Behold the magic that has brought your bloodline back to its rightful place beneath Zimbabwe. Do not hide from your destiny, Rex Khumalo – you are both the destroyer and the father of our nation.'

'Another child.' His voice was heavy with revulsion. 'Killing you now would not rob me of a single minute's sleep, old woman.'

Mutiswa reached out for the corpse, touching, prodding, testing the softer parts with her fingertips.

'The balm is not yet at its best, only when it hardens will

33

the pup be safe from the fly. Come, son of Mashobane, we must hurry. The ghosts of your ancestors grow tired of waiting.'

Rex watched her move from light to dark, so frail were the old woman's limbs that they hardly cast a shadow; roach-like and bent at the waist, Mutiswa shuffled forwards, more akin to a wild animal than any human being. The passage opened – changed to some dark and limitless void, the lamplight now too weak to reach beyond.

'What is this place, old woman? What good has this done, bringing me to this stinking pit beneath the ground?'

Mutiswa turned to face him. Now the light, held close to her hairless skull, showed the full horrors of her afflictions. Dark ophthalmic holes leered up at him and the advanced malignant cells of a deep and virulent melanoma clung to the ruined stump of her nose. In the living light, the canker appeared to Rex as some grotesque and separate beast upon her face, so that he reeled from the horror of it and almost lost his footing.

'You have something for me, Rex Khumalo!' Her mouth twitched just inches from his. 'That which for a thousand years lay buried beneath this ancient city.'

Rex fought back the urge to strike out at the creature in front of him.

'You talk of things you have not seen, old woman.'

'But you have it! I smell the bird of destiny upon your person – my own life is almost spent, Rex Khumalo.' Her face hovered, her eyes hawk-like, fixed to his breast pocket. 'Give me the talisman, that you might glimpse what has been and that which now awaits you!'

Rex drew out the gold effigy – even in that weak light it was still a thing of immense beauty; almost deep red, it glowed the colour of spilled blood.

Mutiswa reached out for it, her hand the trembling waxen foot of a dying bird. For a brief moment she paused just inches from it as if the living metal might turn her

34

fingers to fire. Her mind flew back through the years and once again she saw herself as a young girl – in front of her, the white men who had defiled her and those who had saved her life – as though both good and evil had just that moment stepped out from the dark.

'Take it.' Rex thrust the bird between her fingers.

'Be not afraid, Rex Khumalo. You will live to stand as king of all kings. The spirit of all that has gone before is here amongst us, but to others who spurn your coming there will be famine and great sorrow. The death of thousands will be visited upon those who rule before you and the kings of other nations will turn their eyes away. Though they weep for the dead, none will take up the spear – not until you stand at the head of all our people.' Her eyes were glazed for she was seeing things that to ordinary beings could only exist as fanciful dreams. The drum of iron spears to ox-hide shields, the clattering of modern gunfire, a thousand men lying dead in the rain.

As though trapped by a snow wind, Rex felt the chill of superstition sweep over him. Vast armies of Matabele manifested themselves in the darkness of the cavern, so close and real that he was tempted to call out. Their spears were raised as though in salutation and the soulful stare of a thousand empty eyes were turned towards him.

'You see them!' Mutiswa shrieked. 'You have seen what has gone before, Rex Khumalo!' She grasped his hand and with her withered claw-like fingers led him deeper into the cavern. Rex, as the compliant child followed her, mimicking her shuffling gait, unable to resist.

'Now you shall see that which is yet to come,' she keened, and again raised the lamp to the granite wall at the furthest side of the cavern. 'Behold the birth of a kingdom!'

Rex stared up at the mural and was instantly transfixed by the splendour of the artwork. That same feeling of déjà vu he had experienced with Lee inside the ancient mine workings now came over him. From the style and sweep of the brushwork, undoubtedly, both murals were common to the hand of that same master craftsman.

The final section depicted two opposing armies. One lighter skinned, defending the walls of Zimbabwe; their aggressors, black as fire soot were shown to be overrunning the ancient city's stone parapets. Armed with spears and gnarled battle clubs, to those who stood in their way death was swiftly meted out. Women were slit from the throat to the juncture of their legs – their unborn children torn from the womb and flung from the walls to hoards of devilish carnivores. It was the final cleansing of a land – the destruction of an empire that had ruled ancient Ophir for more than half a millennium and was of that moment being wiped from the face of the earth.

Mutiswa reached out and touched the wall.

'Look carefully upon what has been set for you to find, Rex Khumalo. Through the eyes of one who would lead, not as a servant of those who brought their armies from across the great sea. Not as an underling of one who already stands in the wings and will for a time, through his own failings, bring this land to its knees.'

The stylised figure of a dark-skinned warrior stood more than a foot in height, his upper body clad with the full pelt of a male leopard and upon his head had been placed a crown of snow-white feathers plucked from the tail of a wild ostrich. Set amongst them were those of the blue heron, a show of his high standing. Across his back hung the six-foot span of a giant war bow, one that only a king amongst men might find the strength to draw. With both arms outstretched he held aloft a cast raptor of pure gold – many times larger, though in detail perfectly matched to the one in Mutiswa's hand. With that same terrible countenance it gave impetus to the invading army.

In Rex's mind, doors were flung open. The battle raged within yards of where he was standing. Through the dust the cacophony rose up to him; the sound of steel on steel, the cry and screams of those mortally wounded, the rumble of falling granite blocks and the flute of a thousand arrows.

'Now you must believe, Rex Khumalo. What was won and lost to the white invaders will soon be retaken. Not with the spear or the club, but through the words of a new leader and the barrel of a gun.'

For a moment, Rex saw the slightest of smiles on the harridan's lips, but before he could speak, Mutiswa stepped inside the darkness and left him alone, the lamplight barely alive at his feet.

From deep inside the cavern, she called back to him one last time.

'*Bayete*! I salute you, son of Africa! Take heed of what you have seen, for when the final struggle is over you will indeed be the true leader of all men.'

## -8-

'We need some dogs,' hissed Bella, 'the bigger the better – Ridgebacks or something of that ilk. From now on, I'll have more guns about the house than teacups.'

Lee sifted through the events of that night for a clearer understanding of what had happened. ZANLA insurgents had ripped a hole in his family's life. A hundred years of stability had within that short space of time been turned on its head. Only hours before everyone had been caught up in the congratulatory mood of Karen's promotion – candlelight and heady conversation. Now all that had been soured and pushed aside, no longer of any consequence. Rex and his father had been taken at gunpoint and for all Lee knew, neither one of them might ever be seen again.

'This whole thing is way beyond me.' Karen moved in next to Lee on the sofa. 'In my whole life, I don't think I've ever been so frightened.' She snuggled down with her

37

head against his shoulder. It was two in the morning, but she was incapable of sleep. Her eyes were ringed with dark shadows and every few minutes she would shiver spasmodically.

Bella seemed more awake than any of them. Her temper was still fired up and she paced the lounge floor like an aged lioness spoiling for a fight. Her ivory-handled stick cracked her anger deep into the floorboards. She glowered at her grandson. 'Pour me another brandy. Extra-large, no ice.'

Karen got up from the sofa. 'I'll get it. I need the distraction.'

'Make that two,' said Lee. He followed her across the room then detoured for the storeroom key.

He unlocked the door. The standard lamp had been left uncovered and he switched it on. The stillness and the quiet suited his mood. He stood in front of the rolltop desk with his hands thrust deeply inside his pockets. Karen followed Lee in and left his drink on the desk, his mood now melancholic.

'A century ago we could still run up the old Company flag and to hell with the consequences.' He pointed to the far wall. It was filled almost to the ceiling with memorabilia and faded pictures of family gatherings. He took hold of Karen's hand and led her across the room – together, they stared into the sepia depths of an old photograph. He raised his hand to the glass as though him doing so might bring the picture to life.

'If I could go there tomorrow I would jump at the chance. There's no doubt they suffered for their money, but by God what they achieved they were able to hang on to'

It had been shot by J.E.Middlebrook, a Kimberley photographer of some esteem, on a Lancaster's 1888 *Le Merveilleux*. In places the image had almost faded, though the sombre likeness still portrayed that stark simplicity of the era. Framed along its upper edge by a dark foreboding skyline, the scene was realistic enough for Karen to feel the chill of a cold Karoo wind about her shoulders.

There was a bleakness about the entire landscape, on the faces of diggers who had turned their heads for the camera there were no smiles, no fond expression, just that fading glimmer of hope in their eyes, that they might find and possess the earth's richest prize. It was the beginning of a vast unstoppable empire, one that would power the heart of England's inexorable reach for the continent's dark interior. At the very edge of that hellish pit a woman stood four-square to the hardship and heartache it succoured. She held her son within the protective encirclement of her arms, staring defiantly out from the photograph – an almost indefinable, enigmatic smile on her lips.

\*

# II

# Kimberley, Northern Cape, 1892

# -1-

Catherine Goddard stood within yards of the opencast diggings. She looked down from the unfenced edge of that sombre pit and as she had done a hundred times before, watched a race of tiny insect-like figures risk life and limb for those elusive, precious stones of pure carbon – some no bigger than a single grain of sand, though sometimes for the more fortunate, larger than the egg of the wild Namaqua dove that had once nested there before the trees were felled and the earth laid back to expose the richest diamond mine the world had ever seen. It was more than a mile across and where once the arid ground had risen up as a desolate, thorn-capped hillock above the Boer farm *Vooruitzigt*, now there gaped a deep and ominous scar in the earth's crust and already men as far away as England were calling this phenomenon, The Big Hole.

Below her feet, desperate men swarmed as ants to a broken mound of yellow earth. In their hundreds they climbed and crossed from rickety ladders to narrow causeways, some going even deeper into places that Catherine's eyes were unable to reach. Others rose up for the sunlight and it was on one such ladder that she recognized her son Mathew, coming up hand over hand for the rim on which she was standing. For one indulgent moment, Catherine looked down again into the ominous throat of the great pit, and she remembered that time, almost three years ago when her husband had enlightened her inquisitive mind as to the intricate workings of this

43

vast, all powerful empire.

*Those are the steam engines that power the pumps and winches…*
He had explained, and then together they had looked
down through two hundred feet of dizzying heights to the
chasm's floor where endless haulage ropes were anchored
to their sheaves and men, black as human chips of wetted
coal were filling skips with yellow diamond-bearing earth.
*The full one is winched to the surface – the empty one replaces it…* he
had told her, and she had been amazed, almost
overwhelmed by the complexity of the operation. Now,
through lack of funding and shattered expectations, men
were abandoning their dreams so that gaps of a hundred
yards and more had appeared between the diggings.
Rumours of dwindling ore reserves had been spread
amongst the claim owners by unscrupulous men,
convincing others as to their folly in hanging on to what
would soon be seen as worthless pieces of torn earth, for
the friable yellow Kimberlite oxides were bottoming out.
However, veiled by ignorance and hidden beneath that
diminishing soft upper layer of accessible earth, were the
untouched ores of 'blue ground', a mile-wide pipe of living
rock which in its molten state had been forced by
immeasurable pressure from deep inside the earth's
mantle, and was now a quiescent, sleeping guardian of
uncountable fortunes, though without explosives and hefty
financial backing, harder to break from the depths of that
pit than from the pillars of hell itself.

'I bid you step back from the edge, madam. It would not
do for a woman's body to be found in the diggings.'

Catherine turned on her heels. The reedy clip of the
rider's voice had startled her and she glared at him for his
invasion of the moment, her hair drawn out by the wind to
a lashing, auburn skein about her shoulders.

'And who might you be?'

'Who I am is of little consequence, madam, but I do hold interest in the diggings and therefore would ask of you to move away from company property.'

From the pit's edge, Mathew pulled himself clear of the ladder, his shirt sweated through from the climb, but his breathing was even and un-laboured. At seventeen, he bettered his mother's height by one full span of his own hand, the shape and trim of his body generously altered by a year's hard labour. With a defiant smile he moved in next to Catherine, his face streaked with mud from the diggings and a mop of unkempt, boyish hair a blue-black flashing mane like that of his father.

'Cannot place you sir? Do we know you?'

'Works for the mining people,' Catherine hazarded. 'Apparently, women aren't welcome here.'

The stranger tipped his hat to Catherine, but his distaste for her presence was obvious, then he turned to Mathew and his demeanour softened, though the wanton pallor of the sick man was there about his eyes.

'Take your mother home, young man. The pit edge is no place for a woman.'

'Who are you?' Mathew cut back at him, but the rider had already turned about and spurred his horse for the incoming Kimberley road. Catherine watched him until forced by swirling clouds of red dust to turn her face away. The stranger had an aura about him that unsettled her and though now out of sight, she sensed him there on the street – the way a tiny bird might sense the watchful eye of a soaring falcon. She rested her arm on Mathew's shoulder.

'A letter came in with Zeederberg's mail coach – from your father.'

'From my father – why didn't you tell me?'

'I had to be sure of his whereabouts,' Catherine excused. 'And that what I have in mind is not just some fanciful dream.' She turned away from the diggings, excitement now a fluttering bird inside her chest. On reaching their cottage she took the rickety steps two at a time, unlatched the door and swung it back with a clatter of old timbers then swept into the tiny room, like an eager ship under full sail. She turned to the mirror. Dust had coated her face and she grimaced at the sight of it.

'I know where he is, Mathew,' then without the slightest inkling of doubt, 'we are going to find your father.'

'When?' said Mathew, unable to hide his excitement, then the dull truth of what the journey entailed dampened the atmosphere. 'It will months for us to reach him?'

Catherine spun back from the mirror. 'Time is unimportant; making a start is what matters. My mind is made up. I have had enough of watching my only son go down inside that rathole of a pit. Any longer here and this place will be the end of me.'

'We would need a wagon,' said Mathew. 'Oxen, rifles, provisions to last at least three months. The cost would be mountainous?'

'I have it,' Catherine assured him. 'Your father left me a letter of credit for two thousand pounds. Money from the sale of our claim is still lodged with the Standard Bank in Kimberley.' Her eyes glittered. 'More than enough for all our needs.' She dropped into a chair by the window and started to write. 'If what I have heard is true, we have little enough time to collect supplies before the next column of settlers leaves for the interior.'

Mathew watched her fill the paper. She discarded the pencil and waved her list at him. 'Furguson's store will be as good a place as any for you to make a start.'

By the time Mathew reached Kimberley's Market Square, the late chill of that July afternoon had already worked its way inside the shadows. He took in familiar sights and sounds and committed them to memory, for the stark reality of leaving Kimberley behind now struck home as bitter-sweet. Even the dust thrown up by carts and horses' hooves were given permanent place in his mind's eye. Where once only wood and iron shacks had stood as the backbone of Kimberley's town centre – now buildings, two storeys high, built from brick and roofed with orderly laid sheets of corrugated iron had risen up from the squalor. The painted iron roofs unwittingly matched in winter to insidious clouds of red dust from the diggings, and in the summer when the rains fell in earnest, to ankle-deep glutinous mud the colour of old blood. However, behind this prosperous façade were still the bars and brothels of old Kimberley – canvas wagon-tents stretched to rickety frames and timber lean-tos and all of them faded and worn to the point of tearing free on the next high wind. By nightfall, when lamps were lit, whatever pleasures demanded were unwittingly displayed on the canvas walls as magic lantern shows to those stood outside with a greedy eye for the free perversity. And yet, through all of this squalor and depravation Mathew saw the beginnings of his life in Africa. With a wry smile he closed his mind to the past and cut through a cluttered alleyway for Stockdale Street.

He found the sign, JAMES FURGUSON, WHOLESALE MERCHANT, KIMBERLEY then drew himself to his full height and walked in.

Furguson bore down on him – his moustache twice the regular size, waxed and shaped with military precision, hair slicked with brilliantine and parted down the middle in the traditional style of the London dandy.

'And what can I do for you, young man?' With a persuasive arm, Furguson led him across the store to an expansive sales counter. 'Name the commodity of your desire. A fine waistcoat, perhaps? Something for a night on the town? Or something to woo your lady friend into a state of compliant euphoria?'

Mathew felt suddenly ill at ease and wished he was back outside on the street. A group of men looked on with amused interest. Three of the four were dressed in fine worsted suits, expensive waistcoats and silk ties. The fourth, was roughly done up in faded breeches and open-neck shirt. About his waist had been fastened a thick grey belt of cured elephant hide, trapped between the belt and his waistband was a hunting knife the size of which Mathew had never seen before; the blade threw wicked lights about the room. He stared at the weapon, unable to tear his eyes from that buck-horn handle with its evil length of Damascus steel.

'Guns,' Mathew croaked to the storekeeper, then closed his hand about his mother's list of commodities and silently prayed that no one else had heard.

'What kind of guns?' Furguson's eyes glowed. 'Elephant guns? Mannlichers? Fowling pieces? One with a cork on a string?' The store erupted with men's laughter.

The clenched fist came from nowhere. It took the storekeeper squarely on the point of his piggy nose and clattered him backwards through piles of buckets and broom stales. Mathew vaulted the countertop, his face set with the uncontrolled anger of a berserk street fighter, his fists were flailing hammers, sinking to the joints of his wrists when he found the flaccid folds of Furguson's belly.

'Easy on, tiger!' The voice came from over Mathew's shoulder and he felt himself hooked away from the melee, his right arm locked fast in the grip of the biggest fist he had ever seen. The sonorous drawl of the man's accent linked him undoubtedly to the Americas.

'No need to kill the man, though no one would deny he deserves it.' He held Mathew at bay. 'The man's beaten. Help him up and let the matter lie.'

Mathew fought back his anger, his glare indomitably fixed to the shopkeeper for the rage was still in him. Reluctantly, he stepped forward and held out his hand. About Furguson's eyes were already the first signs of plum-coloured bruising; the bridge of his nose glassy and swollen. Dominated by the younger, fitter man he accepted the truce.

'I misjudged you, young man and I apologise for my stupidity.'

'I should have kept my temper,' said Mathew, 'my regrets for the blooded shirt.'

Mathew caught movement out of the corner of his eye and swung to meet it.

'Hold on there, young man,' the voice was small, none threatening. 'The name's Rudd – like your right hook, though I'm not sure our Mister Furguson here would be of the same mind.' He shot a painful glance at the storekeeper. 'Have the doctor see to your wounds, get him to write off the damage to yours truly. Fortunately for you our Mister Burnham was around or calling for the undertaker might well have been more appropriate.'

James Rudd was smaller in stature than Mathew, but like the man at the edge of the diggings projected immense presence. A single, one-carat diamond stud glowed like a raptor's eye from the centre of his burgundy necktie. A tailored suit hung lightly to Rudd's slight frame; beneath the jacket a gold fob chain crossed the width of his waistcoat. Mathew put the man in his late thirties, hair already well receded, dark, though shot through with tiny flashes of silver, matched to a trimmed beard and splendid moustache.

Rudd sprung the lid to his gold Hunter and nodded to the American. 'Be with you shortly, Mister Burnham. You go on to the club and explain my being delayed.' He turned back to Mathew; 'Didn't catch your name young man?'

'Goddard, sir. Mathew Goddard.'

'And what business do you have buying up guns and the like?' He retrieved the crumpled note from the floor and handed it to Mathew.

Mathew waded in with his explanation. He told Rudd of his intended journey to the interior and of his mother's dogged determination for them to find his father. Rudd listened intently so that his admiration for the boy and his mother grew by the minute. Taking a wagon into little known territory was as courageous as it could be foolhardy – even for hardened, experienced men. But for a woman, and her son barely a few years out of school, the pitfalls were tenfold.

'So with a single wagon, a team of untried oxen and a gun or two, the pair of you will be setting off into the wilderness to search out your father?'

'Our minds are made up,' said Mathew. 'A lot of men have travelled the same road without mishap.'

Rudd recalled his own reckless venturing into the unknown. The boy had something about him – that taciturn look of someone beyond his years, the

50

adventurer's glint in his eye, but alongside these overzealous feelings Rudd sensed a willingness to learn. He started for the door and looked for Mathew to follow him.

'Come along with me. There's someone I want you to meet.'

<br>

## -3-

From the moment Mathew set foot through the Kimberley Club's double doors his aspirations soared inexplicably to new heights. Following the fire of November eighty-six, the club had been rebuilt with finest Kimberley brick and on the instructions of Cecil Rhodes had been afforded every conceivable expense. Seventy-four leading citizens had each contributed one hundred pounds towards the club's refurbishment so that the fittings and furnishings were chosen with a mindful eye for utmost quality. The entrance hall with its circular oak table opened again to an inner corridor, the walls of which were hung with gilt-framed oils and those softer, almost ethereal, watercolour panoramas of a mysterious African hinterland. At the corridor's head, Hubert von Herkomer's portrayal of Cecil Rhodes looked down on an establishment that was now seen as a place more sanctified, more powerful than the seat of legal government in the far Cape.

Mathew looked up at the portrait. The portentous feeling of being watched raked his skin with gooseflesh. He hurried on, past the gentlemen's bar with its spittoons and brass foot rail. On the polished counter, as a symbolic show of the members' unrelenting chauvinism, the black, crenulated boss of a wild ram was displayed as a prominent centrepiece. Mounted on a block of sterling silver and at its peak, made from that same precious metal, a simple snuff box had been filled to the brim with a rich blend of finely powdered tobaccos.

Mathew was walking where Kimberley's elite met to decide the financial fate of an empire. Where deals worth thousands of pounds were struck on the strength of a handshake. Only those afforded a place by invite were allowed to stand where Mathew now waited to enter the inner sanctum of Kimberley's most jealously guarded club.

'Come in, young Goddard.'

Mathew cleared his throat and stepped inside. A simple mahogany table commanded the room's centre and above it, like some Highland mist hung a steel-grey lake of cigar smoke. Next to Rudd, Mathew recognised the big American and at the table's head sat a man with eyes the colour of a clear blue Kimberley sky.

'The fellow at the diggings. I should have known you were one and the same. Sit down – opposite me so I can get a good look at this overzealous young man Rudd has been telling me about.'

Mathew sat straight-backed and looked directly into the unfathomable eyes of Cecil John Rhodes. He knew that all three men were watching him and that his worth was being measured, as though he were now in the presence of some towering Greek colossus.

There was something about the poise of the leonine head, the powerful jaw and raised chin. However, when Rhodes spoke the tone of his voice wavered from a deep, bell-like bass to an effeminate, reedy tremble.

'So tell me young man, what of your background – the abridged version if you would.' Rhodes leant back in his chair, his hair tousled and unruly – his tie overly tight and slipped to one side. He linked his hands at the back of his head and waited for Mathew to begin.

He started with their voyage aboard the Royal Mail steam ship, Dunottar Castle, outward bound from the port of Southampton. '... then by coach belonging to Cobb & Company from our port of debarkation...'

Rhodes recalled his own journeying up to the diamond fields from the Port of Natal. 'A trip not one of us would wish to repeat, hey Rudd?' They laughed in unison. 'I can imagine no worse experience than bouncing my way back from Natal on one of those infernal carts.'

Rudd dismissed the recollection with a perfunctory wave of his hand. 'Never again, I would rather walk.'

Mathew fell eagerly to the rest of his story, relating his family's arrival in Kimberley and their early involvements with the diggings.

'At first we lived on what little monies my father had left over from the sale of our farm. My mother wanted us back in England – she was very nearly at the end of her tether. Food was almost impossible to come by and we lived in a canvas tent no bigger than this room.'

He was enjoying the attention of Kimberley's elite so that he leant forward, determined to give an impressive recount of his father's finest moment – that cold July day when the wind blew in from the east and shrouded the diggings in that fine, grey *guti* drizzle.

'My father came home earlier than usual – I will never forget the moment he stepped inside from the rain, his clothes were sodden through from the diggings.'

'Come on, man.' Rudd pushed him. 'What happened next?'

'Two diamonds,' Mathew grinned, his excitement

53

growing as if it were him who had found them. 'Almost identical, each one of them a shade under sixteen carats.' He looked directly at Rhodes and the sparkle in his eye matched that of the precious stones he had spoken about. 'The very next day he sold his claim for six thousand pounds, to you Mister Rhodes if I am not mistaken.'

'Nathan Goddard! Big chap – black beard!' Rhodes' face lit up. 'As God is my witness I remember the very moment.' Briefly, the dark pallor below his eyes lifted and he was once again infected by that wild uncertainty of working the diggings. 'No. 773 – the furthermost claim on the north-western boundary of the pit. Everyone thought the ground to be worthless – that your father had bought a pig in a poke!'

They studied each other with frank interest.

'You have the means to purchase a wagon and a team of oxen?'

'Enough for the entire venture,' Mathew assured him.

'And the date of your departure?'

'Within the month, as soon as we have a wagon readied and our provisions loaded.'

'Then it is settled,' Rhodes decided and clapped his hands in a show of approval. Now, excitement grown of his own involvement was there in the room – an almost boyish grin had countered his usual quiet, arresting smile and his eyes were alive, bluer and brighter than any Mathew had ever seen. 'A column of mounted volunteers will be escorting settlers and supply wagons bound for the gold diggings springing up near the confluence of the Shashi and Tuli rivers – namely, the re-opening of the Blue Jacket and neighbouring reefs. The column will be going as far as The London and Limpopo Company store at Tati – about twenty miles up from the said river's confluence with the

Shashi. You and your mother will travel as part of that column. That at least will guarantee your safety until you have crossed the Limpopo.'

He watched Mathew's expression for any signs of topographic recognition but there were none; he sighed deeply and clasped his hands on the table in front of him.

'I suggest the purchasing of some form of educational literature regarding the route you will be taking and what to expect of your journey.'

'Baines' books are hard to come by,' Mathew countered. 'I've tried desperately for his *Gold Regions of South Eastern Africa*, but I'm told there is no more call for his writings.'

'Nonsense!' Rhodes swiftly dismissed the allegation with an imperious scowl. 'Whoever said that is a buffoon – an illiterate meddler. Wouldn't know the difference between Baines' brilliance and the boring drivel of some city columnist's frippery! I'll have a copy found and sent to you.'

His face flushed to a deep crimson from the abrupt irritation and he quickly recognised the symptoms: shortness of breath and those constricting reptilian coils thrown about his chest by some cruel genetic freak of nature. He was forced to calm himself and closed his eyes, then breathed deeply for the air that one day would seem more precious than the total wealth amassed by the entire De Beers Company. Not until his breathing had eased did he go on laying out the conditions for his support of Mathew's itinerary.

'Our Mister Burnham will lead the column; his word will hold sway with any matters of importance. Anyone refusing to fall in line with his decisions will be dealt with as he sees fit.' He raised an eyebrow to emphasize his ruling. 'Would I be right in saying you have no objection to what has been covered so far?'

'None whatsoever,' said Mathew. Arguing would only put him at a disadvantage – what he had seen of Burnham was, to date, likeable. The American would prove to be a powerful ally.

'The pitfalls are many,' Rhodes went on, 'especially once you have crossed the Limpopo. I have heard of men being dragged from their tents by hyena and such like. Would the threat of this happening not be of concern to your mother?'

'She will cope admirably,' said Mathew. 'My mother is not one to be put off once her mind has been made up.'

'One more point of worry,' Rhodes added, with that sardonic twinkle back in his eye – for women to him were regarded only as a hindrance. 'Matabele raiding parties roam at will through the areas both north and east of the Shashi River. Their coming across your wagon without the protection of the column would put you at a most definite disadvantage. Rescuing a white woman from marauding bands of Matabele would prove costly and time wasting, as well as unnecessarily dangerous for Mister Burnham's men.'

'That will not happen,' Mathew promised. 'If there were a fight, it would be to the end. Win or lose. That's the way she is – the way we both are.'

Rhodes looked to his colleague. 'So what do you think Mister Rudd? Would the lad end up an asset or a liability to the Company's acquisitions in Mashonaland?'

Rudd smiled at Mathew, from the onset he had quickly warmed to the boy's courage.

'Definitely an asset. Mashonaland would be at a loss without him.'

Rhodes acquiesced. Men of good standing were in short

supply and his fledgling colony beyond the Limpopo would take all that he could muster.

'Then there is nothing more to discuss. A week next Monday. Be ready with your wagon young man – Stockdale Street. Outside of De Beers company offices at nine o'clock sharp or the column will leave without you.'

-4-

'He kind of overpowers a man,' said Burnham. 'Does it to everyone – master of manipulation, Rudd calls him. Damn well right he is too.'

They walked out of the Kimberley Club, into the last showings of late sunlight. A layer of grey smoke blanketed the town's centre and curled back for almost a mile to where upwards of a thousand canvas tents stood out from that dreary landscape – one by one the tents were brought to a dull orange glow by lighted hurricane lamps.

'Rhodes always gets his own way?'

'Never fails to,' said Burnham. He steered Mathew through a narrow alleyway to where the hapless voices of drunk miners and that of an old piano ground from an open doorway. 'Time to clear the dust; you coming in, laddie? We could celebrate your good fortune before going on home.'

Snared by curiosity, Mathew followed the American into the Digger's Rest and jostled for a place at the bar, shoulder to shoulder with some of Kimberley's toughest. Burnham thrust a schooner of beer into his hand just as someone broke into G. W. Johnson's, 'When You and I

Were Young, Maggie', a deep baritone rendition of the miners' adopted song and everyone listened. The applause that followed threatened to lift the roof.

'Brought it with him from the gold diggings at Pilgrim's Rest,' Burnham told Mathew. 'The old man sings the same song every night, and every night they listen; never a bad word.'

'First time I've heard it,' admitted Mathew and looked around the room at a hundred weather-beaten faces. Most were already bleary-eyed and almost off their feet from too much whisky or that virulent blend of rough brandy, the infamous Cape Smoke.

'Rhodes said that you will be leading the column only as far as the Tati diggings?'

'That I will,' said Burnham, 'and what about you? Travelling alone from Tati to the fort at Victoria counts as being kind of crazy in my book.'

Mathew drained his glass; the music seemed louder, driven by strong beer and the loud infectious beat of 'All Around My Hat' from the bar's piano.

By the time the clock above the bar showed eight, the Digger's Rest was in full swing. The old man from Pilgrim's Rest sang 'Maggie' for the umpteenth time and when he lost track of the words, was helped back to his chair and left to sleep it off. Burnham was into his eighth schooner and in full voice with 'Clementine'. He stopped mid-verse and nudged Mathew.

'Now this is what the lads have been waiting for.' He stretched to his full height for a better view of the front door.

Apart for the shuffle of diggers' feet the room fell silent. Only the incoherent mumblings of those beyond caring and the clink of the barkeeper's count could be heard over the rustle of taffeta skirts and the alluring timbre of feminine voices. Mathew's mouth fell open; his grip faltered, almost to the point of him letting the glass slip through his fingers.

'You're gawping, lad – close your mouth before someone takes you for a herring.'

Mathew sucked in his jaw. 'They're almost naked.'

At that very moment Mathew knew that in his entire life he had never seen anything so beautiful.

'Well, not quite,' said Burnham, 'but by the end of the night, by God, I'll wager a pound to a shilling they will not be far from it.' He pointed out one of the burlesque girls. 'The redhead, what do you say to that one?'

Mathew didn't hear him. His life had filled with rouged cheeks and flouncing ostrich feathers, long silken legs that went on forever, lips so deliciously coloured and shaped that to him, were rare, enticing blooms of subtle pinks and violent fiery reds. The crowd parted and in the eyes of drunken men these girls were gilded angels, heaven-sent for rumbustious Kimberley diggers. Cued by the piano they lined up; long legs and pink boas. A man at the back of the room could have heard the drop of a single pin.

'Let's have some order then,' shouted Michael 'Taffy' Thomas, a burly Welsh coal miner, now the owner of claim no. 408 near to the pit's centre. His shirt was opened to the waist where a stomach half the size of a digger's tent sagged to a leather belt. Every man in the bar was waiting, eyes popped like those of lovesick cows for a clear view of these six visions of perfect loveliness.

'The ladies are here by kind request of the management.' His eyes were closed, imparting an atmosphere of mystery and amazement. 'These wondrous creatures have travelled from the high class theatres of Port Natal for the cultural enlightenment of us Kimberley gents.' His eyes opened and glared down upon the multitude. 'So watch your manners. Any rough behaviour and whoever's responsible will answer to yours truly – Michael Thomas.'

'Get on with it, Taffy!'

Men with whisky on their breath and lust in their eyes shuffled forwards.

'Get a bloody move on, Thomas! You're not the friggin' vicar.'

The Welshman stood his ground.

'Last but by no means least, gentlemen, don't be shy with your money – the young ladies will be most appreciative of your donations.'

'I bet they will, Thomas. Now get off the friggin' stage before we damn-well shoot you.'

Cued by one of the girls, the piano player launched into a rackety rendition of Offenbach's, The Infernal Gallop.

Burnham lit a cigar. The ladies from Natal went swiftly into their repertoire – they knew from a hundred similar experiences exactly what the diggers wanted and were holding nothing back.

'Sweet mother of Mary. Would you get a load of that, sonny-my-boy.'

Mathew could not speak. His mouth was drier than the scattering of sawdust at his feet and he was loath to blink for fear of missing any of the lewd contortions being performed in front of him. He was lost between a world of fantasy and the Digger's Rest, not even the miners' ribald howls could turn his interest from these exquisite creatures.

Money flowed, bids were hurled, promises made and the ladies obliged – for the queen's gold coin, men were taken far beyond their wildest dreams.

An auburn beauty with breasts the size of tsamma melons fixed her eyes on the boy at the counter and crossed to where he was standing. Every eye in the room followed the sensuous sway of her hips, the languid slant of her eyes and the way her hair threw glints of copper and gold when she passed within range of guttering lamplight. The crowd parted to let her through then closed again behind her like some ancient biblical sea. She stopped within inches of Mathew – a golden leopardess, a perfumed bird of paradise.

'Come with me,' she whispered, her voice mellifluous, that soft hypnotic lilt of a wild Karoo wind.

To Mathew no other creature could have been created more beautiful than the woman now standing in front of him. His legs were stiff, immobile things rooted to the floor. He stared at her with wide eyes and his young heart raced and reared like wild water through the deep canyons of the Dragon Mountains.

'I am your princess,' she told him, her lips to his cheek, her voice little more than a husky whisper. 'What do I call you?'

'Mathew,' he managed, but with a high unnatural pitch to his voice. 'Mathew Goddard, Ma'am.'

Every man in the room craned his neck for a better view.

'Everyone calls me Molly, Molly McGuire.'

Now the air was stale with smoke and sweat, Taffy Thomas, self-appointed master of ceremonies bellowed encouragement to his patrons.

'And now for what we have all been waiting for! I give you the queen of burlesque. The darling of the diggings. The most beautiful woman for a thousand miles either side of the Kimberley diamond fields!' With outstretched arms and the rough, unkempt panache of an overweight ringmaster he delivered his gift to the crowd. 'Gentlemen! A big hand and an open purse for the girl of your dreams – the most desirable woman between here and Pilgrims Rest!' With a final, brusque roll of imaginary drums. 'The mistress of temptation – our one and only Molly McGuire!'

She winked an eye at Mathew, leant forward and brushed his cheek with her lips. 'Come see me when you're eighteen and I will show you something really special.'

She turned for the stage and with that same licentious sway of her hips, floated away from the bar on a diaphanous cloud of pink and lilac feathers.

## -5-

A lightly sprung Cape cart stood forlornly to the moonlit frontage of the Digger's Rest. Harnessed to it, a mule old enough to have witnessed the early days of the New Rush. Most of the bar's patrons had at some time or other been glad of the service and would without rancour part with the one shilling fare demanded by its owner in exchange for a safe ride home. The sight of the cart weaving through Kimberley's streets had become commonplace, its load of lifeless bodies imbued a sombre air, that of a despised collector of diseased corpses from the fouled streets of London's Black Death.

Burnham loaded Mathew's dead weight over the tailboard and folded his own jacket to double as pillow. The youngster's boots pointed comically up at the stars. Satisfied with his efforts, the American climbed into the driver's seat and clicked his tongue at the mule.

In accordance with Mathew's directions, Burnham steered the rig through the market square, then down alongside the sinister maw of the diamond pit. A full moon lit up a way and in the night behind the cart, a hundred tin roofs showed up as corrugated, silver squares in the moonlight.

'Where am I?' Mathew groaned, then rolled to the cart's side and retched at the dark.

'Up she comes, young fella. Let her go and you'll feel all the better for it.'

'I want to die,' Mathew croaked and levered himself up onto one elbow. 'Have we passed the diggings?'

'Half a mile back, and there's a light up ahead. Would your mother still be awake at this late hour?'

'That she would.' A woman's voice came out of the darkness.

Burnham caught the first glint of moonlight from the barrels of Catherine's twelve bore double-loader.

'What have you done with my son?'

Mathew rolled himself over the side. 'Put down the gun, mother.'

'No harm done,' said Burnham, 'just a couple of drinks at the Digger's.'

Catherine picked up the smell of stale beer on Mathew's breath and realigned the gun with Burnham's head.

'If his father were here he would take a whip to the pair of you. A drunken man can sometimes be excused, but encouraging a boy of barely seventeen years I find abhorrent, and you sir, have done exactly that.'

'Then I apologise profusely, Ma'am. If you would let me try to make amends...'

'No need.' Catherine interrupted him, and cocked the

hammers to both barrels. 'Just turn your cart around and leave us be.'

Burnham tipped his hat to Catherine. Arguing with a gun-wielding angry woman would be at its best, foolhardy.

'Then I'll bid you goodnight, Ma'am. A dose of salts for your boy back there and he'll be right as rain by morning. Don't forget,' he called to Mathew, 'a week next Monday. Any later and the column will be away without you.'

# -6-

That Monday morning howled in cold and cruel from the deep Karoo. On a wind that had risen swiftly there carried the detritus of human squalor, dust from torn earth and the angst of those so chilled by bitter disappointment that they were loathe to move from their tents.

Catherine Goddard stood at the side of the track she had followed so many times. Dust boiled from the pit's edge and she lowered the wide brim of her drover's hat to protect her eyes. She was dressed in calico shirt and breeches and her feet were clad with the tough *veldschoen* boots of the Boer farmer. She turned to her son, her eyes mere slits against the wind and then nodded her head with a finality that would change their lives forever.

'Best we get it over with,' she urged, without the slightest edge of doubt to her voice.

Mathew waited for a lull in the wind and then dropped a lighted Vesta down between the floorboards. The flame fluttered indecisively, as if offering him a final chance to change his mind. It took to the kindling, slowly at first, then, with rampant greed it hurried away beneath the floor. Smoke appeared from cracks and knot-holes in the timbers. Catherine stood back, watching impassively as the fire finally broke through; it was then that she felt her spirits soar, rising up with the flames.

'We should be getting back to the wagon,' said Mathew, but Catherine stayed his urgency.

'Just a few more minutes – then it will be over – there will be no coming back.' She beckoned him closer so that she could rest her head against his shoulder.

Fire engulfed the timber framework and now, against a grey sky towered clouds of acrid smoke. Corrugated iron sheets twisted free of their joists – blackened by heat they rattled as ravens' wings in the vortex. The house that had been Catherine's only tie with Kimberley disappeared on the wind.

-7-

'You have equipped yourself well, young man.'

Mathew looked up from checking the wagon's offside brake-block.

'Like Mister Burnham told me, sir. Leave nothing to chance.'

Rhodes nodded agreeably. 'Sound advice. There are no suppliers to call on once you have cleared the town's limits. It would take a foolish man indeed to leave Kimberley without adequate preparation.'

Rhodes sat his horse with quiet authority, deep into the saddle and long into the stirrups – collar turned up for the wind. He drew out his watch and flicked back the lid.

'You have less than an hour before Burnham takes the column out on the north road. Make sure you have accounted for every need and that your chattels are well battened down. The road is a rough one and knowing our Mister Burnham, he will not take kindly to anyone rattling along like a tinker's workshop.'

'Everything is in order – double checked and enough provisions to last the journey out – all the way to Mashonaland.'

Rhodes kneed his horse into a slow walk alongside the oxen. All sixteen were bright-eyed, their flanks well-muscled from lavish attention, but he knew that in two months' time the tortuous journey would have taken its toll. At least one of them would have died from a broken limb or snake bite. Others struck down by the infectious, bloodsucking bite of the tsetse fly – that tiny, winged insect no bigger than the English housefly. He turned back to where Mathew was shouldering a hundredweight bag of maize meal, up over the wagon's tailboard.

'Who will lead your oxen?'

'Mathew will.' Catherine shot the answer back. 'That is if you have no objections, Mister Rhodes.' She swung herself onto the wagon box. She remembered Rhodes from their first meeting on that cold morning next to the diggings; this time she was prepared. Her hair was tied with a ribbon of silk and hung defiantly to one shoulder – an auburn battle flag. 'Or you could, if you wished, take on the task yourself. Though the pay, I'm sure, would not be to your liking.'

Rhodes' expression hardened, his itinerary spared nothing for argumentative women. He stood the gelding into the bit; with its neck arched the beast stamped and trembled, a show of masculine temperance.

'Then would I be right in thinking, Ma'am, that if your wagon is under threat your son will lead and you, a woman of half his weight, will take up the whip?'

'That would be my intention,' said Catherine, unaware of Rhodes' implication.

'Then let us hope for both your sakes your abilities will prove adequate...' he paused mid-sentence, openly amused by the way Catherine had dressed herself in shirt and breeches. 'Though your dressing in manly attire does not necessarily guarantee manly results.'

'And who perhaps, would be a better judge of that than you, Mister Rhodes?'

The remark angered him. The woman had overstepped her mark but he discarded the incident on the acceptance of her leaving Kimberley within the hour.

'I do not believe you have the strength, Ma'am. Call it as you will, that is the way I see your predicament.'

'Then take up my wager.'

Mathew gave up on loading the meal. There was trouble brewing. His mother had just squared up to the most powerful man in Kimberley. She scowled down at Rhodes, strutty as a bantam cock.

'Five English pounds says I will put the lead animal hard to its yoke with a single stroke of the whip.' She looked around her, aggravated by a growing crowd. All of them men, the opportunist scavengers were gathering for the kill – little boys in mute support of their playground bully. Her eyes glittered; her anger had risen up, but her voice she kept diminutive, deceptively ladylike. 'I will match any wager, gentlemen – pound for pound.'

Within minutes, Mathew had collected upwards of forty pounds; a small fortune. Rhodes reached inside his jacket pocket.

'And my twenty to your five, Ma'am. Like the gentlemen behind me, I say you do not have the brawn for it.'

Catherine drew out the whip stock from behind the wagon box and attached a length of breyed leather; its tapered *voorslag* of supple giraffe hide. The whip had come as a gift, a token of her amicable transaction with the wagon's previous owner. The wagon had cost her two hundred English pounds, its timbers fashioned from iron-hard stinkwood – each of his sleek trek oxen at seventy pounds a head.

*When I was only a small boy,* the old Boer had reminisced, *I watched my grandfather work the wet skin of the Kameelperd for one whole week, and always he kept the leather supple with fat from around the giraffe's own kidneys. But you must pasop,* take care, he warned her, *he made it long enough to reach the furthest ox of eight doubles. Use it only when you have to, for only your best effort will put the whip to its fullest length...*

Catherine uncoiled the lash alongside the wagon. Rhodes' presence alone had swelled the crowd. They watched with jewelled eyes, waiting for Catherine's attempts to flounder.

'Come on sweetheart! Let's see you put up the lash instead of your kitchen curtains.'

In the event of the wagon reaching rough terrain, she would be forced to walk alongside the oxen, from there the shorter whip would prove to be adequate. Rhodes knew this and recognised the futility in what this woman was trying to prove. He saw her cheeks colour and raised his hand for the attention of those behind him.

'Afford the lady a fair chance, gentlemen. Take your time Ma'am, give it your best shot or lay down the whip and save yourself any further embarrassment.'

Catherine waited for a lull in the trailing wind and prayed

for its return at the right moment to give the leather its full flight, anything less and the lash would unfurl with a feeble, impotent slap at the air. Her credibility and contents of her purse destroyed in the winking of an eye. The whip had to be put back along the side of the wagon with a single, fluid roll of the arms; her timing was critical.

Catherine locked her leg against the tent frame and stood at first with her chest and outstretched arms to the front, then, with a prayer on her lips put every ounce of her strength into putting back the lash.

As a fisherman's weighted salmon line the lash curled up and away from the ground in a single, rolling loop. Catherine waited for that tell-tale drag on her arms, only then did she know that the lash was fully out. She reversed her stance, shifted her weight. The wind she had prayed for sprang from the south-west and when coupled to all her strength took the lash away on a shallow, hissing arc.

The sound it made was that of a goose's wings skimming the surface of a lake and then, like the shot from a hunter's rifle, the *voorslag* cracked just inches away from splitting the cupped ear of the lead ox. Wide-eyed the beast lunged forward and snatched its trek chain cleanly from the earth. The rest followed suit and Mathew was forced to run to the span's head to prevent sixteen, half-ton trek oxen from lumbering away with the wagon.

As quickly as it had gathered, the crowd dispersed. Rhodes shook his head, momentarily stunned by what he had witnessed.

'Whatever our differences, madam,' he tipped his hat to Catherine. 'A most commendable performance.'

He reined his horse about and nodded to Mathew.

'Put the winnings to good use, young man – perhaps some embrocation for your mother's shoulder.'

# -8-

Mathew bundled their winnings into his pocket and climbed up onto the wagon. Catherine dropped the whip on the wagon box, from the trembling of his mother's hand, Mathew knew she was suffering the results of her bravado.

'How bad is it?'

'Rhodes was right; I should have swallowed my stupid pride and stood down.'

'You took his wager fair and square,' Mathew insisted. 'Rhodes was toying with you. The money didn't come into it.'

Catherine tried once more to lift her forearm but the pain beat her. Mathew vaulted down from the wagon box.

'Where are you going?'

'To find Burnham.' He slipped the hitch to his horse's reins and swung up into the saddle. 'We need labour, mother. Accept the fact or we are forced to stay behind in Kimberley.'

A contagious air of restlessness hung over Kimberley. People gathered in doorways; expectant, lively faces peered from windows. Horses milled, dogs barked and upwards of five hundred half-ton oxen stood readily to their yokes. East of Kimberley the sky had coloured to that of old slate and in those next few minutes the first fine drops of winter rain alighted on the wagon tents. Burnham looked back along the column and on the raising of his hand the first wagons started forwards. Whips cracked like rifle fire along the full length of Stockdale Street.

By the time Mathew caught up with Burnham, some of the wagons were already a mile clear of the town limits – a slow, meandering snake of canvas and cattle with the American at its front, his Winchester repeating rifle laid across the saddle.

'Well knock me down with a pink boa, if it isn't the man with an eye for pretty burlesque girls.' Burnham waved Mathew alongside. 'Heard about your mother's run-in with Rhodes, would have stumped up twenty pounds of my own just to have seen his face.'

'News travels fast,' said Mathew, his expression grim. 'We need your help – your advice at the least.'

The American knew that the column had suffered its first setback.

'Where have you left your wagon?'

'Still on the street. I need labour – someone to lead my oxen.'

Burnham pushed back his hat and frowned at Mathew. 'A little late in the day for recruiting labour aren't you?'

'My mother has injured her arm – torn her shoulder.'

'Her wager with Rhodes.' Burnham nodded. 'I'm not surprised. Putting out a sixty footer, even for a strong man would take some doing. Should have put up that double-loader of hers instead and sent the man packing.' He shook his head at Mathew's predicament. 'Every labourer within a hundred miles of Kimberley will be down in the pit.'

'No one told me,' Mathew excused, angered by his own stupidity.

'Takes a small army to keep a wagon on the move. Could be you will have to stay behind and wait for the next column?'

'When will that be?'

'Whenever Rhodes finds the urge. Could be a month – could be six.' Burnham looked past him. A lone rider was pushing his mount at a full gallop. 'Looks like more trouble.'

Carlus Pieters swirled his horse in next to Burnham's, his face wan from lack of sleep. The Afrikaner's deep voice roughly edged.

'I have trouble with my family, *meneer*. My children have been struck down by sickness – all four of them. It is God's bidding that I return with my wagon to Kimberley.'

'I'm sorry to hear that, Carlus. Your turning back will be a sad loss for the column.'

The Afrikaner shrugged his shoulders, his eyes deeply ringed with dark shadow.

'I have no choice. If The Almighty has seen it fit for me to stay behind, then so be it. There will be another day, *meneer*.' He held out his hand for Burnham's. '*Totsiens* my friend – God give your eyes strength enough for you to see the road.'

Burnham watched the Afrikaner ride back along the column.

'Get yourself down to his wagon,' he told Mathew. 'Carlus will no longer have need of a full complement – two at the most. Watch your way with him though, or he'll feed your liver to those dogs of his.'

Mathew nodded his thanks to Burnham and turned back towards Kimberley, like Carlus he pushed his horse to the limit; it would not take long for word of the misfortune to reach others. Servants, especially those accustomed to life on the north road would be quickly bargained for.

Pieters had already drawn his wagon out of line with the column.

'What do you want with Carlus Pieters, *Engelsman?*'

Mathew slid from the saddle and respectfully tipped his hat.

'Your servants, *meneer* – I have been told you have no further need of them, I can offer them work with my own wagon. We could perhaps come to some agreement?'

The Boer's eyes narrowed, though it did not hide his dislike for the English. From the depths of his black beard the words came out like angry bees from their nest.

'Like a jackal for the leftovers you come to my wagon. Why should I help a *verdonder* Englishman?'

'I mean you no disrespect *Meneer* Pieters, and I am willing to pay for your trouble.'

Pieters' wife stepped from inside the wagon tent, drawn from the warmth of her cot by Mathew's talk of recompense. Like those of her husband, her eyes were indelibly underscored by fatigue and worry. Her lips were pinched to bloodless lines by uncountable hardships and a mother's angst; her hair black as a crow's wing, plastered by rain across the pale peak of her forehead.

'Take the *rooinek's* money, Carlus. We no longer have need of *padlopers*.' She swung her attention to Mathew and now those sunken eyes glittered. 'How much, Englishman? A price for them all, except for the girl.'

'Five pounds.' Mathew chanced and took the amount from the wad in his shirt pocket, but his reckless showing of that much money was to cost him dearly.

'Ten,' the woman demanded. 'For ten pounds you may take our kaffirs, their pots and sack of meal also.'

Pieters counted the money from Mathew's fingers and shoved the notes deep into the pocket of his moleskin breeches. 'The dogs, you will need them also. In the dark, lions and kaffirs will be up to your wagon without you knowing. Sometimes even the ears of God Almighty are at rest, even for an Englishman.'

'The dogs do not know me – why would they follow a

stranger?'

Pieters shook his head. 'You take a wagon into the wilderness, and yet you know so little of God's creatures.' With an insistent grip on Mathew's shoulder he walked him round to the rear of the wagon. 'The biggest of them you will call him Wolf.'

On hearing its name the hound uncurled from its scrape beneath the wagon, and though rangier than its namesake stood almost three feet high at the shoulder. Mathew likened the dog to a home-bred English lurcher, tucked at the belly, but its quarters were heavily muscled from running down hare and gut-shot antelope. Its coat was roughly brindled, black and brown like the stones of a dried-out riverbed. At the chest and neck the beast's coat was layered with natural armour – mud and fur hardened by a thousand fitful nights beneath a dozen different wagons.

'And his woman,' added Carlus. He clicked his fingers for the bitch to come out into the open. 'Not as strong in the body, but in the head more clever than the fox.'

She came to him side on, crabbing like a buffalo from thick thorn, unsure of the Boer's intentions for from Carlus Pieters a blow with his shovel-sized hand would be just as quickly meted out as a gentle tug to her ear.

'Tiger,' he spoke softly to her and winked an eye at Mathew; she was obviously the Boer's favourite. 'Staying with Carlus will not be good. You must go with the *Engelsman* and watch over his wagon. In Kimberley there will be barely enough money for me to feed my children.' He fingered the soft tip of her ear so that she leant towards him, tongue flopping pink from between her teeth, her grin deceptive and ingratiating, eyes soft as those of a year-old pup though the bitch was quicker and more dangerous than her mate. Carlus had seen her take the head from a rabbit with a single snap of her powerful jaws.

Mathew dropped his hand to a point level with that of the bitch's head. At her shoulder, compared to Wolf, the bitch stood a full inch shorter. She took in the smell of him and watched his face – with that slow beat of a goose's wing her tail started to wag and Mathew found himself ensnared by those smiling eyes – eyes that were never to bear him malice or uncertainty, not once in all the years that were to follow.

'When you take the road, tie her to your wagon and Wolf will follow. Wherever there is the scent of a woman, a man will not be far behind. Feed them well my friend and the dogs will never leave you.'

'What about your driver?' asked Mathew, and looked anxiously along the line of Pieters' oxen.

'I have already paid him off. If you have need of a *voorloper* then better you hurry before you lose him to the pit.'

Mathew swung up into the saddle.

'Two hours at the most. I will be back for the rest of my servants – and for those jackals of yours.' He reached for Carlus' hand. '*Dankie vir jou help meneer.*'

'And to you *Engelsman*,' said Carlus and climbed back out of the rain.

-9-

As a sodden blanket, winter rolled its wind out over Kimberley. Mathew buttoned his jacket against it and drew down the brim of his hat to hold off the drizzle, but the cold had crept inside of him and he was grateful for a meagre sense of warmth that rose from his horse's flanks. From his front, the column's tailing wagon rolled to meet him, then lumbered on past. Close to the wagon's tailboard servants and dogs walked and squabbled playfully, eager for that first taste of the wilderness. Twenty yards in from the roadside, grey smoke leant begrudgingly from a small fire.

'You look down upon Mhlangana Khumalo like a baboon from the hilltop. What do you want with me white man?'

Mathew shook his feet free of the stirrups and dismounted.

'Only that I might share your fire, though from what I can see there is little enough of it to keep even one man from this cold.' He fed the fire with small twigs from about his feet, more a helpless gesture than an attempt to increase the fire's strength. The embers hissed at the rain.

'Pieters – Carlus Pieters. He said that you worked for him?'

'The Boer said many things. He was just as quick with his fists as he was with his tongue. It was a mistake.'

'His children are sick?'

'They are sick.' Mhlangana nodded. 'Around the mines the ground is littered with the graves of white men's children. A price they are willing to pay for their greed.'

'And you are not?' Mathew smiled.

'For stones?' His eyes lifted. 'Look around you, white man. Choose whichever one your heart desires. It will cost you nothing.'

'You know they are not the same,' said Mathew, 'diamonds can bring the wealth of kings to any man who finds them.'

'And to what purpose would I put this fortune?' He waited for an answer, and when none came, chuckled softly at Mathew's lack of reasoning. 'Search for your foolish stones, white man. Leave me in peace with my fire.'

'Work for me.'

Mhlangana shook his head. He held out both his hands – palms upwards. They were thickly calloused, in places, cracked all the way through to the living flesh below.

'Four years I have laboured in the *Umgodi Makhulu*. No more.'

'Not in the diggings,' said Mathew. 'As the leader of my oxen.'

The rain had thickened. Mhlangana shivered from the cold, but already his eyes were brighter.

'And where would I lead this wagon? Which is the road you would have me take?'

'North.' Mathew told him. 'Across the Crocodile River.'

# -10-

Catherine struggled to compose herself and waited for Mhlangana to pull on a pair of her son's breeches beneath his traditional regalia of civet tails and leather apron – for what the Matabele had come to her wagon with, was little enough to save her from embarrassment.

'He's too broad in the shoulders for one of your shirts, Mathew. Take a blanket from under your cot. You said that he worked in the pit?'

'For Blackie McKinnon,' said Mathew, 'four years in the

77

diggings before he took up with Carlus Pieters.'

'Your father spoke often of McKinnon. A fair man with his labour but quick with his fists and one for the bottle, I think was the way he put it.'

Mhlangana walked alongside the lead oxen, across his shoulders, on a strip of hide he carried the assegai, the *Iklwa*, the short stabbing spear of the Matabele.

'Any regrets?' Mathew looked to his mother.

'Only that we did not do this sooner.'

'Amen to that,' Mathew agreed and leant out from the wagon box for one last glimpse of civilization. Kimberley was behind them and the servants Mathew had taken from Carlus Pieters never once looked back. They were encouraging the dogs to hunt. Bright-eyed both dogs meandered amongst grass and low scrub, nose down for new scents, those they had known in Kimberley already forgotten.

After a week's trek the best part of eighty miles lay between the last wagon and the diggings. Now, sweet thorn acacia and *kameeldoring* dominated the wilderness for only the hardiest trees could withstand that time of thirst between the rains. Thorn, hard and sharp as cobblers' needles rattled as flint on steel to dry winds and there was little sign of any human being having ventured there. To the column's western flank the ground had been cropped of grass by nomadic antelope, it was the fiery rim of the Great Kalahari and another three months would pass before the onset of rain.

Catherine took a moment's rest from filling and trimming the lamps and stared with distaste at the dust on her clothes. Her hair, which had once been soft and scented with lavender, was now brittle and dry to the touch, and when she chanced to take out a mirror from

78

beneath her cot, her eyes showed rings of dark shadows from hard labour and her perpetual fight with a cruel intolerant wilderness. About the wagon, where in that last night the cold had come from that open starlit sky, now there was intolerable heat and parched earth. Dust flurried about the cattle as Mhlangana inspanned them; it rose in clouds from servants' feet as they hurried to load their chattels, eager to be away from that place of little shade and no water. Even the dogs seemed part of the ground on which they lay.

'You have a visitor,' Catherine called out to Mathew. The dogs sprang out from their scrapes at the sound of an incoming rider.

Burnham reined his horse alongside the wagon. He tipped his hat to Catherine then turned his attention to Mathew.

'Would I be right in thinking you own a rifle of sorts?'

'8mm Mannlicher,' said Mathew and vaulted down from the rear of the wagon.

'And can you ride? By that I mean, all day.'

'As well as anyone,' said Mathew.

Burnham coughed the dust from his throat.

'Then I'll be back in an hour. Make sure to bring along enough water.'

Mathew called for Mhlangana to saddle his horse then ducked inside the wagon for his rifle.

He smelled the oil; the barrel almost pitch black in the half light of the wagon tent. He pushed home the breech bolt and when he squeezed the trigger the firing pin fell with a satisfying metallic snap to the Mannlicher's empty chamber.

Catherine watched without him being aware of her presence, and indeed, found herself intimidated by what might well be expected of her son.

'Would it not be a good idea if Mhlangana went with you?'

'Not this time, mother.' Mathew buckled the heavy ammunition belt across his chest. 'Get him to stoke up the fire at last light – and sharpen your knives, I have no intention of returning empty-handed.'

Mathew rode head to head with the American. He rode with a natural flair for the mare's unusual gait, letting her find her easiest speed by changing the lateral drive of her legs to that peculiar, diagonal gait of the trippling horse. Burnham brought them to a halt at the edge of a small plateau and they looked beyond it, down into the valley. Short of a small breeze rustling its way amongst scatterings of sweet thorn there was no sound, no sight of a single manmade thing for miles at either hand.

Burnham shook his feet free of the stirrup irons.

'Once we pass that line of hills we're on our own. No houses, no farms, nothing. Maybe the odd prospector or hunter on his way back from the fly country.' He looked to the boy alongside him. 'Just open veld until we reach the Tati River, eight weeks from now.'

'Suits me fine,' said Mathew, 'right now I'm more concerned with the embarrassment of going back to the wagons empty-handed.'

Up to that point they had seen nothing of any size that warranted the use of a single bullet. The scrubby landscape had been stripped clean of all but the smallest signs of wildlife, what remained had hidden away from the heat in deep burrows and thorn thickets, for even at that distance out from Kimberley, contract meat hunters had been busy with their rifles.

Burnham reached for his saddlebag and drew out a brass

telescope. Gently he adjusted the lens to suit his eye then moved the glass through a wide arc. He took time in probing shadows, rocky defiles and those almost invisible scars left by ancient watercourses. Where the veld was thickest he would let his interest linger there, searching out shapes that were irregular to their surroundings. Sometimes Mathew heard the American's breathing catch, and briefly the steady sweep of the spyglass would falter.

'As God is my witness,' Burnham marvelled, 'I don't believe what I am seeing.' He thrust the glass at Mathew. 'That break in the hillside; in my entire life I've seen nothing like it.'

Mathew adjusted the lens. Through a rolling cloud of dust he saw rank upon rank of wild antelope – a single mass of colour; charcoal, gold and flashes of white. As the fingers of some ancient delta the migrating herd spread across the valley floor.

'I see them.'

'That's right laddie, you see them and you will not meet many men who have.'

'What in God's name are they?'

'*Trekbokken*, the Boers call it. Thousands of Springbok. Been known to take upwards of a week for the entire herd to pass the same spot'

*Stay well clear of the trekbokken,* an old Boer had warned him, his wagon battered and scarred where the springbok had dashed themselves to a bloody pulp. *Even now there are pieces of bone still inside the wood. I think more than a hundred were piled to the side of my wagon.* And with a wistful smile recalled the memory of his windfall. *Ja kerel, my butcher's knives were busy for three days – enough dried meat for that whole year and not the price of a single shot from my old roer.*

'So what are we waiting for?' Mathew handed back the

spyglass and gathered his reins. 'We should be up with them while we still have the chance.'

'And how many Springbok would you be planning on shooting?'

'Ten? Twenty? As many as I have bullets for.' Already his rifle was out from its scabbard; so much bounty had awakened the urge for him to butcher out of hand. He followed the American to where higher ground presented them with a better vantage point and again, Burnham brought out the telescope.

'They'll be here soon enough. Nothing short of the Almighty will stop them now.'

The springbok were lean and skittish and constantly moved southwards, the need for fresh grass now paramount. Their speed changed by the second, sometimes slowing almost to a walk where their numbers were forced through narrow defiles. Drawn onwards by some ancient atavism they would again surge as a living tide over open ground.

There was the continuous drumming of hooves. The air shuddered, overpowered by sheer volume of noise. From the broken earth rose veils of choking dust – as a single, sulphur-coloured cloud it climbed above the land. Trees that were there for a hundred years were stripped from the ground; animals too slow in finding refuge were cut down mid-flight, mercilessly trampled.

'The gully!' Mathew shouted. 'They will never be able to jump the gap.'

Both men stood in awe of what they were seeing – both struck dumb by the spectacle.

At first the springbok drew up in tight, excited ranks. Vast numbers crowded the edge of that sixty foot drop to the gully floor, then, as the mile-wide herd of antelope compressed to a solid phalanx, with wild unseeing eyes the forerunners flung themselves outwards into the void.

From the gully floor echoed the cries of the mortally wounded; wave after wave until the ravine was filled with the broken and the dying.

'So many dead,' whispered Burnham, and for three more hours others followed in their tens of thousands, using their fallen comrades as gruesome stepping stones.

By mid-afternoon only the hapless sick and injured still struggled to follow on. Behind them came the scavengers – hyena, jackal and the cape vulture. The sky was already filled with crows, taking time with their feasting – silent funereal flights from carcass to carcass to pluck out eyes and other delicacies, so that they fattened quickly on this plethora of titbits.

'It's over,' said Burnham, thankful of the silence, but he knew that in those next few hours the stench of putrefaction would hang like a tar wind above the valley. Already the hum of greenbottle flies was all around them.

'We need to get on with what we came for. Wait for me on the ridge if you don't feel up to it.'

Mathew put his horse to a slow walk alongside Burnham's. Though he had never seen one, he likened what lay around him to the aftermath of some terrible battle.

Burnham stopped alongside a living antelope and slid from the saddle. The springbok ram fought valiantly to right itself, all four legs were broken – its courage ineffectual. Burnham drew out a knife from his belt.

'Turn away if you haven't the stomach.'

Mathew dismounted and held out his hand for the knife.

'Let me do this. Tell me how.'

'Do it quickly and cleanly, a weak effort could cost you

an eye – even your life.' Burnham straddled the animal's back and took a strong grip of the ram's horns, pinning it there. 'When I turn its head,' he instructed Mathew, 'cut down hard for the bone.'

Mathew spat the dust from his lips. His nerve faltered – the blade hovered, indecisively he touched it against the springbok's quivering throat.

'Do it!' hissed the American and with his voice the trigger, forced Mathew to put the full weight of his shoulder into the killing.

That first stroke cut deeply into the airway. Bright arterial blood sprang from the animal's throat – red and hot with wasting life. As Mathew watched and its eyes let go of the sunlight, something inside of him died.

He dropped the knife and stood up, red with living blood. From chest to waist and the tips of his quivering fingers he was thick with the sickly mess of it – then the flies were on him and the smell and taste were there in his throat and he retched like a man stricken with fever.

Burnham held the ram until the last small tremors of its life abated.

'Always bad,' he told Mathew. 'I mean the first time. Never look at the eyes, worst thing a man can do.' He tested the blade with the ball of his thumb and with a single stroke split the animal's stomach cavity, then handed back the knife to Mathew for him to cut out the entrails.

# -11-

In the weeks that followed, Mathew learned the easy tempo of the wilderness, the way it moved with slow deliberate rhythm – leaves across the surface of a quiet lake. He learned how to distance himself from conflict and how each day became more precious than the one before. He learned to strip, reassemble and fire the Mannlicher with a hunter's skill so that even the American was hard pushed to match his prowess. Burnham would laugh delightedly whenever his protégé beat him into second place. Now, Mathew took the Mannlicher's peculiarities in his stride – the straight, pull-back action of the breech bolt, the top-loading, five round clip that was ejected once empty, and the bullet's arched trajectory from its usage of black powder so that an accurate shot would demand the hunter's succinct feel for windage and elevation. All these things Mathew had learned in a few short weeks and he was now a common sight, sat astride the Arab mare with the results of his day's hunting tied behind the saddle.

Whenever the wagons were outspanned, Mathew would disappear into the veld with the Matabele never far from the mare's flank. Mhlangana showed him sign and spoor left by wild beasts, so that he quickly learned to recognise them apart and give names to the creatures that made them.

'Sometimes a hunter must see with his nose,' Mhlangana expounded, and Mathew laughed at the images conjured up by his imagination. 'Learn how to use it, only then will you put lions apart from buffalo, wild dog from the honey badger or farting baboons from a leopard that waits for you in the shadows.' All that Mhlangana knew he gave to

Mathew, so that together they hunted as a single skilful entity.

When the column reached the western foothills of the Magaliesburg, wild fowl rose in their hundreds from the forest's edge. It was then, in the late hours of that afternoon, Mathew came out from his wagon carrying a twelve-bore double and a full belt of birdshot.

'Time for you to learn how to shoot,' he tossed the gun to the Matabele. 'Let's go find us something to eat.'

Wherever they walked the two of them studied the ground for sign. Many times, Mathew would hold up his hand and listen – the way Mhlangana had taught him. Both crouched low to the ground for them to see beneath overhanging branches where fowl might be feeding.

Mathew was first to hear them. He touched a finger to Mhlangana's arm and pointed at the undergrowth, not twenty yards from where they were standing.

'Guinea fowl,' he whispered and pointed upwards. 'They'll break for that opening in the trees.'

Mhlangana pulled back both hammers and put up the twelve bore, squinting along the barrels for the shotgun's stubby foresight.

The birds came up without warning – fat and noisy, numbering more than Mathew had estimated so that the sky above his head filled with them – drumming the air on urgent, steel-grey wings. Some came to within mere feet of the hide before veering away, clattering through branches for a chance of open sky.

Mhlangana followed their flight and with both eyes open sighted the gun to the densest part of that swirling cloud – then squeezed both triggers and sent a double charge of lead shot hissing into the confusion.

Simultaneously, like seeds from an English Sycamore,

three birds folded mid-flight and tumbled earthwards. The sky emptied and the hunters were left only with silence and the smell of burnt powder.

Mathew shook his head in disbelief. 'Three birds with one shot!'

'It was a good strike.'

'The devil himself could not have done better.'

They set aside the largest of the three – a fat cock bird for Catherine's iron cauldron. Then Mhlangana built up a fire, close to a stream where the bank was thick with clay. Mathew watched him encase the two remaining birds in clay cocoons and when the fire had drawn to a dull red glow, buried them beneath a deep blanket of hot embers.

They sat opposite one another and talked through filled mouths, of what had already gone and what might be waiting ahead of them, their faces streaked with fat and ash from the makeshift oven.

From then on it was the terrain not time that dictated the column's progress. Where the forest broke, the land fell away towards the west. A week's ride with a good horse and the trees would disappear, replaced by short scrub and the vicious *wag-'n-bietjie* thorn. Here, the Kalahari waited with her waterless riverbeds and thick sands.

Burnham swung the wagons more to a north-westerly bearing, pushing hard in the early hours and in the heat of midday, stopping wherever there was shade. By nightfall the column would be drawn up nose to tail in the tight defensive circle of the laager; the oxen outspanned and gaps beneath the wagons closed with sharp thorn against lion and hyena.

Catherine marvelled at a sudden change in the wilderness. Mopani, the axe-breaker tree dominated the veld, their peculiar spoor-shaped leaves edged vertically to the sunlight, conserving moisture. Solitary cream-of-tartar, the great baobab, stood out as grey, arthritic giants above the mopani – some of them more than a thousand years old. From her seat on the wagon box she took in the colours of that changing landscape, most were tints of brown and terracotta, all were products of terrible heat and little water. As a single train of covered wagons they went down into that hot and ancient valley.

'About three miles north of the column,' Mathew reined his horse alongside their wagon. 'The Limpopo – I've seen it!'

Catherine stood up from the wagon box and screwed up her eyes at the way ahead, eager for her first glimpse of the river.

'You are sure of this?'

'As ever I will be,' said Mathew. 'I'm pushing on without the column. You should make the river by nightfall. If not, watch for my fire to guide you in.'

Catherine's heart raced. A few more days at best and they would forfeit the protection of the column. For a moment her courage faltered. Stories of ill fortune had not taken long in finding her – of blackwater fever, a sickness ten times more vile and virulent than the malarial fever that spawned it – marauding savages who in their hundreds fell upon settler wagons and killed for the sheer joy of it. *My husband found the wagon stuck fast to its axles in the bed of the Shashani River* a woman had told her – an Afrikaner woman with the heart and strength of two men. *All but one of them were dead.* Her fists were balled to meaty hammers, her need for revenge dark and unsated. Hatred spat from her mouth. *Four children... in the riverbed with their little throats cut through.* With her face raised up to the heavens she had beseeched a vengeful God; her lust was for Him to bestow a deep and terrible fate upon those killers of little children. Spent from her cursing, she had slumped into her *riempie* chair and held out her glass for another filling of Cape Smoke. *It will be a fight to the end*, she had prophesised. *But it will come, as sure as God gave me, Anna Magdel Bowker the power to foretell.*

The memory of their conversation still lived – every venomous word – every blow-by-blow description of the wagon in the riverbed. Sometimes, Catherine would sit bolt upright from her sleep, her eyes wide and fixed to that dark night outside her wagon tent. When the men were away from the wagons, Catherine would, without compunction take comfort from Magdel's company and learn from her the ways of surviving the wilderness.

Magdel showed off old and practiced skills, second handed from her mother. The making of candles and soap, remedies for colds and colic, the grinding of native tobaccos for her snuff and with a blade made razor thin by a thousand sharpenings she had, in less than an hour, butchered the carcass of a full grown Impala ram – stripping back hide from flesh and flesh from bone. Venison, sliced to the length of a man's arm was liberally mopped with salt and coriander, black pepper and a splashing of raw vinegar to ward off the maggot fly. The meat must always be hung in the shade, and only in winter when the rains are finished or it will rot within a day; high enough for the wild dogs and jackals not to be able to reach it. The biltong would stay fresh and firm for months on end and was the mainstay of a Boer's very survival when game was scarce. With a motherly eye she had watched Catherine stake out the wet Impala hide for the sun and salt to cure, then scour the skin of fat with river stones, tanning it with potent juices taken from roots of the kleinsuurkaree and the bark of sweet thorn acacia. With the hide now stained to a deep red, through patient deliberation and the passing of many days, Catherine learned to work its softness almost to that of a woven blanket.

It will keep out the cold of winter, Magdel had told her and laughed aloud at the sheer delight in Catherine's eyes. God will always provide, *my meisie*. Though Magdel knew, that by his other hand, He might just as surely take away and in the blinking of an eye.

# -12-

For almost six months there had been no hint of rain. The great Limpopo River was now a lethargic string of emerald pools, held together by threads of old water. Elephant and Cape buffalo had ploughed their way through the shallows and their dung lay scattered as fibrous heaps along the shoreline. Everywhere, the rank, bovine stench of the herd draped thickly over the wind. Mathew turned in the saddle; the crackle of dry branches trodden underfoot made him reach for his rifle.

'You won't be taking a bath, then?'

Mathew spurred his horse back up the slope to where the American stood his horse beneath the fever tree.

'How long before the wagons get here?'

'Sundown,' said Burnham. 'There's an old hunter's camp about a mile downstream. We'll be staying over for two or three days before going on to the concession at Tati.'

'Why not push on across the river?' asked Mathew, eager

to be well inside the new territory before nightfall.

'The women haven't seen fresh water for two weeks. There'll be barrels to fill and washing to do. Especially yours,' he jibed, 'you smell like a goat.'

By late afternoon the wagons were outspanned and the cattle led to grass while an army of servants and span leaders cut down thorn for the laager. The ground for a hundred yards around the camp was cleared of scrub, any living creature, human or otherwise would be easily picked out from the moonlight. Satisfied the camp was secure, Burnham called the people together. He raised his voice to carry the hubbub.

'From now on, this is the way it will be. For those of you who have never crossed the Limpopo, once we are on the other side we will be fair game for Matabele raiding parties.' He looked down from the wagon and again raised his voice to reach those furthest away. 'Keep your rifles and ammunition close to hand. Don't make the mistake of underestimating the Matabele, they're hardened fighters, not some home-spun servant girls you left behind in Kimberley.' Subdued laughter filtered back to him. 'Fires will be kept going throughout the night and there will be a watch system put into place. Every man will take his turn and no leniency will be shown to those caught sleeping whilst on watch.' Again he paused and waited for the whispering to die down. 'One more thing, when you go down to the river, go in threes and like I said, take your rifles. And for those who have never seen crocodiles, the Limpopo holds more than you think. Bucket the water well back from the river bank and wash where it's safe to do so.'

Magdel Bowker raised her hand.

'How many are going on to Victoria? When will they

leave the main column?'

'When and where is entirely up to them,' he answered. 'But I would recommend the juncture of the Tati and Shashi rivers.' He picked out Mathew and his mother from the crowd. 'It will take more than a fair share of courage and an eye for quick shooting if that journey were to succeed.'

Again, Magdel Bowker raised her hand. 'You have not answered the question, *Engelsman*, How many? How many wagons will be going on to Victoria?'

'Only one that I know of,' Burnham told her, and the finality of his reply threw stark silence over the gathering.

-13-

'What made you change your mind?' Catherine asked.

'The Lord changed it for me,' argued Magdel, 'I'm going with you. There is no choice in the matter.' She closed her eyes and leant back in her chair. 'Besides,' she went on, 'my philandering husband with his string of coloured jezebels have been seen hunting the Umtelekwe Valley near Victoria.' She growled up phlegm and spat it into the long grass. '*Jong*, when I find that unholy father of our daughter Sannie Louisa, that Johannes Petrus Bowker will feel my hands around that scrawny, chicken throat of his.' She wrenched the cork from the brandy bottle and cocked an eye at Catherine. 'Can you load and fire a rifle? The truth, mind. Where we are going there is no place for a woman who cannot use a rifle as well as she uses her cooking pot.'

'Only if I have to,' lied Catherine.

'Then tomorrow we will start your teaching.' She sipped on the brandy. 'I was fifteen years old when Dawie de Bruin taught me to fire my first rifle. I should have married him, instead of being tempted away by that *duiwel* of a Johannes Bowker.' Her nostalgia eased, 'In my wagon I have four *gewere* – four guns and all of them I can shoot straight with – straighter than any man.' She left her glass on the table and reached inside her apron pocket. Her fingers found a silver box, ornately engraved and appealing to the eye. She sprung the tiny lid. 'Take some. The sneezing will brighten your eyes.'

Catherine declined politely and watched Magdel's finger and thumb nip for a generous pinch of dark snuff. With a snort that would shame a bull rhinoceros, the powder disappeared deep inside the labyrinth of Magdel's sinuses.

'Paradise.' Magdel blinked back the tears, her features screwed to a rotund sphere of puckered flesh. 'Tomorrow,' she went on, 'Sannie will put out the targets along the kopje and I give you my word, after one hour you will shoot them down as good as your son,' she shook her head. '*Nee wat*, not just your son.' Her finger wagged like lamb's tails. 'Better even than the American who leads the wagons – *ja*, that will be good.' Magdel nodded, 'in the eyes of the Lord better than the American will be good enough.'

Within an hour of that next sunrise Magdel had set her trestle and chairs in front of a small hill; her rifles laid out, barrels oiled and blue in the sunlight. Catherine made her way between the thorn trees carrying Mathew's Mannlicher rifle at the trail. Though she was more used to the Metford, the Mannlicher was well balanced and from a dead rest she had seen Mathew take down a rabbit from

93

two hundred yards.

Catherine drew up her chair at the trestle and turned Magdel's attention to fleeting glimpses of a young girl some sixty yards out from where they were sitting.

'Your daughter moves so quickly.'

'Like a *klein bokkie*,' Magdel agreed, 'and always without shoes. One day that *verdwaalde* daughter of mine will tramp the back of a snake and that will be the end of her.'

Catherine watched the girl's progress, mesmerised by her agility. The sun was to the girl's side and sometimes threw her outline against the granite, catching up with her between the shadows. Then, again she was away, jinking from rock to rock like a hyrax fleeing the attentions of a wild cat. The targets were of pale-coloured sapwood, by her clever use of shadows and swaying grasses, Sannie positioned them, affording the shooters varying degrees of difficulty.

She finished her task and in the winking of an eye was down on level ground, unashamedly barefooted and with a lightness of step that caught at Mathew's breathing before he had chance to dismount.

Her hair, though midnight black, flared with an aura of pure gold and held the light about her as though she were an angel and had just set foot upon the earth. She had seen the Englishman before, but only momentarily. Now he was there in front of her, standing with one foot still in the stirrup and it was then Sannie knew that she had caught his eye – that he was watching her. With her head high and with that long, unhurried stride of the young lioness, she walked towards him. Mathew found himself staring. Like an emergent butterfly, Sannie's youthful body strained to be free. A hundred washes had left her garment gossamer thin, so that now it clung to her skin, a fine mist shot through with sunlight. Mathew could not help dropping his eyes to the outline of her breasts, to her waist and beyond; down to the sway and roll of her hips.

'Sannie,' she smiled at Mathew and held out her hand for him, though out of kilter with the timbre of her own language, her voice was mellifluous, softer than a summer breeze.

'My name, *meneer*, is Sannie Louisa Bowker.'

Her hair, combed loosely back from her forehead was darker than his memories of Kimberley's open pit at midnight, her eyes a mix of grey and blue, the colour of deep-running Kimberlite rock that had entrapped those precious stones so many millions of years ago.

'Mathew,' he croaked, and annoyed by his own embarrassment fought the urge to climb back into the saddle and gallop his horse for the deep forest.

She took the bridle from his fingers and with a gentle, almost unnoticeable rounding of her lips blew soft, silent puffs of her own breath into the openings of the mare's velvet muzzle.

'You are so very beautiful,' she whispered, but with her eyes to Mathew's. 'You bought the horse from a Boer, *ja*?'

Mathew nodded. 'In Kimberley; I have named her Amira – The Princess.'

'And is she?' Sannie smiled at him, but with her eyes. 'Is she as beautiful as the princess you had hoped for?'

'More than,' he replied. 'More beautiful than anything I have ever seen.' Then the sudden urgency of Magdel's voice shattered the moment.

'Just like your father. *Los uit die Engelsman*! – leave the man alone, for all you know he is already spoken for.' She shook her head at Catherine. 'Like her father, always ready with cow eyes for anyone new in the camp.' Magdel returned her attention to the attributes of the German made Mauser rifle. 'This is a rifle favoured by Boer hunters.' She worked the rifle's loading bolt, lifted a single 8mm bullet from its five round clip and drove it into the breech. She wriggled forwards in her chair; with her elbows against the table she pulled the butt plate hard-in to the fleshy pad of her shoulder.

'Set your sights to one hundred yards. Any higher and the bullet will be too much over your target's head.' She selected one of the wooden pegs that Sannie had positioned on the kopje then slowly took up the trigger pressure. Her shoulder kicked from the weapon's recoil and the targeted peg leapt like a startled bird from its niche in the rocks.

'As easy as that,' she encouraged, and lowered the Mauser.

'I will try for the peg at the base of the flat stone,' Catherine decided, and allowed Magdel a moment to settle her eyes on the chosen target. She marked the positions of two other pegs, loaded the Mannlicher and took a fine bead on her first target.

The report crashed at Magdel's ears and before the first wooden peg had reached the highest peak of its twisting parabola, another two leapt from the hillside; the gunfire one continuous roll of thunder.

'*Magtig*! You have made a fool of this old woman. In all my life I have never seen shooting like that, Katarina.' Magdel nodded. 'Katarina,' she mused, delighted with her slip of the tongue. 'With an eye like yours a Boer name will suit you better. Those heathen across the river...' she followed Catherine's lead and sent two more targets spinning away from the hillside. 'For their own sakes they will do better to leave us be.'

# -14-

Once they had crossed the Limpopo, for three more days the column moved steadily northwards, and again the land was set upon by surly, heated winds blowing from the interior. At times the air itself seemed scorched and charred of any life for it hung malevolently above a sparse forest – an immobile blanket of seared sky. Like the Limpopo, both the Shashi and Tuli rivers were hardly more than pools of filth, churned repeatedly by vast herds of buffalo and migratory elephant. People were forced to dig deeply into river beds for clean water, sometimes to a depth of several feet.

Burnham called a halt on the north bank of the Tuli River, less than half a mile from its confluence with the Shashi. Four days were spent repairing damaged wheels and repacking axle stubs with fresh grease. Barrels were filled, oxen were led to wherever there was food and before last light were brought back into the laager. Throughout the night, fires were kept to a full burn.

'Tomorrow we leave the column,' said Mathew, his own trepidations of what might be waiting ahead, virulently alive. 'Magdel has reckoned on another four weeks for us to reach the fort at Victoria.'

'Provided nothing untoward happens along the way,' Catherine reminded him and stared deeper into the fire. 'Sometimes I think we should take Burnham's advice and wait for more wagons to come through from Mafeking – four to five weeks he said, before they reach the concession.'

'We have to keep going,' said Mathew. 'When the rains break, Mhlangana is certain Lobengula will push his impis further to the south. We have no choice but to carry on for Victoria.'

Catherine shuddered; the thought of them being attacked by the Matabele tripped her heartbeat. 'Magdel wants to leave the column at first light,'

'As soon as the oxen are inspanned,' Mathew agreed, 'the Bowkers will take the lead. A week to ten days and we should be well out of Lobengula's reach.'

## -15-

'Something tells me that it won't be long before I see you again.' Burnham sat uncomfortably in the saddle. He turned sideways on and lifted the flap to a leather saddlebag. The telescope was just as Mathew remembered. 'Bound to come in handy,' said Burnham and saw Mathew flinch at the offer. 'I would like you to have it. Belonged to my father, reckon it would make the old man proud.'

Mathew forced back the lump in his throat. His voice failed him. Burnham sensed his angst and again reached inside the saddlebag.

'One more thing, then for sure I'll be on my way.'

The casket had been fashioned from cedar and inlaid with mother-of-pearl. Its double clasps were from raw, native silver mined in America's high Sierra Nevada.

'One of a pair, kept one of these beauties for myself,' said Burnham and gently freed the clasps from their fastenings.

'Go ahead,' Burnham urged him. 'Lift her out – she belongs to you now.'

Bought by Burnham's father from Samuel Colt's renowned Armoury on the banks of the Connecticut River, the carved, steer-head grips were made from white, iridescent mother-of-pearl on walnut and the metal parts were still that midnight blue of the unused weapon. The inscription, COLT FRONTIER SIX SHOOTER had been factory etched along the barrel and there was still that faint familiar smell of its last oiling.

'.44 – 40 calibre,' Burnham explained the weapon's attributes. 'Still the old black powder cartridge but plenty powerful enough. Same calibre as a Winchester '73 rifle.'

Mathew lifted it clear of its velvet cushion.

'Single-action Colt,' Burnham went on, 'means you have to cock the hammer for every shot.' Lastly, he handed Mathew a waxed calico bag. 'These will see you through until you find a trader; reckon there's upwards of a hundred bullets in there.'

Mathew swallowed hard to clear the constriction in his throat, but still he could not speak.

'I'd best be going then,' said Burnham. 'Look after the telescope and keep the Colt handy.'

'I will not forget,' Mathew managed.

'I'll telegraph your father once I reach the fort at the Tuli settlement.' He smiled at Mathew and nodded his head one last time. 'Look after your mother,' he said, then turned his horse about and put in his heels; within minutes the haze had swallowed him up.

A bateleur eagle spilled air from beneath her wings. From her height above the wilderness she had seen the wagons and her interest piqued, for whenever these grinding creatures passed there were easy pickings for those quick enough to spot the kill.

With an imperious eye she took up the still trembling form of a snake; now heavily laden, the eagle flogged at the air to regain altitude.

Mathew saw the raptor strike and lift away and already she was feeding, tearing strips of flesh from the twitching reptile as she rose with the thermal. He watched through the telescope until the eagle disappeared, hidden inside the sky.

Mathew swept the horizon with his spyglass, comparing what was there in front of him to Magdel's dog-eared collection of notes and sketch maps. Sometimes the sunlight streamed directly into his face and he was forced to turn away for fear of the sun searing his eyeball. He made sightings on the far horizon and eagerly sought out breaks in the hills, then in the shadow of a wooded ridge he found the opening Magdel's husband had made reference to... *pass with the sun to the span's head and the long hill to your left hand*. So that Mathew knew the Shashani river was some twenty more miles to the east and he estimated the passage of three more days for their wagons to reach there.

Mgandaan, one of Lobengula's most senior Generals stood with twenty five young warriors from the Isizela and Imbezu regiments, just below the crest of a high ridge. Most had seen fewer than twenty summers since their birthing, but their eyes were keen for the exhilaration of that first fight – the first blooding of spears and the respect it commanded.

Something had caught his eye – perhaps the glistening of spring leaves or running water, yet Mgandaan knew the heavens were drier than the ground on which he stood. In reality, whatever had caught the sunlight could only have come from the shiny baubles of a trader's wagon, or the steel of a soldier's gun.

'*MuRungu!*' he hissed. 'White men!' And he marked the place where he had seen that smallest winking of sunlight.

He took the down slope as though the ground and bare rocks were covered with soft river moss, the others followed his speed so that long after their passing a mist of red dust hung in the air. He remembered with sadness, thirty-seven warriors had fallen to the white men's guns. Thirty-seven had died with their spines shot through so that the stream where they had watered ran red with blood and when the darkness came, hyena tore out their entrails and gorged on the dying. The memory of that slaughter made his eyes fill, but a strange madness burned inside him and the blade in his hand scythed back the grass like the horns of the bull buffalo.

He stopped to catch the direction of a slight breeze and from it took the different smells and odours of the forest. Above them, stronger than all the others were the smells of gun oil and wood smoke, the dung of cattle and the rancid smell of fat burnt on a white man's fire, and he drew deeply at the infected air.

'We are amongst them,' he growled, and watched with lions' eyes for their quarry to wander into the killing ground.

# -18-

Already the landscape had changed. Now there was a mixing of mimosa with spring musasa and every sunrise came at the wagons from between the heads of their lead oxen. Mathew urged his horse alongside Magdel's wagon.

'There's our way through. That is if your husband's writings are accurate.'

'And why shouldn't they be, *Engelsman*?' Magdel glowered at him from her seat on the wagon box. 'The cattle need grass. We cross the hills tomorrow or the sun will be gone before we have chance to outspan.' She raised her hand to ward off the sunlight. 'By those trees. I have had enough of this *verdonder* heat.' She pointed out her chosen site to Mathew.

Sannie helped her mother down from the wagon box. As Magdel's feet touched the ground she looked about for snakes and other beings begot of the devil's influence. Anything lying in wait would feel the lash of her hippo-hide sjambok. Her fingers tightened about its stock in readiness.

'Find a place for your mother's chair,' she instructed Sannie, then put her servants to clearing the ground of grass and stones where snakes might lie in wait to nip at her ankles.

With Mathew's help, Sannie offloaded the dead weight of her mother's comfort and silently cursed the Malaccan carpenter who had made it. The wood was blood-red mahogany, heavy as old iron and pegged with dowels of stinkwood, and across the purposely broadened beam, the seat had been strung with *riems* of wild *renoster* hide, strong enough to bear her mother with the added weight of a Mauser rifle rested across her legs.

'And a fire, *my meisie*. Without a fire there will be no coffee, Heaven forbid.'

Sannie dragged the chair into the shade of a mimosa thorn and put up the trestle table. Magdel watched impassively. For supper, there was still the side of a red Impala ram on the wagon floor, wrapped in muslin and salt and less than a week old. From a skillet of hot lard she would coax out pumpkin fritters – fat and fried and thickly snowed with sugar and cinnamon. '*Ja*,' thought Magdel, 'for tonight that will be enough. In the morning the *Engelsman* must go to the forest with his rifle. If luck is with us, perhaps a pig or two from the reeds near the river.'

She would boil off fat for soap and candle making. Make sausages, thick as *Pofadders*' tails. Magdel nodded appreciatively at the wisdom in her decision making and lowered herself into the chair; her head bent forward for Sannie to drop in a filled pillow of goose down, then leant back and took on the peace of her chosen spot beneath the tree.

She sat with half closed eyes. Sannie moved as a yearling filly about her business of setting out a cleared space between the wagons. Magdel watched her – willowy as spring flowers – lithe as a hunting otter in the Tugela and she smiled at a time when her own body had been just as sleek, just as firm and compliant to eager fingertips – though by a woman of her age, quiet solitude was welcomed as a blessing. Now there was time for memories and an appreciation of fine foods, the blossoming of her own flesh and blood and the smell of mimosa blossom above her head. Yellow stars on a green sky. Perhaps, if she liked this place, they could camp for a few days – maybe three or even for an entire week if the wild pigs were down by the river like they were for her husband all those years ago. 'That *verdonder* husband,' she reminded herself, 'what is he doing so long away from his wife and child – I think when I see him again it would only be right for me to shoot the *bliksem's* head off.' Again her face softened and whilst others laboured, she drifted with her memories, up inside the soft, green canopy of mimosa leaves. 'Sannie,' she called to her daughter, still with her eyes half closed and the goose down pillow now perfectly shaped to the back of her neck. 'Bring my *geweer* – the Mauser, and the box of bullets from beneath my bed.'

Sannie brought down the rifle and set the box of ammunition on the table. She did not question her mother's reasons for needing the weapon – that way her life was easier and the hours would ebb and flow without argument. Soon the fire would be hot enough for coffee and with plenty of sugar she would take a cup of it for herself and sit up on the wagon box, perhaps with a flirting eye for the Englishman.

Magdel slid a five round clip down through the Mauser's open breech and quietly pushed home the loading bolt. The awkward angle of her seat made it difficult for her to hold the rifle steady. She was forced to take her time, waiting for the rhythm of her breathing to settle before drawing back on the trigger.

Apart from the orange flash at its throat, the snake's colouring blended perfectly with the leaves, both iridescently green so that Magdel found it difficult to set them apart. Only when the young boomslang breached gaps between the branches could she make out the slender, thumb-sized head with its tiny coloured collar, bright as orange naartjie peel against the sky.

The single shot clapped like thunder and rolled amongst the hills. Mhlangana dropped his axe and ran for the wagons but Mathew was there before him, the Colt already drawn from his belt. Then he saw the reason for the shooting, writhing on the ground at Magdel's feet.

'There was no need for the rifle. The noise will have carried for miles, you could have shouted for either one of us?'

'Magdel Bowker sorts out her own problems.' She lowered the Mauser across her thighs.' Wherever our wagon stops there are serpents waiting to eat at my legs, but not this one. This one I have sent him back to the devil.'

Sannie lifted the snake by its tail. The contorting body seemed aware of her touch and coiled back on itself, wrapping about her forearm, stiffening against her flesh. Purposely she stared at Mathew and she smiled at him, but with her eyes so that only he would be aware of her thoughts. She lowered her voice; it barely carried the distance between them.

'I have held much bigger ones than this, *meneer*.' Knowing the advantage was with her she rolled her arm free of the coils then flung the twitching serpent out beyond the wagons.

'You must dig a hole for the *slang*,' Magdel warned, 'or its family will pick up the blood scent and come looking. The camp will be filled with those devilish creatures.'

'Anyone within five miles of here will have heard the shot.' Mathew swung his attention back to Magdel, his mood transparent.

Magdel shook her head. 'A snake or a springbok – *maak nie saak nie* – it does not matter, there is no difference. A shot is a shot. Every Boer has the right to fire his rifle, be it for meat or killing the heathen. All is sanctified by the Almighty and if He means for the Matabele to hear the bullets of Magdel Bowker then so be it.' She dismissed the altercation with a perfunctory sweep of her hand. 'The matter is closed. The Matabele will only leave their precious villages after the first rain, and that is still a week or two away.'

Sannie lifted a pan of boiling water from the fire, filled the billy well short of the brim then added a muslin bag of ground coffee and pressed down the lid. The coffee was rough ground and black as old gunpowder. Magdel rolled her eyes at the smell and beckoned to Mathew.

'If you are still so afraid for our safety, *my seun*, perhaps you might go with my daughter, our water barrels are almost empty.'

Sannie unhooked a pail from its peg on the wagon. '*Kom, meneer*, take up your gun,' she smiled at him, eager for him to follow. 'I will wait for you by the river.' She ran from him, barefoot through the veld. Mhlangana leant on his axe and with knowing eyes watched Mathew lengthen his stride to keep up with the girl.

Sannie waded out to where the water ran fast against her legs. Mathew lay on his side, the heel of his hand to his chin and watched her dip the bucket beneath the surface. Her dress was wet to a foot above her knees and Mathew stared at the transparency of the cloth, tipping the brim of his hat to hide his eyes.

'Do you not swim, *meneer*?'

'I do swim,' he told her and flinched at a sudden tightness in his stomach, 'if I were of a mind to. What about you?' he countered weakly.

'Sometimes,' she told him. 'Sometimes when the sun is hot I swim for the water to keep me cool.' She set down the bucket. 'And now the sun is hot, but that is not why we came here. Is that not so, *meneer*?'

Mathew shook his head. The words stuck fast in his throat. Sannie had already loosened the buttons of her bodice, on tiptoe she lifted away her dress – then let it fall to the ground; a fragile wisp of cotton.

Without speaking, Sannie moved away from him and found a ridge of soft sand just beneath the stream's surface – she followed it out to where the water swirled at its deepest – dark, forbidding eddies about the juncture of her legs.

'Am I not to your liking, *meneer*?' Now her breasts were tipped to a dark and trembling pink from the chill of fast water.

'More than anything,' Mathew croaked, and not for a second could he tear his eyes from her.

'Then I would like it very much if you were to stand beside me.'

Mathew stood up and looked back at the way they had come – the canvas tops of the wagons were barely visible through the trees and he could still hear the solid strike of an axe to the base of a sweet thorn.

'I will turn my back for you,' she encouraged. 'Then I will count to ten.'

He hesitated a moment longer.

'... three, four, five, six...'

He dropped the Colt on a tussock of grass and stripped off his shirt and boots.

'... seven, eight...'

He reached her on the count of ten – her hair a black and gleaming cloak about her shoulders.

'You can touch me if you wish,' whispered Sannie, her voice soft but now unsteady – trembling like reeds to deep running currents.

Mathew wrapped his arms about her waist so that she could lean against him, her head against his chest and with her hands behind her back she reached for him inside the water. She felt him waken, slowly at first, then turned to face him and still her fingers worked their magic so that his eyes rolled in their sockets like those of a lovesick bull for a field of heifers.

'Past those reeds,' she whispered into his open mouth and led him with the current to where the stream shallowed. The bank, by that last year's seasonal flood had been spread with a white arc of virgin sand.

Sannie pushed him down, still with her face to his and with her tongue so very much alive inside his mouth that he was forced to hold her off to catch his breath.

'Lie still!' she laughed, and pinned his arms against the sand. 'Now you are mine and I will have whatever I wish from you.'

Mathew closed his eyes, but not completely so that he was still able to make out the exquisite shape of her mouth whenever she lifted her face from his, and when she moved over him her breasts brushed against his chest and left whatever he tried to say pinned to the back of his throat.

'Be quiet,' she whispered, and smiled at him through a halo of sunlight, 'the time for talking is long past.' She was so very clearly in control and delighted his senses in ways that he had never imagined – taking him on thunderous wings to the very brink of ecstatic vistas, and then, expertly she would bring him back with a sudden, experienced releasing of those slender, wicked fingertips. 'Do you like what I am doing for you?'

'Oh yes,' whispered Mathew, 'I surely like what you're doing to me, miss Sannie.'

'And what if my hand does this?' she drew her nails across the muscled flat of his stomach and laughed delightedly when the muscles twitched from her teasing. 'Then again,' she whispered close to his ear, 'this might be even better?' She lowered her face to his chest, deliberately taking one hard nipple between her teeth so that he shuddered and groaned beneath her.

'Someone might hear you,' she admonished and laughed with him, but with a wicked edge to her voice. 'Your mother would kill me for what I am doing to her son.'

'She would kill us both,' said Mathew.

'You are more handsome than all the others. Stronger – and bigger down here,' she giggled, and reached for him.

Now her hand rolled back and forth, brushing between them, coaxing the heat she had kindled from a warm, quiescent flame to a towering inferno, firmly filling her hand until her girlish, slender fingers could no longer encompass the girth of him. Again, Sannie leant forwards and put her lips to his ear so that her voice was a hot and roaring wind.

'For this you will remember well of me, *meneer*.' Then with an expert angling of her wrist she guided him between her legs and loosed the stallion free for its first unhindered run at the open veld.

# -20-

Mhlangana froze – the axe still raised. Sounds filtered out from within the stockade; those of pots being put to the fire, the murmur of busying servants and Magdel Bowker's stentorian voice chivvying them on. But these were not the sounds that had stayed his hands. What he listened for now had come to him before on the lonely killing fields of spent battles and in those brief few moments before their starting. Now he stood silently in the shadows and that same feeling of mortality came over him.

All sound had gone from the wilderness. Only the far-off cry of rock hyrax and foraging baboons echoed from higher ground and in the very air hung a deep and ominous threat for those who sensed it, as if a storm had built above the wagons and was poised like some terrible entity, ready to engulf them.

Mhlangana ran with the axe hefted across his shoulder and when he reached the wagons beckoned urgently to Catherine.

'You must prepare yourselves. Look to your weapons before it is too late.'

'What is it?' she demanded of him. 'Where's my son? He went to the river with Sannie, you must find them.'

'*Verdonder* kaffirs!' hissed Magdel and pushed herself up from her chair. 'Help me into the wagon.'

She ushered Catherine forwards. 'There are things to be done. God willing He grants us the time.'

Magdel reappeared from her wagon tent, her arms loaded. She handed the guns down to Catherine. 'Now the boxes, take off the lids,' Magdel growled, 'then bring out that rifle of yours and whatever else you have to fight with.'

Catherine wrenched back the lids. The boxes were filled to the brim with brass cartridges for the Mauser and paper-covered Peters buckshot for Magdel's big twelve bore double. She tore her eyes from them and ran for her own wagon; the fear that Mhlangana had left her with now scurried rat-like for her throat.

'*Kom nou*, Katarina!' Magdel shouted after her. 'We must hurry. Bring out your guns or the kaffirs will kill us all!'

Catherine stripped the Mannlicher out from its scabbard. She struggled to hold her grip steady – her heart now a powerful beating drum inside her chest.

'You can do this – stay calm, stay calm!' She steadied the rifle across her legs and reached for ammunition. She dropped a full clip into the Mannlicher's breech and slammed the bolt forward. 'Now we shall see how well you fight,' she goaded and looped a bandolier of fifty rounds across her chest. She was no longer so afraid. For her son and for the others who had travelled with her she would fight with all her being, with all her soul.

'Nathan's twelve bore double,' she remembered and reached between the wagon's outer wall and her own cot. Mathew had oiled the weapon and wrapped it with calico.

111

She tore back the covering, opened the breech and dropped in two fat, brass-cased cartridges. Buckshot. Nathan had warned her. At ten paces a single load will cut out a man's stomach – at three it will take off his head. She left both hammers un-cocked and carried the shotgun forwards to where Magdel was waiting.

'I have this surprise for the *duiwels*,' Magdel gloated, and handed an ancient flintlock to Catherine. 'Hold it steady whilst I make ready the powder and shot.' A readiness to fight had stripped all fear from Magdel's face. God Himself was with them. 'It was my father's,' she exulted, 'and his father before him fought the Zulu savages at Inkanyana and Ulundi with this same *donderbus*.'

Magdel took back the weapon from Catherine, half-cocked the striker then gripped a paper envelope with her teeth and tore it open. She ran a tiny pinch of black powder into the open flash-pan then reseated the striker to hold the flash-pan closed. With the weapon pointing skywards, Magdel poured the rest of the powder down inside the barrel.

Catherine watched her labour. A nimble-fingered armourer could not have done it better. With a quick and practiced eye, Magdel primed her evil flintlock blunderbuss for battle.

'And now these,' said Magdel, 'as you English would say – the parts that do the business.' A measured handful of shot – each separate piece of lead had been cast in her gang mould and was the size of a single pea. Finally, to hold the charge as a firm plug inside the barrel she drove in a strip of greased wadding with the flintlock's ramrod.

'Now it is ready,' Magdel breathed, and sweat from her hairline ran as rivers across her brow. 'Save only to draw the striker fully back and then pull the trigger.' She leant the weapon against the wagon and looked to the ashen-faced woman standing next to her. 'All we can do now is pray that Mhlangana will be the first to find our children.'

## -21-

Mhlangana found their clothes and the American six-shooter on the riverbank, but he could see no sign of Mathew and Sannie. He knew they would not be far from where he was standing, and then he heard the faint sound of Sannie's voice above that of the stream. Only when Mathew answered his warning did he move back from where the clothes had been discarded.

They dressed quickly and started back for the encampment, Mathew with the Colt cocked and held to his front ready to fire. Sannie stayed close to his side and already horrific memories from her childhood were sweeping in to haunt her. She recalled the screams and shattered bodies and the burning. Suddenly the stench of it was there in her nostrils and her eyes were wide from the terror of those moments. She ran barefoot over drifts of sharp stone and without feeling the cruel stab of devil-thorns, and when they reached the wagons her mother saw the fear in her eyes.

Magdel loaded a twelve bore double with buckshot and thrust the weapon in Sannie's hands.

'You know what to do child, fight like the devil himself or the kaffirs will cut out your heart.'

Mathew checked the Colt for a full load and pushed it behind his belt – then took up his father's twelve bore

Winchester and filled his pocket with cartridges. He looked to his mother. Catherine stood grim-faced, her head high; the Mannlicher loaded and cocked. Neither one of them spoke. All around the tiny stockade the forest had stilled. When an owl called out from the treeline, Mhlangana nodded and looked to the man at his side.

'They will be here soon enough. Should it come to the ending of our lives, do not let the women be taken.'

'I understand,' said Mathew, and rested the shotgun's long barrels against the wagon.

# -22-

There were women's voices and the bellowing of oxen – the slog of an axe being put to trees and Mgandaan felt the eagerness to kill rise up inside of him.

'I see only two *amadoda*. The rest are women and the dung-eater half-breeds that serve them.' And yet he knew of the dangers. The white settlers were outnumbered though had the advantage of quick-firing guns, in a short time many of his warriors would lay dead on the battlefield, but already the sun was low in the sky and his men were restless from their waiting.

Mgandaan cupped his hands together, forming the shape of a hollow gourd and with his thumbs pressed to his lips blew between them with a long breath. It was the call of the waking owl, the long and eerie wail of a bird just risen from sleep. With hardly a sound his warriors stood up from their hides and went down to the wagons.

'Could it be that you were mistaken?' Mathew chanced and hoped that Mhlangana's instincts had been misguided.

'I made no mistake. The way the Matabele fight has not changed. They will not come in the darkness for fear of witchcraft.'

'What of their numbers? Five guns and a handful of servants against a Matabele raiding party?'

'There will be many,' Mhlangana agreed, 'but if we fight as men there is still a chance.'

It came from the forest's edge – a thirty yard wall of long shields; each one locked to the next and like the scales of a snake, covered the forward thrust of their attack. Black and white, cut from the hides of royal Nguni cattle, hardened by a hundred winter suns – these were the war shields of the Isizela and Imbezu regiments.

There were tails and strips of civet, lion and golden leopard, plumes of ostrich feathers, a terrifying imminence, the rustling of bare feet and the rattling accoutrements of war that were tied above them.

'Wait until they reach the cleared ground before you fire!' Magdel shouted. She had selected her target and watched the line of shields surge as a black sea for the stockade. Mathew and Sannie braced themselves for the wave of violence that was about to come over them. Only an hour ago they had been together on the riverbank, drowsy from their loving in warm sunlight. Now their lives might well be forfeited. Sannie reached out for him and he squeezed her hand. He sensed her trembling. Behind them, the dogs had picked up on the threat and had made their way through gaps in the thorn. They walked with their hackles raised and their lips drawn for they sensed the conflict and hungered for it. Magdel touched a finger to Sannie's cheek – then with a final look to the heavens faced the front; sighting along the Mauser's barrel she squeezed the trigger.

Catherine followed Magdel's lead and fired just as the phalanx of shields reached the chosen killing ground. Two Matabele went down at the first volley. Like weavers' shuttles the loading bolts flew back and forth, every shot a solid strike, then the Matabele broke formation and came at a full run for the wagons, baying for blood.

'Look to your side! They will come from behind the wagon!' Magdel shouted to Mathew and saw him swing the shotgun through ninety degrees.

They came up over the wagon box. Magdel's servants fell to their knees, their hands outstretched to the heavens in helpless supplication. Left and right, Mathew fired both barrels. Two warriors were caught in a hail of heavy buckshot; one squarely across the stomach. His innards spilled – his balance faltered and he fell backwards from the wagon, ropes of blue intestines tangled about his feet. The second had been struck in the shoulder, but only by a single ball of lead shot so that he steadied himself and jumped down inside the enclosure. Before Mathew had chance to reload, the skull of Magdel's servant girl had been cleaved through from pate to her lower jaw.

Magdel discarded the Mauser and took up her blunderbuss. Four sons she had buried in the shadow of a hardekool tree on the banks of the Tugela; their throats slit across. All four had died in front of her. There would be no more. No more pain for her to bear alone – no more dead to put in the ground.

'*Kom nou!*' she raged at the warriors in front of her, and in their own tongue she mocked the warriors of the Matabele.

116

In that smallest of moments a tell-tale flirt of smoke showed from the flintlock's flash-pan. Magdel pressed her back to the wagon for she had primed the heavy barrel with more than the normal charge of powder.

Like thunder, the *donderbus* bellowed out smoke and flame from its flared barrel. Five warriors were caught in a withering hail of lead shot – four perished mid-stride then Sannie fired the twelve bore double and the fifth collapsed just yards from her mother's feet. Catherine stepped forward; lowering the Mannlicher's barrel to the back of his head she fired a single ball through the warrior's brain.

# -23-

Those left unscathed looked down with suspicion on the settlers' encampment; only women possessed of devilry could fight as these had done. Talk of witchcraft and wizardry whispered amongst the Matabele for half their number lay dead or mortally wounded, and from the highest point on the settlers' barricade a man dressed in the fighting regalia of the blooded warrior taunted their ears.

'Enough of your children! Send us your *amadoda* that we might fight as men!' Mhlangana let the insult hang then vaulted from the barricade and drove his spear into the earth; 'With the assegai!'

Shamed from their hiding place, one by one the Matabele stepped into the open.

'You mock us like a baboon from the cliff tops, but you stand with the white man's guns at your back and yet you call on the children of the Isizela and Imbezu *amabutho* to fight in open fields?' They laughed at the challenge and again moved back for the protection of the forest. 'Go back to your masters, old man. Soon, we will finish this. I myself, Ndumiso Khumalo will cut out your liver and leave your body for the crows and jackals to fight over.'

Mhlangana froze where he stood. The name was as familiar to him as the air he breathed and through all his time at the Kimberley diggings had cherished it more than his own. He searched for the source of the voice and his chest was filled with a deep, unfettered longing.

'My name is Mhlangana!' He let the words hang on the breeze. 'Let the one who calls himself Ndumiso step forward. Or like the baboon, does he lack the courage to taunt the leopard from open ground?'

A single warrior stepped out from the treeline. Like the man who chastened him he was tall, though far lesser in years and lithe as a young impala ram – in his eyes there lurked the impetuous urgency of a young warrior keen to blood his spear for the first time.

'I am that one, old man.' He shouted across the open ground, 'I am Ndumiso Khumalo.' Now his voice was thickly edged and he stared at the Induna with the hesitant eyes of the fledgling eagle. Between them had breathed the soft words of uncertainty. Again, Mhlangana called across the clearing.

'You are barely more than a boy and yet you run with the colours of the Imbezu regiment at your shoulder? Step closer that I might see the face of this *umfana*, of this youth who taunts me from a distance.'

'So that your bullets can find me?' Ndumiso countered.

'So that I can see if the woman who succoured you is indeed Imbali, the mother of my child; the one who carries my heart in her hands.'

Ndumiso drew in his shield as if this man were himself the embodiment of some evil spirit.

'How would you know this? How would you know Imbali is the woman who bore me if you are not a wizard?'

'Because, I am your father. Blood of Mashobane, Descendant of Mzilikazi, The Great Elephant.'

For long moments there was silence. In his mind's eye Mhlangana saw the boy he had left behind. Ndumiso started towards him and the clash of breech bolts sounded out from behind the barricade.

'Do not fire!' Mhlangana threw up his arm and watched Ndumiso cross the clearing. The youth spoke with his eyes for the tightness about his throat prevented words from leaving his mouth. Then, with a supreme effort he shook himself free of the pain and looked to the man in front of him.

'We feared you were dead, my father. Others came back from the great hole and spoke of terrible things, of men being made to live and work as vermin below the ground.'

Mhlangana traced the line of his son's jaw with his fingertips. 'And the boy that I left behind is now a man. If I had not heard your name, you might well be lying out there with the dead.'

Ndumiso reached for his father's hand. 'In three days you will be back amongst the sacred Matobo. Many have longed for your return.'

Mhlangana shook his head. 'I cannot follow you. Not until the rains have set. I have given my word.'

'But they are the white *umlungu*?' Ndumiso growled.

'And without them I would not be standing here with my son,'

'Then if only for one night,' pleaded Ndumiso.

'Mgandaan is with us. There is much to speak of, one night will be barely enough, my father.'

Mhlangana nodded. 'Tell Mgandaan to take up the dead. Wait for me at the forest's edge.'

# -24-

Amongst the tall *umbuze* acacia, Mgandaan and nine other warriors sat with their spears to the ground. The dead were gone, buried in shallow scrapes and rocky alcoves high on the hillside. A low fire and late moon lit up the gathering. Mgandaan's eyes were thin – dark slits below his brow. He spoke with resignation, for years now he had watched a trickle of white hunters become manifest, the forerunners of a vast relentless flood.

'The soldiers gather as flies to blood. Soon their numbers will equal those of the elephant and the buffalo.'

'What are the words of Lobengula?' Mhlangana asked him. 'How does our king see the way for his people?'

For a long time, Mgandaan was silent, staring into the embers as though he had not heard him speak; he lifted his head and sighed deeply.

'He knows that what has been given cannot be taken back. His mark has been put to the white man's paper and carried south. Like the *umuhlwa*, the white ant, already the settlers devour the earth and burrow through mountains for gold, but it will not end there, not until the elephant's bones are stripped bare.' He looked up at the sky; the portent shape of an eagle owl soared high in the moonlight – hunting the treetops. Superstition raked his skin.

Respectful of their General, the others watched in silence.

'Tomorrow, Mhlangana. Take the *abelungu* and their wagons amongst the Mashona. The white soldiers have built their fortress close to Zimbabwe, the place of stones. Count their numbers and listen. Become a dog at your master's fire. You will know when the time is right. When the white man talks of war, take up your spear – your king will be waiting.'

# -25-

Absentminded, Magdel toyed with the flintlock's trigger.

'If we are still alive by morning, we must leave this *verdonder* place and push onwards for the Lundi River.'

'They won't come back,' Mathew assured her. 'Mhlangana gave me his word. He will be with us at first light, the fighting is over.'

Magdel looked about at the devastation. The Matabele had spirited away inside the forest and with them, carried on makeshift litters had gone their fallen. The servant girl lay buried amongst the roots of an old sweet thorn. To ward off scavengers, Mathew had piled the grave with rocks from the riverbed. Sannie scattered handfuls of dry earth to hide the marks of their conflict and then, gathered about the grave they sang, Nearer My God to Thee. Catherine had cried softly against Mathew's shoulder and Sannie had stoked the fire and dragged out a full jug of Cape Smoke from their wagon chest.

Long ago, Magdel accepted without rancour that wherever Boers went, be it westwards to the great Kalahari or north beyond the Soutpansberg, there would always be graves to dig. That was the way it was. The way it would always be, for God had laid down his price for their taking up of these new lands. Magdel leant her gun against the wagon wheel. Her moment of private contemplation calmed her and she sighed that long exhausted sigh of a woman beggared by age and perpetual weariness from journeying into the wilderness.

For two hours they sat with rifles close to hand. They sat with their cups filled and refilled with coffee from Sannie's fire. At first with straight backs and stiff tongues from the shock of what had happened and later, slackened by Cape Smoke and the warm flicker of firelight, with softer eyes for what they journeyed for.

'My husband is a good man,' said Magdel, 'but he has been misguided by the devil.' She drained her mug and flicked the dregs at the fire. 'The *bliksem* has always been easily led, but I will find him and never again will I let Piet Bowker away from my sight.'

Catherine's thoughts were still of the fighting.

'We could not have held them off – not just the three of us.' She reached for Magdel's hand. 'We are indebted to you for our lives.'

'It was a small thing,' replied Magdel. 'God gave you the courage to venture into the wilderness, my Katarina. Without his help, none of us would have lived to reach this far.' She squeezed Catherine's hand and then leant back, deeply into her goose down pillow – now with her eyes closed. 'The first time was much worse – many of our people died – whole families were murdered by the Zulus. Thirty-six graves were dug on that day. Thirty- six men, women and children were put inside the ground and as God is my witness, such a killing will never happen again.

Not as long as I have two feet to stand on and a loaded gun in my hands.'

'Losing a child would have finished me,' marvelled Catherine, 'how does a woman carry on after the loss of so many loved ones?'

'Like everything else, there is no choice in the matter.' Through gritty eyes, Magdel scoured the forests and far hills. 'Sometimes I think this land has been cursed by the Almighty Himself.' She reached down and scooped up a handful of soil. 'The colour of blood,' she whispered and let the red earth trickle away from between her fingers. 'Some say for all the children laid beneath it. White, black, Boer, Englishman or Zulu, this land has no concern for which one of us it takes – but take of us it will. Today's killings will not be the end of it, *my meisie*.' She shook her head and the dust from her hand. 'It can never end, not even from the passing of another hundred years. Black will never be at peace with white, for to each the colour of another race is as a red rag to the raging bull.' She smiled at Catherine, her eyes soft, though clouded with exhaustion and the numbing effects Cape Smoke. Sleep was not far away and she longed for the peace it might bring her. 'Never will it end,' again her voice trailed off to a whisper, 'for that is the will of God Almighty and the will of this *verdonder Afrika*.'

*

# III
# MASHONALAND

# -1-

Nathan Goddard drew out a single piece of paper from his breast pocket and for the umpteenth time that day, smoothed out the folds with his thumb and forefinger. The message had been keyed from the Company's telegraph station at Fort Tuli. Each time he looked at the words it was with increased anticipation and his hands trembled. He read aloud for fear of missing a single letter, the reality of what was happening sent both shivers of concern and those of sheer excitement along his spine.

WIFE AND SON EN ROUTE TO VICTORIA. SUGGEST YOUR EARLIEST SUPPORT.

More than a week had gone by since it reached the telegraph office at Victoria and he silently cursed his luck for not being to hand when the message came through. To his front, a pair of glistening telegraph wires strung as delicate metal threads for as far as the eye could see, their furthest reaches blurred to an innocuous copper smear by the haze. A black sky curtained the far horizon, and even with that distance between them, Nathan could hear the deep bass growl of thunder.

He pocketed the telegram and without looking back kneed his horse to a slow canter, determined to reach the wagon drift on the Lundi River before nightfall.

# -2-

'We will never make it across!' Catherine shouted, and looked upstream to where the storm had blackened the skyline. Many times she had seen rivers rise from nothing but dry sand to raging torrents within the space of a single hour. The Lundi River, though at that moment almost empty, was wide enough to take a span of sixty oxen standing nose to tail – dry reaches of white sand strung between the shallows, but from the high carry of a north wind the first fat drops of rain had already slapped to the wagon tents.

'We have no choice,' countered Magdel, 'either we cross now or wait for however many days or weeks it takes for the river to empty.' She looked to her daughter. 'We must lighten the load or sink to the axles. Carry what you can on the horses.' She turned to Mhlangana. 'Double span the first wagon. And hurry – our time is running out.'

Within the half-hour both wagons had been stripped of irreplaceable powder, shot and cartridges for the rifles and double-loaders. Sannie horse-backed their essential provisions across to the far bank and set them down where she knew the water could not reach, then covered the precious cache with a light canvas sail to keep powder and cartridges safe from the rain.

A sky the colour of black iron engulfed the wagon drift – fingers of white, excited lightning crackled inside of it and like the African night, the rain came swiftly. It fell with violent disregard for everything in its way so that the once dry earth was thrashed to the colour of raw meat. As an ominous wall it moved across the landscape – deep ravines were flushed of debris and creatures slow to move were drowned in their burrows. Gullies that had seen no rain for those long dry winter months were filled beyond their banks, linking one to the other, rivulets to streams to hurrying glides amongst the trees so that everywhere the earth moved as a single expanse of living water.

The air filled with smells released by the deluge and amongst them hung the acrid fizz of ozone from the nearness of lightning strikes. At the lowest point of the valley, like an impatient lover the riverbed waited – ready to take that first spate.

## -3-

Nathan stood in the stirrups and screwed his eyes at the sweeping vista to his front. The storm had ridden in with him from some fifty miles to his right hand and now, like an ominous shroud hung black as a widow's cloak above the upper reaches of the Lundi River. With a keen eye he traced the river line for movement.

He found what he had prayed for – a single wagon had reached the near bank and a second, double-teamed, rocked and yawed in its wake. Then he saw the flood water and his heartbeat skittered.

\*

Mathew fired a single shot above the oxen, forcing them to a quicker pace across the sandbanks, though to Catherine, the far bank might well have been a hundred miles away. At the span's head and with all his strength, Mhlangana put out the whip and held the lead pair to wheel ruts left by the first wagon. The oxen lunged at their yokes, their eyes rolled to a crackling sky. They sensed the imminence of the flood waters and bellowed fearfully at the incessant sound of thunder.

On the far bank, Magdel stood bolt upright from her seat on the wagon box.

'*My liewe God*!' she screamed to Catherine. 'I can see the water. Get out of the river before you perish!'

It broke from the final bend as a sliding wall of white water – teams of white-maned horses thirty abreast. Mathew spurred his horse to within arms' reach of Catherine's wagon.

'Let it go!' he shouted and held out his arm to lift his mother away from the wagon box. 'For God's sake, Mother, it's not worth losing your life for!'

'There's still a chance!' Catherine waved him off. 'The rope from Magdel's wagon, run it back from that big Mopani and make it fast to the transom!' She sensed Mathew's uncertainty and rounded on him. 'Do it, Mathew, or by God our journey finishes here in this riverbed!'

'Run out a rope!' Mathew shouted up to Sannie and then spurred his horse up the bank.

Sannie climbed past her mother and dragged a coil of thick manila rope from behind the wagon box. She vaulted clear of the wagon and drew out the loose end. Together, they threw a double loop around the girth of the biggest tree. Mathew ran out the slack and tied off the rope to the wagon's forward transom.

'Bring them up from the water!' Magdel screamed and in awe of Catherine's courage, raised her eyes to the heavens.

At first the wagon stood stubbornly into the flood, its

own mass and the constant strain of the double team anchored it fast to the riverbed, then the water engulfed the wheels and swirled as hungry, licking waves about the oxen. Catherine abandoned the whip and braced herself against the wagon box. Beneath her the wagon twisted and reared as though some mythical creature were rising up from the riverbed. On the bank, the lead oxen faltered, drawn to their knees they stood gallantly into their yokes.

Catherine clung desperately to the wagon box. She had gambled on her wagon being swung through a steady arc for dry ground – then the front right wheel struck sand and as a child's doll she was flung from the wagon. Mathew saw her surface only once, then the river drew her down and she was gone.

Nathan broke from the treeline with his feet already hanging loose from the stirrup irons. He saw the river reach beneath the wagon's underside – the agonising shudder of wood and canvas being lifted from the riverbed. Catherine's wagon reared like a stricken animal and tipped sideways into the current.

Like a steeplechaser in sight of the winning post, Nathan drove his horse up and out from the riverbank. Both horse and rider shot beneath the surface, Nathan with the reins wrapped about his forearm and his fingers locked to the gelding's mane.

'To your left hand!' Mathew shouted and ran to keep pace with his father.

Catherine flailed her arms above the surface, striving for a firm grip on overhanging branches, but the powerful drag of the current tore them from her hands. Twice she went under and twice it let her go again, just long enough for her to fill her lungs with precious air then it stirred her in with eddies and whirlpools and took her down once more. She came up thrashing at the water, but now the will to live was no longer so important. A deep tiredness came over her, and then, as if from a dream she was lifted out from the river.

-4-

The storm swung southwards and left openings between the clouds – blue sky and yellow sunlight. When Catherine opened her eyes the face above her was lost to a halo of bright colours. She tried to speak but her throat convulsed from the ingress of river water and she coughed violently. Nathan gently rolled her onto her side and waited for the paroxysm to abate.

'Tell me I'm not dreaming?' she managed weakly and turned to face him. 'Or that I have died in the river and gone to heaven?'

Nathan brushed the wet from her cheek. 'Then I have gone there with you, my sweet.' Gently he stroked a lock of hair away from her forehead.

The remaining hours of daylight were used to right and haul the upturned wagon from the riverbank, once the oxen were freed of their yokes, Mhlangana led them away to where a carpet of spring grass had magically appeared between the trees. Within earshot of the wagons he built himself a fire of old Mopani and green thorn; flames to ward off lion and smoke to hold at bay bloodsucking insects that already swarmed as black, incessant clouds about his head.

Nathan stood with his arm around Catherine's waist and

132

together they watched Mathew repack the wagon's axle stubs with a mixture of tar and tallow fat.

'I still can't believe that you are here,' said Nathan.

'Nor I,' said Catherine. 'There were times I thought we would perish out there in the wilderness.' She reached for his hand. 'Walk with me. There's still time before nightfall. Mathew can lay the fire and put up the lamps. It's been so long.'

Once again, her man was there at her side, tall and broad-shouldered with a Winchester repeating rifle casually held at the trail. Nothing could hurt her now – neither the river nor a thousand Matabele would stand a chance against this towering god-like being. She talked incessantly, unable to sate her need for his attention, and the sun's late angle lit his features with a halo of golden light so that she could not help but stare at him. Wolf and Tiger caught up with them. The dogs delighted in a chance to hunt the riverbank and willingly came to heel whenever Nathan called to them. They followed the river's edge for almost a mile before turning back and even by then the flow of water had still not eased from the high flood mark. Bank to bank the water boiled with foam and detritus brought down by the run-off. Occasionally, to the south-east the storm still growled.

'You almost drowned,' Nathan gently chastised.

'And put in that situation again, I would do the same,' she countered. 'We had come too far, my heart. Losing our wagon was not an option.'

Their walk to the wagons was spent in silence, but they were constantly touching as though each were afraid the other might disappear. Nathan would sometimes stop and draw her to him, sometimes a little too hard and a little too long so that she was forced to call out for fear of his strength squeezing the breath from her, but always with her face buried inside the open front of his shirt so that he could not see her smiling.

Mathew collected logs from the river's high-water mark and, on a bed of hot coals Catherine arranged a skillet and her three-legged iron pots. Magdel brought out sweet potatoes and the last of her Cape-grown pumpkins.

'We shall make a feast,' Magdel decided, 'a feast to remember the crossing of a great river – a celebration.' She looked about for Sannie. '*Brandewyn* my kind; a full bottle! Set an extra place for the *meneer*. Tonight is a special occasion – we have a guest. And your mother's chair!' Magdel boomed. 'Or am I expected to get it myself?'

The iconic throne was set in the fullest part of the firelight and as usual, to its right hand, Sannie erected the trestle; setting it with glasses and old but twinkling cutlery.

'You will take a *dop* with us, *meneer*?' Magdel cocked her head at Nathan, but she had already decided for him and poured his tumbler full to the brim with Cape Smoke. She shouted instructions for hurricane lamps to be hung high on the branches of sweet thorn and now they threw good light to the fireside. 'Your wife already knows,' she told him, 'always I look for snakes. I cannot bear those slithering creatures anywhere near me.' With a deft flick she put the whip to a stone and sent her pretence spinning away beneath her wagon.

Jars of peach, apricot and watermelon conserve were spirited out, the extravagance warranted. Bread to go with them came up golden brown and mountainous from Sannie's baking pot, and in a skillet of hot fat, quartered guinea fowl were turned and spiced one last time. Magdel looked on and smiled appreciatively. God had shown them mercy – delivered them from the wilderness.

134

'Sannie, *my liefling*. Bring out your father's concertina for me to make some music with.'

Magdel settled herself in front of the fire and everyone listened. She sat with her eyes closed; in her mind's eye were the social gatherings of her childhood. Trek Boers would come from a hundred miles and even further for the occasion of a wedding or birth of a child, gifts would be exchanged, sheep roasted, skewered above the braai pits, still dripping with fat they were feasted upon. Thanks would be given to The Almighty and when the wagons were properly laagered and lashed together with trek chains, men with a love for the wilderness burnt in their eyes would waltz their sweethearts to the strains of lamenting fiddles and concertinas. Later, where the firelight did not reach, they would roll out blankets made from soft Karoo wool and make love with only the stars to watch them.

'So long ago,' whispered Magdel and emptied her mind to the music. To Magdel, the past was more worthy of contemplation – people were happier, fearful of their God and without question or forethought had always bowed to His rulings. Horses were faster and men were stronger, with muscled backs and beards as black as thunder. Her countenance hardened, but the music went on. The Lord had given her children; all but one, He had taken away – without reason – without thought for a woman bereft of her sons and still with her time on earth strung as a lifeless road before her. Now, only her daughter, her music and her jars of Cape Smoke were left to comfort her. Where the road would lead it did not matter, one day the wagon tracks would peter out to nothingness and she, Anna Magdel Bowker would be left to lie in the wilderness – merely another name carved into the heartwood of some

135

gnarled and ancient hardekool. She caught her daughter's eye and without deliberation, Sannie rose from her stool and refilled her mother's glass with brandy.

'I love you, *my meisie*,' Magdel whispered, and it was then she saw in her daughter's eyes the first glimmer of another life – the first stirrings of some tiny spirit. From the falling of that first rain the seed had struck, God was sending to her wagon a grandchild and with it, the strength for her to carry on.

'*Ja*,' mused Magdel, the way ahead had been shown to her. Still there were hopes and dreams to be tended to, fields to till and the seeds from her buck skin bag to be planted – and beyond all else, her man, Petrus Bowker would be brought back to the fold, for it would not be right in the Lord's eyes for a child to be raised without a grown man's knee to ride upon. 'A grandson,' Magdel whispered. There was much to do – much to prepare for and she gave thanks for the blessing and now her fingers and feet were expectant, lively things in the firelight.

For three more nights they outspanned amongst forests of gnarled mopani, then on the morning of the fourth day when the wagons were readied and the oxen restless again for the road, Nathan led them out of that last oppressive valley to where the breeze blew fresh and sweet about their tiny column. A gentle increase in elevation encouraged fields of long and slender grasses tipped with seed the colour of rose quartz. The trees were lush with spring foliage, some tall as ships' masts. Many of the highest branches interlinked and at any time of the day would shield the wagons from hot sunlight.

To Magdel, they were being led from the arid deserts of Egypt to the verdant gardens of Babylon and she stared, wide-eyed from her place on the wagon box, for now the track was good enough for the wagon to move on an even keel and she took advantage of its gentle roll between the trees. Nathan rode on a loose rein for the fear of attack had gone out of him – he slackened the horse's pace to a slow walk and at the edge of a wooded vlei, waited for Mathew to catch up.

'Three miles beyond that rise and you'll judge as to whether or not it has been worth you leaving Kimberley.'

Mathew stood tall in the saddle. 'Why not ride on ahead and take a look? We could be back within the hour.'

Nathan shook his head. 'We go in together,' he insisted.

Catherine's interest lay with her first sighting of Victoria. What she saw filled her with trepidation. What buildings there were had been thrown together from thatch and sun-dried brick, and the feelings she incurred from seeing them made her want to turn the oxen around and make again for the established towns of the far Cape.

'We have come so far,' she whispered incredulously, 'and for what? A ramshackle collection of huts no better than the cottage we left behind in Kimberley?'

Nathan sensed her anxiety.

'We'll outspan near the river. A day's rest for the oxen and they can take us on to your new home.'

'You never said?' Catherine challenged his hiding the truth from her.

'In the morning,' Nathan teased her. 'I will tell you about it in the morning, once you have rested.'

'You will tell me now!' Catherine insisted, and her voice bubbled and raced, almost too fast for him to comprehend. Fresh excitement flashed in her eyes. 'You let me think I would be living here? In this... this rathole of a mining camp?'

'The spring runs all year round,' he told her, 'cool, sweet

137

water and less than twenty yards from your kitchen door.' When he described the view across to the mountains, her eyes softened and he thought he saw the first glistening of a tear before she blinked it away. Now, with a change of heart and from seeing another woman wave to her from the doorway of Slater's Auctioneers, Catherine's spirits lifted. Men with battered hats and curling beards glanced up at the wagons, only mildly interested in the new arrivals for they had seen it all before. Occasionally, someone would wave and those who knew him would shout encouragement to Nathan.

Magdel watched from her own wagon, her rotund frame set stoically square to the wagon tent, but her eyes were into every open room and window and every face on the street was scrutinised for some familiarity. She studied them with a punitive eye and at each new possibility, tightened her grip on the hippo-hide sjambok.

'Have you seen anything of him, Ma?'

'*Nee my liefling*. Maybe we are too late. Perhaps your devil of a father has moved on.'

'He is here,' said Sannie, and shivered at the thought of him watching, peering like a fugitive from behind some curtained window. 'I feel him close by.'

'Then we shall root him out,' hissed Magdel and strengthened her vigilance.

Nathan led the wagons to a quiet stretch of open veld at the town's edge, close to the river and where the bank's gentle gradient was suited to drawing water. With Mathew's help, Mhlangana freed the oxen from their yokes, he let them drink, wary of the crocodiles that he knew would be watching from the reeds.

'The journey is over and yet your eyes are sad?' Mathew hefted a filled bucket onto the riverbank. Mhlangana took it from him and set it down between them. His breathing was quiet and his eyes were soft for the setting sun.

'The years away have made me hunger for my own people.'

'Then it would be right for you to go to them,' said Mathew.

Mhlangana paused before replying – it was a decision he had not made lightly for the bond struck between him and Mathew's family was almost as strong as that with his own kind. 'Your father spoke of clear water and rich earth. Before I leave it will be good to see what we have journeyed for. '

'Will you ever come back this way?' asked Mathew.

'I will return,' Mhlangana told him.

-5-

It was the smell of tobacco smoke, human sweat and the need for other men's company that drew Mathew in a straight line for The Thatched House. However, there was a restrained eagerness about him, for he had not forgotten his first night in the company of hardened Kimberley diggers and the dozen or so burlesque girls up from the Port of Natal. Memories of Molly McGuire's perfumed promises were still very much alive and for every night since their meeting, her soft, imagined voice had seen him off to sleep.

Nathan brushed through the batwing doors, raised his hand to the barman and mouthed the word, 'beer' above the clatter. A face came out of the smoke and hovered moonlike in front of Mathew's. Light from overhead hurricane lamps brought out the ravaged pall of the hardened drinker, and when he attempted conversation, the smell of rotten teeth and foul innards rocked Mathew back on his heels. Nathan shouldered the drunk out of his way and steered Mathew for an opening in the crowd.

'Over by the wall.' He pointed out a gap at the bar counter.

Nathan watched his son's reactions from the corner of his eye – the sudden turning of his chest to meet a stranger head-on, his clenching of teeth or narrowing of eyes that signalled how close the youngster was to lashing out with his fists. The barman moved with them and for Nathan's readied money pushed two schooners of beer across the counter.

'So you brought in the wagons, then?'

'Safe and sound,' said Nathan, and then returned his attention to Mathew. 'Your mother mentioned your relationship with Magdel's daughter.'

'All in the past.' Mathew grinned, though not convincingly; he knew the contrived bravado would not satisfy his father for long. 'Think nothing of it. Flash in the pan, father – nothing more.'

'So having Magdel for a mother-in-law would not concern you?'

Mathew choked on his beer.

'And whilst we are on the subject,' added Nathan, 'over by the piano – the rakish fellow – take a good look at him.'

'What of him?' Mathew keened.

'Say hello to your father-in-law.'

The creature Nathan had pointed out seemed more akin to a stork than a human being, hung with the drab attire of a man on his uppers. His hands were knuckled and gnarled as the roots of an old tree. Whisky and harsh sunlight had wasted the flesh from his face, though above that hawkish nose there glittered cold, invasive eyes – the colour of black ice.

Bowker turned his head and stared in their direction as if he had sensed them watching him. He smiled at Mathew, seemingly aware of his daughter's fortuitous dalliance. Mathew shivered at the thought of what might have been.

'Not if he were the last man left on earth,' he growled just as both saloon doors flew back against their hinges.

Johannes Petrus Bowker froze where he stood. For more than a hundred nights a dream had come to him, always in the small hours and always with the hobgoblins of delirium chasing him through the dark. He was always running, but there were no features for him to recognise, none for him to run to, just darkness stretching away in front and his feet were heavy, cumbersome things trapped inside the morass of his own nightmare. Now, the subject of his worst dreams had become reality. With the eyes of some vengeful soul just raised from the dead, the nightmare stepped towards him.

'Four years,' Magdel growled and the barroom fell silent. 'Four long years I have gone without the comfort of a husband, Johannes Petrus Bowker – and *ja*, not a single thought for your child whilst you were hiding in the wilderness with your *verdonder* whores and whisky.'

The tip of her sjambok whispered serpent-like about her feet. To Johannes, Eden's snake had coiled itself about his woman's arm and its head was her fist, clenched and ready to strike, ready to slash and lunge for his wasted body.

'May the heavens forgive your sins of the flesh, Johannes Bowker,' and with the skill she had learned from her father, put out the hippo-hide lash to the skinny half-moons of her husband's trembling buttocks.

He leapt backwards, arching his body to avoid the flickering leather tongue, but the movement lacked timing and speed from the damning effects of strong liquor. Had Magdel put the full force of her shoulder behind it, the whip would have laid him open, but part of her remembered the time when he would come to her with flowers and promises of tender moments. It was these faint memories that curbed her ferocity so that only two or three times did she purposely lay the whip to him, dancing him over the floor; a gleeful girl with her favourite whipping-top.

Johannes squealed louder than a clipped piglet and scrabbled for cover, but a shove from a digger's boot sent him sprawling back within range of the lash – at each near miss the room erupted with shouts of encouragement and offers of money for every welt raised – then as suddenly as she had begun, Magdel lowered her whip and crooked her finger to winkle him out from the crowd. She shook her head and her countenance changed.

'Do you not love me anymore?'

Johannes seized the moment and stood up. 'More than my useless life is worth, *my liefie.*'

'Then why do you live with a nest of whores in your wagon?'

Johannes looked down at his feet.

'Because living alone in the wilderness has made your husband weak. The devil has found his way inside of me, *my lammetjie.*'

Magdel weighed the possibilities of what their reunion might bring. She remembered how good he was with a rifle and how his bony fingers were more adept than hers at reloading cartridges or giving fine edge to her precious biltong knives. The more she thought about her life the more difficult it was to see reason in it, to choose between a life without a man or for him to share her bed and sit with her through the ravening cold of July nights. Perhaps it would be right to put what had happened behind her and take her husband's sins as punishment for her own failings. She nodded retrospectively. The decision had been made. Together, they would carry the cross of reconciliation and go forward as they had before – husband and wife before the eyes of God Almighty. Between them it would be as it was and she smiled at her man and held out her hand for him to follow her back to the wagon. Later, when it was quiet and while Sannie was curled down deeply in her wagon cot, she would tell him about their grandchild, and far into the night, talk with him of what might be.

## -6-

Though little true emotional attachment had grown between them, Mathew still found it hard to say goodbye. Petrus Bowker had already left on horseback, his aim to clear a site and make it ready for Magdel's wagon. Sannie sat demurely next her mother on the wagon box, dressed in that same, almost worn through cotton frock that Mathew would remember for the rest of his life. As it had done on that day of their first meeting, early sunlight played through Sannie's hair and put a halo of gold about her shoulders, he saw in her a vibrancy for this new adventure for already her eyes were keenly seeking out what might be waiting ahead.

'We will miss you all,' said Magdel, having exhausted every excuse to linger. She reached down from the wagon box and touched her fingertips to Catherine's cheek. With a strained voice Magdel whispered down to her friend.

'God keep you from harm, *my klein* Katarina,' then Magdel turned her face to the front and without looking back, shouted to her *voorloper* for him to put out the lash.

-7-

Mathew rode on ahead and picked out ways between trees and rocky outcrops more suited to the wide span of their wagon. He welcomed the solitude, the freshness of deep forest and a clean, exhilarating sky above him. Not until they were less than a mile from the homestead did Mathew first catch sight of a thatched roof with its stone chimney. He waited for the wagon to catch up, not wishing to rob his mother of her moment.

Catherine stood up from the wagon box and cupped her hand against the sunlight. Her breathing skipped – excitement burst from inside her and she looked to her son with the impatient, laughing eyes of a young girl.

'Your horse, Mathew.' She vaulted from the wagon box and then crooked her knee for him to help her into the saddle.

Catherine rode stirrup to stirrup with Nathan and where the ground was firm, at a full gallop. She was first to the homestead's frontage, leaping clear of the saddle she ran for the door and with bated breath reached for the latch.

Without warning, her legs were swept from under her and with the toe of his boot, Nathan pushed back the door.

He set her down gently, and still within the encirclement of his arms. For a long moment he covered her mouth with his, and in the coolness of that empty parlour, Catherine felt the fatigue of twelve long weeks lift as a heavy cloak from her shoulders. She wriggled free and in seconds was through the inter-leading door. She stood at the room's centre – quietly in awe of what was around her.

'Where in Heaven's name did you manage to find all of this?'

'Dealing and thieving.' Nathan laughed and made light of his efforts.

Catherine ran her fingers over the bevelled edge of a black iron stove. To either side, the walls had been lovingly fitted with shelves and pegs for her pots and pans.

'And this will be your pantry,' Nathan went on and again the walls were decked with wooden shelving, cut and planed to a smooth finish from the timbers of some derelict wagon. The air, like that of a Cape wine cellar was cool and smelled of thatch. Nathan had purposely built the walls two feet thick to hold off the heat of high summer.

'Food will last for days at least, even without salting,' Catherine delighted, and followed him back to the parlour.

Doors had been set in the wall at either side. One of them had been left open and drew in the breeze from a single window.

'Mathew's room,' he told her, then crossed the parlour and pushed back the remaining door. 'And this, my sweet, is ours.'

The bed was wider than the wagon she had shared with Mathew through all those weeks of travelling up from Kimberley. On it, Nathan had plumped a goose feather mattress, taken from the proprietor of The Thatched House in full payment for a debt incurred at the crown and anchor table.

'To sleep in a proper bed will be paradise…' Catherine mused, and before she could finish talking Nathan dropped the latch on the door.

They lay in each other's arms, quietly contemplating the goings on of those last few days. They talked about fertile ground stretching away below the homestead – what they would plant and after a full year, how many cows would graze the rich pasture close to a stream that Nathan had pointed out to her.

'Mhlangana could bargain with the local chief; at least twenty cattle to start with.'

'And fowl.' Catherine insisted. 'No more than a dozen mind – but young enough to give us eggs for at least a year.' She sighed contentedly, for the first time in two long years she would sleep without fitful dreams as perpetual bedfellows. 'There were times when I thought I would never see you again. I had dreams – bad dreams,' she went on, 'that you were alone in the wilderness. There were men – all of them with blood on their face and you were there amongst them, but I could not see your eyes.' She shuddered against him. 'Only then would I wake up from it and lie there alone, listening to the wind outside my window; too frightened to close my eyes for fear of it starting over.'

He stayed until her breathing quietened. Only when he heard the approaching wagon did he gently lay her aside and stand up from the bed.

It took the remainder of that day for the wagon to be offloaded. Mhlangana led the cattle to where the grass grew thick and green and the horses to their paddock

146

behind the homestead. Mathew brought in wood for the kitchen and soon, Catherine had the makings of a first meal.

They ate outside, seated around the wagon's trestle table and for those last few moments of daylight, watched the sky turn through all the colours of a cathedral window before Mathew put up hurricane lamps in the trees.

'I wonder where Magdel will have outspanned for the night?' said Catherine.

'Not more than ten miles out from Victoria,' Nathan hazarded. 'If there's truth in what I've heard, her philandering husband has found work with the Cambrian Gold Mine, close to the junction of the Shashi and Ngezi rivers.' He pointed due west. 'About forty miles as the crow flies.'

Catherine looked up at a sky shot through with tiny pinpricks of white light. On the far horizon lightning clawed at the clouds. When the breeze picked up, the drone of men's conversation drifted across from where Mathew and Mhlangana had set their fire, and from the high forest, baboons barked down from rocky cliffs. A fanciful twist of Catherine's imagination took her back along the road from Kimberley. She shivered with trepidation and imagined Magdel sat in her stinkwood chair, alone in the lamplight; watching the night for snakes, her sjambok and Mauser rifle on the trestle close to her elbow.

# -8-

For three weeks it rained in the middle hours of every afternoon – the seeds Magdel had given Catherine were all well set, and along orderly rows of tilled soil the fecund warmth of late November had worked its magic. Peach, apricot and lemon had opened their first leaves, all jealously guarded and encircled with thorn to ward off rabbits and antelope that might come to feed surreptitiously in the small hours. Nathan had built up mounds of red earth and Catherine had planted them each with six white seeds from her precious store, already the mounds were massed with the creeping tendrils of her first pumpkin plants. For those same weeks, Nathan related to little more than past forays into the mountains. Mathew listened intently; enraptured by tales of ruined cities and his father's stories of raw, native gold he had taken from the riverbeds.

'I grant you these are smaller than a pinhead,' he told Mathew, 'but there could well be a fortune waiting for the man who finds the main reef.'

For the third time that morning, Mathew prised a glass stopper from a tiny medicine bottle and tipped the contents into the palm of his hand. In the open sunlight the grains of raw gold came alive, reflecting that deep, emissive glow of a setting sun.

'There has to be more,' said Mathew.

'Gold fever,' Catherine chipped in. 'You have the fever, Mathew, the same as your father.'

'And the cure mother?'

Catherine shook her head. 'Gold placates gold, my son. There is no cure.'

'Surely if we find the reef...'

'How many men have said the same?' Catherine interrupted. 'How many have poured money into worthless holes in the ground?'

'We are not your, many men.' Nathan countered.

'The two of you are more than enough,' said Catherine. 'For weeks now, all I have heard is talk of gold.' She squared her shoulders. 'Take Mathew with you. Go and find your gold mines; a day, week, whatever it might take. Men should be out of the house doing things, not here hanging about my kitchen.'

'I need a few more days to finish your garden?'

'The garden can wait,' she insisted.

'We could stay for a few more days?' Nathan suggested, but Catherine quickly brushed the offer aside. The permanence of men about the house had driven her to distraction.

'Tomorrow morning.' She scowled emphatically at Mathew. 'I will put up food enough for three days. The both of you will be out of my kitchen by sunrise.'

## -9-

For an hour they rode north-eastwards, following narrow valleys between the foothills. In all directions the veld had thickened and even the trees seemed to have doubled in size since Nathan was last there.

'Soon we will have to dismount; we've come as far as we can on horseback.'

Mathew found himself strangely at ease with his new

149

surroundings.  Fed by fresh rains and run-off from the hillside, plant life had burgeoned. In the uppermost branches, purple-crested turacos and gold-coloured orioles flapped and called through the foliage.

'There's my mark.' Nathan pointed out deep cuts he had made to the trunk of a young fig. He swung down from the saddle and gestured to Mathew. 'Walk your horse on a short rein and bring her through.'

He lifted aside a gate of rough saplings. The makeshift paddock was large enough for both horses and well watered. The grass was ankle deep and would last out the week if needed. They off-saddled and stowed the livery beneath a rocky overhang. Nathan drew out his rifle from its scabbard and along with a canvas bag of provisions, slung it across his shoulders.

'We follow the stream,' he told Mathew.

'How far?'

'An hour's steady walk,' said Nathan. Mathew shouldered the axe and shovel and secured the Colt behind his belt. In his free hand he carried his father's battered and blackened prospecting pan. Eventually, just before midday, Nathan lowered the canvas bag. Alongside a small pool were knee-high heaps of discarded gravel.

'You have to go in deep,' he told Mathew, 'down to bedrock – that's where the gold is lying'.

Mathew waded into the middle. He dug until the spade struck rock. Nathan filled the pan with sand and gravel from the deepest part of the diggings.

'The skill is in keeping the lighter, more buoyant waste riding close to the surface.'  He worked the pan with a practiced rolling of his wrists so that the contents spun as a vortex of water, sand and gravel. 'Minerals differ not only in colour and shape, but in weight also.'

'As compared to sandstone or quartz,' Mathew hazarded, 'iron or gold being the heavier should settle at the bottom?'

Nathan concurred. 'And if the pan is tilted thus, the sand can be discarded, but carefully – keep on going until only the heavier concentrates are left behind.'

For one last time, Nathan flooded the pan with clean water.

'Tell me I'm not dreaming,' Mathew croaked, 'that the light is not playing tricks with my senses?'

'There's the truth in what I've been telling you,' said Nathan, he handed the pan to Mathew. 'Take it into the sunlight.'

Mathew climbed out from the stream and stood where bright, natural light filtered down through the canopy. What he now looked at, though small in quantity was to him, more alluring than the diamonds he had seen in Kimberley. Should the grains of gold be fused together they would barely have covered the head of a match. Carried up from the earth's core, the precious metal, entrapped by bands of grey quartzite had over millennia leached from the rock – carried from it by the violence of a million storm rains. For the gold to travel mere yards took more than a thousand years, and for it to find its way along fleeting rivulets took ten thousand more. Then, in the final part of its journey to the valley floor it was caught by the urgent rush of sometimes, almost vertically flowing streamlets, sped from its place high up on the slopes of the Nyanda mountains to where now stood a creature evolved from that same, prehistoric time; a time of immense geological upheaval. It glowed enticingly – delighting the eye of the man who now gazed down upon it.

'I'll settle for a reef six feet wide and a mile deep,' said Nathan.

'Going ounces of gold to every ton mined,' Mathew added, and both men laughed at their fantasies. 'So where do we go from here?'

'Leave the pan on the bank,' said Nathan and pointed out a break in the trees. 'The ruins I told you about; we can see them from up there – a small diversion, an hour at the most.'

Mathew followed his father away from the valley, they climbed steadily upwards, and at a similar pace, Mathew's patience frittered away.

'How much further before we see this ruined city of yours, father?'

'From that ridge to your front,' Nathan encouraged.

Mathew reached the vantage point and slumped down against his pack. Park-like, the land a thousand feet below swept away before them, thick with island forests and grassland, dotted across with granite kopjes. He reached inside his haversack for the spyglass, eager for his first sighting of the ruins.

'Not more than a mile or two at the most from where we are sitting,' said Nathan. 'Those wooded kopjes – right of that ridge. Put your glass to them and look carefully; the walls are covered in vines.'

Mathew followed his father's line of sighting. At first, the countryside on which he gazed was blurred by shadow and distance, cluttered with strange uncertain shapes of rock and burgeoning undergrowth – slowly, his eye grew accustomed to the magnification. Aloes flamed from cracks in the granite, rock rabbits and klipspringer antelope stood in open sunlight, unaware of being watched from so great a distance.

'What do you make of it?'

'Stone kopjes and a lot of trees, it would take a hundred men more than a month to cut their way through.'

'Give me the telescope,' said Nathan, frustrated by the delay. 'The trees inside the walls were darker, more established than those outside. The larger of those two granite hills,' Nathan committed, 'a half mile or so to the right of it.'

Mathew retrieved the scope. 'Someone has beaten us to it – the clearing to the right of the wall – they have a fire going.'

For a third time the telescope changed hands. 'Two men,' Nathan growled. 'Fossickers!' The word spat from his mouth. 'Grave robbers – Rhodes' men will have them dancing a jig at the end of a rope.'

Nathan tried as best he could to follow their movements, driven by anger he was unable to steady the scope, then the crack of a rifle shot broke his concentration.

# -10-

'Would you look at that, Mister Chulmleigh? A more marvellous sight I swear I've never before clapped me eyes on.'

Again, O'Reilly plunged his fist into a bucket of water, rubbed his find between thumb and forefinger and then held the shining artefact to the sunlight. 'And I tell you, Chulmleigh. Never in a dozen lifetimes would I prefer the company of whores and whisky to that of this little beauty.'

No bigger than O'Reilly's little finger, a golden replica, that of a winged beast, half bird half reptile had been skilfully brought to life by ancient goldsmiths and even though it had been hidden beneath the ground for more than a thousand years its original form remained unblemished. The melancholic colour of that precious metal was still very much alive; red and raw, as though only that morning it had been poured from the smelter's furnace.

'Should we be handing it in to the Company's ancient ruins people d'yer think?'

'And the mother of all pox on Mister bloody Rhodes' company.' Chulmleigh sniggered. 'It goes in the bag with the others and we'll have the buggers melted down and sold before his committee tumbles to our little scheme.'

O'Reilly opened the neck of a hessian sack and peered inside.

'I'd say not far off a goodly fifty ounces or so.'

The finds were made up mainly of beads and beaten foil, all of that same precious metal – some still fixed to remnants of wood and yellow ivory, held in place by exquisite bindings of drawn gold and tiny, hand-forged copper nails. A few of the treasures had been cast as solid pieces, portrayals of wild animals – buffalo, rhinoceros and even a cobra's likeness; the snake's hood fully blown – portentous and threatening, its eyes were cruel reptilian slits set deep inside the gold. O'Reilly discarded the bag with casual disinterest; to him the treasures were merely an easy means of lining his pockets. His thoughts swung more to filling his belly.

'Bloody starved I am, time to get some grub on the fire.' He crossed to what was left of a butchered impala ram, cursed the early signs of putrefaction and slapped the palm of his hand to the beast's rump to clear the flies. He drew his knife along the soft indentation of the animal's haunch so that the copper-coloured hide parted to expose clean pink flesh beneath. He put the weight of his shoulder behind the stroke and sliced down through muscle and ligaments; cutting deep into the animal's hip to break the bone free from its socket. He dropped the hind leg on a tussock of grass then wiped his hands on his breeches.

'Rake up the coals,' he told Chulmleigh, 'while I fetch us a little something to wash down our dinner.'

They sat with their backs to a wall of granite blocks, sixteen feet thick at its base and built to reach up thirty feet above their heads. O'Reilly perused the stonework – each block had been cut from living granite, shaped and squared to fit the one before it.

'So whose name would you put to having built this place, Mister Chulmleigh? Blacks couldn't have done it, not too good with the old straight lines these Shona lads. Not in a thousand years could they build a place like this.'

'Don't give a damn. Made ourselves a tidy profit and that's what matters. Blacks or us Irish, I don't give a monkey's turd.'

O'Reilly passed him the bottle. His hand wavered – now his eyes were fixed upon a gap in the stonework.

*

Only when the moon had halved and showed itself as a tipping, silver bowl in the afternoon sky was the girl assured of coming rains, for when the moon was at its fullest the rains would hold off – hot winds would burn all life from fields – where once there was water, cattle would die of thirst and the nights would fester with evil things.

Shapes would be seen to move in the shadows and ears would be pressed to walls for the sounds of a witch's familiar laying her spells at a victim's door. All of these things the girl had been tutored in, and though fey of smile and more beautiful, more lithe than a gazelle upon her feet, she was more dangerous than the beast which sat within reach of her outstretched slender hand.

'My beautiful *horomba*,' the girl whispered, her voice so soft that it could have been merely a breath of restless air amongst those ruined corridors of hewed stone. She sought out a pad of pliant flesh beneath the animal's powerful lower jaw and worked her fingers in amongst the softer, underlying hair; dark ecstatic eyes rolled within their hooded sockets and though denied any understanding of her words, the baboon sensed a tenderness in her fingertips. It raised itself from its place in the sunlight and stood equal in height to that of the girl, with an almost human-like awareness of their friendship the animal touched a hand to Mutiswa's shoulder.

A sound – the touching of steel to stone – a slight, unnatural invasion of the quiet, though it was enough to alert her senses of another human presence.

'*MuRungu*!' Mutiswa hissed, and the animal standing with her turned its head to the breeze. She felt the beast's hackles rise, and already its lips had curled back to expose vicious yellow fangs – at their base, thick as the girl's fingers; to their tips, longer than those of the full grown leopard.

\*

'Hand me the rifle,' O'Reilly whispered. 'Slowly now, Mister Chulmleigh, we have visitors. You get on down there behind the wall whilst I sort out our peeping Tom. Don't let the little black lassie slip through your fingers, mind.'

O'Reilly waited for Chulmleigh to make his way back inside the labyrinth of stone passageways. He fired from a sitting position with his knees drawn up as steady support for the rifle. From a distance of only fifty yards the bullet struck exactly where he had intended, high up on the ape's chest.

*

'A girl with a monkey as big as herself, Mister Chulmleigh? What need do you suppose she had for an ape that size?' He made an obscene gesture with his thumb and forefinger. 'You don't suppose she was having a bit of the other with her man in the fur coat now?'

'Wash out that mouth of yours, Mister O'Reilly and we'll have no more of your unkind words for the lassie.'

'It's more than words that I have in mind for this one, my friend – and it won't be my tongue that gives the little darlin' a lashing either.'

Chulmleigh threw back his head and roared through a full mouth, then he tightened the rope at the girl's throat and his expression hardened.

'You be a good girl now and me and O'Reilly over there might think to letting you go – once we're all done with you that is.' He dropped the rope at O'Reilly's feet. 'Best we get on with it then. I'll be going in first so if you wouldn't mind, Mister O'Reilly, sir, I would thank you to hold the wench to an even keel.'

Three years had passed since he had left the goldfields on the Witwatersrand, since he had felt the urgency of a paid-for slattern straddled across his gut, so that now his entire body trembled with perverse anticipation. The coupling of lust and the rampant malaise of his own diseased heart thumped inside his chest.

'A gazelle, Mister O'Reilly, I would say we have done ourselves proud, sir.' Chulmleigh wiped the venison grease from his chin and shuffled forward; gluttony had forced apart the buttons of his filthy waistcoat. The ginger-haired folds of his gut doubled over his belt and his eyes were greedy twitching things to the juncture of the girl's legs.

'And a fine young gazelle she is at that, Mister Chulmleigh. Best you be getting on with it before the lassie's daddy comes a looking.'

Chulmleigh wrapped the rope around his forearm and jerked Mutiswa's head to below the level of her knees.

'Chulmleigh's the name, ma'am. Popular with the girls back home on the Reef I am.' He looked past her and grinned at O'Reilly. 'They don't call me donkey-ride-Chulmleigh for nothing, do they Mister O'Reilly?'

He freed the belt at his waist and kicked down his breeches. The girl's whimpering served only to heighten his fervour, now more animal than human and with thick excited fingers he pawed at her secret parts.

'Get into her Chulmleigh before I burst in me breeches!' O'Reilly snatched at the rope but Chulmleigh slapped him away and with his free hand, spun the girl around then reared against her, driving deeply inside her sex with that perverse force of a rutting boar.

'Like a wild horse, Mister Chulmleigh! Short of a good tuppin' the lassie was.' He lifted her face in line with his. 'Looks like today's your lucky day my little darlin', our Mister Chulmleigh here is almost up with blowing the lid of his billy.'

Chulmleigh's cheeks rose and fell like an ironsmith's skin bellows – his face bulged from that final furlong's gallop – his arms stiffened, then his eyes flew wide open and in that short euphoric moment, Chulmleigh danced his jig with the devil.

Nathan raised himself above tall grasses at the forest's edge, making sure of the Winchester's balance. There would be no room for error. The rape of a native girl would hardly warrant a raised eyebrow; though killing a white man in her defence would bring more than an even chance of the hangman's rope for the perpetrator. He stroked the trigger and O'Reilly's bowler hat spun like a startled fowl into the air.

O'Reilly went for his rifle but he stumbled over loosened breeches and fell face first against the masonry. Chulmleigh stayed pressed to the girl's rear and like a drunk coming out of his stupor, stared with bemused surprise at what was going on around him.

Mathew was quick to cross the open ground and stood over the Irishmen with the Colt cocked and ready to fire. O'Reilly slumped sideways onto to the grass. He pressed a soiled handkerchief to his cheek and glared up at the intruders.

'You'll pay for this, as God is my witness I'll make you bastards pay for what you have done here.'

Nathan slipped the noose from the girl's throat. Pain prevented her from straightening up and she clutched at her groin with both hands.

'Best get your things together,' Nathan growled at Chulmleigh, 'before I let the girl loose on you with a knife.'

'I know you, Goddard. I've seen you around Victoria. Rest assured we will be seeing you again.' He held the front of his breeches closed and with his free hand reached

159

for the canvas bag, but Nathan pinned his arm with the heel of his boot.

'The bag stays. Take your hat and your rifle – that is all.'

'There's upwards of a day's work in that bag?'

'And I will bear that in mind,' said Nathan, 'when I hand it over to the proper authority.'

'Bloody Rhodes' men. Toffs the bloody lot o' yer. Like bloody Masons all pissing in the same bloody pot and the hell with everyone else.' He nodded to O'Reilly. They would accept their losses for the time being; next time things might well be different. There was a score to settle and money to recoup. 'Like I said, Goddard, you and that pup of yours have not heard the last of this.'

O'Reilly fingered the damaged hat – the bullet had slit the bowler's crown, almost from front to back.

Chulmleigh tucked his shirt inside his breeches and leered at the girl. 'And to you my little black darlin' – if it be a boy that I have planted in your belly, Michael Patrick Chulmleigh the Second would be my choice of names for that bastard of yours.'

## -11-

Mutiswa covered the beast's face with scarlet blooms from the lucky bean. It was her final gesture of farewell. Mathew helped her close in the creature with blocks of granite taken from the wall. Until that moment she had kept silent. Now she looked to Nathan for his understanding. He saw in her a strangeness of being – happenings that had already fled her life, and in the darkest depths of her eyes were those yet to come.

'Your name, *musikana*? What is your name, girl?' He used the soft dialect of the Shona people and though his tone was amicable the girl's eyes fluttered wildly, watching for that slight movement of his hand, the subtle raising of an eyebrow that would signal the violent ending of her life.

'My name is Mutiswa, lord'

A slight breeze skittered inside the collar of Nathan's shirt. There was a difference in her, one that he had seen before in the dark-eyed stare of a gypsy seer. That same madness was once again there in front of him, lurking beneath the gentle façade of a girl's innocence.

'I owe you my life, lord'. He was different – though still the white man looked upon her with the aloof glare of the conquering eagle, and yet, she saw no harm in him. 'These broken walls are my home,' she told him, and spread her arms to encompass all around her. 'Since I was a small child, I have lived amongst these hills.' Now, she laughed at his curiosity; her pain and loss seeming to have disappeared as smoke on the breeze. 'My people are everywhere – they are the wind, the moon and the sunlight about my being.'

Mathew spread the contents of the fossickers' canvas bag on the ground.

'You cost our friends a pretty penny, father. There has to be a small fortune in gold here.' He picked out one of the pieces and held it to the sunlight. 'What would you say to this one? Some sort of bird creature?'

'More bird than anything else,' said Nathan and took it from him, 'an eagle, perhaps – or a falcon.' He studied the detail. 'A talisman of sorts.'

'The girl,' warned Mathew, 'what's wrong with her?'

Her eyes were wide open and yet, Mutiswa saw nothing

of those who stood in front of her.

'What has gone and that which is still to be has been put to the Great Wall.' Her hand rose up as if to seize the bird from Nathan's fingers. 'Thousands will perish. None will take up the spear against him – not until the son of your sons and those of ancient kings see as one through the eyes of all the people!'

Nathan closed his hand about the talisman. Mutiswa swung her eyes onto him and like those of the deeply insane they rolled inside her skull until only the whites were visible. Nathan reached for his rifle as the chill wind of superstition came over him. Mutiswa spun on her heels and like the fleet-footed klipspringer antelope was away through a break in the wall; in seconds she was lost to the ancient temple's maze of stone corridors.

# -12-

'Your putting a bullet through O'Reilly's hat really put the wind up both of them.'

Nathan smiled at the recollection. 'The scum deserved more. A good beating would not have gone amiss.'

Mathew put the toe of his boot to the fire and marshalled the embers closer in to the billycan.

'The girl's premonition – put the shivers up me, I'll give her that.'

'Likewise,' Nathan agreed and like Mathew, mulled through the happenings of that previous afternoon.

They ate cold ham and maize bread that Catherine had wrapped in muslin, and washed it down with the sweetened coffee. Sunrise flooded the high ridge where they had spent the night and with his telescope, Mathew was quick to find the ruined walls he had begrudgingly left behind, unexplored.

'No sign of the girl – or the Irishmen. I was convinced our fossicker friends would follow us.'

Nathan led the way back to the stream. In turn they dug out gravel and panned the concentrates for signs of free gold. Eventually, after having moved a further two hundred yards along the stream bed, only a tail of grey iron coloured the bottom of the pan; the tails of fine gold had disappeared. Nathan turned his attentions to higher ground.

'The gold must be coming from up there,' said Nathan, 'somewhere inside the treeline. Leave the spade and the pan on the bank. The rest we'll take with us.'

'How do we know where to look?'

'We don't,' said Nathan. 'Watch for outcropping quartz reef, anything that stands out as being different to the ironstone.'

They climbed upwards from the stream and quartered, back and forth across the hillside – every outcrop scrutinised and broken into. Not until the sun was directly overhead did Nathan find the first signs of what he had been hoping for.

The piece of weathered rock was no bigger than a hen's egg, naturally stained by the leaching of minerals from cracks and lateral flaws in the quartzite. When Nathan split the rock with his hammer, powdered yellow limonite stained his fingertips. Unlike the barren ironstone the rock was heavily mineralised, cut across with layers of coloured quartzite, tightly formed by intense pressures and unimaginable heat – vibrant pinks, purples and reds of a

163

dozen different hues and along those layers cast inside the stone were grains of yellow metal. Nathan touched the wetted tip of his tongue to the rock and those tiny flecks of raw gold flared from the sunlight.

'Fool's gold,' Mathew dismissed. 'A cruel imitation – I've heard it talked about.'

'Imitation be damned. You're looking at the real thing; fool's gold shows up dull when it's wet – more of a brassy colour.'

Mathew learned to recognise which types of rock warranted a second blow with his hammer. Gold favoured the more colourful quartzite, whereas the whiter, glassier looking rock would prove to be barren. His impatience grew; every rocky outcrop had the hammer put to it. Nathan struggled to keep up and called out for Mathew to slow down. He rested with his back to the ironstone and took stock of what they had found. In his hand, he held a lump of gold-bearing quartz, half the size of a builder's brick.

'We're close, unless rocks like this are all that's left of the reef.' He gauged the distance they had climbed from the stream. Even with steam- driven pumps, lifting water to that height would prove almost impossible. A track would have to be cut for mules and wagons. They would need powder and fuse and a strong labour force to bring up equipment and supplies. The first insects of disappointment rustled about his feet.

'We need a reef and water,' said Nathan, 'and so far we have neither.'

Mathew pointed diagonally along the hillside. 'That gulley – there could be water?'

The ravine had formed as a deep tear in the hillside. After centuries of rainstorms most of the low-lying rock formations had been laid bare of soil and plant growth. The makeup of the rock itself had been thrown open to the sunlight and apart from narrow shaded strips away from the gully's centre, the ironstone had been swept clean of forest detritus.

'Close in to the sidewall.' Mathew pointed.

'Ferns,' Nathan realised. 'They wouldn't be there unless there was water.'

'Could just be seepage?' Mathew countered, 'hardly enough water to run a mine with.'

'Below those trees,' Nathan shot back at him, his spirits buoying. Where the ground dropped away, acacia saplings stood six feet tall from the gulley floor. Just yards beyond the saplings, the dense upper foliage of a wild fig bridged the ravine. 'Run-off from the hillside could have backed up against the ironstone. We could recycle the water – use what seepage there is as a top-up. Filter the mud out with settling dams before pumping it back to the mill.'

'The ledge,' said Mathew and drew his father's attention away from the fig tree. 'One thing's for certain, those holes in the rock are man-made. I'm going down there.'

## -13-

Nathan ran his fingertips round one of the indentations in the ironstone. The sides had been worn smooth, the bottom ground to an elliptical shaped bowl by the pounding action of stone pestles. Some of the ancient mortars had been worn to more than a foot in depth. Mathew counted thirty in total, set in rows of ten across the ledge and with room enough between each for a man to work unhindered by others to either side of him.

'Thirty men,' said Nathan, 'the noise would have rivalled a stamp mill.' He was now unstoppable. 'And they must have had water. How else would they have separated gold from waste?'

From where they were standing the ledge fell off at a steep angle, almost vertically.

They climbed diagonally, as close as they dared to where the fig's matted canopy breached the gap between the gully walls. Mathew pulled back layers of rotting leaves to make a window for the sunlight. It streamed inside; a bright, finger of white light, angling down for the gully floor.

For the first six feet, Mathew was forced into using his axe to clear a way through the branches. Growth had been vigorous, sustained by roots driven deep into the hillside and even through those long cloudless days of the dry season the tree had successfully drawn out moisture from fissures in the ironstone. Mathew worked his way down inside the darkness until he could lower himself to the gulley floor.

He stood ill at ease, his back to the gully wall and with the Colt levelled at the darkness in front of him.

'What can you see?' Nathan called down to him.

'Nothing as yet. My eyes need time to adjust.'

Apart from the rustle of green pigeons amongst the upper branches, he could hear no other sound – then, as if from melting ice, a single drop of water plinked to the pool at his feet.

'We have water!' Mathew grinned at the face peering down at him through the foliage. 'And plenty of it!'

'You've seen it?'

'In front of me – you were right. A pool backed up

against the ironstone.'

'What else?'

'Broken rock – piles of it.'

'I'm coming down,' said Nathan, his voice thickly edged with excitement.

Mathew watched his father through the foliage. Cloud shut out the sun and what light still reached inside the gully was little more than a dull shadow.

'A candle stub,' said Nathan, 'and Vestas.' He passed them to Mathew. 'Light her up. Let's see what we have here.'

Mathew struck a match against the ironstone. The dark fell back and the surface of Mathew's pool shone black and quiet as a moonlit lake.

'Over there,' said Mathew. 'What do you make of it?'

The ore had been left heaped against the sidewall. Nathan selected a fist-sized piece of quartz and held it to the candlelight.

'Would you look at it,' he said softly to Mathew. 'It doesn't come any better than this.'

The rock was laced with veins of yellow gold. The quartz had been sheared through, shattered by ancient miners – part of it still black, the edges glassy and smoothed by fire.

'Straight from the reef,' Nathan realised, 'ready for crushing.'

'So why did they leave it?' Mathew shot the question and Nathan shook his head. There was fire in his eyes.

'Only one thing will make men leave ore like this behind, and that's trouble. This was dumped in a hurry. What we need right now is to find out where the ore was mined.' He buckled the rock inside Mathew's haversack. 'Start looking. The reef has to be near here – somewhere inside this gully.'

Several paces beyond the ancient tree, Mathew found leather buckets rotten through with age. In their haste to abandon the workings the ancient miners had flung them aside. Like others, they had been filled with rich ore from the reef. Nathan could not resist the temptation to select another choice piece from the rubble at his feet. Again, he held it in close to the flame. For long moments his eyes played over the rock's surface and his imagination ran unchecked.

'If we both live for another hundred years, neither one of us will see anything as rich as this.'

'But from where?' Mathew reminded him.

Nathan took the candle from him and held it at arm's length above his head. Where there was once a thick matting of dead leaves, now there was rock. At waist height and at a slight incline, a dark hole loomed in the ironstone.

-14-

'How far in have we come?' asked Nathan.

'I'd say about thirty yards.'

Hot wax from the candle stub had encased Mathew's thumb and forefinger. He guessed what remained of the candle's life — twenty minutes, nothing more. The flame wavered slightly, caught by a gentle ingress of fresh air.

The shaft had been cut with iron gads and wooden barring tools, with hardwood wedges driven inside the reef. Fires had been set to the face; the incessant pumping of skin bellows would have created temperatures equal to those of the smelter's furnace. When suddenly quenched with cold water the tormented rock would have split wide open, loosened enough from the reef for the ancient miners to lever it out with their barring poles.

The incline twisted right and left, at a slight downwards angle, but always in sympathy with the reef – a four foot wide quartz intrusion that in its molten state had squeezed through fissures, pushing its way from the earth's mantle before coming to rest in tandem with the ironstone.

Dust rose up from the floor. The smells were those of a thousand years ago. Apart from the spoor of insects and those of inquisitive rodents, no other marks were there for Mathew to follow.

'The roof's getting lower,' he warned and was forced onto all fours. A halo of dust settled about the candle. Childhood phobias crept up on him and just as he readied himself to turn and dash for the sunlight, the hanging wall of rock above his head disappeared.

A cavernous void stretched way beyond the reach of their candlelight. From a narrow fissure in the high roof the smallest glimmer of natural light barely managed its way through. The roots of ancient trees hung as matted ropes, almost to the floor.

Both men stood in silence – gradually their eyes grew accustomed to the emptiness.

'We're not alone, father.'

Where light from Mathew's candle made the nearest sidewall, macabre shadows danced against the rock.

'By all that's holy Mathew, there are dead men down here!'

The candle flickered – almost went out.

'We're losing the light,' said Mathew. 'We need hurricane lamps – two at least.'

'And we still have work to do,' said Nathan, eager for the sunlight. 'Our friends over there can wait. Best we register our find with the Mines Office before the Irishmen and half the world gets wind of what we have here.'

-15-

They left their horses tied to hitching rails outside the Chartered Company buildings – brick under iron, the walls limewashed and pristine white in the early sunlight. The commissioner's office was empty of custom and they found Vigers hunched squirrel-like over a week's worth of paperwork. A droplet of sweat hung precariously from the very tip of his beaky nose.

'Nathan Goddard?' Vigers stood up from his desk. 'Heard you had gone south – someone said you had gone back to Kimberley?' He reached for Nathan's hand. 'Fort Victoria would have been the worse off for it, but obviously that does not come into it – I mean, seeing as that you are still here and not in Kimberley.'

'Kimberley had its uses,' said Nathan, but the dapper little company man had already turned his attention to Mathew.

'And this might be?'

'My son, Mathew,' Nathan introduced.

'But of course I should have noted the obvious likeness. Forgive me my manners – unfinished paperwork. Dampens the old brain, I'm afraid. Welcome to Fort Victoria and if at any time you are in need of any assistance in the mining field please do not hesitate to call on yours truly.'

'That's what we are here for.' Nathan cut through the pleasantries. 'Three blocks of gold claims, east of Providential Pass. We've come to register our rights to mine them.'

Vigers quickly donned his commissioner's hat; 'And would I be correct in assuming the strike is on new ground and not the re-pegging of an abandoned property?'

'New reef,' confirmed Nathan, and drew out a plan of the claims from his shirt pocket.

Vigers scrutinised the plan's layout and that included in the drawing, were all four points of the compass and the date and hour of the pegging. He noted also that all corner and intermediate beacons had been correctly identified and that the distances between them were in strict accordance with the laws of his department.

'I see your project is within a few miles of the Cotapaxi claims?'

'Four miles out from their northern boundary,' confirmed Nathan, 'and a good six miles or so east of the Dickens.'

'Ah, yes. The famous Dickens Mine,' said Vigers. 'Rumours of a buy-out by a more powerful player are rife, even as we speak. Mr Albert Grey's Northumberland Syndicate, if I am not mistaken.' His fingers busied with pen and paper whilst his mind shuffled ahead of the moment.

Without looking up from his work, Vigers quoted a sum of seven shillings and sixpence for the registration fee.

'That will be for all three blocks of claims, of course.' He cocked a querying eye at Mathew's father. 'Your property, how should we call it?'

'Empress Deep,' said Nathan, openly relieved by the

171

success of their transaction. In the eyes of the law the reef was now legally his.

Vigers penned in the name and the date of its legal registration, making sure the ink had dried before handing over three separate certificates. He dropped the registration fee into his cash box, then as an afterthought; 'I should make sure all your boundary lines and beacons are in good order, only yesterday afternoon did two other gentlemen bring my attention to their interest in that same area – asked for credit in lieu of registration fees. Bit strapped for cash they said.' He paused, not sure if Nathan had heard him. 'Two Irishmen, I believe – a Mister Chulmleigh and if I am not mistaken the other gentleman was a Mister O'Reilly.'

# -16-

'The scum followed us from the ruins.' Mathew lengthened his stride to keep up. 'We should be out there now, putting up claim pegs.'

'Not before I'm done here,' Nathan brooded. 'If our Irish friends are still in town, this is where they'll be.' He brushed aside the hotel's batwing doors. Men stood three deep to the bar counter, miners and prospectors most of them. Piano music tailed to nothing and before Nathan had reached the counter most of the drunken banter had all but dried up.

'You're a wee bit late, boyo. O'Reilly saw you coming. He and his Mister Chulmleigh friend left ten minutes ago – via the back door.' The drunk stood an inch taller than

Nathan, built like a buffalo across the shoulders but heavy in the gut. He lowered his eyes. 'Told us about you two thieving their spoils out at the old ruin.' A thick, tobacco stained finger hovered in front of Nathan's face. 'Almost killed him he said. Showed me the hole in his bowler. An inch lower and our Mister O'Reilly would have been stone dead.'

'Little enough punishment for what they did to the girl,' Nathan countered. 'O'Reilly had her trussed like a pig.'

'And a pretty little pig I believe she was. Reckoned on you and that boy of yours wanting her all to yourselves.'

Nathan hit the drunk in the stomach. His head dropped forward and Nathan hit him again – at the point of his thick nose. The drunk fell backwards and lay bleeding into the counter's brass spittoon.

'Chulmleigh said you stole their claim?'

Nathan searched for his new aggressor – fists clenched and ready for another fight. The speaker detached himself from the crowded bar – shorter than Nathan, but broad-shouldered and with a three inch moustache drooped to either side of his mouth.

'Though better men would only judge a man after hearing his side of the story.' He grinned at Nathan and stepped over the prostrate drunk – his voice thick with Scottish brogue. 'The Irishmen painted too grim a picture of their assailants. I would be more than surprised if any of it were true.' He extended his hand. 'Allow me to introduce myself – Allan Wilson.'

'Nathan Goddard.' Nathan accepted the hand.

'There's a private room at the back. I'll have some refreshment brought through.' Wilson gestured to the hotel proprietor and ushered Nathan and Mathew towards a locked doorway.

The room had a businesslike feel to it, the entrance blanketed from prying eyes by heavy curtains; the windows were draped with that same green velvet. Once the curtain and door were closed, noise from the bar disappeared. Mathew recalled his experiences at the Kimberley Club and half expected Cecil Rhodes and Charles Rudd to walk in on them.

'Please,' Wilson invited. 'Sit yourselves down.' He waited for them to settle, then, still unseated, reached inside his jacket pocket. 'This, I'm afraid, is what your Irish friends were touting around the bar.'

At first, Nathan was loath to touch it. Light from a single lamp fell to the fist-sized lump of rock Wilson had placed at the table's centre; it glowed enticingly, though at the same time, Nathan sensed the threat of him losing everything.

'From our claims,' growled Nathan and picked up the sample of rich ore. Every quartz reef had its own peculiarity – no two were exactly alike. Nathan recognised the rock's natural colouring, the insets of bright, mulberry coloured quartz and the way those specks of raw gold were cast inside the stone.

'Thought it might be,' admitted Wilson. 'You have them registered, of course?'

'An hour ago,' said Nathan, 'Vigers told me what the Irishmen were up to.'

'And you came looking for them,' proffered Wilson, 'understandably so.'

Nathan pushed back his chair, like Mathew he was more than eager to be on his way.

'Here me out, Nathan – give me ten minutes of your time and I'll explain my reasons for bringing you here.' Wilson came straight to the point. 'On behalf of the

Victoria Mining Company, I would like to express my interest in your mining venture. As you most likely know, our own Mister Morrish has already re-pegged the Electric claims to the south of you and renamed the property as, The Cotapaxi. What I have in mind is a central milling point, a ten-stamp battery that would take ore from both properties. Under one banner the company's mining interests would be guaranteed. In short, the said properties would complement one another.'

'You would make an investment,' said Nathan, intrigued by Wilson's offer, 'based on a single piece of reef?'

Wilson retrieved the quartz and held it into the lamplight.

'Assuming the find to be substantial and of similar grades to this – then yes, we would be interested in either a direct purchase or a fifty-one percent shareholding. With the Company bound to supplying equipment and labour for the ongoing development of your claims.' He replaced the lump of quartz. 'We would, of course insist on you holding the position of mine overseer. Our man on the ground as they say; trustworthy managers are scarce, especially where gold production is concerned.'

'What about the Mashonaland Agency?' Nathan asked.

Wilson smiled at the comparison. 'Pretty well have their hands full, as I see it. Their people are busy erecting a five-stamp crushing battery at the Victoria. The agency already owns six of the nine most promising properties on the Victoria Goldfield.'

From the look on Mathew's face, his resistance to selling the Empress Deep was obvious.

'And were we to keep it?'

Wilson held a match above the lamp glass; the Vesta flared and he took time in rolling the tip of a Julieta cigar inside the flame. The Cotapaxi reef wouldn't last forever. The Empress Deep might well be what the company shareholders needed to stay afloat. He drew on the cigar then exhaled a perfect ring of grey smoke. Like a noose it hovered above the gold ore.

'Then you would be subjected to the full force of the Chartered Company's rules; in a nutshell – Mister Rhodes takes half your profits.'

# -17-

Catherine served up stew and dumplings and later, chunks of fresh bread that Mathew smothered with butter and honey. Nathan swirled coffee grounds round the bottom of his mug then watched them settle as a dark tail around its base. In his mind's eye they were grains of fine gold, but from amongst the dregs, O'Reilly's face laughed up at him.

'We'll leave at sunrise. Axes and rifles are all we need. For their sakes I hope the Irishmen stay clear of our claims.'

Catherine felt his anger.

'Take Mhlangana with you. You might well need an extra pair of hands.'

'What if they come here?' warned Mathew.

'They won't,' said Nathan. O'Reilly would have the entire garrison after him and he knows it.' He stood up from the table and crossed to the window – sunlight seared the western horizon then slipped below the hills, within that next half hour the sky would be pitch black.

'You'll be away for one night?' asked Catherine.

'Tomorrow night,' Nathan confirmed. 'As soon as the lines are cleared and the beacons up we'll be on our way home.' He could see Mhlangana's fire from the kitchen window. He nodded to Mathew. 'Best you tell Mhlangana to be ready at first light. Food for one night, his spears and a blanket; we might well be sleeping without a fire.'

*

They rode out from the homestead just as the eastern skyline changed from black to pink and pearl-grey, the colour of a dove's breast. Nathan went in front with a loaded .44 Winchester rested across his legs, but with the hammer forward. He kept his horse to a slow canter, only yards ahead of Mathew. At Mathew's left flank, holding on to the stirrup leather, Mhlangana kept pace with the horse. When they reached the makeshift paddock and whilst Mathew corralled the horses, Mhlangana cast ahead for spoor.

They caught up with the Matabele and knelt alongside him.

'What do you see?'

'*Ize*,' said Mhlangana, 'nothing – since the last rain no one has passed where we stand.'

Nathan looked across the ridge to where they had first climbed inside the ravine. There was little breeze and again, the rustle of green pigeons was the only sound.

'There is no one,' whispered Mhlangana. The breeze came from their front. A pair of kudu bulls browsed on young acacia leaves, unaware of being watched. Their horns were heavily spiralled and, as the antelope lifted their muzzles to feed, tilted backwards to the level of their shoulders.

Nathan stood up. Immediately the antelope took fright and spirited away, striped wraiths between the trees.

'Take Mhlangana and a lamp with you; see if the Irishmen found their way to the reef.' He slung the Winchester across his back and picked up the heavy, woodcutter's axe. 'I'll start with our registration pegs. When you get back we'll work on the boundary beacons until the light fails.'

This time, Mathew secured the rope directly above the opening. Below the matted foliage the darkness itself was thick with smells of rotting leaves. He set down the hurricane lamp and waited for Mhlangana, then held a lighted Vesta behind the lamp glass. Within minutes the pool and entrance to the ancient shaft were bathed in yellow light. Mhlangana lifted his assegai and stared with trepidation at the opening to the tunnel.

'There are ghosts here,' he told Mathew. 'I would rather fight a hundred men than walk beneath a mountain.'

'I have seen you fight, and yet you fear the dark?'

'Not the dark,' said Mhlangana. 'Here there is witchcraft; Shona *mahondoro* and *mtagati*.'

Mathew put up the lamp and drew out the Colt from his waistband.

'Then I will leave you to watch for your ghosts. Tell my father I have gone in alone.'

Mhlangana caught up with him before the first twist in the tunnel. Nothing was said, but Mhlangana's eyes were wide and sweat had sprung as glistening beads across his forehead. In the dust, Mathew recognised his own spoor and that of his father; no others had overlaid them. Now the light engulfed the sidewalls. It reached the cavern's high roof and from against the furthest wall, slumped shoulder to shoulder the same mummified remains

Mathew had seen earlier witnessed another intrusion.

'In my father's name,' Mhlangana whispered. 'Find what we have come for and let us leave.'

Mathew knelt to the footwall and held the lamp in close. 'Children,' he realised, 'or women – they would have barely stood tall enough to reach my elbow.'

About their necks, glass beads the colours of peacock feathers hung loosely about the upper vertebrae.

'Do not touch them!' Mhlangana pleaded. 'On both our lives do not touch the dead.'

Mathew straightened up; attracted by the uniformity of the cavern wall he drew his hand across its surface.

As snow from a church window the dust fell away as a thin expansive sheet – in the lamplight the rock beneath was smooth as alabaster.

'Leave me here. Find my father. Tell him to join me – tell him I will not leave here until he does so.'

# -18-

Nathan set down his haversack. The rock face was bathed in yellow light and, like the penitent worshipper, Mathew crouched silently before it. For a long moment both men stared in awe of the discovery.

The colours were vivid, overly bright as to appear garish – blended tints of iron ochre, oxides of native copper, fiery reds, azurite blues and malachite greens of a hundred different shades, all of them brought iridescently to life by exposure to the lamplight.

'The ruins,' Nathan realised, 'where we found the

Irishmen and the girl.' He pointed out the ancient stonework and those same towering trees that even now guarded the outer walls – all of it, through the artist's skill reproduced in exquisite detail.

Mathew enlarged the window, sweeping away more of the dust with the back of his hand. From the first setting of hardwood fires against the reef, to the transportation of mined ore in those same leather buckets, a complete pictorial record of the ancient mine was there on the wall. Mathew traced back along the mural with his fingertips.

'The holes we found on the ledge.' He pointed them out. Behind them, a stone mullocker the weight of twenty men – a rocking stone levered about its point of balance like a child's see-saw was being used to crush the gold- bearing rock.

'Crude but very effective,' said Nathan, 'then from there to the mortars, thirty of them, each with their own attendant.'

Mathew moved his hand further to the right. 'The pool,' he realised and shook his head in wonderment. 'Here they're panning off gold from the quartz.' He stepped back from the wall, overwhelmed by the implications of what they were looking at. Nathan touched his arm.

'We still have to cut the lines. Best we get it done before the Irishmen do it for us.' They started back along the shaft, eager for fresh air and sunlight.

For as long as daylight lasted the three of them worked on marking out boundary lines. They cut their pegs from living trees and fixed them in cairns of heavy ironstone. The peg displaying registration number and name of the licensed holder went close to the shaft entrance, as close as Nathan could establish to the centre of the reef. By nightfall all the pegs were in.

'Put in a fire,' said Nathan, 'we'll stand the risk of someone seeing it.'

Mhlangana dug out a shallow scrape; partially hidden, the flames were kept to a low burn. Left alone with Mathew, Nathan broached the subject of going to war with Lobengula.

'There's talk of Rhodes using company troopers to fight the Matabele,' said Nathan, 'Jameson's also touting for volunteers. Some sort of militia. Convinced he will have Lobengula on the run within a fortnight.'

Mathew's interest piqued.

'Sounds as though you have already decided to join with him?'

'Not yet,' said Nathan, 'though if I was asked, refusing would prove the harder option. Every man able to fire a rifle will be stepping forward.'

'Rhodes must be dangling a juicy carrot or no one would volunteer?'

'Twenty gold claims and generous land grants,' Nathan elaborated – his mood transparent. 'We would double our interests.'

'Triple, if I were to come with you.'

'And your mother would have the skin from my back if I so much as hinted at your joining forces with some militia. Get some sleep. We leave for home first thing tomorrow.' Silently, Nathan cursed himself for broaching the subject of war with the Matabele. When sleep eventually came to him it was on clouds of dark thoughts.

Mhlangana scouted a quicker route to where they had left the horses. Within minutes of them leaving the paddock the sky covered over, the quiet whipped away on the back of a northwester. They rode in the rain, like glass fingers it cut through the forest canopy and drummed the earth to red slurry. Not until the storm eased did they make out a twinkle of welcoming light from the homestead window.

Catherine watched her husband in from the rain and while water still ran from Nathan's beard she kissed him full on the mouth.

'Someone to see you.'

'Saw the horse – who is it?'

Catherine looked past him and nodded her head to Mathew.

'Ask your son, I think he might well remember him.'

Mathew was first through the kitchen door.

'Burnham!'

'Came to see if you still had the Colt?'

'Sleep with it under my pillow – we're inseparable; never go anywhere without it.'

'Forgive my impoliteness.' Burnham turned to Nathan. 'Frederick Russell Burnham and you, sir without a shadow of a doubt, are Mathew's father.' They shook hands and immediately, Nathan warmed to the man. The adventurer's glint was there in his eyes and the strength in the American's handshake easily matched with that of his own.

'You'll take a drink with us? And supper?'

'I would object to neither,' said Burnham.

'Then stay the night?' Mathew suggested. 'Take my room. I insist.' He looked to his mother.

'You can leave in the morning, Mister Burnham. The rain should have cleared by then.' She saw relief in Burnham's eyes, but there was something else – something more sinister behind the smile. She took down a bowl and ladled it full with stew and at its centre, dropped in two large boiled potatoes and a thick slice of corn bread.

'Take this to Mhlangana,' she told Mathew. 'In this wet I'm sure he'll be glad of some hot food.'

Mhlangana had slung a canvas sail between the trees. He struggled with wet wood, but slowly the flames took hold. Mathew crouched in close to the fire. From overhanging leaves, rainwater splattered against the canvas. With an open hand, Mhlangana wiped the rain from his face.

'My woman, my son and the hills of *Thabas Indunas* – the time has come for me to be with them again.'

'A man should be with his family,' Mathew agreed, 'but it will be with a heavy heart that I watch you leave.' He fed the fire with chips of wood. 'You have heard of Cecil Rhodes' mistrust of the Matabele?'

'I have heard it said.'

'There will be war,' said Mathew.

'The fighting will come,' agreed Mhlangana. 'There is place only for one king. When the buffalo fights with the lion, one of them will die.'

Inside the homestead, Catherine stood at the kitchen window, alone with her thoughts. The manly smell of freshly lit cigars drifted in from the sitting room; the sound of men's voices she found to be comforting. However, when she joined them at the table, the conversation shrivelled.

A dark presence had found its way inside the house; Catherine sensed it there, mocking her from where it had seated itself alongside the men. Nathan leant over and held the tip of his cigar inside the lamp glass.

'Sit down, my dear. Burnham has been telling me about Rhodes' plans for opening up land west of the Lundi River.'

'Matabeleland?'

'That's what some are calling it,' said Burnham. 'The Matabele have, shall we say, been making a nuisance of themselves.'

'In what way?' asked Catherine, readying herself for confrontation with Cecil Rhodes' emissary. 'Surely the Matabele are entitled to do as they wish in their own country?'

Burnham lifted his glass and sipped at the brandy. He smiled at the comment. Catherine had already voiced her opinion of Cecil Rhodes' grandiose ideas for a new colony. Rhodes she saw in the same light as Genghis Khan and Saladin, repugnantly unstoppable – quick to spur the Imperial war horse over anything that stood in his way.

'Settlers are constantly being harassed by Lobengula's impis,' Burnham continued. 'They're being attacked with increased ferocity. Some have abandoned the journey even before they have reached the Limpopo.' He turned his attention back to Nathan. 'Preparations for the invasion of Matabeleland are already under way. Money and equipment were dispatched from Kimberley some two weeks ago.'

'So why exactly are you here, Mister Burnham?' But already Catherine knew the answer. The presence she had sensed was still there in the room, now more powerful; twisting in its seat to face her head-on.

'I apologise for my assuming your support, Ma'am, but through circumstance I'm forced to ask for your husband's help.'

184

'You would take my husband to war, Mister Burnham?'

Mathew came in from the rain and sat opposite the American. He listened avidly and quickly picked up the thread.

'How many men are you looking for?'

Like a wild beast protective of her young, Catherine glared at him.

'As many as we can muster,' Burnham replied. 'Every able-bodied entrepreneur in Mashonaland will be putting their names to it. Twenty gold claims and three thousand morgen will go to everyone who signs with the militia.'

'More land than we could ever hope for.' Nathan whistled softly. 'Who will be leading the column?'

'Major Allan Wilson will lead our Victoria Rangers. A column from Salisbury under Major Forbes will rendezvous with Wilson's rangers at a spot near Iron Mine Hill, some one hundred miles northwest of Victoria.' He turned to Catherine. 'We need to be rid of the Matabele, Ma'am, once and for all.'

'Rid of them, Mister Burnham? And why not? In Rhodes' eyes the Matabele are worth little more than worn-out chattels.'

Nathan did his best to temper her abhorrence.

'Let it lie, Catherine. Rhodes has taken the wellbeing of hundreds of settlers squarely across his shoulders – if it hadn't been for his foresight, we would still be living in that shack alongside the Kimberley diggings.'

'What about Mathew?' Burnham ventured.

'What of him?' Catherine hissed. 'Convincing my husband of your need for an extra gun is one thing – taking my son to war as well, is a possibility neither you nor the devil could ever hope for.'

Mathew opened his mouth to speak but with an

185

imperious sweep of her hand she silenced him.

'Do not even think of it, Mathew. When you're of a rightful age and not before – then you may decide these things for yourself.' She looked Burnham squarely in the eyes. 'Until such time, if Cecil Rhodes and his warmongers want my son they will first have to come through me.' She stood up from the table; her voice shook. 'If you will be kind enough to excuse me, perhaps a little time on my own.' Nathan heard the snick of the latch when Catherine closed the bedroom door behind her.

Burnham was first to speak. 'I can't see our run-in with the Matabele lasting more than two weeks, Nathan – three at the outside.'

'This promise of Company land grants? Nathan queried. 'Would it be in writing?'

'Black and white; whatever else people might think, Rhodes is still a man of his word.'

Nathan stood up from his chair and crossed to the window. The sky had cleared. Stars, tiny pinpricks of white light shone down from the firmament.

'I'll come with you. But there will be conditions.'

'Excellent!' said Burnham. 'Name them.'

'Should anything untoward happen, my claim to the land and mining grants would immediately go to my family.'

'Without hesitation,' assured Burnham. 'What are the others?'

'That I would be given the rank of Captain in accordance with past experience and finally, Rhodes will have to waive his normal fifty percent levy on our mining interests.'

'The last I cannot vouch for,' said Burnham, 'not without direct consultation with Mister Rhodes. Everything else, I can find no problems with.'

The three of them talked long into the night. Catherine

heard the clink of glasses and from her cupboard, the sound of Nathan reaching down a second bottle of brandy. As the level inside the bottle lessened so did talk of war reach its crescendo.

When Nathan came to bed, Catherine, though still awake turned to face the window. Eventually, sleep overtook her but the horrors of war were waiting. The sand inside her hourglass was quickly running out.

# -20-

Nathan reined his horse into the shade and waited for the others to catch up. Talk of Rhodes' land grants and the rights to twenty gold claims had spread rapidly; mercenaries and lawless drifters from every quarter of the colony were making their way to Victoria.

'Another mile and we'll be within sight of the fort. It would be wise for Mhlangana to stay well clear of it. Any man with a rifle and an eye for a fight will pick him off without so much as a second thought.'

Mhlangana had stripped himself of the white man's paraphernalia. Now he stood almost naked, except for a simple apron of soft leather and the gummed head-ring of the Matabele Induna. In a canvas bag, across his shoulders he carried enough food to last the five days it would take for him to reach GuBuluwayo. In his left hand he trailed the assegai – the blade bright as new frost from a recent honing.

Mathew slid from the saddle and put forward his best efforts into saying goodbye.

'Come back to us.'

'You have my word,' replied Mhlangana, and marvelled at the sadness in Mathew's eyes.

'And I will hold you to that,' said Mathew. There was little more to say. 'Go well, my friend.' From the constriction in his throat his voice barely made it above a whisper.

*

On the fifth morning, Mhlangana rolled clear of his sleeping place in deep scrub and shook himself free of that last night's rain – the storm had come at him in the early hours – whichever way he turned the howling wind had found him. Now he stood with his back to the sun, the cold fell from him and when he lifted his eyes to the western horizon the joy that leapt from his heart was almost too much for him to bear.

To his right hand, *Thabas Indunas*, Hill of the Chiefs crouched as a sleeping lion to a pale sky – to his left and as far as he could see, the hills of his beloved Matobo stood round and grey as the backs of browsing buffalo – in their tens of thousands – ringed with spring musasa and at their very peaks, shaded the colours of dawn and steel by early sunlight.

He drank water from a rain-filled depression in the rock and from the bag at his shoulder took out the last remnants of roasted maize. He ate quickly, the urge to run now paramount and with an eye for a far ridge, Mhlangana relaxed into that steady, swinging lope of the distance runner.

When the sun had reached its highest point, Mhlangana was afforded a first sighting of his birthplace. In that moment he caught the familiar scent of cattle and that of smoke from a thousand cooking fires. The vastness of it astounded him, for the fields where once his son had played as a child were covered end to end by the beehive shaped dwellings of the Matabele. From each side of Lobengula's GuBuluwayo, stretched herds of royal Nguni cattle, and had he been of a mind to, would have needed no less than a full day for him to count their numbers.

'My father tells that staring into the distance is a pleasure enjoyed only by women and old men?'

The small voice spirited out to him, its source hidden by tall grasses. Mhlangana smiled at the child's bravado, from the timbre of his voice, he guessed the boy had seen little more than eight full seasons.

'And calling from the hillside is favoured only by baboon and wild *imbila*, the rock rabbit, not by sons of the Matabele.' Mhlangana taunted skilfully; a game he had played a hundred times with his own son. 'Perhaps it would be safer for the rabbit if he stayed hidden? If you are truly a warrior, then step into the sunlight that I might see your face.'

'We have decided,' the boy announced, 'that we will spare the stranger's life.'

'So, you are many!' Mhlangana shot back at him. 'Show yourselves. Or like the black eagle I will swoop from the sky and devour you!'

Two heads bobbed above the grass, their eyes were wide and watched him intently, like those of mice for the hunting eagle owl.

'We are the sons of Mthunzi, the Shadow. We look to the safety of the king's cattle.'

'And what of your brother?' Mhlangana pointed his assegai at the youngest sibling. 'Does he not have the

189

strength to speak or have your mother's chickens plucked out his tongue?'

The youngest sprang to life, his attention caught by the plaited ring of hair on the warrior's head.

'You wear the head-ring of the king's Induna, and yet you carry no shield? The shield is the totem of the Matabele nation, it would not be deemed as right for a General of the king's impis to take the road without it. Mthunzi, my father, speaks often of this truth. Tell us your name, stranger. Show the sons of Mthunzi you are truly a warrior of the Matabele; that we, as guardians of the king's road might grant you safe passage.'

'My name is Mhlangana, descendent of Senzangakona and the royal house of Khumalo, and he demands the right of safe passage.'

The heads disappeared. Now there was the slight trembling of uncertainty in their voices. For a moment there came a stillness amongst the rocks and tall grasses – then, with a flurry of small feet the boys were there, knelt before him with heads bowed to the earth in a remorseful act of supplication.

'Forgive us, lord. Seeing you come from the east struck fear in our hearts. We thought you to be a spy. Shona imposters watch like jackal for the chance to steal the king's cattle.'

Mhlangana shook his head and laughed softly. 'I will spare you this time. Rise up and show me the road, I yearn to be with my people.'

They ran at the front, the eldest always a step ahead of his sibling – throwing sticks held at the ready and with an ear for tiny, clattering hooves; those of the dik-dik antelope, or as a lesser prize, the plump, copper- coloured partridge.

'*Amathendele!*' The boys would shout when the birds flushed from the undergrowth; fleeting as copper sparks in the sunlight.

At the final ridge, Mhlangana called them to a halt.

'From here I can find my own way. Your work is done, my little warriors. Go back to your cattle.'

'You will tell of our bravery?' pleaded the youngest.

'The king himself will hear of it,' Mhlangana assured him and with a father's hand encouraged them back to where they had left their cattle. He watched until the boys were all but specks on the horizon, then turned on his heels and went down into the valley.

## -21-

Before dawn, the king himself summoned Mhlangana to the royal enclosure. Fresh from the sleeping mat, Mhlangana stood naked to the warmth of a small fire whilst his woman, Imbali, gazed upon him with soft eyes. With fat from the hump of a bull eland, she lightly anointed his body, so that now he glowed with that same, deep patina of black granite.

'You are indeed the king's man, my heart. Should another woman look upon you with cow's eyes I shall be forced to cut out her tongue.'

He clothed quickly and in the full regalia of his high standing. To each muscled arm were tied medals of his valour; tails from the whitest of royal cattle, culled in their prime – each one given to the Induna by the king himself. At his waist hung a kilt of soft hide, adorned with the

191

black-ringed tails of civet and for the length of a man's arm above his head, a plume of coal black ostrich feathers. To Imbali they were the storm clouds above the sacred hills of Matobo.

Against his skin, hers was the lighter, more subtle of colour – that of turned earth to warm rain. Barely reaching his chest with her forehead, she stared up at the king's favourite and marvelled at the face above her, black as the night itself, godlike in the firelight; throughout her entire life she had never seen another more beautiful.

'Were it not the king who summoned you, lord. I would love you until every glimmer of strength was drawn from my body. One night was not enough,' she whispered, and let her hands wander beneath the skirt at his waist. She felt his passion rise, cobra-headed from the soft caress of her fingertips and she teased him lightly.

'He still hungers, lord.' Though sorely tempted, Imbali forced herself free of his arm. 'Go now, my husband, do not stay for another moment or not even the strength of a hundred great elephants will be enough to take you from me.'

-22-

From open fire pits an aura of deep red veiled the sky above the royal enclosure. Mhlangana knelt on one knee, his head bowed, as yet the right for him to gaze upon the face of the king had not been granted. Though it was almost dawn, from a black sky, a river of stars, the souls of a million dead looked down upon Lobengula Jando

Khumalo, the last great king of the Matabele.

'Rise up, my cousin, we are of the same blood, turning your face to the earth will serve neither one of us.' He slapped the palm of his hand to the great drum of his own stomach. A woman, barely more than a girl stepped from the shadows, naked except for her *betshu*, an apron of bright beads and soft leather. She made place for Mhlangana, covering the ground with the skins, those of black-backed jackal and the spotted furs of wild civet. She was slender – beautiful, still in those magical years of her early womanhood – lithe as an otter, long limbed, light on her feet as the slender river Jacana. Mhlangana settled to his place at the king's fire and with the unhurried countenance of a wise man he waited for Lobengula to free the way for him to speak.

From the mere raising of his little finger, the young woman like some dark, exotic butterfly prostrated herself before the royal platform. With her forehead touched almost to the earth, bathed in the glow from the fire pits she was more beautiful than the sunrise.

'Thabisa, my youngest wife and bringer of joy.'

'My king,' she answered coyly, for she knew that she was still his favourite. 'Do what you will with my worthless life, lord.'

'You are the brightest star in your king's night,' Lobengula whispered unashamedly. 'Go now. Bring food for the king and his cousin.'

Thabisa shuffled backwards into the shadows, still with her eyes averted. Lobengula watched her until she disappeared through an opening in the thatched wall.

'Why is it that nothing remains as it first was, my cousin? In my sleep I see a great river. The water is filled with crocodiles; too many for my eyes to account for their numbers.' He slumped back against a mattress of deep furs and sighed like a man beggared with age. The mountainous dome of his belly rose and fell with his breathing, heaving for air like the great bellows of his ironsmiths. 'Their jaws are open and to the backs of each one a white soldier rides with the *isibamu* in his hand and greed in his eyes.'

Superstition curled at Mhlangana's feet and for an instant, he saw the first signs of remorse form as tiny stars at the corners of the king's eyes.

'They will take it all; from the gold beneath our soil to the eagles in our skies. The white soldiers will not rest until the Matabele sit as dogs to their master's fireside.'

The sun broke clear of the horizon, tempering the glow from the fire pits. For as far as a man could see, GuBuluwayo, the nation's heart had awakened as a single yellow flame in the sunlight.

'Were I to be given my time again, the white *abelungu* would never so much as walk upon this land. There would be but one voice, one kingdom – that of the Matabele. From the southernmost river to The Smoke that Thunders in the kingdom of the Makololo. Every man, woman and child would pay homage to the son of Mzilikazi.' He stared now at the man across the fire and his voice carried with it the heavy spear of regret. 'Only then, if we were to stand as one great kingdom could we defeat the soldiers.' He raised himself onto one elbow and the royal platform creaked from the shifting of his weight. 'They will come for us, Mhlangana. Already my spies bring word of a hundred wagons and a thousand soldiers gathering like vultures to the east.'

'Then we ourselves must make ready, lord. To our thousands they are but a few. The king has only to raise a finger for his people to fight to their last breath.'

Lobengula smiled at the whimsy; for a moment his eyes clouded. The fantasy manifested itself through droves of multi-coloured cattle standing rank upon rank beyond the enclosure. To him, they became as warriors, their colours matched to the long shields of his regiments – long horns, peculiar to the Nguni breed were blades of bright steel – assegais tipped with sunlight.

'*Bayete*!' he whispered the royal salute, but his vaporous army merely disappeared amongst the grasses. 'They will bring their guns; those that stand with iron legs and shout with voices quicker than rain. The *isigwagwagwa*,' he whispered and the name alone was enough to invoke in him a feeling of terrible dread.

*The Maxim machine-gun can deliver six hundred rounds a minute – the equivalent firepower of thirty rifles.* Mathew's father had expounded. Mhlangana remembered the devastation Nathan had spoken of. *For a hundred yards, nothing, not the trees nor even the grass had been spared.*

At the king's beckoning, Thabisa stepped forward – laden with baskets of beef straight from the cooking fire. As decreed, the meat had been left bloody and thickly curtained with yellow fat. Thabisa laid the smaller of the two baskets at Mhlangana's side and then, like some repentant child with her arms outstretched and eyes again turned to the ground, shuffled on her knees to where Lobengula Khumalo, Shaker of Mountains and father of the Matabele nation waited with aching eyes.

'Come closer, *intombaza*.' He gave himself up to watching his consort. Her skin gleamed and her hair shone as crushed coal from a rubbing of fat and sweet smelling herbs. She settled at his side – the act itself was practiced and purposely effusive – a sensual folding in of slender limbs. She took up her sharpest knife and with dainty fingers freed a balanced choice of meat and fat from the beef in her basket. Like a mother with her cosseted child, Thabisa fed her king with titbits, proffering the meat only when he nodded for her to do so. With a selective eye, Lobengula singled out the more succulent cuts of beef, pausing between each mouthful for Thabisa to hold the beer pot up to his lips. His face and chest glistened with unguinous juices and when he belched, the sound rose up from his gut; the sonorous bass rumble of the Great Black Elephant. The king's upper arms were thickened with fat and muscle, though his hands were those of a woman, narrowed and slender to the tips of his tapered fingers. To the rolls of fat at his waist hung pendulous breasts and as the sun rose higher, sweat from beneath them ran as glistening rivulets. He nodded his head, without speaking, Thabisa took up her basket and left the enclosure.

'There were times, my cousin when for a hundred days a man could travel alone through the wilderness with neither sound nor sign of any white man.' A breeze came from the north, rolling onto his side the king lifted his face to it. Clouds, poised though still quiescent had gathered on the horizon. By late afternoon they would all be dark as thunder. 'Like flies to a wound in my side they come from everywhere. I fear them, Mhlangana; as the old elephant fears the hyena and the jackal.'

His gaze turned back from the heavens. Beyond the enclosure the insect-like shape of a single runner broke from the eastern skyline – the blade he carried caught at the sunlight like the portentous eye of a signaller's mirror. His speed was that of the long distance messenger and though almost a mile out from the king's enclosure, Lobengula was able to pick out the colours of the warrior's shield – black and white, the battle ensign of the Imbezu *ibutho.*

'Mjaan and Manondwane have sent word. What we spoke of has already begun.'

Like that of a young boy to his father's beckoning, the runner's pace did not falter. For three days the warrior had run from sunrise to dark, stopping to drink and rest only when that darkness closed his eyes to the road.

A stark silence fell over the royal enclosure. When the runner came to stand at its entrance, Lobengula called for him to come forward.

'What words do you carry? Through the eyes of your Induna, tell your king what you have seen.'

'Soldiers, my king. Close to *Thabas Insimbi*, the Mountain of Iron. They swarm as fleas to the back of a jackal.'

'You have seen them?'

'With my own eyes, lord.' Prostrated, with his cheek pressed against the earth he was aware only of the king's voice. To raise himself or to look upon the Great Elephant without consent would bring only death, for beyond the enclosure, grotesque bald-headed vultures looked down upon the royal kraal; willing servants to the king's executioners.

'What of the Mashona?'

'They follow like dogs, my king. They clean the white man's camp. Their tongues are as those of women at a beer drink. Our spies learn much from their yapping.'

'But they do not march?'

'The soldiers sit as locusts amongst the trees, oh great Stabber of the Skies. They wait for others to join them.'

'What others do you speak of?'

'From the place they call Victoria, *Obaba Nkulu*. The king's eyes are everywhere.'

'Go,' said Lobengula. 'Make a place for the night and eat

the food of ten men. Tomorrow you will take back the King's word to the Imbezu and Insukameni.' He rolled onto his side; his stomach heavy with meat and his eyes small from the beer pot. As a sated lion, Lobengula settled himself for sleep. Through hooded eyes he looked to Mhlangana.

'We still have much to speak of. Tonight my cousin, when the moon is full you will come to me.'

# -23-

Save for the yapping of dogs there were few other sounds when Mhlangana covered Imbali with a kaross of soft furs and then stepped out into the night. The moon, bright as a silver sun patched the great kraal with light and shadow – jackal and genet vied for scraps of offal and excrement. Cooking fires still smouldered – a child cried, a man cursed and women quietened their children with old stories. From every roof, a heron's feather of blue smoke leant with the breeze, gathering as a lake where a quiet stream went down to the valley floor. At a low port, Mhlangana carried a battleaxe, hafted with dark tamboti. The blade shone wickedly sharp in the moonlight. In the near distance the glow of red fires led him towards the royal enclosure, and on the breeze the portentous throb of ancient songs quickened his heartbeat.

'Only a fool or a brave man would approach the king's household unannounced. Which of those are you, stranger?'

Mhlangana froze mid-stride. His reply would be afforded

little time before the king's guard loosed his first spear.

'I am Mhlangana, father of Ndumiso. Cousin to the Great Elephant. Step out from the darkness that I might see your face.'

The reply invoked a low murmur of laughter; the warrior made no attempt to hide the scorn in his voice.

'To walk without a shield does not show the wisdom of a king's Induna – I say that you are a spy, an assassin.'

Mhlangana stepped away from the moonlight.

'Then speak with the king, you eater of dung. Let The Great Elephant himself decide the fate of his Induna.'

Through the clean air the spear made but a slight whisper – the sibilant flight of a night bird. A tiniest spark of moonlight flicked from the blade and from it, Mhlangana realised the whereabouts of his aggressor. In that same instance he spun on his heels and at the peak of its powerful arc he released his grip on the axe.

The guard's arm came off cleanly, just inches below the shoulder. At first there was no pain, the mere brushing of a wind, but instinctively the warrior reached out with his left hand and found the stump of raw flesh. Bright arterial blood leapt from between his fingers and when he fell, Mhlangana, like the mongoose to the mortally wounded snake was already standing over him.

In the moonlight the blood was thick; a black and oily pool. The man's eyes flickered. He lay with his face upturned to the sky and although the night was warm, as his life ebbed, a feeling of terrible cold rose up from his feet and he shook violently.

Mhlangana stooped in close and marvelled at the spectacle.

'When you see the ghosts of our fathers' fathers; tell them it was I, Mhlangana, cousin to the Great Elephant who has sent you there.'

Where the king waited there was no light, save for that of a full moon and the crimson glow of fire pits. Apart from the head-ring of his status, Lobengula, Lord of Thunder, lay naked as a child just born, spreadeagled upon a thick mattress of furs taken of lion, leopard and civet. Where a carved rest of native timber might have supported his head, there was now the golden skin of a male lion, its own great head wider than the war shields of the Matabele. Like that of the man who lay upon it the beast imbued feelings of menace and foreboding; with empty eyes it stared above the fire pits. Where once from its throat there had come the deafening roar of kingship, now there was only silence.

His skin glowed from a fresh covering of bullock fat, for with the first showing of a full moon to the granite shoulders of *Thabas Indunas*, the ritual had begun.

Thabisa, naked apart from her beaded skirt of the married woman, glistened as an ebony wraith at the king's side. Her fingers moved as gentle rain about his form, her arm the long and slender neck of the egret, to and from the earthenware pot at her feet. Wherever her fingers touched his skin she left behind a spark of moonlight, brighter than any morning star.

'I see you, my King.' Mhlangana knelt on one knee, his battleaxe laid to the ground.

Lobengula smiled without taking his eyes from the heavens, for the night sky was vast – brighter and more beautiful than any he had ever seen.

'Mhlangana,' he spoke softly. 'Blood of my blood. Sit closer, my cousin.'

While the king talked, Thabisa worked her magic and the ululations of a hundred virgins swept as warm spirits above the fire pits. Now the moon, cartwheeling to its highest place above the royal kraal was at its brightest and for the entire length of his body, Lobengula Jando Khumalo glowed as a single spiriting flame in the moonlight.

'Are these not the finest stones from the white man's, *Umgodi Makhulu*?'

'They are, my king. Though in the face of the one I bring you they are but grains of sand from the river bed.'

Mhlangana held out his hand to Thabisa. She took the stone from him, her hand trembled. Larger than a dove's egg, and though now there was no sunlight for its natural colour to feed on, still it flamed as a falling star.

Lobengula rolled the diamond between thumb and forefinger – a single octahedral crystal. Apart from the smallest inclusion the stone was perfect. At its centre there glowed a tremulous eye of coloured light – part silver, imbued by moonlight; the colour of sharpened steel – part red, drawn from withering coals in the fire pits, the colour of blood. By daylight, Mhlangana had witnessed a blaze of lemon and starlight; so alive was the gem that he feared the ghosts of past empires might well be trapped inside of it.

'A stone such as this should be looked upon only by kings,' breathed Lobengula

'I have seen powerful men fight as wild dogs for a hundred times less, my lord.'

A small flame rose from the embers. A solitary owl called from far forests, its voice sharp as the moonlight. Far to the east soldiers sat to their fires and oiled their guns. Lobengula sensed their gathering – as an ageing bull elephant might sense the closing in of the hunter – the antelope, the lion's presence or the rabbit the mamba's scent permeating the burrow.

'You have seen them with your own eyes; the road from

the south is deep with wagon spoor. Soon, my cousin, like the honey bird to the filled hive they will come for me.' He looked to the granite dome of *Thabas Indunas* – crouched as though asleep, foreboding and leonine to the horizon. Had he the power, the mountain would be made to stand as guardian; an impassable stone sentinel.

'Before the rising of the next sun you will leave GuBuluwayo.' He turned to Mhlangana. When he spoke, the heavy burden of the Matabele people passed between them. 'Find a place where these stones will be safe from the soldiers, where only spirits and the eagle might chance to gaze upon their sacred resting place. No one must know of its whereabouts – not even our own people.'

## -24-

Nathan Goddard pushed back his chair, closer to the window. The makeshift conference room was awash with stale air – every other man was smoking a cigar – thick, stylish Julieta that the Posselt brothers had shipped by Zeederberg coach from Kimberley. There were shadows of thoughtfulness in his eyes and the stark possibility of war with the Matabele weighed heavily upon his mind. He watched Mathew's excitement flair at the mention of rifles and quick-firing Maxims, but in his heart of hearts he prayed that his son would see sense in his argument and find good reason for staying behind.

Rhodes' administrator, Leander Starr Jameson sat at the table's head and whilst others talked he watched for those first tell-tale signs of dissension. However, he found nothing short of total support for Mister Rhodes' abhorrence of the bullying Matabele. The task of commanding the Victoria Volunteers he had given over to Major Allan Wilson and, as was relevant to his usual strength of character, Wilson quickly took control of the floor.

'Gentlemen and fellow officers,' the Scot raised his voice above the banter. 'I'll cut straight to the chase. Either we crush the Matabele or abandon our efforts to colonise Mashonaland.'

He searched the faces in front of him for any show of disagreement and like Jameson, found nothing short of the Chartered Company's expectations.

'In July past, the Matabele killed more than four hundred men, women and children. Most of them local Mashona. Their being butchered within the immediate vicinity of Victoria, I find most disturbing. Though it is true that not a single white man was murdered, the killings did little other than create an atmosphere of panic amongst our settler population. One, which I might add, we can little afford to lose.'

He allowed the facts to sink in then went on. 'The Company's choice as to when and where we invade Matabeleland has already been made, gentlemen. Our lot will meet up with a contingent of the Salisbury Horse at Iron Mine Hill. Under the overall command of Major Patrick Forbes, we will push on across the Lundi River and engage with Lobengula's impis – more than likely, somewhere in the vicinity of GuBuluwayo. Mister Rhodes insists on our capturing Lobengula alive. You, gentlemen, as men of rank would do well to bear this in mind.'

'So when exactly do we leave for Iron Mine Hill?' asked Nathan, and every man in the room listened intently.

'Two weeks from today, Captain.' Wilson himself was eager for the fight. 'With good fortune on our side we should all be home for Christmas.'

## -25-

Already the threat of war had spread its cloak above Victoria. As a woman, Catherine Goddard found herself mystified by men's inability to co-exist with others of different race. What Nathan had told her had in the matter of a few short moments, taken on ominous form and now the threat of personal loss was there, circling vulture-like above their home.

'Men are cursed with suicidal stupidity. They consider little, other than drinking, fighting or killing one another.' Catherine paused, expectant of some rebuke, then, when none came; 'Mathew is barely eighteen and you would have him lose his life in pursuit of some heathen warlord. Whom I might add, was and still is I should imagine, content enough to be left alone. Or has this seemingly insignificant matter of legal sovereignty conveniently slipped your Mister Rhodes' land-grabbing little mind?'

Nathan held up his hands at her onslaught.

'I cannot argue with that,' he admitted, 'but neither you nor I will deter Rhodes. He sees nothing less than his furtherance of the Empire.'

Catherine shook her head and again, Nathan saw that flash of angry eyes.

'Short of physically restraining you both, I cannot keep you from going, but I will say this, Nathan Goddard; come back from your crusade without my son and I swear by all that is holy, your Mister Rhodes will have me and a Mannlicher rifle to answer to.'

'That will not happen,' Nathan did his best to reassure her. 'I will be with him for every waking minute away from Victoria. The column will have the protection of over five hundred men armed with rifles and Maxims. The war with Lobengula will be over before you know it.'

'Then more's the stupidity of Rhodes' little band of Company vigilantes for thinking that,' hissed Catherine and gathered herself in defence of her reasoning. 'Or have you forgotten that your son and I have already experienced the Matabele at first hand?'

She moved to the window. Across the valley seasonal changes had overtaken the forest, groves of slender musasa were now a dozen vibrant colours about the hillside.

'Sometimes I find myself wondering if we would have been better suited to having made a go of things in Kimberley.' For a moment, her mind wandered back across the Limpopo. 'When will the column be leaving?'

'Two weeks from today.'

'And what of me?'

'You would move into Victoria, of course. George Hughes' wife has suggested you should stay with her. It would be good company for the both of you.' Nathan went to her and slipped his arms about her waist. She leant against him, but stiffly as an old woman; the fear of losing her family already a dark and heavy hand on her shoulder. She reached behind and pulled his face closer in to her neck so the thick curling mass of his beard brushed her skin with gooseflesh.

'You will be gone for at least a month – perhaps even

forever.'

'Less than a month, my sweet. Lobengula's impis will be sent packing and that will be the end of it.'

'If only things were ever that simple,' Catherine whispered. The thought of losing her men and living out her life alone filled her with trepidation. Silently, she prayed that it would not happen.

## -26-

To Catherine, her allotted fourteen days came and went with impunity. From the street's edge she watched her menfolk, along with Victoria's youngest and fittest form their column of twos.

'When you're ready, Nathan, fall in your troop behind Fitzgerald's lot.'

Major Allan Wilson looked across the street and respectfully tipped his hat to Catherine. 'Five minutes, Ma'am. That's all I can spare before the off.'

A slight wind scurried the dust about wagons and horses. The union flag, emblazoned with the British South Africa Company lion and tusks roundel fluttered at the column's head; an arrogant warning to be flown in the face of the Matabele. Stringing back from the column's mounted contingent were the mule wagons, loaded with general supplies, munitions, small artillery pieces and between them, mounted on galloping carriages were the lethal, three-legged Maxim machine guns. To the rear, native handlers marshalled their strings of loose horses.

The sun came up; half the street turned yellow, slashed

along its length by slanting shadows. Mothers held up their children – fathers and sons leant from the saddle for one last kiss and for some, the scent of downy hair brushed against their cheek. In his fighter's regalia, Mathew fitted the part of some young subaltern, criss-crossed bandoliers, Metford rifle, the .44 Colt six-shooter pushed behind his belt. In Catherine's eyes, in the spate of a few months her son had crossed the line; the boy she knew had been left behind in Kimberley.

'You are by far the handsomest here,' said Catherine, and though she put on a mother's smile the act was weak and fretful. She reached for him and drew him down for her lips to touch his forehead.

'No tears, mother,' In the face of other men, Mathew made light of his feelings. 'We will be home before you know it.'

'Watch for your father. Come home safely.'

'I will,' said Mathew, 'that I can promise you.' He reined his horse back to into line, affording his mother and father those last few precious moments together.

Nathan dismounted. On a slack rein, Luke stood quietly to his side.

'It has all been said,' whispered Catherine and struggled valiantly with her angst. 'I want you to take this with you. When you look at it I will know – every hour of every day you must have it with you, my love.' She pressed a slender locket and chain to the palm of his hand. 'Promise me that, promise me above all else that you will keep it with you.'

'You have my word on it.'

'Every waking moment my love will be with you, my sweet.' She broke from his arms, unable to prolong the agony. 'Now go,' she pleaded with him, 'your men are waiting.'

Nathan buttoned the locket away in his breast pocket. He swung up into the saddle and leant to her one more time for her to touch his face.

'Be strong, Catherine. Whatever happens, be strong. My love will always be with you.'

Allan Wilson touched his spurs to the flanks of his big grey. Like a serpent freed from winter hibernation the column shuddered with excitement – from Victoria's single, dusty street, mounted men and wagoner's stirred for the offing, ready to follow their leader into the wilderness.

With their children, women gathered as tight circles and took solace from one another. Stripped of their men, even the smallest amongst them now took up the heavy burden of provider and guardian, for now they were their children's sole protectors. With heavy rifles in their hands and bandoliers across their bosom they walked with dark intent to where they had left their wagons.

Catherine stared after the column until its trailing edge played tricks with her eyes, blurred by distance – merely a smear of dust – loneliness already the spiteful, careless companion as she climbed into the driver's seat of her Cape cart.

-27-

'October sixteen, gentlemen,' Wilson nodded his appreciation to Burnham, the column's scout. 'A day ahead of schedule and setting aside our Mister Robertson's fall from his horse, we are none the worse for wear.' He handed back the telescope to Nathan. 'Iron Mine Hill, Captain; what do you make of it?'

Nathan panned the glass slowly across the ancient hillside, their position of latitude now a hundred miles north of Victoria, almost to the yard.

'No sign of the Salisbury contingent, Major. Either we have beaten them to it or they have gone on without us.'

'I suspect the latter. Take our Mister Burnham with you and see what you come up with. Be back before dark, Captain. Pass on my pleasantries to Major Forbes should you be fortunate enough find him.'

The countryside was short-grassed, open parkland that allowed them to ride abreast. Both men rode with rifles drawn from their scabbards, rested across the saddle. Though they talked openly, not for a second did their eyes stop searching the way ahead for sign of the Matabele.

The sun was well up before they reached Iron Mine Hill. After scouting the area for any show of recent occupation, Burnham again met up with Nathan.

'Wilson was right, the Salisbury lot left here two days ago.' He handed Nathan a note he had found on the kopje. Forbes himself had signed his name to it.

*Come at your best speed. Will encamp close as is practical to GuBuluwayo.*

'Damn the man's impatience,' Burnham growled. 'He should have waited for us.'

Nathan saw the first inklings of resentment; the opening up of an old and festering wound.

'You don't agree with Forbes?'

'Arrogant fool,' said Burnham. 'Forbes considers no one but himself.' He pocketed the note and reined his horse about. 'Best we be getting back or we'll be riding in the dark.'

# -28-

For millennia the Matobo hills had been left untouched, save for the coming of storms and the raging of forest fires. As a whole, this vast expanse of igneous rock stretched in length and breadth for a hundred miles; a gargantuan granite batholith, in many places, stone *dwalla*, ancient granite hills towered a thousand feet above surrounding forests.

Cooled slowly beneath an overlay of dolerites and sedimentary limestones and exposed over aeons by climatic changes and natural erosion were the feldspars and quartz that gave the granite its dawn hue; through rose-pinks to subtle blends of mother-of-pearl. At the onset of winter, dampened by fine *guti* drizzle, the hills stood row upon row as the backs of a thousand sleeping buffalo, grey giants protruding from the forest canopy. At its extremities, and where even now formations of weathered limestone still reached amongst the granite outcrops, encouraged by deep and fertile soils the trees had burgeoned, standing as tall guardians to a thousand valleys.

By dawn of the third day, Mhlangana reached the northernmost rim of the Matobo hills. Across his chest he carried the *isikhwama*, a bag of soft goatskin and inside of it, sewn into the belly skin of a slaughtered yearling calf was a fortune vast enough to rival that of Cecil Rhodes. In another, he carried food and from chance findings added to it – harvesting the wild *inkowane*, mushrooms thicker and wider than the span of his own hand. At night he lay with his back to the warm granite, his eyes bedevilled by vast rivers of stars. However, he slept only fitfully, with his

210

spear and axe close to hand for the granite hills were home to leopard and rock python. Each morning he rose at first light and with the rising sun to his left shoulder pushed deeper inside the spiritual home of the Matabele.

On the seventh day, with a blood sun a red and portentous eye in the heavens, Mhlangana felt the magic of the land about him. In the lee of a granite cliff he built a fire. For that entire night he sat with his back to solid stone and in his hands, again he held the assegai and the battleaxe. Only when the night had almost ended did he lose the will to stay awake. Dark and heavy with dreams, waves of exhaustion crashed over him.

Like gunfire, the storm broke. Lightning, as white capricious fingers groped through mountainous thunderheads and the rain, incessant and heavy poured out from them. It ran as silver sheets across the granite, each a separate torrent, eventually linked together by fissures and deeply worn out ways in the living rock. The run-off gathered speed and volume. Sometimes, where the granite plunged as a sheer face, the water would turn wild and unpredictable; smashed to a mist it would hang veil-like above the far footings of the hills.

Awakened by the sound of thunder, Mhlangana opened his mouth and drank from the rain. Before him, the summation of the storm's anger rolled amongst the granite hills.

Attacked by countless tropical storms the more degraded limestones had eventually succumbed – burrowed into by natural carbonic acids. Ringed by forest, the dark throat of one of these ancient sinkholes loomed at Mhlangana's feet. Like a child fearful of the dark, he knelt on one knee and peered inside a cavern wide enough to take six oxen standing shoulder to shoulder across its entrance. From

211

beyond the boundaries of his imagination the hobgoblins of all his superstitions drew up alongside him. Voices made silent by the passing of a hundred years breathed from the darkened pit – this was a portal to the underworld – a witch's lair.

'Your spear is dull with old blood and yet you fear the darkness?'

Mhlangana spun around, but there was no one; butterflies, yellow and white rose from salt rich soils – as vibrant, silent clouds, they hung on the sunlight, then again, drifted earthwards. A breeding pair of tiny, klipspringer antelope watched him from their place amongst the rocks, eyes wide, unmoving, pools of black light. Only their noses twitched.

Again Mhlangana heard the voice; broken Ndebele, but familiar enough for him to understand.

'You carry the spear and axe of a great fighter, but your hands tremble like those of a girl?'

'Yet you hide from me?' Mhlangana hissed. 'If you are neither spirit nor wizard step into the sunlight.'

'Then give me your word, Induna.'

Mhlangana tightened his grip on the assegai and with the power of his right arm hefted the wicked battleaxe up to his shoulder.

'Step from your hiding place. On your life do not try to deceive me.'

Like a quick wind, a man, barely greater in height and build than a pubescent Matabele girl stepped from the forest. In his hand he clutched the hunter's bow, its entire length no bigger than a child's plaything – a slender, bone-tipped arrow nocked and readied for flight.

'I am N'go, the caterpillar!'

'*UmuThwa!*' Mhlangana recalled the name given to the

212

Khwai Bushmen by Zulu mineworkers on the Kimberley diamond fields. Only once before had he seen these little, amber-skinned people of the deep Kalahari. Small eyes, thinly slanted as those of a snake – the poison that tipped their arrows just as deadly. As forest wraiths they would appear from nowhere. Like ghosts, fleeting as desert winds, on sinewy legs they would match the stamina of any antelope – with a jackal's cunning and an unmatched hunter's eye they would strike at will.

'This is not your place, *umuThwa*. Where is your clan?'

Birdlike, N'go perched to the crest of a boulder, as a nervous finch he was ready to dart for cover. He arched a slender arm towards the west.

'Makgadikgadi.'

'The Great Thirst.' Mhlangana knew of the name. As a small boy hunting ostrich with his father he had glimpsed the Bushman's strange and shimmering land, a full twenty day's march further west into the driest heartlands of the Kalahari; six thousand square miles of arid scrub and parched earth where vast migratory herds once wallowed in the shallows of a great lake. Now, set apart from the lush oasis of the Okavango, only the giant salt pans of *Ntwetwe*, *Sua* and *Nxai* with their islands of igneous rock remained.

N'go stared down from his stronghold. His eyes now those of the meerkat, watchful of the cobra's every move. In the time it would take for an owl to blink he could release the arrow and as a puff of wind be away inside the forest.

'Why does a son of the Matabele come alone into the wilderness?'

'Perhaps I am not alone, *umuThwa*.'

'You are alone. For two suns I have followed your

213

spoor.'

'Then you also are alone.'

'Perhaps.' He freed the arrow from its bowstring and without taking his eyes from Mhlangana, slid the precious tool back inside a quiver cut from the bark of the Kokerboom. 'Perhaps as the wind, my people are everywhere.'

Mhlangana lowered his axe. A single, yellow butterfly hovered undecidedly over the Bushman's head; then, soft as yellow sunlight it touched his nose and alighted there.

'*Uvemvane!*' N'go whispered, delighted by the tiny creature's preference. Cross-eyed he watched the yellow wings fold and then extend. Like a child he raised a little hand and gently brushed the creature away.

'What do you guard so closely, Induna – that it clings like an ape to its mother?'

'A curse,' said Mhlangana.

N'go's eyes narrowed. 'Then cast it off – only a fool would choose to carry it with him.'

'I have given my word.'

'What words are these that you would put your life at risk to the wilderness?'

'You pry too much, *umuThwa*.'

N'go's face puckered –  more wrinkles than a lizard's throat. He smiled, delighted by his own astuteness.

'Show N'go this curse, Induna. I do not fear the magic of your witch. Only that of *Heiseb* or *Kouteign Koorou*, the serpent.'

'To those who do not know they are merely stones.'

'But still you fear them?'

'They bring death.'

'I do not fear death, Induna. Show me these stones. Lay them out for N'go to piss on this magic.'

Mhlangana lowered the weight from his chest. With the tip of his spear he plucked the knots from the leather bindings.

From the sun's angle, a thousand colours fell upon the precious hoard. Most were stones of the first water, none smaller than the first joint of Mhlangana's middle finger, though still as nature had left them – fashioned by God's hand many were crystals of almost perfect symmetry. The largest, a diamond that Mhlangana himself had spirited out of the Kimberley diggings, lemon coloured, bright as hoar frost to the tips of winter grass. As a nations heart it pulsed with sunlight.

'A child's baubles.' N'go snorted. 'The riverbeds beyond the Makgadikgadi are filled with stones such as these.' He sneered at the Induna's stupidity. 'What will your masters have you do with them?'

'That I find a place,' said Mhlangana and peered sideways to the cave's edge. 'One where others will fear to enter. It is the bidding of my king.'

'A place beneath the earth?'

'It would be wise to choose so.'

N'go plucked the yellow diamond from the pile, held between his face and the sky, the gem filled with fire – bright as the sun itself. Inside the stone, colours swirled as portentous mists – shadows. N'go shivered. The first tiny wings of  superstition were fluttering over his skin. He abandoned the gem to the pile and as though only moments ago he had grasped the poisonous stem of the tree nettle and shook his fingers to free himself of the curse.

'There is a place.' He looked towards the cave and with a small voice spoke as if others might be listening. 'No one will enter. Others have perished trying – there are

215

guardians.'

'Ghosts?'

'Not ghosts,' N'go hissed, 'the guardians live.'

Mhlangana gathered up the diamonds. 'If I smell treachery, *umuThwa*, I will kill you.'

'A hundred times I could have ended your life, Induna. Take up your stones and follow N'go.' He looked to the north horizon and nodded his head. New clouds were already forming. 'Soon the rain will return, without it we cannot pass. Tread warily and you will live – as a fool and you will be dead before the next sunrise.'

# -29-

Between the granite hills the earth is soft and deep, deposited there by natural erosion and unfathomable hours of rotting down – streams run thick with sediment, the remnants of all life. Timed by the season of rain and high temperatures the air is laced with powerful odours, to humankind most are undetectable, but to the swarming life of the forest floor these scents become the very reason for their being, triggering the urge to hunt and reproduce – sometimes swelling their numbers by tens of millions.

It was these conditions that set in motion the nomadic instincts of *Dorylus wilverthi*, the driver ant. Marching columns converged to become a single, voracious file of more than a metre in width and so many were their numbers that it took half of one full day for them to cross the high dome of living rock at the valley's head. Fledglings were stripped from their nests, newborn antelope devoured where they dropped – reptiles, asphyxiated by sheer weight of numbers were dissected and then devoured from the inside, their skins and skeletons left as empty husks on the granite.

Each worker carried with it a small white larva, a genetic replica of its kind; all were driven by the urge to find a guarded place where their young could pupate. At the forest's edge the column slowed, becoming indecisive, then, as if guided by some predetermined signal, poured like a black tide through a break in the limestone, following the roots of the wild fig to a place where the air was warm and moist – where their numbers would increase a thousand-fold.

As a single living organism they settled there; the dark beneath the ground now thickened with pheromones and the stinging smell of formic acid. Balled together as a glittering, sibilant nest the ants were restless – the workers eager to hunt – now a hundred times more dangerous than the adder or the lion.

## -30-

The Bushman, artful and focused, spun the wooden drill between the palms of his hands – fast enough for it to make its counterpart beneath squeal and smoulder. Satisfied that a spark had taken hold, N'go laid aside his fire sticks and, with a lover's touch and the velvety fur scraped from the seed pod of the *umshonkwe*, lifted the glowing ember to a waiting pile of dry tinder – fine yellow grasses – mosses taken from the dry undersides of trees at the forest's edge. The tinder smouldered; with it cupped between his hands, N'go gently fanned the makings with his breath, coaxing the infant spark to a dancing adult flame before placing it amongst the kindling.

'Without fire we cannot see.' N'go nodded with commitment as a tendril of blue smoke curled serpent-like from its nest of twigs. 'Without fire we cannot pass.'

Instinctively, Mhlangana raised his spear; belly high, ready to take the charge of some imaginary aggressor. N'go laughed at him. The act was pretentious, futile.

'Lower your weapon, Induna. Not even your king's regiments will pass beyond the gate of death if the guardians see fit to hold them at bay.'

'Do not mock me *umuThwa*. Save your ghost stories for the children of Makgadikgadi.'

N'go watched the fire mature, then raked out coals from its glowing heart. With bare fingers he juggled the best of them into a clay-lined gourd, covering them with bark and droppings left by the rock hyrax. From a skin pouch tethered at his waist he poured the gourd full to its brim with a mixture of dried root scrapings from the violet tree and the powdered pods of the *umketsheketshe*, the snake bean. Smoke poured out from the gourd, becoming darker, more redolent. Mhlangana turned his face away; the air now thick with strange odours.

'Soon it will be time.' N'go pointed to the eastern horizon. The moon, as though tipped by the sun on celestial scales rose above the hills.

N'go built up the fire with slow-burning hardwoods. Light from the freshly risen moon now angled deep below the ground and the thunder of another storm growled from twenty miles behind the first. Crouched against his heels, Mhlangana peered inside the cavern, fearful of what

218

might be waiting there inside the dark.

'Take up your axe, Induna, be as my shadow, speak only when I speak – still your feet if I do not move. The eyes beneath the ground are as stars in the night sky, never do they sleep.'

On the incline, the sinkhole twisted away from the moonlight. N'go's firebrand lit up the walls and, as yellow eyes, reflected from pools in the cavern floor. In place of stars, crystals of calcium carbonate threw back light from the cavern roof, most were opalescent, some almost pure and clear as spring water – as glittering colonies they clustered about the calcium rich seepage that spawned them.

As a wraith, N'go led Mhlangana deep inside the ancient cavern, every footfall placed with trepidation, the only sound was that of the stream where it whispered away inside the dark. A down-drafting flow of air drew out smoke from the gourd, deep in the earth the pungent smell of burning snake bean found its way through fissures and secret places. N'go raised the burning firebrand above his head, then, stepping to the side touched the flame to a shallow niche in the sidewall.

With its innards scooped away, the seed pod of the Cream of Tartar tree had been filled with tallow. At first the lamp merely guttered, like a candle from being left out in the rain – then the rush wick softened and from the melting fat at its tip there bloomed a smoky, yellow flame. N'go lifted out the lamp and raised it high enough to light the cavern wall.

'The beginnings of my people,' he whispered.

Where the yellow light fell, limestone and hard granite conjoined; the limestone rough and nodular and in its entirety, had been deeply scarred by acid seepage. But the granite was left untouched – a hundred times more resilient. Above the highest mark left by a thousand angry floodwaters the stone was still that pearlescent tint of first sunrise, its texture as that of lustrous marble. Mimicking a teacher of small children, N'go used his guttering torch as a pointer; the meerkat tutoring the mighty lion and his rheumy eyes glowed with satisfaction.

'My father's father – hunting the great eland, the elephant and the *ibhalabhala* – the striped kudu.'

Protected by the darkness the ancient rock art still retained a vibrancy of colour; reds and yellows, pigments of raw sienna and dark, midnight blacks mixed with the rendered fat of wild animals to ensure longevity – the artist's brushes fashioned from nothing more than the feathers of some tiny bird.

'This one?' whispered Mhlangana, and lifted the tip of his spear to touch the wall.

'The rain bull,' N'go explained, 'the bringer of great storms.' Larger, fiercer than the elephant, surrounded by prancing, stick-like images of Bushmen, the mythical creature rolled as a dark storm across its granite landscape; its belly the black and ominous cloud, its powerful legs limned by falling pillars of rain. 'And here, the Mantis and *Kouteign Koorou*, master of the water, a serpent greater than the hippopotamus and the crocodile.'

The cavern wall was filled with ancient artworks, one upon the other, often overlying those that preceded them; scenes aged less than a hundred years were intertwined with those of more than a thousand.

'I have seen enough, *umuThwa*. Lead on before your lamp fails. Show me the secret place you spoke of.'

'Then prepare yourself, Induna.' He gently blew into the gourd; the contents crackled awake. Again, from the pouch at his waist he pinched a generous measure from the concoction of herbs and root parings, then sprinkled it in amongst the embers. Only when the smoke was like a mist about their heads did he gesture to Mhlangana. 'Do not forget. Stay close. Make no sound unless I bid you to do so.'

# -31-

As if devoured by N'go's mythical serpent, the sinkhole swallowed them further beneath the forest floor. Where once there had been a single cavern, now there were many. Lesser tunnels spread from either side like the roots of an ancient tree and from them came the smells and sounds of things condemned to a world of perpetual darkness. Superstition, now the silent tormentor dogged Mhlangana's footsteps, his only way back to the surface through that tiny, flickering light – one that should it go out would leave him there to die, a blinded man trapped beneath the earth.

N'go raised his arm and he listened. There was sibilance, leaves whispered by wind over hard stone. In the darkness ahead, Mhlangana sensed a portent – a gathering of evil, a malevolent force that watched him from a distance. With every second he sensed it moving closer and instinctively his fingers tightened about the wooden haft of his battleaxe.

'Step into the pool,' N'go told him.

Rooted to the granite floor, Mhlangana peered into the gloom for the first signs of movement.

'Step inside the water,' N'go warned him again, 'or on my life the guardians will devour you.'

Like hot tar spilled from the caulker's fire, the cave floor glistened; changed from stone grey to pitch black, the floor undulated like the surface of a lake. The air above it was thick with the stench of formic acid and, though blind from birth, in their tens of millions, carnivorous driver ants, excited by the disturbance surged across the cavern floor. With the lamp held above his head, N'go waded, waist deep into the pool. From the gourd at his shoulder, acrid smoke drifted with the air currents.

'We must hurry – what the devils cannot smell they will feel; the magic will not hold them back for long.'

Mhlangana followed him, only once did he look back over his shoulder. The pool's edge seethed with insects, those in front forced by those behind to form as living rafts – locked together one upon the other. Though the ants were driven by instinct, the drugging effects of N'go's concoction confused them so that now they swarmed about the water's edge as some leaderless army.

'They do not follow, *umuThwa*! But the way back has been closed to us.'

'Stay close to the light,' said N'go, 'Walk where I walk, Induna – watch your footing and stay silent.'

'The water?' Mhlangana realised. 'It grows hotter? What magic makes the smoke rise up like this?'

Heated by deep-running thermal springs the water bubbled with sulphurous gases, fear of the unknown rose up cold and serpent-like from the pit of his stomach. 'We should turn back, Bushman. I have no desire to be boiled alive in your devil's kitchen. Where does this wizardry come from?'

'From The Place of all Life. Deep beneath the rock on

which you walk. Be quiet, Induna. Take the lamp, do not let it slip from your fingers or we will perish here.'

Reluctantly, Mhlangana took hold of the lamp. N'go's outline drifted spirit-like in front of him then in an instant the Bushman disappeared.

# -32-

Like a child afraid of the dark, Mhlangana fought off fear that had coiled about his throat. He steadied himself against the sidewall, the lamp in his hand felt weightless, almost empty – soon the dark would fly at him and with it every imagined horror of the underworld.

'A curse on your father's grave, *umuThwa*, where are you?' His voice echoed about the cavern. As ghosts, clouds of steam drifted in and out of the lamplight then something touched his shoulder and Mhlangana spun about as though the devil himself had reached for him.

'Do you not hear it?' N'go placed a pink palm against the sidewall. The thunder, Induna – the Rain Bull has again wakened the storm.'

'I feel nothing. You speak in riddles, Bushman. Lead on before you kill us both.'

N'go took the lamp from him. 'Follow closely. Before the water rises we must pass between the stones.'

From the storm, rainwater found its way inside the sinkhole, reaching the cavern's lowest point it slid inside the pool. Mhlangana felt the cold current surge against his legs. N'go's lamp flickered indecisively, the tallow that fuelled it almost exhausted. Where he led, the cavern pinched to a narrow cleft so that Mhlangana was forced to sling the skin carrier side-on for him to pass through. Now, as a single, unbroken barrier the granite stood to their front and already the water was rising.

'We cannot go back,' said N'go. 'The ants will devour us.'

'Then we will die in your rathole, Bushman.'

N'go held the lamp above his head. Detritus, brought in by the fresh run-off swirled about his face. The outgoing fissure had been overwhelmed by the sudden ingress of floodwater.

'Climb with the water, Induna. Like smoke from a fire, it will rise only if the way above is open – without the storm we cannot go forward.'

'Tell me you have been this way before, *umuThwa*?'

'As a small boy,' N'go told him, 'with my father's brother and like you, I feared I would die here.'

N'go found keeping his head above water effortless. However, burdened by weapons and the weight against his chest, Mhlangana found it hard to stay afloat. Like a scrambling lizard he searched out cracks and leverage points in the sidewall to stop himself from going under.

'I cannot climb like this for long, *umuThwa*. My strength is failing.'

Light from the lamp ebbed and flowed, the source of its power now almost spent. Above them, the darkness appeared as some infinite abyss.

'Reach up!' N'go yelled. 'Take up the lamp from me once you are inside!'

Mhlangana stretched out his arm; 'A hole, *umuThwa* – but I see nothing!'

'Wait for the water to reach it,' N'go instructed Matabele, 'then pull yourself inside, Induna – do not be afraid.'

With every muscle screaming for surcease, Mhlangana trod water until his head drew level with the granite ledge. With a supreme effort he was able to drag himself inside the hole. The water followed, gushing past him for a way out. Mhlangana reached back for the little bushman and drew him out from the flooded shaft.

'We are safe now.' N'go grinned; the sparkle was back in his eyes. He lifted the guttering flame and stood upright. A cavern, smaller than the one they had left behind opened up to the front – to their right hand the floor fell away at a steep angle. A steady stream of floodwater followed the natural decline. Mhlangana could see it tumbling away through an aura of weak, natural light. He followed N'go to where the rock was dry underfoot.

'Only when the Rain Bull awakens does the water flow through the mountain. When the storm dies the river that brought us here will disappear.' He urged Mhlangana forward. From a niche in the sidewall, N'go lifted out another fat-filled lamp and from the flame of the first the wick caught and spluttered to life. With his arm outstretched he held the thriving flame above his head.

'Between the living and the dead there stands a gateway to another place, Induna. Behold the world of the long dead.'

For a moment his lips moved – some silent incantation. Thrown by a nervous flame the shadows danced a macabre jig inside the alcove.

'A king of kings, Induna – look upon the father of the Matabele.'

# -33-

On the king's orders, women took up their offspring and found refuge amongst the sacred hills of the Matobo.

Where once there had pounded the vibrant heartbeat of a vast and powerful empire, now only crows and vermin looked for food about the cooking fires of GuBuluwayo. At night, emboldened by the silence, hyena and jackal spirited in from dark fields, shouldering aside ruined doors to peer inside for those without the strength to walk.

In the royal kraal, fire pits smouldered unattended, strewn with the offal and bones of slaughtered cattle, the smell of putrefaction hung for more than a mile about the enclosure. Here again, the crow and the vulture watched with infinite patience for they had long since learned to read the signs of ill fortune.

'Leave nothing standing, son of the king's cousin.'

Ndumiso bowed his head, already a hundred fires bled into the sky – it would take him and the other *abafana* two more days to finish the burning.

'It will be as the king asks, whatever the Great Elephant decrees it shall be done.'

'When the soldiers are close enough to feel the earth thunder, then only you, Ndumiso Khumalo, son of Mhlangana, will put fire to my powder store. Neither a keg of powder nor a single bullet will be left for the white *umlungu*.'

Again, Ndumiso bowed his head, but in his heart the pain was that of a son for his dying father.

Lobengula Khumalo, Shaker of Mountains, son of Mzilikazi, reached down from his litter of leopard and civet and his eyes were heavy.

226

'When your father returns, bring him to me. The spoor of my wagons will lead you north to the great river.' His fingers touched the woolly pate of the youth's head, there was still so much to say but the oxen were restless and the wheels of the king's wagon were already turning.

# -34-

Heeding Burnham's recommendations, Wilson swung the column's march to its new south-westerly bearing. On the following day, by late afternoon they had cut the spoor left by Forbes' wagons. A week later and still some twenty miles from GuBuluwayo, two men made their observations from a wooded ridge overlooking the Bembesi River.

'Forbes doesn't know they're there,' said Burnham. 'Hard to tell from up here, but I would hazard a force of at least a thousand warriors.'

Nathan quickly picked up on the plight of the Salisbury contingent.

'The Matabele are waiting for him to take the column across the river; Forbes' lot won't stand a chance.'

Upwards of a thousand Matabele crouched to either side of the natural drift, their leaders had pre-empted Forbes' choice of crossing place with pinpoint accuracy. Concealed by thick riverine undergrowth they were well hidden – sunlight flicked from their spears – warriors of the Imbezu and Ingubu regiments lay as hunting lions to a water hole. Nathan pulled his rifle from its scabbard and in quick succession fired off three rounds into the air. He prayed for the sound to reach the column; it was the universal signal of men in dire need of assistance.

The column slowed and then ground to a halt. From its head, a single, tiny puff of smoke; a moment later, the acknowledging report from a carbine echoed along the valley.

Forbes was waiting for them, he watched them down from the ridge, from the way he sat to the saddle his annoyance was obvious.

'Burnham. I might have known you had a hand in this.'

'Major Forbes, sir.'

'Every Matabele within a five mile radius will have heard your shooting. I trust your reasons for halting the column will convince me it was worth the effort. To be frank, I see your actions as those of an imbecile.'

'Then I would suggest you check your way forward, Major.'

'And you are?'

'Goddard, sir. Captain, B Troop, Victoria Rangers. It was I who fired the shots, not Burnham.'

'Then explain yourself, Captain.'

'The Matabele are waiting for you to cross the Bembesi. We saw them from the ridge. We had no choice but to warn you.'

'Major Wilson? How far behind you?'

'An hour at the outside. Under the circumstances, I suggest you wait for his column to catch up.'

Forbes reined his horse about and gestured to the nearest trooper. 'Go with Burnham and Captain Goddard. Report back directly to myself and be sure of your sightings, stragglers or otherwise I need a good account of any Matabele you come in contact with.' He turned back to the American. 'For both our sakes, Mister Burnham, I pray the

Company's efforts are not being wasted.'

*

Under Burnham's guidance they rode out from the
protection of the column. Burnham put the trooper's age
at little more than nineteen.

'What's your name, boy?'

'Warren, sir.'

'English?'

The boy grinned. 'From Macclesfield, sir and proud of it.'

Burnham liked him. The boy, though somewhat bolshie
was keen to impress. His eyes were everywhere – bright
with young excitement.

'Never seen one, sir; I mean a real Matabele. Wouldn't
know one of Lobengula's lot if he jumped in front of my
horse.'

Nathan threw up his arm. Though the air hardly moved,
the scrub to either side appeared to undulate, like a field of
corn disturbed by the wind.

From the undergrowth the Matabele rose up in their
hundreds, almost silently the elite of Lobengula's warriors
swept from their hides as hawks on rustling wings, long
shields snowy white, flecked with black like the breast of
the martial eagle – others were tints of copper and pale
ivory. A divine madness fell upon the Matabele, as a red
mist it bloodied their eyes and now their hands were filled
with the assegai or heavy axe – the full and terrible battle
dress of the Imbezu and the Ingubu regiments.

Nathan and Burnham reined their mounts about and at
the same time snatched their rifles clear of their scabbards.

'Warren!' yelled Nathan. 'Get out of here, boy! Back to
the column!'

From both flanks the Matabele put out their fastest runners and from the beating of spears to long shields the voice of a thousand drums reached its crescendo. Trooper Warren screwed up his face at the noise, unable to close his ears to the onslaught, unable to move – terrified by the thunder. Like an ox committed to the slaughterer's yard he had been struck dumb by the spectacle.

'Cover me as best you can!' Nathan shouted to the American and then spurred his horse back towards the drift.

Alone, Burnham could only hope to delay what he now perceived as inevitable. To either hand the Matabele swarmed as black ants, many were little more than boys, like cubs to the heels of lions they hungered to be first in line for the kill, the coveted first blooding of spears – the boy becoming the man – the *indoda*.

At a full gallop, Nathan fired as soon as the Winchester's butt plate touched his shoulder, but already trooper Warren's little mare had suffered a mortal blow. Spinning sideways on his heels the warrior had swung the assegai underhanded and in an upward arc. The razor sharp edge like a foot-long knife had split the animal's stomach – almost front to back – spilling her entrails as thick blue ropes about her hind legs. Burnham emptied his rifle into the melee, but as quickly as warriors fell to the ground others were there to fill the gaps.

Warren frantically kicked his heels at the mare's flanks, bravely she went forward, but the life was ebbing from her.

'Take my arm!' shouted Nathan and reached across the gap for Warren to grab a hold.

The mare floundered just as Trooper Warren kicked his feet free of the stirrups, the moment his hand locked to

Nathan's wrist he was wrenched from the saddle like a child from a spinning carousel.

'My stirrup!' Nathan shouted down to him and slowed his mount long enough for the trooper to find his footing. Desperately, Warren pulled himself across the saddle. Nathan put in his heels and drove the animal forwards. Slowly they gained speed and drew away from the baying Matabele.

Forbes was waiting for them, an air of superficial calm about his group of favoured underlings. The Maxims were still secured; roped to a wagon bed and covered over with thick canvas. Forbes purposely ignored the American and focused his attention on Trooper Warren.

'Where's your horse, boy?'

Warren struggled to regain his breath, wide-eyed he blurted out his report.

'Killed her, sir! They nearly had me, Major, sir! Captain Goddard saved my life, sir. Without him and Mister Burnham's help they would have had me skewered like a pig on a bonfire!'

Burnham cut in – every second counted if they were to set up adequate defences.

'Those we saw would amount to well over one thousand, Major.'

'More like ten!' Warren insisted. 'The woods were alive with savages, sir! Big black buggers with spears – screaming like mad'uns they were!' Expectantly, Burnham looked towards the river crossing.

'Ten minutes and they will reach our wagons, Major – I suggest you stand the men to and run out the maxims before it's too late.'

Forbes glowered at the American; 'And were I in need of your suggestion, Mister Burnham, I would ask for it.'

Burnham shrugged but made no reply. Again, Forbes pushed the trooper for information.

'You're sure of what you saw?'

'On my dead mother's grave,' said Warren. 'More Zulus than you can shake a stick at, sir.'

Nathan caught Burnham's attention and pointed to a gap between the wagons.

'Wilson's here. Best we get on over there.' They galloped the quarter mile to where Allan Wilson rode at the head of the Victoria column.

'Thought you two had absconded!' The Scot was in high spirits and obviously pleased to see them. 'Beginning to think Forbes' lot had gone in without us.'

'Give it your best speed, Major – pull the column in alongside Major Forbes' wagons and have the men stand to.'

'Matabele?'

'More than Major Forbes is ready to believe,' said Nathan. 'No more than a mile out.'

Orders were shouted back along the line; within minutes the column had surged forwards. On drawing up some fifty yards from the Salisbury Horse, both Maxim machine guns on their wheeled carriages were freed from their mule teams.

'And the seven-pounders, Captain Lendy.' Wilson rallied his men. 'Stand to and watch your front!'

Between the wagons and the forest the valley was carpeted with dry grass the colour of corn stubble. What breeze there was had disappeared and on the western horizon a band of cloud hung thick and black to a sombre sky; they were the strange and ominous colours of war.

'They're watching us from the treeline, Nathan.'

'Now that they've seen the re-enforcements they might think better of it and leave us be.'

'They'll come for us,' Burnham countered. 'The Matabele would rather die than run from a fight, no matter what the odds are.'

Allan Wilson moved in between them.

'Mathew's with Captain Lendy's lot, Nathan. The lad's keen enough to learn the Hotchkiss and seven-pounder.' He looked to the American. 'What do you think, Mister Burnham? What are we up against – Lobengula's best or cannon fodder?'

'Hard to say, Major.' Burnham panned his binoculars over the treeline. 'A lot of them carry black shields; either Lobengula's personal guard or young recruits.'

'Nonsense.' Forbes stepped up alongside Allan Wilson. 'What difference would the colour of their shields make? Another one of your fanciful stories, Burnham. Popinjays in fancy dress are all that they are.' He grimaced at the American, his eyes glittered, leopard-like. 'You're not fighting Red Indians now, old chap – it will take more than a handful of savages with spears and coloured shields to frighten Englishmen. Let them come, I say, black shields *et al.*'

'Then I suggest you tell that to their General, sir.'

Burnham handed the binoculars to Forbes. 'Top of that hill, Major; though I would say, more the eagle than the popinjay, old chap.'

Mjaan, Commander of the Imbezu *ibutho* surveyed all that lay before him. Plumage taken of ostrich and crow stood as a crown of feathers about his head, black as the sky behind him. The shield was almost as tall as the man who stood beside it, cut from the hide of a royal ox it was of a single colour; that of hoar frost – white as buck quartz – the mark of a General. In his right hand he carried the *umkhonto*, the same Zulu war spear once carried by his father, the blade bright as a mountain stream from a thousand sharpenings. From his waist hung tails of civet and jackal and at his upper arm were amulets of fur and tassels of valour. At his throat were strung the claws of leopard and the blood-red feet of the bateleur eagle. As though he had sensed the white man's scrutiny, Mjaan turned his head and looked down upon the column. Like that of the black mane lion, so the threat of death was there in his eyes.

Forbes' skin flushed with gooseflesh.

'Mister Wilson, sir. Have Captain Lendy bring the Hotchkiss to bear on the hilltop.' He gave the American little more than a sideways glance. 'Show our Mister Burnham here just how quickly his Matabele friends run from a taste of good British gunnery.'

Mathew stepped forward and helped Corporal Whittaker slew the Hotchkiss round to face the target. His eyes were bright with excitement. Whittaker opened the breech and nodded to Mathew.

'Load for me.'

Mathew seated the first round and watched the Corporal ready the weapon.

'We're good for two miles,' Whittaker pointed. 'One disadvantage though, the shells only explode on impact; too small to be made with airburst fuses.' He adjusted the gun's elevation and line of sighting. 'A thousand yards, I'd say – lucky for us there's little or no wind.' With an experienced eye Whittaker checked his settings then nodded to Mathew. 'Reckon we should be pretty well on target laddie; let her go.'

From the granite kopje, Mjaan watched the warriors of the Imbezu and Ingubu regiments gather along the treeline, amongst them were those who had not yet reached their twentieth summer though as privileged sons of veteran fighters were eager to prove their worth; the *Zansi* – boy soldiers – their black shields mingled with the black and white of the Imbezu and they looked to their General for the raising of his spear.

From the column's front a flower of white smoke rose up from between the wagons and then, as if struck by lightning, the living rock jumped beneath Mjaan's feet.

'Take her up one more graduation,' Whittaker instructed and from the corner of his eye watched Mathew make slight adjustment to the gun's elevation. Travelling at more than twelve hundred feet per second, the second shell took little enough time to reach the summit. Mathew saw it burst against the granite; a cloud of white smoke before the sharp clap of the explosion crashed in his ears.

'What do you say to that one?' whooped Mathew. 'Any closer and we would have dropped it on the bugger's head!'

'There's no telling whether we got him or not,' said Whittaker. 'They're crafty devils.' He slapped the palm of his hand to Mathew's shoulder; the forest's edge seethed with Matabele. 'There's your answer, boyo. Level your gun to three hundred yards and reload. Looks like the savages are bringing the fight to us.'

From the forest a phalanx of tall shields came forwards at a full run.

'Run out both maxims and stand to!' Wilson shouted above the melee. They had been afforded little enough time to form the wagons into a defensive square. The Maxims were mounted on galloping carriages; already freed from the horses they were swung round to face the Matabele. Both guns had been pre-ranged at three hundred yards. Within that minute the first 250-round canvas ammunition belts were drawn out from their wooden boxes, threaded between the carriage wheel spokes and with their metal leader tags, fed inside the open breeches.

'Load!' Wilson ordered, and heard the tell-tale crash of the loading mechanisms. Both gunners perched to built-in metal seats on the gun carriage transoms – with the safety locks already opened they leant into the double pistol grips; their thumbs hovered expectantly above the firing buttons.

'On my order!' Wilson walked between the gunners, cajoling them with a slight touch to the shoulder; the odd word of encouragement. In the face of so large a threat, panic was never too far away.

'Stay calm, lads – stay calm. Hold your nerve, boy. Remember what you're here for.'

Positioning himself between the Maxims, Wilson's own heart fluttered wildly. As a thousand charging buffalo the Matabele thundered towards the guns.

'Coming at us head-on, Major – either they are fools or brave men.' Nathan wondered at the spectacle. Like a roaring wind from a valley head there came that wild drumming of spears to ox-hide shields. Where there had been grass and shallow undergrowth now there was ruined ground, only thicker trees stood up to the onslaught.

Fifty yards to the right, Forbes had at last ordered the off-loading of both his Maxims. Both weapons were freestanding – mounted on tripods, their gunners hurried to set the elevation screws to three hundred yards while their loaders ran in the canvas feeder belts. About the Maxims, six hundred men with Metfords, single-shot breech-loaders and Winchester repeating rifles knelt or stood in rows to face the Matabele.

From behind the Hotchkiss field gun, Mathew stared in awe of what he was witnessing, his eyes wide; heart in his mouth.

'They're close now, Mister Whittaker, sir?'

'Hold your fire, laddie. Wait for the Major's orders now, there's a good fellow.'

Before every battle there falls a silence about the men who stand to take the sword. In every mind, silent prayers are said – within those next few minutes a thousand men would perish.

At three hundred yards, Allan Wilson barked out the order to open fire. The Matabele shuddered to a standstill. As charred grass to strong winds their front ranks disintegrated, blown apart by shells from the field guns and withering fire from the Maxims, and still the Matabele's rear ranks stepped up eagerly to replace the fallen. Three times they gathered strength and surged forward, and just as many times were they torn to shreds by the Maxims.

'Cease firing! Reload and watch your front!'

Smoke had spread as a blue shroud above the killing ground. Nathan lowered his rifle. Emptiness and shame, the aftermath of so much slaughter stood beside him. Thankfully, the quiet held and he hawked the acrid taste of bile, guilt and burned powder from his throat.

For a long time no one spoke, they had been the first of all Her Britannic Majesty's soldiers to employ the Maxim gun on African soil. First-hand they had witnessed the devastation and whilst many stared in shocked silence, others wretched and turned their heads from the killing. Spent casings and canvas ammunition belts lay thick about the gunners' feet. Mathew kicked aside a dozen Hotchkiss shell casings and straightened up from the field gun. His voice trembled and the words came out as small things over the quiet.

'They've gone, Major. All of them.'

-36-

Not since his boyhood had Mhlangana seen the man now sat before him. Where once there had been bright and lively eyes, now in death only empty blackened sockets stared out from that ruined face. A paper thin covering of dried flesh hung about the forehead and high cheek bones, though the lower jaw had completely fallen away. To a withered left hand, Mhlangana recognised the *izagila*, the gnarled fighting stick of the Zulu warrior, cut from the branch of a knob-thorn. In the other, trapped by claw-like fingers and small as a child's plaything was the wooden spear of kingship. To some it would appear only as a harmless toy – to those who knew, this perfect miniature of the warrior's assegai invoked a greater fear than any quick- firing rifle.

Still in place, almost touching the forehead was the

elliptical head-ring of his status, the *isicoco*, held there by the interweaving of hair with natural resins and beeswax; the only show of vanity, a modest crown of three green feathers, plucked from the tail of a wild parakeet. A single string of small blue beads encircled the shrivelled neck and where once there had been a corpulent waistline, now there was left only bone to support a royal girdle of leopard tails.

'Babamkhulu,' Mhlangana whispered and fell to his knees. 'Son of Matshobana Kamangete. I salute you Mzilikazi! Father of the Ndebele people and sire to the Great Elephant; your firstborn son, Lobengula Jando Khumalo – Shaker of Mountains – The One Who Drives Like the Wind!'

Set to either side of the mummified corpse were the accoutrements of the ritual interment; earthenware pots, once filled with millet beer and native tobacco had been left in rows against the granite. About the dead man's withered shoulders had been sewn the green skin of a black ox. At his feet, spread upon the granite ledge were the kaross of leopard and civet. For twenty five years the skins had suffered of dark and isolation, and yet in the light from N'go's lamp the furs were still those tawny shades of copper and gold.

'For twenty rains my father gave himself to guarding the king's resting place.' N'go's eyes glittered. 'Since my father's death, five more rains have passed and for as long as N'go might live I have pledged to do the same. Those who would rob the king of his treasures will die beneath the ground.'

'EnTumbane,' Mhlangana realised. 'You have led me to the graveyard of the Kings'.

'Is it not a fitting place for your king's baubles, Induna?'

N'go delighted in their surroundings and with the lamp above his head danced as some forest sprite about the natural alcoves of his secret place. 'Come with me,' he beckoned to Mhlangana, 'there are many things for you to see.'

As a vaulting cathedral roof the cavern's hanging rose beyond the reach of N'go's lamp, like a desert wind the air was warm; the living rock beneath their feet dry as the sacred hills with the sun at its zenith.

'The stone, *umuThwa*? What sorcery lives beneath that I can feel its fire?'

'Spirits of kings live beneath the floor, Induna. If your heart is true there will be nothing for you to fear.'

At a point furthest from the cavern's entrance, the sidewall folded away, almost at a right angle.

'The story of enTumbane!' N'go piped, revelling in the moment like an enraptured child. Back and forth he swept with his lamp, pausing only to highlight more of the treasures. 'Teeth of a hundred *izindlovu*!' He raised his hand to the nearest tusk. 'The spear of the great bull elephant; not one of them is smaller than N'go.'

At their tips, where the stain of plant juices had been held at bay, the ivory was still that soft colour of fresh buttermilk, smooth to Mhlangana's fingers. A magical silkiness that for hundreds years had brought in elephant hunters from as far afield as the southernmost Cape and from the great Arab trading portals of Sofala and Quelemane on the Indian Ocean. Each tusk, heavier than a grown man. At their base, where once they were held in place by casings of thick bone to either side of the pachyderm's jaw they were thick as a girl's waist – carelessly marked by the axe and heavy knives of their butchers.

240

Propped against the granite were the tools of the hunter's grizzly trade, brought overland by Portuguese explorers. Smooth-bore flintlock rifles that if the hunter's aim were true and his nerve held, could kill an elephant or buffalo with a single shot, hurling an eight ounce slug of lead through the animal's brain.

'Red iron from the mines of Ndanga,' N'go went on. Ingots of red, native copper cast in the shape of the cross – stacked in piles it would have taken the strength and patience of ten men to correlate their numbers.

'What of these?'

Porcupine quills, in their hundreds, bound together and stored in plaited baskets. Mhlangana drew one out, at its pale base the quill's anchor point had been cut across and then sealed again with beeswax. Mhlangana broke away the seal with his thumbnail.

He angled the quill to the palm of his hand. From its open end grains of yellow sunlight ran like fine sand.

'Gold, *umuThwa*. White men would kill us both for what you have shown me.'

'No white man has set foot in the tomb of Kings, Induna.' N'go swung the lamp closer to the wall. 'Behold the father of your people; the king's final journey to enTumbane. There are few who know of it.'

Through the skills of N'go's father, the story of Mzilikazi's last journey had been set to the granite wall. Upon a litter, laid to a bed of furs, the first great king of the Matabele was being brought to his final resting place, enTumbane, The Little Hill – preordained burial place of Mzilikazi, The Black Bull.

Mhlangana followed the little bushman to where they had entered the cavern and is if by the sorcerer's magic, the walls about the king's alcove were aflame with blue fire. From the movement of light it seemed as though Mzilikazi himself were about to throw aside the wrappings of his burial and step out from the alcove. N'go stood with arms outstretched; excited tongues of blue flame about his body.

'Bring your stones, Induna. Rid yourself of the burden. Let the spirits blind those who would take the king's treasure from enTumbane.'

Mhlangana fell to his knees and slid the leather thong from his shoulder, for ten days he had suffered the weight so that now, gratefully he set it down at the king's feet and pulled away the bindings.

'As tribute from his firstborn, I will leave the spirit of Lobengula Khumalo; it will be fitting.'

Though they lacked the sparkle of the cut diamond, still the stones drank in light from the air about them. In turn, they glowed as ghostly embers looked upon by Mzilikazi Khumalo, first great king of the Matabele.

'I have kept my word, *umuThwa*. Now I would leave this graveyard, I wish to feel the sun on my face.'

'Already the sun is with us, Induna.' N'go doused the lamp and still there was light enough for them to see. 'Look around you.' He replaced the lamp in its alcove and beckoned to Mhlangana. 'The way out has been shown to us.'

From the cavern's lowest point that same pale light, as the colour of open sky reflected from the granite walls. With trepidation, Mhlangana edged forward and peered inside the opening.

'I see the sun as though we stand beneath the water?'

N'go nodded. They had reached the burial chamber's final secret.

'We stand above and yet we are below, Induna. What you

see are the fingers of first sunlight. You see what other men cannot.'

The floor dipped away at a steep angle, smooth as marble from a million years of rushing water. Tentatively, Mhlangana crouched against his heels and tested the rock with his fingertips. Slicker than the blade of his assegai, there would be no footing; a single step would see him flung into the narrow shaft.

'Only ants and lizards can descend walls such as these, bushman?'

'Then only lizards can ascend for the king's treasures, Induna.' N'go placed an open hand against his breast bone. 'Do as I do. Fill your chest with air, as the otter follows the fish, once you are in the water you will follow N'go's feet towards the sunlight.'

Without waiting, N'go crouched against his heels and inched his way past the point of no return. Like a man losing his footing to a muddy riverbank he shot forwards and disappeared inside the shaft. The sound of him striking water echoed back up to the cavern – agitated light danced excitedly above Mhlangana's head. Before his courage failed him, Mhlangana gritted his teeth and pushed away from the edge.

Flung clear by his own momentum, with flailing arms he dropped away from the granite; feet first he struck the water. Drawn like a moth to the light he kicked against the weight of the axe across his shoulders and slowly, through clouds of iridescent bubbles he rose up to the surface of a warm pool.

N'go crouched at the pool's edge, knees drawn up under his chin, the tiny flap of leather suspended from his waist, pushed between his legs. In the broken sunlight, his childlike form blended with that of the forest. He waited for Mhlangana to drag himself out from the water.

'For as long as *Kouteign Koorou* brings rain, the way inside enTumbane will be safe from thieves, but you must tell no one of its secrets, Induna.'

'It shall be as you ask, *umuThwa*. What of yourself? Where will you go?'

'My home is here.' He spread his arms, as thin branches in the sunlight. 'Like my father, I will die here, but there is much to do – stories to leave for others who might follow; stories that only those descendent of Mzilikazi will understand.'

Mhlangana turned his face to the sun. With his eyes closed he let the warmth flood over him. It was time for him to leave, his yearning for GuBuluwayo now strong and titillating.

'Then I will leave you here, *umuThwa*. My road home is a long one.'

There was no reply. Where N'go had warmed himself at the water's edge the rock had dried. Where the little Bushman had crouched the only life was that of a single butterfly – on silent yellow wings it spiralled upwards, high above the ancient pool.

-37-

Mhlangana heard the explosion when he was little more than a mile from GuBuluwayo. The flash from it ripped across the horizon just as first light touched to *Thabas Indunas*, the Hill of the Chiefs. He stood in awe of the phenomenon and was unable to tear his eyes from a towering pall of black smoke that had risen spirit-like above the treetops. Already the sky for as far as he could see was flecked with scavenging birds, it was then that he realised the final act of Lobengula's defiance, for the old king had ordered the burning of his own great city.

The sun was an hour short of its highest point before Mhlangana reached what was left of the royal kraal.

'Baba, my father, I feared you would not return.' Ndumiso stepped out from behind the charred walls of the king's store house. 'I see you my father and my heart is glad.'

'Ndumiso, my son. What of your mother?'

'My mother is safe. What she could carry she has taken with her. It was on the king's word that the women and children should flee into the hills.'

'And the king? I see no dead? No blood has been spilled and yet our houses burn?'

With his assegai, Ndumiso pointed northwards. 'They have loaded the king's wagons and trekked towards the kingdom of the Makololo; towards the Great River.' He looked about at the havoc, the destruction was total. 'The king's house and the powder stores were the last to burn. You will have heard the thunder?'

Mhlangana nodded, but the spectacle was too much for him to comprehend.

'Why did the king not command his Generals to stand and fight? Or do his regiments find it easier to run with the women than to protect their heartlands? What of Mjaan and Mgandaan?'

'Many were slain at Bembesi,' he told his father. 'Cut down by the *isigwagwagwa* and the smoke demons that leap from the earth. The king has taken with him what is left of his regiments. Mjaan, the king's General, the Imbezu, the

Ingubu and the Insukameni stand with him. From the cover of the forest, like the leopard they will strike when least expected.'

'Then we will join with them,' hissed Mhlangana. 'Where are the soldiers now?'

'They are close, Baba, before dark they will reach GuBuluwayo.'

-38-

'Tell me what you make of it, Nathan.' Burnham handed him the field glasses. 'Other than mangy dogs and a few crows there appears to be nothing left.'

Nathan adjusted the focus. As the remnants of some great pyre GuBuluwayo smouldered – pillars of acrid smoke reached skyward, joining with the low cloud. The rain they had all been dreading would be there before nightfall. Nathan was satisfied that the valley had been emptied of Matabele; he turned in the saddle and through the binoculars found the remains of the king's kraal.

'Brick-built. Most of the walls have been razed. Has to be where the old king kept his powder and munitions.'

Burnham drew out a pad from his breast pocket and scribbled a note to Forbes.

*Bulawayo has been abandoned. Come at your best speed.*

Already the Ndebele name for the king's kraal had been shortened to suit the British tongue. He called over one of the native runners and handed him the note.

'As fast as you can. Give it to Major Forbes.' Burnham watched the runner away and then kneed his horse alongside Nathan's. 'We should be up with Lobengula before the week's end. He could not have got very far. The greedy old beggar will not have left his comforts behind, rest assured he will be with his wagons — somewhere north of here, I would say.'

'Why not south? Or even to the west?' Nathan suggested, but the American scout shook his head and smiled at the supposition.

'South would take him towards the fort at Tuli and the king knows that the Company has a fair few men garrisoned there. To the west, there's little or no water. It has to be north, I'll stake a year's pay on it.'

They reached the remains of the king's own buildings just an hour after midday, there was little left of the brick-built living house and the wagon store. The acrid stench of burnt powder was still strong and the ground was heavily littered with shattered munitions boxes and brass cartridges.

'No sign of any wagons,' said Burnham. 'I was right, the old devil's packed up his kit and gone north.'

# -39-

For five days Mhlangana and his son pushed northwards towards the Zambezi, their food was that which they gathered from the wayside. From GuBuluwayo the wagon tracks had been easy to follow, though on that last day had they almost disappeared for the rain had filled them with black mud.

They went down into the valley, Mhlangana leading his

son at a fast pace and with each mile covered, the stronger scent of wet oxen, the distant creak of timber and the crack of the driver's whip seemed just that little bit closer. From either side Mhlangana knew they were being watched by hidden eyes, for Lobengula's impis guarded his road to the north, a road they knew the white soldiers would follow.

'*Hau*! Mhlangana. We feared that you had been taken by the soldiers.'

Mhlangana lowered his spear and his eyes were bright.

'Mjaan! Are your warriors all asleep that their General must wait by the road for the old lion and his cub to follow on?' His smile faded. 'What of the fighting? I searched for the glory of battle, but found only the breaking of spears?'

Mjaan's face hardened, images of the slaughter at Bembesi were still vivid; the bodies of a thousand warriors he had been forced to leave behind. The stench of putrefaction stayed with him, like the grinning tormentor the memory of their defeat was never far away.

'Neither the axe nor the assegai can stand against the white man's three-legged guns, my brother. With a sad heart I watched the *isigwagwagwa* pour death upon our warriors. Now we must be as the fox and the jackal; the soldiers will follow the king's wagon into the thick forests, there we will strike them down. As a mongoose strikes for the Cobra's throat, so will our *amabutho* overrun them.'

'I see you, Mhlangana. Blood of my blood. Come forward that your king might look upon his cousin with clear eyes.'

Mhlangana stepped inside the makeshift enclosure. Canvas had been stripped from one of the wagons and slung between the trees as a protective awning. Naked, save for a small apron of soft leather, the king had seated himself amongst a bed of his favourite leopard skins. Thabisa, his most junior wife sat close to the royal litter, her eyes were filled with fear  for she knew the fate of the Matabele had already slipped from king's hands. The air was thick with humidity and the wild scents of the fever-ridden lowlands.

'Tell me what has become of my city, Mhlangana.'

'There is little to tell, my king.'

Lobengula lowered his head. A bank of dark cloud covered the sun and the first distant sound of thunder rolled out above the clearing.

'What you say darkens my eyes.' He swivelled round on the cot and wafted flies from his face. 'What of the soldiers?'

Mhlangana shook his head. 'Like ticks to a dogs back, my king. Mjaan tells me many were lost to the soldiers at Bembesi.'

The king nodded. 'The *isigwagwagwa*; I have heard of its voice – spitters of death.' He looked towards GuBuluwayo. 'We cannot stand against them. Mjaan and Mgandaan will take their warriors into the forest. For the soldiers to follow my wagons they will be forced to cross the Shangani.' He looked up at the darkling sky. 'The river will soon run at its fullest. By tomorrow's last light those left of my warriors will make ready for the final battle. The elephant can no longer find the strength to carry on.' His eyes softened; no longer weighted by the burden of his own future. 'What of the stones?'

'They are safe, lord. For seven days I journeyed into the sacred hills. No man will find them.'

'Then you have chosen well, but there is one more task that your king must ask of you.'

'My king has only to speak.'

'As well as the lion's heart you will need the buffalo's strength, my cousin. In the wagon behind you – a thousand gold queens. With his own eyes the one the soldiers call *Doktela* must see the price I am willing to pay for him not to follow.' Lobengula urged him closer to the fire. 'But first you must eat and rest. At the showing of first light you will find this *Doktela*, tell him the king's heart is heavy with sorrow; the eagle has become the sparrow, it looks only for a place to sleep.'

'What if still they follow, my king?'

'Then we will fight,' said Lobengula, 'and their women will lie alone in the night.'

-41-

'Over there, Chulmleigh, at the edge of those trees, what do you make of it?'

Chulmleigh put up the glasses and focused them on the place O'Reilly had pointed out. Shadows played tricks with his eyes and for a while he struggled to find anything out of the ordinary – then his vision settled and he saw the tall figure of a Matabele watching their movements from the treeline.

'You were right, boyo, there's a blackie spyin' on us. Doctor Jameson don't pay us enough for chasing after savages. We'll wait here and see what the bugger's up to. We're on picket duty, not scouting for Captain bloody Goddard and Yankee Doodle bloody Burnham.' He spat a stream of spittle into the grass. 'Goddard and his pup are still due their comeuppance, and they'll be getting it soon enough, mark my words, Mister O'Reilly, or my father was born an Englishman.'

'Stay out of their way,' warned Chulmleigh. 'If they remember us from the ruins our number's up. When were ready for them, whichever way the penny lands, at least one of them won't be goin' home to that sweet little lady I saw them with in Victoria.' He handed the glasses to O'Reilly and blinked his eyes at the sunlight. 'You have a go. Keep your eyes on the black feller; if he moves, let me know.'

O'Reilly steadied himself against a tree and put up the field glasses.

'Watch yourself Chulmleigh, the bugger's coming straight for us.'

Chulmleigh watched Mhlangana make his way across the clearing.

'Any shenanigans and he'll be getting a bullet between those fancy skins of his. Can you tell if the bugger's carrying a gun or not?'

'Can't see one. Bloody great axe in his hand and something on his shoulder – a bag of sorts?'

'D'yer think he knows we're here?'

'Oh, he knows all right. Looking straight back at me, he is. Cheek of the devil he has for coming up to us like this.'

Mhlangana walked until he was within hailing distance then held up his hand – palm towards the soldiers.

'I bring a gift from Lobengula! A gift of gold queens for your General, *Doktela*.'

Chulmleigh lowered his rifle.

'You speak a bit of their lingo, Mister O'Reilly. What's the bugger saying?'

'Something about a present for *Doktela*.'

'And who be damned is *Doktela*?' mused Chulmleigh. Mhlangana slapped his hand to the canvas bag on his shoulder.

'Gold queens for your General, a gift from the great king, Lobengula.'

O'Reilly's fingers froze around the field glasses.

'Our ship has just come in, by God.' His eyes glittered and a single droplet of spittle hung from the rubbery welt of his lower lip.

'The bag on his shoulder, Chulmleigh.' He grinned at the Irishman. 'Stuffed to the brim with gold sovereigns it is, stuffed to the bloody brim!'

Chulmleigh's eyes widened and he lowered the rifle.

'Bring him in nice and easy then, and none of your usual abusive banter, Mister O'Reilly, can't have him doing a runner with our severance money.'

'Nice as pie I'll be, Mister Chulmleigh. For a bag of gold sovereigns I'll kiss the black bugger's arse.'

O'Reilly called Mhlangana forward.

'On the ground, sir.' He pointed with his rifle. 'Nice and gentle like.' He waited for Mhlangana to drop the bag and step away. O'Reilly pressed the toe of his boot against the bag.

'Open her up, Mister Chulmleigh. Let's see if our Zulu man here is telling us the truth.'

Chulmleigh drew out the knot and opened the canvas bag wide enough for light to drop inside of it.

'Would you look at that,' he croaked and lifted out a handful of gold coins. 'Enough in that bag to get us back to Dublin and go equal shares in the Brazen Head down Bridge Street.'

O'Reilly's eyes bulged in their sockets for the gold was more alluring than anything he had ever seen. He held his tone steady, masking his excitement.

'For *Doktela*, you say?'

Mhlangana nodded his head.

'Lobengula will wait for your Generals on the banks of the Shangani. He wishes an end to the killing.'

'You tell your king that *Doktela* will be pleased with the gift.' He switched back to English. 'So don't you go worrying yourself sick now, there's a good fellow. You tell old Lobengula, Doctor Jameson will be pleased as Punch with his present.' He winked an eye at Chulmleigh. 'And you can rest assured that me and old Chulmleigh here will take it straight to him. Won't we Chulmleigh?'

'Like an arrow, Mister O'Reilly – like a friggin' arrow.' He waved Mhlangana away from the bag. 'So you cut along back to your king now and tell him everything is just hunky-dory and that Misters Chulmleigh and O'Reilly will definitely not be fighting with his impis. Or anyone else for that matter.'

Allan Wilson edged his horse alongside Burnham's. The rain had come back and now hung as a drab cloak between the sky and fields of black mud. Burnham drew in the neck of his cape, leaning sideways from the saddle he pointed out veiled remains of wagon ruts; to either side the ground had been deeply churned as though vast herds of antelope had migrated northwards.

'Two thousand warriors with him, maybe more. But that would be a guess, Major.'

Fires still smouldered at the centre of a makeshift thorn scherm, the entire enclosure was littered with hides and bone. More than a hundred Nguni cattle had been slaughtered, roasted and devoured in the space of two days.

'Forbes would disagree,' Wilson mused. 'His estimations are more along the lines of two or three hundred.'

'Forbes can think what he likes,' countered Burnham, 'for all our sakes, Major, hopefully you have a better eye for the situation than he does'

Wilson turned his attention to Nathan.

'What about you, Captain? Forbes or our Mister Burnham here? Who do we go with?'

'I'm with Burnham,' Nathan insisted without hesitation.

'And so say all of us, Captain. Unfortunately, we're stuck with Forbes.' He turned back to the American scout. 'Your best guess, sir – how far ahead would you put the Matabele?'

Burnham looked ahead to where the wagon ruts dropped towards the riverbank.

'All I can tell you, Major is that the Matabele crossed the

river sometime this morning. Couldn't say how close they are – not until I've scouted the far bank.'

'Then you will be doing that soon enough,' said Wilson, 'Forbes has ordered that I take a contingent of Victoria Rangers across the Shangani and try to make contact with Lobengula.' He turned back to Nathan. 'Your son, Nathan?'

'What of him?'

'He has insisted on going with you.'

'How much time do we have before we leave?'

'As soon as the men have drawn rations and extra ammunition – an hour at best.'

'The Maxims?' asked Nathan.

Wilson shook his head. 'No Maxims. Forbes dug in his heels. The mud would be up to their axles; dragging them through this quagmire will hold us up. If we are to catch up with Lobengula then our need to be quick off the mark will be paramount.'

'The river's coming up fast,' said Burnham. 'Once we cross to the other side our chances of getting back before tomorrow night will be slim.'

'Marooned on the other side of the Shangani with two thousand Matabele baying for my blood?' Wilson reined his horse about. 'Not a situation I would relish. 'Come with me, Mister Burnham. We'll talk to Forbes, perhaps we can persuade the man to rethink.'

*

'Your apprehension has been duly noted, Mister Burnham.' Forbes struggled to control his temper. The American's overbearing masculinity irritated him. Burnham was as an outsider and showed little regard for seniority. 'Though I find it necessary to remind you of my own experiences, most of which were accrued campaigning against the Natal Zulu shortly after their unsuccessful confrontation with the Queen's soldiers at Rorke's Drift.' He spoke with his back turned and stared out from the shelter of a canvas buck sail. 'You will leave this camp within the hour as Major Wilson has already ordered. If, when your patrol returns, the Shangani is in spate and the Matabele are in pursuit, then the Maxims will give you covering fire, but from this side of the river.'

Forbes squared up to the scout. 'I think, Mister Burnham, I have made my reasons for your crossing the Shangani simple enough – even for an American.' He revelled in the victory, being Commander designate of the first substantial Company force to fight against the Matabele invigorated him. He glared at Burnham and like some belligerent British bulldog openly invited his retaliation.

'Would there be anything else, Mister Burnham?'

'Plenty,' Burnham growled, 'but it can wait until I get back.'

'Should I take that as a threat?'

'Take it how the hell you like,' hissed the American and followed Allan Wilson to where Nathan waited with the horses.

-43-

The Shangani was running belly-deep to the horses when Major Allan Wilson took a twelve man mounted

256

contingent through to the far bank. The entire column had been made up of men from the Victoria Rangers and though he was proud to lead them, like the American scout, he had been left with the foul taste of Forbes' unwillingness to see folly in his own judgement.

Climbing out from the river brought an eerie silence about the patrol, save for the creak of wet leather and the hissing of rain there were few other sounds. Burnham spurred his horse in next to Nathan's.

'I can feel their eyes on us, Nathan. Sending out twelve men and no support from the Maxims is nothing short of madness. Chelmsford made a similar mistake fighting the Zulus in Natal.'

'The Zulus?'

'Fourteen years ago,' Burnham confirmed. 'A place called Isandhlwana. The aristocratic fool left a thousand British dead for the vultures to feed on.'

Nathan looked over his shoulder, back along the column. Wilson had put Mathew alongside Trooper Michael Dillon; both were of a similar age.

'Forbes was never the right man for this,' said Nathan.

'The man's a pretentious fool,' Burnham agreed. 'Textbook soldier; can't stand the man and he knows it.'

Nathan drew in his cape. The American's eyes were never still. Every sound from the forest drew Burnham's attention.

'Do you ever stop watching and listening?'

'Only when I sleep,' joked the American then put up his hand to halt the column. 'Over to your left. The base of that tall mopani, we have ourselves a Matabele, gentlemen.'

Major Wilson came alongside. 'What is it, Burnham?'

'An old man, probably a straggler. Best you wait here, Major whilst I find out what he's up to.'

257

Burnham reined his horse out of line and rode to where the solitary Matabele sheltered from the rain.

'I see you old father, what are the needs of a man that he must stand alone in the forest?'

The old man leant on his spear, his body more wrinkled than the bark of the tree under which he sheltered.

'I watch only for the warmth of each new sun, *umlungu*. What is it that you seek in the kingdom of Lobengula, calf of The Black Bull?'

'We search for the king, but we are few and our guns are cold. We mean the king no harm. What is your name old man?'

'What you ask will serve no purpose, white man. Names are for men who will live to greet each other again.'

'Then why do watch for our passing?'

The old man clicked his tongue against the roof of his mouth. Though his hair was frosted with age still his eyes were sharp.

'Is it wrong for a man to stand and watch by his own wayside? Do the birds not watch the passing of lions from their place in the trees?'

'It is not wrong,' said Burnham. 'We seek only to end the fighting. The time has come for the Matabele to put aside the old ways, the white Indunas speak only of peace. The ways of killing are over.'

The old man's eyes glittered. What he had seen in the past would span the white man's life twice over.

'Only a fool will lead a few against a thousand buffalo. Already the king's Generals know you are here. Go back to your people before the spirits of your forefathers reach out to you from the forest.'

Burnham shivered at the warning.

'I would ask for an audience with your king. The man

258

who sent me would be greatly angered if I failed him.'

'Then this man has the wisdom of a small boy. The only voices you will hear are those of the king's *amabutho* before the vultures pluck out your eyes.'

'Show me the road, old man that I might reach Lobengula before nightfall.'

The old man smiled at Burnham's insistence and for a long moment studied the man looking down at him: the crushing blue eyes and deeply cleft chin, the barrel chest – that of a young ox, the oiled cape that threw off rain like the feathers of the *ikewu* water fowl. All would be consumed and left for the forest to cover. In the time it would take the moon to fade from full to its last quarter, all that the white men were would be forgotten – their women would find no comfort when reaching out in the night.

## -44-

A fresh wind whipped rain beneath the awning. Mhlangana knelt before his king, his heart heavy and his features drawn from lack of sleep.

'My regiment, lord, Mjaan has taken them back towards the soldiers.'

'And you are wondering why I keep you here?'

'That is true, *Baba Nkulu*.'

'Your dying would serve no purpose, my cousin. Your king's need of you is greater than that of the white man's *isigwagwagwa*. The soldiers have crossed the river. They take my gold and still they follow like jackals.'

'I am but one man my king. What might one man do to stop them?'

'Leave the fighting to those who thirst for glory, my cousin; the Imbezu, the Ingubu and the Inyati. Mjaan and Gandang are with them and the fighting will be bloody.'

Lobengula leant from his cot. 'Thabisa, the youngest of my wives; it is known only by a few that she carries the child of a king in her belly. Before the soldiers crossed the Shangani she was set upon the road. Soon, my cousin, Thabisa, the flower of your king's life will reach the Matobo and your own woman, Imbali will be charged with her keeping. When the fighting is over, seek out the sacred caves where they hide from the soldiers. Take up your woman and the king's Thabisa. With my blessing take Thabisa as your own; somewhere beyond the reach of those who have killed me.' He slumped against the cot, his breathing heavy. His eyes closed to the malaise of gout that ravaged his body. 'If the child delivered of her is a boy then my eyes shall see through his.' He rolled his head to the side and looked at Mhlangana. 'Through him the blood of my father's father shall live on. The next king of the *AmaNdebele* will be as your own son.'

He turned away. 'Now you must leave me, Mhlangana, blood of Mashobane. Turn your eyes to the road and remember well of your king.'

-45-

Nathan rode with his rifle across the saddle. On the strength of Forbes' whimsical guesswork a dozen of the

Company's finest men were blundering deeper inside forests that were familiar only to the Matabele. Every hour away lessened their chances of making it back to the Shangani before it burst its banks and cut them off from the main column.

'To our right!' shouted Burnham. 'There's your answer, Major. A curse on Forbes' assessment – no more than two or three hundred the idiot said. I would put their numbers closer to a thousand.'

'More to our left!' shouted Nathan. 'The savages are trying to get behind us!'

Wilson spurred his mount alongside the scout. 'The devils are everywhere; from your own experience how do you see our situation?'

'Dire,' hissed Burnham. 'Pull the men back to the river before the Matabele outflank us.'

'Take the lead, Mister Burnham. I suggest we make the most of what little daylight we have left.' Wilson looked up at the sky. The cloud had thickened. 'Halfway back to the main column is the best we can hope for Nathan. Hold the men together. Weapons cocked and at the ready, I have a feeling we will shortly have need of them.'

Burnham forced the pace, nose to tail through the rain and as hard as the sodden terrain would allow. They rode in silence; every man kept his eyes to the front for now a thirteenth visitant warrior rode alongside them.

\*

Nathan sat with his back to a tree, run-off from the leaves splattered against his hat. Mathew sat next to him, staring out at the forest, straining his eyes for movement. As a welcome blanket, darkness enveloped the soldiers. Mathew closed his eyes and his thoughts drifted homewards.

'Burnham says the Matabele won't attack when it's dark. Frightened of ghosts he told me.'

'True enough,' said Nathan, 'but they know that we're here. At dawn the savages will be at us.'

'I'm scared,' said Mathew, 'Ma won't cope on her own.'

Nathan reached out for him. 'It isn't over yet. Forbes might well send a relief column out at first light.'

Burnham stepped out from the darkness.

'Wilson's sent Captain Napier and two others back to Forbes' lot for reinforcements.'

'When?' asked Nathan.

'Best part of an hour ago. There's been no shooting so the chances are he got through.'

When the wind turned, the battle songs of the Matabele drifted in with the rain.

'You still carrying the six-shooter I gave you?'

'Always,' said Mathew, thankful of the distraction.

'When they come,' said Burnham 'wait for them to get in close – and mark your man. Shoot when you're sure of a hit.'

'What are our chances?'

'Depends on Napier,' said Burnham, 'if he makes it through to the column then our chances are pretty fair.'

'And if he doesn't?'

'He has to laddie, or by this time tomorrow night we all will have doffed our caps to the devil.'

'I can hear horses.' Mathew stood up. A slender seam of first light hung above the forest. There were breaks in the cloud, momentarily the rain had stopped. Allan Wilson stepped from cover to guide the riders in.

'A welcome sight, gentlemen!' Wilson looked back along the line of riders, his eyes strained for a glimpse of field guns and the Maxims. He reached for the nearest horse and held the bridle for the trooper to dismount. 'Major Forbes – how far behind is he?'

'You had best talk to Captain Borrow, sir. Forbes is still on the other side of the river.'

Borrow reined his horse in next to Wilson and slid from the saddle. As soon as his feet touched the ground Wilson was at him.

'The letter I sent with you, Captain – did Forbes read it?'

'He did, sir.'

'And did Captain Napier emphasise our need for support?'

'Enough for Major Forbes to threaten him with arrest should he have continued. Captain Napier gave his best efforts to coming back with us, but Forbes would hear nothing of it.'

Borrow reached under his cape for Forbes' reply. Wilson held the letter close to his face; the light was still weak – the trees still shadows.

*You will know to act as best you can under the circumstances. The Shangani is on the point of flooding. It would be foolhardy of me to bring the column across before the flood abates.*

Wilson buttoned the letter inside his breast pocket. His hands were shaking; along with the cold, disbelief had slipped beneath his cape.

'Thank you, Captain. Put your men in with the others, rest while you can, this might well be your last opportunity to do so.'

## -47-

At dawn, though crippled by rain clouds, daylight felt its way inside the forest, it was then that Mjaan, the king's General marshalled his regiments. With them and eager for battle were those who had survived the slaughter at Bembesi; the *Zansi* Imbezu, the Insukameni and remnants of the Ingubu *ibutho*. With their eyes red for the killing they went forward in their thousands.

## -48-

Rain, light as mist drifted on an easterly wind, fine *guti* drizzle that sometimes might last for weeks before relenting; so much quieter than the high rolling eye of a powerful storm. It touched upon the tall trees as some vaporous entity, where the sounds of battle and the cries of stricken men were loudest it mixed with fear and acrid gun smoke. By midday only a handful of Wilson's men were left standing, the ground about them littered with dead and the dying.

'Mark your targets!' shouted Wilson, his voice now

tremulous from his constant shouting and the pain; that sickening ache that he knew would never go away.

Six men cursed the rain – steam rose up from warm carcasses and heated rifle barrels. Trees were stripped of their leaves, bark shattered, blown away from bleeding sap wood. Mathew fought alongside his father, to his right hand, Burnham and trooper Michael Dillon fired almost incessantly into a flanking wall of Matabele. Dillon was shooting blind, both his eyes destroyed by a ricochet. Above their heads, incoming rifle fire cracked through the canopy.

'They're pulling back!' shouted Mathew.

Wilson called across to him. 'Collect what ammunition you can find before the savages come back.' He beckoned to Nathan and the American. His arm, like that of a discarded marionette hung lifelessly at his side; an inch below his elbow the bone had been shot through. He gave the order through gritted teeth. 'Burnham, you will make every effort to reach the main column. Tell that bastard, Forbes just what he's let us in for.' He turned to Nathan. 'Mathew will be going with him. Two minutes with your son, Nathan, that's all the time I can spare you.'

Only the better marksmen amongst the Matabele still favoured their rifles, most discarded them with contempt for these were not the weapons of their forefathers. Mjaan lifted his spear to the sky and every voice fell silent.

Nathan heard the start of it. From the forest, as a wind it came about their makeshift fortress. With one voice, two thousand Matabele closed on those who were left; the final killing.

'Take this with you,' said Nathan. 'Be with your mother when she opens it.' Mathew stuffed the canvas wallet inside his shirt. The happening was surreal; the innards of a nightmare. His hands shook and like the hollow drum of surging Matabele his heart pounded. Nathan pulled him close and for one last time breathed in the smell of him. 'Now you must go,' he told him, 'ride like the devil before it's too late.'

'I will come back,' said Mathew; the words barely cleared his throat. 'I swear by all that's holy, I will come back for you.'

'Take my horse.' Nathan hurried him and thrust Luke's reins between his fingers. He nodded to the American. 'You had best be going, Mister Burnham. I look to you for my son's life.' He legged Mathew up into the saddle.

'I love you, Mathew. If for no other reason, my son, remember me for that.'

Mathew reined his horse in only once, that for one last indulgent moment he might look back at his father. Blurred by rain the scene was that of an artist's sketch; black and grey, devoid of other colours – a lake of grey smoke, a veil about the soldiers' final redoubt. Tall against the trees, Nathan stood four-square to the onslaught; to his right hand Allan Wilson and Trooper Dillon were barely visible through the gun smoke. The shots were sounding further apart.

'Keep pace with me or die where you stand!' Burnham barged his horse into Mathew's. 'For God's sake boy, keep going!'

With the killing madness upon them, the Matabele swept in from either side. Mathew gritted his teeth and put his heels hard in to Luke's flanks. He rode with the Colt's hammer at full cock. Head to head both men galloped their mounts blindly through thickets of young saplings, their legs numbed from a continuous thrashing.

'Get ready to swing left!' Burnham yelled to Mathew.

Less than twenty yards out from the Matabele, the American changed direction. Leaning out from the saddle he fired three rounds into a line of howling warriors. Mathew swung for the gap. However, others had pre-empted the scout's manoeuvre and from where they were hidden, stood up from amongst the mopani. Burnham saw them at the last minute and fired with the gun's barrel barely a yard from a warrior's face, but the warrior's club had already completed its arc. Burnham's horse shuddered beneath him; angled from waist height, like some heavy scythe the gnarled club smashed through the gelding's leg. The animal galloped for all of a hundred yards before it went down, the shattered leg folding inwards as Burnham jumped clear and windmilled into the scrub.

'Take my arm!' shouted Mathew then pushed his horse just fast enough to give momentum to the scout's western style vault behind the saddle. Burnham still had his pistol. With his arm locked around Mathew's waist he emptied the gun at the screaming Matabele.

'Bear to the right!' yelled Burnham. Mathew kicked more speed from his horse, gradually, the roar of pursuing Matabele faded. The forest had opened up; a hundred yards of short grass took them down to the riverbank.

## -49-

Wilson was firing single-handed, rifle propped against the belly of his downed horse. Strangely, his fear of dying had been replaced with a grim acceptance.

'Burnham got through Nathan, or these savages would

267

have brought them back and butchered them both in front of us.' Incoming gunfire withered and then fell silent. 'Giving us a last few minutes to mull things over, gentleman-like of them, wouldn't you say?'

Besides Allan Wilson only three other men were left alive. Trooper Dillon, Nathan Goddard and the towering Scot, Jack Robertson. The others, along with their mounts, lay where they had fallen.

Nathan pushed himself upright. A bullet had lodged in his thigh; the pain now almost unbearable. He was light-headed, the desire to sleep unrelenting, heavy about his shoulders.

'Damn them all. What are they waiting for?' He fed a fresh cartridge into the breech of Dillon's rifle. Incessant cold and loss of blood cramped his fingers.

'Have they gone, Captain?'

'Keep your finger on the trigger, boy.' Linen bandages, black with blood covered most of Dillon's face. 'Fire when you hear them come in close.'

'Are they coming back, sir?'

'Anyone special back home?'

'My mother and father, and a girl.' Dillon's mouth softened. 'Mary. Pretty as a picture, sir. Lives with her mother. Hurst Green, a small village in the north of England.'

'Best be ready, lads,' warned Jack Robertson. 'The beggars are coming back.'

At first, the sounds were no louder than a light drumming – distant – rain on canvas tents.

'I can hear them,' said Dillon. 'Captain Goddard, sir – I can't see. Will you stand with me?' The sound of rain became the thunder all around them. A thousand spears to long shields.

'I'm here, boy.' Nathan drew Dillon's head against his shoulder. At twenty yards both men heard the rasp of short spears being wrenched from their leather thongs; with his free hand, Nathan levelled the Boxer-Henry.

'Can you hear me, Dillon?'

'I can hear you, Captain. Will it hurt, sir? When they kill us.'

# -50-

A slight wind moved amongst the dead as though gathering up souls from the fallen. Upwards of a thousand warriors stood about the killing ground – not a single man dared speak.

Alone, Mjaan paused at every soldier's corpse to marvel at the devastation wreaked upon it – some were little more than boys, though they had fought with the hearts of lions. He walked slowly from the killing and at the edge of the redoubt waited for the silence to become total.

'No man shall defile the dead nor speak ill of them or he will die by my hand!'

Thunder growled above the battleground; the eyes of the *amabutho* were all upon him.

'Take up your dead, oh sons of Mashobane! Leave the soldiers where they lie. I say to you, warriors of the Matabele – besides these men we are as timid girls – for they were men of men, and their fathers were men before them.'

Cecil Rhodes rested his arms to a modest desk, his leonine head moved in time with the characteristic, untidy sweep of his longhand. He replaced the pen in its glass well without lifting his eyes from the letter's contents, taking time to check the legality of his writings before reaching for a brown, manila envelope. Outside, the early January heat had already started to build so that he was glad of a constant through-flow of air beneath the thatched roof. The cottage, though barely adequate complimented his need for a solitary existence. Rhodes looked up and for a long moment let his eyes wander over the land outside the window. He had it all. Lobengula had been beaten; the place he had renamed Bulawayo was his, though bitterly won.

'Come inside, young Goddard. I will be with you in a moment.'

Mathew stepped through the doorway. Light from the window flooded most of the room. Stacked on makeshift shelves were the necessities of Rhodes' nomadic lifestyle, books on English law and burgeoning, leather bound journals, scribblings of ideas and grandiose dreams of empires in the making, for Rhodes was a man of perpetual mental motion and even in the dark, early hours before dawn, plans were hatched and stored for future reference. There was the warm smell of cologne, freshly laid thatch and rough, native furniture.

Rhodes swivelled his chair to face Mathew.

'Jameson tells me you are going back to the Shangani?'

'In the morning.' Mathew nodded.

'And you'll be going alone?'

'The Matabele will pay little attention to one man.'

Rhodes stood up from the desk, though smaller in stature, swiftly he took control of their discussion.

'You're aware of what might well be waiting for you?' His eyes were fatigued and ringed with shadows, but still Mathew recognised that indomitable force of the man behind them.

'I have little choice, sir.'

Rhodes acknowledged Mathew's dilemma. 'The personal trauma of losing a loved one. Your father was a good and loyal ally and God knows I could have done without losing him.' He handed Mathew the envelope. 'A small token of my gratitude. You will excuse the inadequacy of the text but I was never blessed with an artistic hand. If you would show its content to Mister Vigers, the Mining Commissioner in Victoria, I'm sure all will be made clear to you.'

Mathew went to open the letter but Rhodes shook his head dismissively.

'In your own time. You have much to prepare for. Take what you need from the Company stores. Tell our Mister Dawson to put my name to it.'

# -52-

Though more than a month had passed, still the desperation and the horror of what had happened contaminated the forest. Mathew shivered in the sunlight and for an hour he held back, unable to dismount. The urge to turn his horse about was strong. Trees that were stripped of leaves had replenished their losses and where men had fought to the death, grass, that quiet deceptive carpet, now completely covered the battleground.

'I was beginning to think you weren't going to make it.'

Mathew spun round in the saddle, the Colt already out from his belt.

'Coffee's on the fire and you sure look like you could use some.' Burnham stepped away from the tree. The same battered hat and Winchester rifle.

'Rhodes sent you?' Mathew guessed. Burnham shook his head.

'Dawson told me you were coming out here.'

Mathew kneed his horse forward.

'When did you get here?'

'Early this morning. If we work together we can be away before nightfall. Don't much relish the thought of being out here in the dark.'

'What about the Matabele?' Mathew asked him.

'Seen nothing of them. Word is the old chief's pushed north for the Zambezi with a few of his diehards. The rest have had enough. The fight's gone out of them.'

Mathew dismounted and tethered Luke next to Burnham's horse. Thirty yards from the camp, Burnham had dug a hole – a yard deep between the roots of an old tree.

'Best I could come up with,' Burnham explained. 'Buried what I could find. Reckon on scavengers having taken the rest.'

Mathew forced himself to look inside the grave. At first, his eyes were unadjusted to the half-light, then his vision cleared and for the first time the reality of what had happened reared up at him from that dark hole. Though the pain went deep it was not unbearable. Only their bones were left, the men had gone.

'We should mark the grave,' said Mathew. 'Others will come back. Without a mark of sorts no one will find it.'

'The tree,' said Burnham. 'Use my knife; make your mark and then we must leave.'

For that next hour while Burnham closed in the grave, Mathew cut his mark, the cross of Jesus Christ and below it, simply inscribed, he cut the words: *To Brave Men*.

He stood with Burnham in front of the grave. 'I shouldn't have left you, Pa...' the words, though contrite sounded out of touch with reality; at any moment, Mathew expected to see his father strolling towards him from the forest, then, as a cold and biting wind the finality of his father's death wrapped around him.

'Best we be getting along now,' said Burnham, 'with luck, we can be across the Shangani before nightfall.'

*

With only minutes of last light remaining, Burnham found the place where he had previously crossed and urged his horse belly-deep into the water. Without incident, both horses climbed out onto the far bank.

Mathew built a fire of dried mopani, above it, Burnham slung an enamel billy filled with clear water. They drank overly-sweetened coffee and roasted the remainder of Mathew's bread over open coals. Mathew let his mind wander, it helped him cover the pain and for a moment the smallest of smiles threatened his lips.

'That was my first time ever inside a bar.'

Like Mathew's, Burnham's eyes softened.

'The comely, Molly McGuire?'

'Don't reckon I'll ever forget her. Don't suppose I'll see

her again though?'

'Don't be too sure,' said Burnham, 'women like her have a habit of turning up when you least expect it.' He banked up the fire with the heel of his boot. 'Right now your lovely Molly will be out where the money is. Trust me laddie, you don't want to know the half of what she does to get her pretty little hands on it.'

'You ever been married?' asked Mathew. 'It's just that I have never heard you speak of anyone.'

Burnham nodded his head. 'You'll meet her soon enough. Blanche is not the kind of woman who cherishes being left behind. Reckon she will already have set her sights on coming up to Bulawayo. Likes to be where the action is.'

Other memories of their journey up from Kimberley sprang to mind.

'What about you?' he urged, 'I seem to recall you showing a fair amount of interest in the Bowker girl?'

'Sannie,' Mathew recalled, 'might well look her up when I get back home.'

A horse whickered. Burnham's hand closed around the butt of his pistol and he swivelled sideways-on to the forest.

'Put the gun away, white man. I am alone and wish you no harm.'

'Why do you follow us?' Mathew cocked his pistol.

'We follow the same road.'

'Then show yourself.'

Mhlangana stepped out from the dark.

'Well I'll be...' Mathew lowered the Colt. 'I thought we had seen the last of you.'

'I gave you my word. Sometimes the bee flies far from the hive, but always it will return.' The joy of their reunion quickly disappeared like sparks above the fire.

'I was with the king when our regiments fought your soldiers at Shangani. Mjaan, the king's General spoke of the battle.'

'My father was amongst the fallen.'

'As was my son,' said Mhlangana. 'It can be said that we have both suffered a great loss.'

Again, Mathew struggled with the pain; it rose up cold and mercilessly from deep inside him.

'At sunrise,' he told Mhlangana, 'I will be starting for Victoria. I would want you to come with me.'

'I will make my fire alongside the road,' said Mhlangana, 'together we will begin the journey.'

## -53-

To their left hand, *Thabas Indunas* crouched as a lion. To the front, the skyline blazed with dawn sunlight.

'Guess this is where we part company,' said Burnham.

'My mother has waited long enough,' Mathew replied.

Burnham nodded. 'I reckon that's a fair enough reason.' He leant between the horses, his hand outstretched. 'You take care of yourself. Keep an eye out for Molly McGuire, she might just decide to pay you a visit.'

'Only in my dreams,' said Mathew.

'I'll look you up. Soon as the dust settles.'

'I'll be watching for you,' promised Mathew.

Burnham wheeled his horse about. Bulawayo still lay some twenty miles to the south.

For most of every day, Catherine Goddard would sit with a clear view of the incoming track, but the eyes that watched were dulled from grieving and from their corners, now there spread the creases of heartbreak and hardship. Every waking hour of every day she prayed for a glimpse of inbound riders and though only a month and a half had passed since her men had left for Bulawayo, those silver streaks borne of her worrying were plain enough to see. Begrudgingly, she forced her attentions away from the track and onto the gardens; each of the fertile beds repeatedly cleared of weeds, the red earth raised and furrowed on either side to take water she had diverted from the stream, the furrows crisply cut and lined with stone in a way that Nathan had shown to her. Had he suggested she planted the pumpkins first? She could not remember; it seemed too long ago. Cicadas whined in the treetops and a single, yellow-billed kite soared directly above the homestead, a cushion of breathless air beneath its wings.

What Catherine saw, at first seemed little more than a wisp of smoke. Perhaps the light had tricked her eye, but the wisp became a feather and in defiance of slanting sunlight she shielded her face and stood upright from her chair.

'Please God, let it be,' she prayed out loud, frightened even to blink for chance of what she was seeing might disappear.

Two men came out of the haze, one on horseback, the other close to the rider's flank, his arm entwined with the stirrup leather. Catherine held her breath as the runner dropped away. Freed of its extra burden the gelding gathered speed.

From a quarter mile out, Mathew recognized the stoic figure of his mother and his blood chilled. From the way she was standing he knew the tragic news had reached her. It was then the enormity of a future without his father fell upon him like a ravening wolf.

Luke whickered, after almost two months away the sights and smells were still familiar. Mathew swung his leg across and slid sideways from the saddle. No longer able to stem the pain, as a river in spate the sorrow flooded out from him.

'I should not have left him.' Mathew choked, but Catherine put her hand to his lips.

'Don't talk,' she pleaded with him. 'Not yet.'

# -55-

From first light to sundown, Mathew filled his days with work. Like some runaway engine he refused to stop and the days and weeks flew past in a blur of speed. Already he had cut wood enough to see them through that next full winter, but still his axe rose and fell. Mhlangana worked alongside him; both men felled and stacked the wood in abject silence. Catherine brought out food and they ate in the shadow of a tall *mnondo*. Then, again they let their work and the forest engulf them.

They widened and relined the stream with flat stones from the hillside and given of the extra water, the gardens burgeoned. They built fences and paddocks for the horses and where the earth was soft they cleared the ground of rock and trees, extending the lands for Catherine to plant her orchards.

The nights were the worst for Mathew. Besides his own grief, Catherine's crying filtered out from behind closed doors, for every night his father's letter was read a hundred times before exhaustion took his mother to sleep. When the fires were lit and the moon rose up from the high forests his father's memory was all around him, as if from an open wound the pain was always ready to bleed profusely. Until the small hours he would sit with only the wavering light from a hurricane lamp for company. A hundred times he took down rifles from their hangings; stripped, cleaned and reassembled them, sometimes in the pitch dark. More than once he had fallen asleep in his father's chair, a Metford carbine rested across his knees. It was after one such night that Mathew woke with the winter sun full on his face.

He walked outside; the frost was there, crystals of white ice where the sun had not yet reached. Luke whickered to him from the paddock and for the first time in six long months, Mathew caught himself smiling. He knew that what he had lost was irretrievable and yet, the pain had eased – the time for brooding was over.

From the kitchen, he heard the clattering of pans – Catherine shouting the dogs to get outside – the crackle of hot fat. When he walked back to the house, unfamiliar pangs led him straight to where his mother stood squarely to her stove. The kitchen smelt of bacon and wood smoke and his senses flooded.

'Whatever it is you're cooking, mother, I'll have a bucketful. Double as much again for afters.'

'How did you sleep?' she asked him. Although still slight,

a sparkle showed in Catherine's eyes; the sullenness was disappearing.

'In the chair,' said Mathew, 'for the last time, though. Tonight I sleep in a bed before I forget what it's like to straighten my legs.'

Whilst they ate, they talked. Quickly, Mathew prioritised. 'First the Mines Office to sort things out with Vigers. Then we'll clean out Slater's sale yard.'

He would make a list – his mother would negotiate costs and supply dates. Catherine was an accomplished haggler and would cut the time and expense of his own blunderings by a third, at least.

'Machinery and labour?' Catherine drew him back down to earth. 'Now that the Dickens is up and running, prices will be high.'

Mathew pushed his empty plate to one side and spread the tabletop with paperwork. Rhodes' letter to Vigers was first to hand. It was then Mathew realised to what extent his life had changed. The extra concessions won from Rhodes' Company would double the farm's acreage; mining rights either side of the Empress Deep's main reef would increase three-fold. In terms of natural assets, Mathew was already a wealthy man. His father would always be there, but now was the time for Mathew to walk on his own; it was time to let go of his father's hand.

# -56-

Mathew quoted verbatim from Rhodes' instructions. 'At the Company's discretion the abovementioned is entitled

279

to a grant of two hundred gold claims and thirty thousand morgen of arable land. That there will be no enforcement of the Chartered Company's standard levy of fifty percent on gold produced by the Goddard family for as long as they hold the rights to the said claims. This grant will stand as a token of the Company's gratitude and will run for perpetuity.'

He nodded his head at Vigers. 'A mistake or two, but enough to give you the gist of things.'

'A magnanimous gesture on Mister Rhodes' part – you're very fortunate.'

'Now comes the hard part. I need machinery – picks, shovels, dynamite and drill steels. A stamping mill and an engine to run it. Where do I start looking?'

Vigers handed back the letter. Mining equipment was at a premium. Every day new claims were being registered; the goldfields were booming.

'Wherever you're lucky enough to find it would be the short answer. What about capital?' Vigers asked without looking up.

'Couple of thousand.'

'That will barely get you into the running. As prices are at the moment, a thousand will buy you little more than someone else's scrap.' Vigers liked him, he saw no sign of Mathew baulking. 'Get yourself over to the Thatched House. Talk to John Dickens, tell him I sent you and show him some respect or you will get little more than a blacked eye for your trouble.'

Mathew crossed over from the Mines Office and walked into the hotel. The bar was full, prospectors and miners most of them – those who knew him smiled or nodded sympathetically. By most, Mathew's father had been well thought of. He ordered a beer.

'John Dickens, where can I find him?'

The barman looked sideways; Dickens always sat near the wall.

'The feller with the beard. Watch his temper mind, doesn't take kindly to strangers.'

Mathew waited for the crowd to thin before going over. Dickens leant on one elbow. Likening the burly miner to the American grizzly bear, Mathew could not have encompassed his neck with both hands.

'Mathew Goddard.' He left the beer on the counter and extended his right hand to Dickens. 'Vigers said you were the man to ask for advice?'

'Nathan's boy?'

Mathew nodded. His father's name tripped as cold fingers inside his shirt.

'I need a mill and an engine.'

Dickens drained his glass; froth stuck to his whiskers, but he made no attempt to wipe it away.

'How much money have you got?'

'A little more than two thousand.'

'Your claims?' Dickens went on. 'All pegged and legal like?'

Mathew nodded.

'What about water?'

'Enough to start with – close to the reef.'

'And labour? You'll need at least ten men – more when you start producing.'

Mathew kept his composure. Dickens was digging deep; gauging his metal.

'One good man, that's all,' said Mathew, 'but I will find others.'

For the next hour, Dickens pumped him dry of information; it took more than money to open a gold reef.

He leant against the bar counter and pushed his empty glass at Mathew.

'The Cotapaxi, you heard of it?'

'Four miles south of my place.' Mathew caught the barman's attention; the glass was refilled and paid for. 'The old Electric claims?'

Dickens nodded. 'Rhodes' men are putting in a new ten-stamp Sandycroft crushing battery. The old three-stamp has already been stripped out – she's lying next to the mill site along with her boiler. A case of first come first served so best be getting yourself up there and tell that Morrish layabout, it was Arthur John Dickens who sent you.'

-57-

'John Dickens, you say?'

'Big fellow,' Mathew confirmed. 'I believe he owns the mine just to the west of Fern Spruit?'

'Co-owns it,' Morrish corrected him, 'a Mister Ledeboer and two others hold interests in the Dickens.' Morrish stepped away from the shade of his makeshift office. Cicadas shrieked in the treetops – the sun now directly overhead. 'Walk with me.' He waved Mathew to where the installation of the new Sandycroft crushing battery was in full swing. Though he walked with a slight limp he was broad across the shoulders, his forearms thickly set from years of manual labour. Men swarmed like ants over dismembered machinery and lifting tackle. Rectangular shuttering boxes had recently been thrown full with concrete; solid immovable bases to take the weight of the mill's two giant mortar boxes. Separated from the others by a few yards, another plinth had already hardened; the timbers stripped away – a grey and glistening concrete slab with its mounting bolts ready to take on the weight of the engine's massive iron cradle.

Mathew watched with interest as the first of two supporting king posts was hoisted into position; twenty feet long and thick as two men standing back-to-back. Cut from seasoned Oregon pine and at more than ton in weight it swayed like a drunk to its iron footing, upended by squealing block and tackle. At the rope, twenty native labourers grunted under the strain – all of them powerful men. In his mind's eye, Mathew saw them working alongside him at the Empress Deep, though for a moment, the sheer magnitude of what he had taken on threatened to overwhelm him.

'Ten stamps,' said Morrish. 'Two banks of five – both off the same line shaft. She'll give us thirty tons for every twenty-four hour shift – three times the output of the old three-stamp.' Morrish pointed their way between footings and dismembered machinery. 'Best you have a look at what you're up against before parting with your money.' He looked over his shoulder and shouted a flurry of instructions to the men erecting the king post. He shook his head and grinned at Mathew. 'Need eyes in the back of your head; any chance they get to malinger. What about reef, how much have you opened up?'

'Two hundred feet,' Mathew hazarded. 'Four feet wide, give or take; at best six feet, but all of it showing payable gold values.'

From a clattering, proud giant, the three-stamp crushing battery had been stripped to a tangled pile of rusting iron; grass stood two feet tall from between the dismembered mill parts. The boiler had been dumped alongside and, like the rest of the equipment, had been scarred brown by the corrosive effects of weathering.

'So young feller, what do you reckon?'

Like a latecoming lion to a kill, Mathew climbed amongst the crusher's iron bones.

'Worse than I expected. The whole lot looks about fit for the scrap pile.'

'You're reading it all wrong, young feller. Two months ago this little darlin' was up and running sweet as a new clock – clear the rust and grease her up and she'll be crushing your reef as if the devil himself were swinging the hammers.'

'It's all here?' Mathew queried.

'Everything,' Morrish assured him, 'and there's a new set of shoes and dies in my store. I'll throw them in with the mill.'

'How much?' Mathew asked. The money he had to hand now seemed pathetically inadequate.

'A months labour and I will consider the debt written off.' Not since their parting of ways in Bulawayo had Cecil Rhodes spoken to Mathew. On horseback, he had come upon his manager's transaction under cover of noise from the mill site. 'Prove your worth as a mining man and the mill is yours. Fail and I will have Mister Morrish here cut her up for ballast.'

At the edge of Kimberley's diamond pit, Mathew the boy, had faced the lion. Now, as a man though not yet nineteen he was being offered a token place at the lion's kill.

'I accept – when do I start?'

'You already have,' said Rhodes and gestured to Morrish. 'Post-date a bill of sale for the three-stamp. Thirty days,

Mister Morrish. We'll see if this prodigy of yours has stomach enough to make the grade.'

*

For thirty nights, Mathew shared the lean-to Mhlangana had built for them at the forest's edge. Thatched with tall elephant grass the roof sloped down to touch the ground, barely thick enough to hold off cold south-easterly winds that came at them in the early hours. They ate what Morrish gave them; maize meal porridge and beef before they slept as dead men, wrapped in blankets huddled close as they dared to the fire.

From dawn to sunset, Morrish pushed the pace and in those twelve hours of each day, Mathew learned how to use the level, the square and the plumb line. At the blacksmith's forge he learned the ancient art of drawing and welding iron; bringing the pieces to a white heat for him to twist and lap the metal. He shaped and sharpened drill steels, heating the tips to a deep cherry red before quenching them in buckets of cold brine, hardening them enough for the hammer boys to drill their holes in the living quartz – deep enough for Morrish to charge the Cotopaxi's reef with dynamite.

At the rock face, Mathew stood shoulder to shoulder with the lashing crews, after a week of breaking rock with a fourteen pounder and shovelling ore to fill the cocopans, the pain drained away from his shoulders and the palms of his hands were thickened with calloused skin. Alongside the big Matabele he toughened to whatever work Morrish gave him, he looked forward to the start of every shift, his back and shoulders heavy with new muscle.

On the evening of the thirtieth day, Morrish signalled to

the mill operator for him to 'lift stamps'. He was smiling and a mischievous glint in his eye put Mathew on his guard.

'You can do the clean-up by yourself,' said Morrish. 'Bring the amalgam down to the office when you're finished. Lock the table before you leave or that savage up there on the mill will steal us blind.'

'On my own?'

Morrish nodded. 'On your own, laddie and make a good job of things, Rhodes is waiting in my office.'

With some trepidation, Mathew gestured to the operator for him to shut off the water supply to number one mortar box; from a steady stream over the copper plate the water reduced to a shallow skimming – then, reluctantly it slowed to little more than a trickle. Mhlangana stood alongside him; in his hand a square of heavy fabric ready for the amalgam. Mathew leant over the amalgam plate so that he could reach to its centre with a softwood spatula – for a moment his hands hovered there, then, strengthening his resolve, he started scraping together a thick mixture of precious gold and quicksilver.

Tinted by trapped gold, the mercury was now a pale, buttery yellow – the colour of early sunlight.

-58-

Cecil Rhodes freed himself of the customary woollen jacket and tie; he sat with his shirt sleeves rolled up to the elbows and with the neck of his linen shirt wide open. Mathew sat across from him, in contrast to Rhodes' pallid features he was burned to a deep brown from his month's labouring in open sunlight. A ball of silver amalgam the size of a large grapefruit took centre place on the office table.

'So how say you, Mister Morrish – a good result? Or does the three-stamp go to Slater's scrap yard?'

Morrish cocked a doubtful eye, but unable to carry the weight of his pretence any longer, nodded his head to Rhodes. Mathew's hands were heavily calloused, his nails split from wrestling broken ore from the reef; for thirty days he had done the work of a dozen men.

'I think we have the makings of a gold miner, Mister Rhodes.'

Rhodes skipped the conversation forwards

'What about transport for your mill?'

'I can bring in a wagon,' said Mathew

'Strong enough to carry the engine and boiler?'

Mathew nodded. 'That won't be a problem.'

'Then our Mister Morrish here will help you load. Now that the installation of the Sandycroft is complete, we have more men in our employ than is needed.' He looked up at Mathew. Like all builders of great empires he was always one step ahead of whatever game had been set in motion.

'You could do worse than taking some of our native labour for your Empress Deep – good workers, most of them.' He leant back in his chair. 'How do you stand financially?'

'Low in the water.' Mathew admitted.

Rhodes' eyes glittered.

'Then we will talk again, young man.' He stood up from the table and extended his hand to Mathew. 'You may leave us now. Mister Morrish and I have much to discuss.'

## 59

Alongside the wagon, Mathew rode Luke at a slow walk. Weaving the gelding between the trees his mind drifted. Nostalgically, he recalled the long trip up from Kimberley, loaded with chattels, guns and hundred-weight bags of maize meal. Now the wagon was empty – stripped of its canvas tent and cots, it was the bared bones of a transporter's flatbed. It took twelve muscled oxen to pull it the five mile distance to the Cotapaxi. Mhlangana, in khaki breeches and barefooted coaxed his span with gentle words, for with the wagon empty the strain on their yokes was light and the whip was seldom needed.

'We need labour,' Mathew called across to him.

'There are many to pick from,' answered Mhlangana. 'Choose wisely – I have watched them. Some have only the worth of old baboons.'

'There are good men amongst your baboons. Find me ten, those who can use their brains as well as they swing their hammers.'

By mid-afternoon they had reached the mine, as before the first sounds were those from iron stamps, men's voices and the ring of hammers to rock and steel – the Sandycroft mill, a demanding iron colossus.

As some pagan idol on concrete altars it towered above the site. Men on wooden platforms shovelled rock into the crusher's iron jaws so that it fed and disgorged constantly. Against the skyline it was a monster, at its side its iron cohort – a hissing bitch of an engine, excited by flaming, waist-thick logs in her firebox. Through her power and gearing down of giant pulleys, inexorably she turned the mammoth camshaft, imparting the strength of thirty Shire horses, all of them working in unison.

'We've upped her tonnage to maximum!' Morrish expounded, forced to shout above the din. 'Thirty tons, yesterday – should be same today!'

Like a child to fire or running water, Mathew was drawn to the base of the giant crusher. Imprisoned by concrete and thick bolts the mill shook and thundered; each of the stamps weighing in at over a thousand pounds. One by one they were lifted, then in turn, disengaged from rotating, cast iron cams they would fall free, crushing the rock inside their mortar box to gold- laden slurry.

From that steel heart-beat, a trained ear could gauge the efficiency of the crusher; whether to increase or reduce the feed, slacken or turn up the supply of water, or, if the iron shoes or dies were wearing down and when, to within a half day, they would need replacing. Mathew knew it would take time; for him to learn control of his own machines would take months of dedication. It made no difference. He relished the challenge, eager for his acquisitions to be loaded he shouted across to Morrish.

'I'll be needing the loan of your sheer legs – and if you can spare me some of your men?'

'Behind your wagon – all the parts are accounted for and stacked ready for taking away.' He took hold of Mathew's elbow. 'Let your driver supervise the loading, there's one more thing for you to watch before I let you loose on those claims of yours.'

Morrish lifted the butter-coloured ball of gold and quicksilver out of the company safe. Still wrapped in heavy drill, the last day's production was again placed at the table's centre. He looked across at Mathew.

'Your views on retrieving the gold, how would you do it?'

'I know that heat is used,' offered Mathew, 'though I

have never seen it done.'

Morrish nodded and stood up from the table. 'Bring the amalgam with you – time to watch and learn.'

Behind the makeshift office a fire had been set, now it was thick with hot embers, from the slightest movement of air the coals took on that dark red eye of a blacksmith's wakening furnace.

'Put your amalgam into the retort pot.'

Made of cast iron, the retort, a foot deep with a concave bottom stood as a witch's cauldron to its three iron legs. Morrish bolted down the lid and positioned the retort to the hottest part of the fire.

'Make sure you keep the outlet pipe under water or the fumes will kill you. Once she's up to temperature the mercury will start to boil off.'

From the retort's lid, an iron condenser pipe angled downwards to beyond the fire's reach. Morrish filled a battered prospector's pan with water and positioned the pan so that it covered the open end of the pipe.

'Give it fifteen minutes or so.' He squatted alongside Mathew and waited for the transformation to begin.

Mathew watched the first bright droplets of reclaimed mercury appear beneath the surface of the water. They joined together forming a trembling silver pool at the bottom of the pan. When the flow of mercury ceased, Morrish lifted the retort away from the fire.

'Give her a while to cool down; any leftover fumes will change back to mercury.'

An hour later, Mathew came back from his wagon. Morrish slackened off the clamp bolts and lifted the lid. Inside, a pock-marked cake of sponge-gold covered the bottom; yellow as sun-ripened corn.

## 60

Three times, Mathew brought his wagon to the Cotapaxi, each time he came away the wagon creaked and groaned from its load of heavy iron. Before the final journey home, with Mhlangana's guidance, he wheedled out the best of Morrish's surplus labour, those who had worked alongside him and could wield the heavy pick and fourteen-pound hammer. Mhlangana was quick to spot the shirkers and he sent them packing, only the best now walked behind the wagon; blankets and chattels strung on twine across their shoulders.

From alongside the lumbering oxen, Mathew looked back at his caravan of men and machines and the feelings they invoked were those of excitement and optimism.

'We have our mill and it cost us nothing!'

'But in sweat and blistered hands we paid a thousand times.' Mhlangana reminded him. 'And we will pay again. Soon the wagon will be of no use – the hill is too steep.'

'We have men. Where there is no road we can push one through. With the money saved on the mill we will buy fuse and dynamite. Nothing will stop us from reaching the reef. Should it take us six months or even a year, then so be it.'

Behind the homestead, the dismembered mill and engine were stacked on log pallets to keep them clear of the ground; cleaned of rust, every moving part, every nut and bolt was greased before being stored. While Mathew and his men worked, Catherine sketched and logged every metal part to the pages of her inventory and with a woman's intuitive eye she looked ahead for pitfalls and costings. Picks, shovels, axes and dynamite were added to her list. Mules would be needed to carry in labourers' rations and smaller items, saving the greater trek wagon for the transporting of heavier machinery. Already the Shona labourers were restless for hard work and they yearned for Mathew to point out a way for them to follow.

'Time for us to spend some money,' said Mathew.

'In the morning,' Catherine agreed, 'I'll take the cart. Slater's auction starts at ten o'clock. We'll be there at nine sharp.'

'An hour early?' Mathew cut in incredulously. 'We'll be riding in the dark?'

'Then we'll be the first there for the best of what he has,' said Catherine. 'I will take what we want before the auction gets under way. Slater has never been known to turn down a good offer. The sight of gold coin makes his mouth water.'

\*

At the auctioneers, Catherine steered Mhlangana between piles of used equipment, sorting good from scrap she haggled with renewed determination over the pricing.

'Prices are climbing faster than you realise.' Slater bemoaned the knocked-down selling price. 'Last week a wagon load of cement was sold even before it reached Victoria.'

'And your next shipment?' Catherine pushed him. 'When will it arrive?'

'Two weeks,' hazarded Slater, 'give or take a week for any delays.'

'Twenty pockets – two pounds a pocket – that's two shillings a pocket over and above your usual saleroom price.'

Slater seemed perplexed by the offer and screwed the stem of a fresh pipe between his teeth.

'Paid upfront?'

'As we speak,' said Catherine, then closed the deal by counting out the exact amount. 'A bill of sale, Mister Slater? With your intended delivery date and signature, if you please. The price of your picks and shovels we will discuss later.'

Slater winced at the threat of further marginal profits and left Catherine to find her own way about the yard. Other men were filing in through the gate, eyes already sifting through what was on offer, though within that same month most of them would be making their way back across the Limpopo, relieved of what money they had and with the dark cloud of bitter desperation hanging over their heads. Raw-boned and disillusioned they rummaged with calloused hands; glassy-eyed they fought as scavenging birds over the scrap piles. However, there were others less concerned with bargaining for Slater's mining supplies.

'Would you be lookin' over there, Mister Chulmleigh – that sweet little thing in breeches and shirt. With hair like that I'll wager a shilling to one of your gold pounds the lassie be not long out from old Dublin Town.'

'Already seen 'er, Mister O'Reilly, were I standing next to the wench I knows exactly where my hands would be.'

O'Reilly spotted Mhlangana. 'Best be careful, Chulmleigh. Brought along her savage for the fetching and carrying.'

'Or for the tuppin'.' Chulmleigh sniggered.

'What's the black bugger staring at?' O'Reilly dropped his hand to the butt of his Webley pistol. 'By all that's holy, Mister Chulmleigh – if the bastard keeps on staring he'll be feeling the toe of my boot, to be sure he will.'

Mhlangana lowered his eyes.

Slater handed the pre-paid bill of sale to Catherine.

'No guarantees on the delivery date, Mrs Goddard; you'll have to take it as and when.'

O'Reilly steered Chulmleigh towards the back of the sale yard.

'The redhead,' O'Reilly kept his back to Catherine. 'I'll be damned if the little darlin' isn't our dead Captain's missus.'

'You're talking in riddles, Mister O'Reilly?'

'Goddard, you bloody Irish fool! Big feller – black beard; got the chop with Wilson's lot at Shangani?'

'The ruins,' Chulmleigh recalled. 'Gave us a whipping for what we did to the black wench, if I'm thinking straight?'

'That you are, Mister Chulmleigh, that you certainly are.' Absentmindedly, O'Reilly fingered the hole through his bowler. 'Time for his missus to square the debt, wouldn't you say?'

Chulmleigh's eyes glittered. 'That it is, Mister O'Reilly. That it is.'

## -61-

'The weight of one more shovel, mother and we'll be back in Slater's yard bargaining for a new axle.'

Catherine didn't hear him, she looked beyond her son to the frontage of Vennell's printing establishment; pinned to the timber wall was a handwritten, cyclostyled page from *THE NUGGET*, the town's advertiser. The writing had almost faded, the paper itself badly weathered.

'What is it, mother?'

As though caught up in a dream, Catherine brushed past Mathew and stepped up from the street to a wooden veranda.

Together they read a list of names that had been posted there. It took only a moment for Catherine's trembling finger to find the one she loved. She read aloud, but as a slight whisper – unable to still the words in her mind.

*Captain Nathan Goddard of the Victoria Rangers – gladly he paid the ultimate price – far from hamlet, town or city.*

Again she felt the pain of her loss and the deep raw ache of it frightened her.

'No more crying,' she pleaded. 'No more tears, my sweet, I beg of you.'

Very slowly, the pain eased and as if by its own accord, her finger slipped from his name and settled across another. Her breathing tripped when she read again of a soldier's obituary.

*Trooper Johannes Petrus Bowker – bravely did he stand his ground.*

'Magdel's husband,' Catherine realised, 'I had no idea that he was with your father at the Shangani.' She turned to Mathew and her face was stricken with concern for her friend.

'I must find Magdel. For all we know she is alone with Sannie at the Cambrian mine.'

'I will come with you,' said Mathew, but Catherine vehemently shook her head. 'I must go alone,' she insisted. 'In the morning. First we will see to getting this equipment back to the house, there will be plenty for you to do whilst I'm gone. The road through to the mine must be finished before the start of the next rains.' She took out the whip from its scabbard before climbing into the driver's seat of her Cape cart.

## -62-

'Four days, Mathew. If I'm not back by then, your coming to find me will be justified. Not before mind.'

Mathew gave his mother a leg-up into the saddle. He had insisted on her taking his horse and slid a freshly oiled Metford carbine into the scabbard.

'Thirty miles west of the fort,' Mathew reminded her. 'The wagon ruts should be enough to lead you in.'

'And I shall follow them all the way, my darling, over-worrying son.'

'You have food and water enough for both ways?'

'Several times over.' Catherine chuckled, and bent for Mathew to kiss her cheek.

'Tell Sannie I may well pay her a visit.'

'Knowing Sannie, she will have wasted little time in finding herself another beau,' Catherine admonished. 'Every young man within twenty miles of The Cambrian will be sniffing around Magdel's wagon like a jackal.' She flashed a smile at her son and at the same time touched her heels to Luke's flanks. Mathew stood and watched until the image of horse and rider melted in with the mist.

There were moments when the reasons for Catherine's concerns for Magdel were almost forgotten. Thankful of her time alone she watched the forests and hills fold back at either side, some still lush with growth and others, where the frosts had caught the open parklands had already turned from green to brown by the cold breath of winter.

There were flocks of noisy guinea fowl flushing as steel-grey clouds from their feeding place amongst the grasses, so many of them that Catherine could only contemplate their numbers. At every new twist in the road exciting moments delighted her eye and when quick enough, she caught the sounds and sight of startled antelope crashing their way through the forest.

By mid-afternoon, red hills loomed to her right hand. Devoid of trees, only hardier grasses and short scrub coped with the sour red earth of this eroded, range of ancient serpentines. Now, in that late sunlight, their western slopes were daubed the colour of fire and cinnabar, but where the shadows fell to rocky crags and deep gullies, the earth had turned the sinister colour of wasting blood.

An hour before dark, Catherine crested the spine of a low ridge and took in her first sighting of the Shashe River. Dropping the brim of her hat against the sunset she picked out the glow of hurricane lamps and from a vast unspoiled wilderness there rose up sounds of people talking. The soft, melodious lilt of a trek Boer's concertina gave the little mining camp an air of peaceful melancholy. However, within minutes of Catherine reaching the encampment, her first impressions were shattered. Now she felt compelled to turn her horse about and gallop for home. Amongst the shadows and lamp-lit tents she found the pervasive cancer of misfortune; at its side, as a sickly child there crawled despair. Where once the Cambrian's reef had gone down rich and deep, now only barren quartz came up from the face; the stamping mill stood as a redundant giant against the skyline.

Backed amongst the velvety growth of old Kigelia trees, as a wrecked ship, Magdel's wagon leant precariously to the broken stub of its rear axle. Again, Catherine sensed those feelings of adversity that so valiantly she had fought to be rid of. Dogs slunk out from beneath the wagon, whereas a month earlier they would have growled and barked at any stranger. Now with tails tucked between their legs they could find the strength only to leer and whimper.

'Katarina!' Magdel came out from the leeward side of her wagon; beneath her eyes the skin was deeply shadowed by long nights and deprivation. She moved stiffly with the frailty of an old woman and held Luke's bridle for Catherine to climb down. 'As God is my witness – it is so good to see you again. Let me look at you, *my lieflike* Katarina. How have things been with you these past months?'

'Difficult to bear.'

'I heard of your loss, so many brave men.' Magdel lowered her eyes. 'My Petrus also was taken from me.'

For a long moment, they clung to one another and took comfort from the intimacy of their friendship – there was nothing that could be said, no words could make their losses more bearable. In Magdel's hair there was the sour smell of old sweat and river water.

'*Kom*,' said Magdel and led Catherine to where a second chair had already been set in close to the fire. The same hippo-hide sjambok had been laid out on the trestle table, but there was no enamel billy and none of Magdel's enamel cups were put ready for filling.

'I took the liberty of bringing a few things with me.'

Magdel nodded, her eyes, glittering like those of starving sparrows had already found the canvas carriers slung across the bridge of Catherine's saddle. Catherine slipped the buckles and reached inside.

'Coffee, sugar and your favourite, Cape Smoke – on my doctor's advice, of course – and rusks,' she added. Like a mother at Christmas time her life was being enriched by this simple act of giving.

Magdel watched in awe of the bounty. Without looking up she beckoned to the coloured girl.

'Boil water, Anna. God has sent to us an angel – and bring cups, girl, the biggest you can find.'

Anna raked up the fire, brought out the filled enamel billy from the wagon and balanced it between two hearthstones. Catherine piled the table with the rest of her provisions; soap and candles – a loaf of home-baked bread, salt and a smoke-cured ham wrapped in muslin.

'And this.' She drew out a small tin and held it to the lamplight.

Like a child for its mother's hand, Magdel reached out, fearful of Catherine's gift suddenly disappearing on the wings of a spiteful dream.

'*My liewe God*!' Magdel whispered. The tin, inscribed with Gallaher's Scented Snuff glowed as a bar of yellow gold in the lamplight.

As an expectant connoisseur, Magdel carefully prised back the lid. Her senses reeled. Unable to resist for even another second she took up a generous pinch. Though laced with cinnamon, still there was that powerful, underlying smell of raw, ripe tobacco. Magdel sniffed up the powder, the sneeze, when it came, was thunderous – the pleasure rippling inside her head almost unbearable.

'If I die tomorrow, Katarina, I will have already seen a tiny piece of paradise!' Again, Magdel's eyes flooded and again the camp echoed with her sneezing.

For half the night they reminisced, only when the fire had died for a second time and the level of Cape Smoke had fallen below the bottle's middle did Magdel, with Anna's steadying hand take herself off to her wagon.

Catherine fed the fire with thick mopani from the log pile, with the Metford nestled into her side she drew a woollen blanket up beneath her chin; within minutes, not even Magdel's snoring could keep her from sleep.

-64-

The morning was fresh and cold from the night's frost. The billy simmered above the embers and whilst the loaf Catherine had brought from home was still soft, Magdel cut slices from it; thick as her hand and then thickened again with salty yellow butter. Without expression, Magdel spoke softly to Catherine.

'My Sannie died a week ago on this day.'

Again, death had come to Magdel's wagon and she had been forced to step aside. What God decreed she had accepted – that was the way of the Boer.

'Had I the money, my wagon would have been made

right and there would not be the need to tell you. I would have been gone from this place and the truth with me.'

Sara, Magdel's servant girl stepped out from behind the wagon – compared to Anna's slightness of limb, she was still in that first full flowering of motherhood. Naked, apart from a small leather apron she walked with voluptuous disregard for those about her. Like a quarter moon to a dark sky her smile was white as vlei frost, her body heavily fleshed, bright and shiny black as a moonlit stream. She lowered herself to the ground at Magdel's feet, close enough to the fire for it to ward off cold from the child at her breast. Magdel watched Catherine's face for signs of her abhorrence, but she found only bewilderment.

At a week old the child was rose-pink and cherub-like, its tiny head from birth was capped with fine, dark hair the colour of midnight. With persistent tiny fists and a mouth no bigger than that of a mewling kitten it snuffled insistently to the burgeoning black breast of its wet nurse.

Magdel smiled at Catherine, but it was the smile of a broken woman.

'God had not the need to take them both from me.' She reached over and gently touched her fingertips to the child's forehead. 'His father's hair, perhaps – but the eyes,' whispered Magdel, 'as surely as God made us all, these are my daughter's eyes.'

They relapsed into silence; Magdel waiting – Catherine's maternal instincts now in turmoil. Frightened by what she had found, she counted back through the months. A thousand questions, as drops of rain they fell about her, but already she knew the answer to them all. For that next hour it took all of Catherine's strength for her not to seize the child from Magdel and run for home. Again, that feeling, one of total, inconsolable loss hung above her as some dark malicious cloud.

*

From the saddle, Catherine looked down at Magdel. The sun was now directly overhead and dropped only small shadows about the Kigelia trees. When Sara rose to take the infant back inside the wagon, Catherine felt as though a part of her was dying; many emotions were warring inside of her.

'I have left a purse with Anna, enough for repairs to your wagon and to get you away from this godforsaken place.' She paused to compose herself, pitying Magdel would serve no purpose. Already the Afrikaner woman had suffered more than most and though still she burned inside, like others cursed with deprivation she had denied herself the luxury of mourning. Hardened by the happenings of her lifetime, as a ship to relentless seas, Magdel would turn and stand again, four-square to the wind.

'Where will you go?' Catherine asked her, knowing full well that these were the last few moments they would spend together.

'East,' said Magdel. 'There are seventeen wagons already crossed from Bethlehem in the Orange Free State. I will join with them.'

'Thomas Moodie.' Catherine realised. 'I have heard talk of him and his column making for Gazaland?'

Magdel nodded. 'It will be a good journey. If God sees fit to spare me one more time it will be my last.'

Catherine drew a deep breath, the melancholy of her surroundings had all but finished her – those last few hours draped as a leaden shawl about her shoulders, and though her face was expressionless, Magdel could see the play of emotion in her eyes. Catherine reached for Magdel's hand. There was little left to say.

'I cannot stay any longer, love the child enough for both of us. God go with you both, my dearest friend.'

'And with you, my Katarina.'

# -65-

'Time we wasn't here, Mister Chulmleigh, your fancy piece is on her way.'

'Where is she? Damn these eyes of mine – give me the spyglass.'

O'Reilly turned his back. 'Patience, my fat friend whilst I make sure of our lassie's intentions, wouldn't do for us to be taking off down the wrong road now.'

'What's she wearing?'

'That would be telling now, Mister Chulmleigh, wouldn't be right for a man to get himself all worked up like.'

'Damn you, O'Reilly! What's the bitch wearing.'

'Moleskins and blouse – be buggered if they aren't men's breeches.' He paused to adjust the focus; theatrically, he sucked in air between his teeth. 'Coming straight for us, she is. Rides like a man – legs either side of that big bastard horse of hers and, oh by all that's merciful I don't think I should be telling you, Chulmleigh. Best for us both if I covers me eyes.'

Chulmleigh grappled for the spyglass. 'Give me the glass yer Dublin donkey before I suffers a seizure.'

He wiped the eyepiece clean of sweat and quickly picked

up on the white of Catherine's blouse. At a slow canter, every part of Catherine's supple body rocked and swayed in time with the horse's gait. From the sun's angle, every fold in her blouse, every dark crease in her moleskin breeches was accentuated.

'Sweet mother of Mary, I can even smell the bitch's sweat. There's neither lump nor crack on the wench's body that I cannot see, Mister O'Reilly.'

Where the track narrowed, Catherine gave more slack to the reins, letting the gelding pick its own way between the rocks. Her hips swayed in sympathy with Luke's slow walk and from her hairline, sweat ran down inside her collar. Silently, she cursed her own stupidity for leaving the Cambrian when the sun was at its highest. She slipped the first button of her blouse and by leaning forwards allowed a trickle of cooling air inside.

'I swear the bitch is tormenting us,' whispered Chulmleigh. His hands were shaking and from the very tip of his vulturine, beaky nose a single drop of sweat trembled loose and fell away. 'She's stopped, so she has.'

'What for?'

'Not sure; she's getting down – you won't believe me.'

'Believe what, Chulmleigh? What is she doing?'

Chulmleigh stiffened, though silent, his breathing quickened.

'In memory of me own sweet mother, Chulmleigh, what's she fuckin' doing?'

'Slackening her belt.'

'Give me the glass back.'

'Undoing her buttons, so she is.'

'The glass, Chulmleigh – give me the bloody spyglass.'

'The bloody horse is in the way, now – I can't see her; only her face. I think she's takin' a piss.'

304

O'Reilly tore the glass from Chulmleigh's fingers.

'Bring up the horses, yer fat Irish fool before she gets away from us.'

Catherine drew up her breeches and re-buckled her belt. In the enervating heat of noon, the wilderness was completely still and yet for one brief moment she shivered and instinctively swung her gaze to higher ground.

'I swear she's looking straight at me.'

'And why would she be doing that?' mused Chulmleigh, 'you bein' uglier than a Belfast trollop. We're too far away for the wench to see us up here.'

Catherine shook herself free of the portent. 'Grey goose walked over my grave,' she told herself and smiled at her own foolishness. Like a man she swung up into the saddle and again opened her blouse to let in the breeze.

*

She has to stop,' said Chulmleigh. 'It will be dark soon enough.'

Catherine rode close in to the leeward side of a granite kopje. Here the trees were taller with ghostlike silver bark and wide, outstretched limbs. The ground was soft, though still she was able to pick out deep hoof prints from her last crossing. She followed her own spoor to where she had found the stream the day before.

'The wench is looking for a place to bed down. We had best get over there, Mister O'Reilly; we're not losing this one – no siree. Captain bloody Goddard and his whelp won't be stopping us this time.'

Satisfied that he had done enough, Mathew left his axe buried deep inside the heartwood of an old acacia, for that first half-mile, straight as a track- layer's line the ground had been cleared of trees. Where there was rock, his men had set to it with fourteen-pounders, breaking out the ironstone for others to roll it aside. Where the ground sloped it was levelled, the trees cut and left as stumps less than a foot in height – low enough for wagons to pass over without damage to their axles. The track was now level enough for them to carry steel and cement without losing their precious load to the forest.

At night, Mhlangana built his fire away from the others, for he was a Matabele, an Induna and leader of the king's men. His birthright alone preferred him a sleeping place away from the rabble. Mathew ate and slept alongside that same fire, they talked of past times, often with the fighting at Shangani ready to spill from their lips, but neither one of them finding the courage to let it out. The wounds were still open and raw edged. However, Mhlangana saw no other way open to rid himself of a burden he had carried with him from that battleground.

'The place you call, Slater's yard'

'What of it?'

'Two men.' He went on. It was obvious to Mathew that he was ill at ease. 'The smaller one covers his head with the strange *isigqoko*. Black and round like the calabash; when the other one spoke with him, O'Reilly was the name that he used.'

The Irishman's name ground like steel on flint to Mathew's ears.

'The man who spoke to O'Reilly, what was he like?'

'Fat,' said Mhlangana and stretched his arms away from his sides, 'as the wild pig with its belly filled.'

'Chulmleigh.' Mathew realised. 'Rogues, the both of them, they were with Wilson at Shangani.'

'Both men lived,' said Mhlangana. 'They did not fight alongside the others at Shangani.'

'Why are you telling me this?' But already the recollection of his run-in with the treasure hunters had joined him at the fire. Rumours of their desertion had once been common talk. Some men swore they had been left amongst the dead at Shangani – others said differently. However, back from the fight with Lobengula's impis, with their military obligations honoured, most had quickly shrugged off any allegiance to the Company. In a land thickening with newcomers it had not been hard for rogues and vagabonds to lose themselves to the hubbub of a booming mining town.

'It was I, Mhlangana Khumalo who carried the king's gold to the soldiers at Shangani.'

Slowly the full implication came to him. Rumours of Lobengula's peace offering of a thousand gold pounds had been dismissed as nonsensical. Supposedly, the gold had been sent to dissuade the soldiers from following after the king. Few had taken the story to heart.

'You gave the gold to the Irishmen?'

'They swore the gold queens would be taken to the white Induna at GuBuluwayo.' Mhlangana dropped his eyes to the fire. 'It was a mistake.'

'You were not to know,' said Mathew. 'You have told no one else?'

'No one.'

Mathew stood up from the fire. A thin line of last light

307

slipped behind the far horizon. A cold breeze slid inside his shirt.

'What were they doing in Slater's yard?'

'They whispered as thieves,' said Mhlangana. 'They watched with jackals' eyes.'

*My mother*, Mathew realised. *They were watching her*. His eyes flew back to the western horizon; the chill breeze now greedy fingers raking along his spine. 'Fetch your spears,' he told Mhlangana, 'as soon as the moon is up we ride for the Cambrian.'

## -67-

Taking a dead-rest against the granite, Chulmleigh leered at the image inside his spyglass.

'Our lovely's thinkin' of taking a bath in the stream – we should be getting on down there.'

'Give the wench chance to settle,' O'Reilly countered, 'we'll go in all gentleman-like or the Captain's widow will be up and at us with that rifle of hers.'

'Shirt's comin' off.' Chulmleigh stiffened behind the glass. 'She's smilin' bejesus!'

'Thinking of what's in store for her.' O'Reilly chuckled and drew out the cork from the bottle between his knees. 'More's the pity her husband and that pup of his won't be around to watch.'

'Sweet mother of Mary Magdalena!' Chulmleigh thrust the telescope at O'Reilly. 'I can't be watching anymore; tits like a wild horse she has!' He took the bottle in exchange and pulled long and hard at the fiery mix of rum and Cape

Smoke.

Like Chulmleigh, O'Reilly splayed his elbows against the granite. Catherine had a fire going; close to the bank where she had lowered herself into the water. Firelight caught the fullness of her breasts and from the chill of that moving stream their tips stood dark and firm as ripe Damascus grapes.

'Come on out my little beauty; let's be seeing what nestles between those long pretty legs o' yours.'

Catherine reached for a small towel and stood up – half-turned towards the fire she relished its warmth and stepped out from the stream. In the moonlight, her skin showed up porcelain white. Like a leopard from the high kopje, O'Reilly watched her every move.

'Big as a tom cat's ruff, Mister Chulmleigh – thick as me grandmother's whiskers – cracklin' red I'll wager; like a burnin' bush rustlin' under me fingernails.' He shoved the glass at Chulmleigh. 'Take a look for yersel' boyo, a finer one you'll not be seeing anywhere else this side of God's own Limpopo.'

Chulmleigh took the glass from him. The only sounds were that of his own breathing and the far-off yip of a lone jackal. With each item of her clothing, Catherine lent her time to warming them over the fire.

'Pullin' on her drawers, O'Reilly. What do you say to us going a callin'?'

'Another ten minutes, Mister Chulmleigh. Show the girl some respect. Keep that fat friend of yours buttoned away inside your breeches for a little while longer.'

*

Catherine heard the Irishmen long before O'Reilly called

309

to her from the shadows. She stood away from the firelight with the Metford cocked and loaded, resting against her hip.

'Who are you and what do you want?'

'We saw your fire,' said O'Reilly. 'An hour's warmth and we'll be on our way, me darlin'.'

'Where are you from?'

O'Reilly grinned; some of the tension had eased from the woman's voice.

'Across the Shashe. Ten miles or so west of the Cambrian, just a couple of old prospectors, Ma'am. Neither one of us would harm a flea so we wouldn't.'

'And where are you bound for?'

'The fort at Victoria. We're Rhodes' men. Company prospectors, Ma'am and that's the truth of it.'

Catherine eased off her grip on the trigger. 'Step forward – into the light so I can see you.'

'Misters, O'Rourke and Daniel Cunliff, at your service, Ma'am.'

The lies rolled easily from O'Reilly's lips. With a flamboyant sweep of his arm he bowed from the waist. 'Only ten months up from the Cape and not long out from the old country; Dublin, Ireland to be precise.'

Catherine looked to the night behind them.

'Where are your horses?'

'Tethered, Ma'am. Thought it better we came across on foot.'

'Turn around.'

'If its pistols you're looking for, neither of us uses the cursed things.'

Catherine scrutinised the pair for weapons tucked inside their belts. There were none. For long moments she stood in the dark, unable to make up her mind. With the opportunity slipping away, O'Reilly played his final card.

'Begin' your pardon, Ma'am I think it's best if we were on our way then. Not wanting to frighten a good lady such as yourself.'

'Wait,' said Catherine. 'I see no harm in your sharing my fire. A hot drink, but nothing more mind – coffee is all that I have. Then I will ask you both to leave.'

'And thankful we will be for it.' O'Reilly tipped his hat. 'Though it would be seen as more polite if myself and Mister Cunliff here could put a name to our goodly benefactor?'

'Catherine Goddard.'

'Your husband's name, Ma'am, if you wouldn't think it wrong of me for asking? Chances are we might well know him.'

'Nathan,' said Catherine, but the words did not come easily. 'My husband was killed at Shangani. I live alone with my son.'

'A terrible battle so we were told.' Chulmleigh feigned sympathy. 'Lost a dear friend of my own to those same murdering heathen so I did.'

'You were there?'

Chulmleigh shook his head. 'Not meself, Ma'am – Catherine, if I might be so bold; I haven't the stomach for killin' and fighting.' He removed his hat and like the tearful sympathiser, clutched it close to his chest. 'A dear friend of the family's – with Wilson's lot when they were all struck down.'

Catherine visibly straightened up. 'My husband was amongst those thirty three, what was your friend called?'

'Dillon, Ma'am. Trooper Dillon – Dennis Michael Cronly, hardly more than a lad. Studied alongside my nephew at Stonyhurst Jesuit College before taking the call

311

to come out here. Looked to becoming a man of God so he did.'

'Brave men, all of them,' said Catherine, 'come forwards – make yourselves a place by the fire.'

## -68-

The track was little used, though in the moonlight it stood out as a dark indelible line.

'Your mother crossed the stream here,' Mhlangana pointed out the deep prints for Mathew, 'and here is the spoor of others following the same road.' Even in the half-light the spoor was still distinct.

'Two riders,' said Mathew and silently he cursed the lack of daylight. 'The Irishmen,' he hissed and from the moon's angle measured the distance he had covered. 'I should have gone with her. How much longer before we reach the river?'

'When the moon is above us.'

'Take my stirrup,' said Mathew.

Wraithlike, they moved as fast as Mathew dared, making good their time where the countryside opened up, then forfeited those same minutes to the dark when deep forest closed in around them.

Where the track rose up they stopped to rest. On the crisp air, sounds from as far away as ten miles drifted up to them. As if on cue, a single shot, clear as the crack from a drover's whip, cut through the silence.

For more than an hour, Catherine listened to the Irishmen's repertoire of stories, three more times she refilled their mugs with coffee. The fatter of the two became agitated; he was no longer the amiable guest. For increasingly longer moments she watched him from the corner of her eye – her trust failing. In the firelight his features were drawn and wolf-like, his eyes followed her every move – those of a drunk or the opium addict. The Irishmen were overstepping her hospitality; she stood up from the fire with the Metford rifle still cocked, but held at the trail.

'I need to sleep and the coffee is all but gone. I must ask you both to leave.'

O'Reilly grunted his distaste at leaving the fire. He gestured to Chulmleigh.

'Better we make a move, Mister Cunliff. The lady's been patient enough with our ramblings; time we got a scurry on.' He pulled up his collar against the chill. The moon had halfway crossed the firmament, away from the fire the air was cold – the veld was quiet. O'Reilly knew they were alone.

Chulmleigh's speed was that of a man half his weight. The blow, though open-handed, was struck with the full force of his right arm; it sent Catherine reeling backwards from the fire. The Metford fired, triggered by the reflexive tightening of Catherine's fingers. The shot flew wide, missing O'Reilly's head by mere inches. He snatched the weapon out of her hands and ejected the spent casing.

'You sit there nice and quiet like, girlie or you'll be upsettin' our Mister Chulmleigh here. Gets all excited for

313

nothin', so he does.'

Catherine tasted the salty tang of her own blood; the edge of her tongue was bitten through. Her eyes seethed with hatred.

'You're scum the both of you.'

O'Reilly grinned; his eyes in the firelight were dark and empty – those of a snake.

'That's twice I've almost lost me head to a Goddard bullet.'

'Third time lucky,' hissed Catherine. 'Rest assured you Irish wastrel, my son won't miss.'

'Irish wastrel, the lassie called you, Mister O'Reilly!' Chulmleigh pinned her arms against the ground, with his face only inches from Catherine's he breathed the words into her mouth. 'Your dead husband thought the same of us, Ma'am. Took our gold and the black lassie we was giving a seein' to, he did. Not this time though, me feisty red-haired darlin'.' The stench of rum and the diseased canker of rotten teeth swept across her face. 'This time there's no one around to hear you screaming.' He nodded to O'Reilly. 'The rope on your saddle, Mister O'Reilly – truss her up and stoke the fire so's we can see what the Captain's wife has tucked away inside her breeches.'

-70-

Mathew knee-haltered his horse no more than a quarter mile from where he had seen the flickering light, through the spyglass he watched the Irishmen laying on wood to their fire. On the crisp night air Chulmleigh's voice was wild and high pitched. Spreadeagled close to the fire, like a victim readied for some ritualistic slaughter, the summation of all Mathew's worst fears took shape inside the lens.

'The scum have my mother!' He saw her head move; they had stripped her to the waist – from the blackest depths of Mathew's being his anger, like a black wind, rose up in him.

*

'In all of yer life, Catherine have you ever seen a finer sight than Patrick David Chulmleigh's, man-o'-war?'

Looking down at her, Chulmleigh, the triumphant conqueror, stood with his fists balled and breeches buttons fully opened from the waist. In the firelight, his body hair sprouted as ginger tufts from a soup of freckles and pallid flesh, but below the flesh was firm and arrogant; distended by excitement, like a condemned man fighting the hangman's gibbet it swung and twitched just inches from Catherine's face.

'If you would do the honours, Mister O'Reilly – we'll be having the lassie's breeches down before she loses interest.'

O'Reilly dropped the empty bottle, toad-like he shuffled in next to Catherine – her mouth bled from the pressure of his leather belt between her teeth.

In desperation, Mathew replaced the spyglass with his rifle, but he quickly realised the futility in what he was doing.

'Too many trees – got to get closer.' Chancing a bullet from inside the forest was not an option, the rifle's sights were indistinct – he was still too far out from the fire. The slightest snick from a leaf would send the bullet a yard wide of its target. Again he cursed himself for not having found his mother before dark.

O'Reilly cupped a filthy hand to one, fat round breast. Between finger and thumb he squeezed her nipple. Like a terrified filly, Catherine lunged at the binding; her wrists and ankles already rubbed raw.

'I think the lassie's enjoying the attention, Mister Chulmleigh – methinks her not having the Captain around all these months has left her well short of a good bit o' cock.'

Lasciviously, like a leopard cleansing the fur of its mate, O'Reilly dragged his tongue over Catherine's bared breasts. Chulmleigh watched him, then driven by alcohol and his own perverse excitement he straddled Catherine's legs and set to freeing her belt.

'Hold her still, O'Reilly – the lassie's breeches front's done up tighter than a smouse's purse.'

'Your knife, Chulmleigh; use yer bloody knife!'

Chulmleigh fumbled a clasp knife from his pocket; the blade, razor-sharp slashed through the leather. Catherine turned her face to the side. Overcome by the pain in her mouth and the incessant degradation she closed her eyes.

-71-

Mathew eased the Mannlicher's barrel between the branches of a young tree. From where he stood the way ahead lay open; his line of sight to the camp now unobscured. Little more than moonlight and cropped

316

scrub covered the ground. Like that of a man already driven to the very edge of insanity, O'Reilly's voice keened through the quiet.

'Once we're done with you, sweetheart, we'll be payin' that lad of yours a visit.'

Catherine stared up at him, unable to speak, through her eyes the hatred screamed at him.

'Thought that would get yer attention, lassie. Hold still now there's a good lady.'

His hands were rough – his whiskers frantic, crawling things on her skin. Catherine reared up against her bindings; about her waist her clothing hung in tatters. Chulmleigh held the clasp knife to Catherine's face, the tip of it pressed against her skin – a tiny jewel of bright blood followed the line of her jaw.

'Give us what we want,' breathed Chulmleigh, 'or you might well end up in the same pickle as that husband o' yours.'

The bullet took Chulmleigh two inches below the juncture of his shoulder, like a boxer's heavy fist to the soft, unresisting flesh of the armpit. Both lungs were ripped through. Chulmleigh felt nothing. The knife fell from his hand and for an instant he stared at Catherine – his expression bemused, then that deep insidious cold reserved for dying men came over him.

Catherine found herself unable to tear her eyes from the spectacle. Though Chulmleigh's eyes were wide open he was seeing nothing. Slowly, from the waist he toppled forwards; blood from his ruptured lungs welled from his throat. Before Chulmleigh's lifeless face hit the ground, O'Reilly had chambered a bullet and pressed the Metford's barrel hard to Catherine's head.

'Step into the light!' O'Reilly shouted into the darkness.

'Now, or by Jesus I'll shoot the woman!'

Mathew came out from the shadows; his rifle at the trail.

'The Captain's whelp – I might have guessed you'd be along. He stood up. 'Drop your rifle and come forward – slowly mind. Any funny stuff and your mother won't be around to watch the sun come up.'

Mathew lowered the Mannlicher to the ground and started across the clearing. Mhlangana had disappeared – neither sound nor movement gave any warning of his whereabouts.

'Let my mother go.'

'No demands, laddie-buck – let's not forget who's holding the gun. You just do as you're told now.' O'Reilly put his boot to Chulmleigh's corpse and rolled it clear. 'Made me a wealthy man, you have. Old Chulmleigh here is worth a bob or two. No family so I suppose I'll be takin' charge of what he has. No point in wastin' good gold, I always says.' O'Reilly cocked his head to one side, distracted by what he thought to be the whisper of night birds' wings in the forest behind him.

To O'Reilly it was merely the closing in of dark clouds for the life had already gone out from him. He pitched forwards, head first into the fire; his hair flamed – a halo of tiny sparks fled upwards with the heat. Mathew watched him burn. Without speaking, Mhlangana stepped from the shadows and wrenched the axe from O'Reilly's skull.

*

There was still the taste of fresh blood on Catherine's lips, she dabbed the wound with her tongue; the taste of it bitter-sweet. She waited for Mathew to light the tinder and then, wary of the flames she lifted the crackling bundle and dropped the firebrand deep inside the heart of the wood pile. Neither one of them spoke, together they watched the fire take hold; within minutes the flames were treetop high. Forced back by scorching heat they went to where Mhlangana waited with the horses – by morning there would be nothing left.

'We still have a long way to go,' said Mathew, but Catherine lingered; her head cocked to the pyre. To her, the howling of boiling sap and flame were now the tormented screams of her assailants.

## -72-

Two men watched the night fall, the road they had laboured on for weeks showed as a dark scar in the red earth – now indelibly scoured from the passage of heavily laden wagons. Where the valley narrowed, cooking fires winked as fireflies and on the cold air, smoke from them threaded as grey yarn through the forest. Close to where they were standing, Mathew could hear the horses in the paddock and a sense of deep contentment came over him.

'We've made a good start, I will grant you that, but there is still so much for us to do.'

Mhlangana nodded his head. 'With the first rains come the flying ants. In a single day they will dig their holes beneath a stone while the earth is still soft. They look for nothing more.'

Mathew chuckled. 'Your ants are like old men. They have a lifetime in which to build their mountain. We have little more than three months before the rains break.'

'And in a single day you move more earth than the termite moves in a lifetime. I see no problem. The road is almost finished – before the rain comes your machines will be ready.'

Mathew leant on his rifle, with soft eyes he stared across the valley.

'Sometimes, when a man has wealth and cattle enough to fill the lives of ten men, still his own may seem empty.'

'Those are the words of a man who lies alone at night,' said Mhlangana and smiled at the insight.

Mathew recalled the time he spent at the Digger's Rest in Kimberley, carousing with Burnham; his first meeting with strong beer and the lascivious Molly McGuire. Since that night she had plagued his dreams and left him sweating like a man beset with fever. He shook himself free of the memories. He had witnessed the beginnings of a lifetime, the years that lay ahead were not for him to see.

'We have a mountain to move,' said Mathew.

'This is true,' said the Matabele and together they went down to where Mhlangana had built their fire.

\*

Ten more days it cost him before Mathew's team of labourers reached the place where he and his father had first corralled their horses. The hillside had already been cleared of trees and the route upwards to a proposed mill site surveyed and marked out with wooden pegs as parameters for the labour force to work to. Where there was solid ironstone, holes were drilled; the sound of hammers to drill steels a permanent voice about the valley. Mathew charged the holes himself, driving in the sticks of dynamite with wooden poles, so as not to cause a spark.

Then he would watch Mhlangana put fire to the fuses before running back along the hillside to where there was shelter. Like staggered canon fire, each shot fired in sequence, blasting out the solid rock. Pieces the size of sledgehammer heads flew as far as half a mile before crashing back to earth.

The road had been laid at varying angles to cope with the gradient, back and forth, always driving upwards for the mill site. The bends had been widened enough to take the sweeping arc of a wagon with its twenty mules working two abreast.

'Tomorrow,' said Mathew and walked with Mhlangana to where they had left the horses, 'Bradfield will be here with his wagons. The lighter pieces first, as a trial run. The heaviest we will leave till last.'

'Even with twenty men,' said Mhlangana, 'the task will prove a hard one. Moreso where the road twists back like the neck of a snake.'

A lightly sprung Cape cart came towards them; mules rigged to the traces. Mathew recognised the lumpy countenance of both passengers.

'We have visitors. Go on without me. Wait for me where we left the wagon.'

The cart pulled up alongside him. Vigers, the Mining Commissioner sat in the driver's seat. Sweat had soaked through his shirt front and his tie seemed more the hangman's noose than a comfortable accessory.

'Gentlemen.' Mathew smiled. 'Mister Rhodes, sir, what brings you all the way out here to the Empress Deep?'

'Business,' Rhodes intoned and shuffled sideways to avoid the sunlight. 'Vigers here has been bombarding my ears with your entrepreneurial skills.' He looked tired and ill. The heat had swollen his face; his colour high and blotched with purple, but his eyes were still that pale arctic blue and his voice was clear.

'Come on up.' He cleared a place alongside him. 'Mister Vigers, if you would find us all something to drink. This heat is intolerable.'

Vigers reached behind him and slacked off leather straps from the lid of a wicker basket. He drew out three crystal glasses and a flask of cool water. While Vigers poured, Rhodes turned his attentions to Mathew.

'This road of yours – how much longer before you're ready?'

'Tomorrow,' said Mathew, 'twenty mules and a flat-bed wagon.'

Rhodes peered inside the basket. Silver salvers had been wrapped and stacked with linen napkins between them. Stuart crystal caught at the sunlight.

'I believe there is ham and roast chicken in there somewhere. Help yourself.'

Mathew reached out a fat chicken leg and sprinkled it with salt from a sterling silver pot. It was then he saw the first flicker of amusement in Rhodes' eyes.

'Bradfield – the contractor?' Rhodes guessed and Mathew nodded.

'That boiler of yours is awkwardly shaped; heavy as a bull elephant. What if the mules cannot cope with the gradient? Mules are unpredictable creatures, you know – what if they panic?'

They were both silent, each man watching the eyes of the other.

'Then we lose our mill,' countered Mathew, 'but that will not happen. Bradfield's the best there is, he assures me a week at the outside to transport the bulk of my machinery. God willing, there won't be any problems.'

'I have broached the subject before, I know, but what about capital?'

'I manage with what's available,' said Mathew. 'What we cannot afford we will do without.'

Rhodes sighed and with the back of his hand wiped the sweat from his brow. The man was persistent, a tougher nut to crack. In those last six months Mathew's business acumen had climbed another rung on Rhodes' ladder.

'Labour,' Rhodes went on, 'you started with ten men?'

'I now have twenty.' Sweat snaked inside his shirt, but he ignored the discomfort. 'When production allows it, I will be in the market for perhaps another twenty.'

Rhodes handed his empty glass to the Mining Commissioner.

'Vigers tells me your reef is up to six feet wide in places?'

'And in others as little as three,' said Mathew, 'but with high values.' He discarded what remained of the chicken. Within seconds of it hitting the ground it was overrun by scouting hordes of black ants. All three men watched them; the relentless cutting and lifting would soon consume it totally. Rhodes was first to speak.

'I believe the late Mister Wilson forewarned you of my interest in your Empress Deep?'

Mathew kept a good face. 'Before my father died at Shangani, since then the matter has not been discussed.'

Rhodes looked up at the high cliffs, struck across with ironstone bastions they shimmered in the heat. Though lesser than a true mountain, the hills upon which Mathew and his father had struck their claim lines were to most men, well out of reach.

'Then now would be as good a time as any for me to repeat the offer. On the return of a favourable report from Vigers here, I will make available to you a sum of fifty thousand pounds sterling to meet development costs of the property known as, Empress Deep.'

Mathew nodded his head, hearing that amount was in its own right powerful enough to flush his skin with gooseflesh.

'More than most will see in a lifetime,' Rhodes added.

'And should I refuse your offer?'

From within that pallid facade, Rhodes' eyes glittered.

'Though I do not doubt you have the will, Goddard. Without my help I doubt you will find capital enough to drive the project forwards. Sleep on it. I'll be staying at the Dickens Mine for one more week before leaving for Kimberley. The terms of my involvement are as before. Should I leave earlier than anticipated, Mister Vigers here will telegraph your answer through to Kimberley. For both our sakes, I hope you do not disappoint me.'

# -73-

With a tripod gantry and rope blocks the first dismembered parts were slung aboard the contractor's wagon. Bradfield had brought his own labour force and already their backs were slicked with sweat.

'Four turns in the track before we reach the top – the last will be the bitch that gives us trouble, I can smell it coming.' He looked to Mathew for help. 'I need you to work as my swamper; my right hand man. It'll take a clear mind as well as a strong back to get your mill round these bends.'

Mathew nodded. 'Tell me what I must do.'

While the load was being secured, in the sand at his feet, Bradfield sketched out a plan of what he expected. Mhlangana also watched and found little difficulty in taking on board the rudiments of the contractor's directions. Compared to oxen, Bradfield's mules would prove quick on their feet, like a team of Alaskan huskies already they looked eagerly to their driver for the command to pull. Each mule knew its name and would in the winking of an eye respond obediently to their wheeler's instructions.

'I will ride the left hand or, 'nigh-wheeler' as it's called.' Bradfield pointed out the nearside mule, harnessed closest in to the wagon. 'From there I can control the leaders and if needs be, make it onto the wagon seat for the brake.'

'Who will lead the team?' asked Mathew. Bradfield spat a plug of tobacco from behind his lip.

'No need. I will drive the leaders from the wheeler.'

'And how will you do that?'

Bradfield straightened up and Mathew followed him to the front of the span.

'Got freight bells on 'em, see.' He reached across and showed them to Mathew. Fastened to the lead mules' harness, the freight bells jangled when he tapped them with his fingers. 'The others listen for 'em; wherever the leaders go, the rest follow. Trust 'em they do.' He took Mathew back to the wagon. 'This 'ere's the jerk line. I keeps a hold of it all the time, see. Runs front to back, hundred and twenty feet of her; goes up through rings on the harness of the nearside animals, right up to the leader. Steady pull on the line tells the mules to go out left; jerk it sharpish like and they'll turn to the right.'

'And what do I do?' Mathew asked. Bradfield led him round to the span's far side.

'Make sure the sixes do their job. Otherwise the leader mules will drag us through the break and she'll tip.'

'Sixes?'

Bradfield nodded his head.

'Get the buggers to skip the chain and pull at right angles to the leaders.' Again he drew in the sand. 'First six mules after the wheelers; first two are called pointers, next pair, sixes and the last, the eights. Been trained special, see. Once I give 'em the order, the left siders'll cross over the chain.' He drew a line perpendicular to the span. 'Then all six'll pull the chain into the bend and walk sideways on until the wagon's round the corner.'

Mathew shook his head at the ingenuity. 'I understand. When do we start?'

'Soon as my boys have lashed down the load, I'll give you the nod when we're ready.'

Mathew watched them work, shoulder to shoulder with his own crew. Like ants they lifted in unison and they sang the songs of their fathers, it was their way – the way of Africa. To pass the time, Mathew found himself scrutinising Bradfield's wagon, compared to the Boer trek wagon, this was a leviathan of wood and iron.

The rear wheels were six feet high, the front would measure up at four. Forged from iron, the tyres were four inches wide and almost an inch thick. The spokes were of split English oak, from five inches wide at the hub to three and one half at the point.

'She'll carry ten tons, depending on the ground,' Bradfield told him. 'Only one of her kind between here and the Transvaal goldfields.'

'The wagon is strong,' Mhlangana nodded his head, 'I will watch with open eyes.' He stroked the heavy tyres in wonderment, not even the Matabele ironsmiths would match them.

It was midday when Bradfield climbed into the saddle of the nearside wheeler. As if the lead mules had sensed the difficulty of the terrain they turned their heads and looked up at the hillside. Though the animals made no noise, a definable air of uncertainty hovered vulture-like over the wagon.

'Had me another teamster up till yesterday,' said Bradfield, 'lost him to Doel Zeederberg. Son of a bitch promised him more money. Could have done with him on the whip for the way up – might well need your help with that one if the mules go lazy on us.'

'For a small reduction in your charges, Mister Bradfield, I would happily take the teamster's place.' Catherine drew level with the wagon. Dressed in khaki and with her drover's hat pushed back from her forehead she looked every inch the veteran teamster. Bradfield tipped his hat to her.

'Missus Goddard, Ma'am. I might be right in thinking a woman's place is not in the driver's seat of a haulage cart. Dangerous enough for a man...'

'And I suppose doubly so for a woman,' Catherine interrupted. 'Heaven forbid the very thought of a woman teamster, Mister Bradfield.'

'Don't be fooled.' Mathew grinned. 'My mother can handle a team as well as any man. Let her take the teamster's seat, either she proves herself by the first bend or on my word I will take her place.'

Bradfield spat a stream of tobacco juice; 'Black-skin snake whip – forty feet long with a handle taller than this boy of yours; could you make the darlin' sing?'

'Better than most, Mister Bradfield and I would thank you not to refer to my son as 'boy'. Bigger men than you,

327

sir have needed the services of a doctor for less.'

Bradfield capitulated. 'Till the first bend then. Whatever I tell you, Ma'am, quick off the mark or my wagon and mules will end up smashed to bits and back at the start.'

Mhlangana led Catherine's horse away; knee-haltered it was left to graze at the forest's edge. Catherine climbed up to the driver's seat and took out the whip from its bucket. She nodded her head to Bradfield.

'I'm ready.'

'Then you must excuse my language Ma'am, without a few choice words these lop-eared barren whores will refuse to move.'

'If that's what it takes then swear away, Mister Bradfield.'

'*Bvakacha*! Move my lop-eared darlings! Up *mutungamiri*! Get off your arse you fat idle baboon – take us to the top!'

Pulverised rock spat from the wheels. Combined with the weight of Bradfield's wagon, Mathew guessed the total load on the axles to be more than fifteen tons.

'Pull you devils! Pull *marovha*. *Dhonza* you slack-brained donkeys or tonight I'll feed my dogs with yer innards!'

Catherine held the whip at bay until the road turned up from level ground, she watched attentively for trouble, then, aggravated by the extra strain on its harness a middling mule threw its head. Before Bradfield could open his mouth to curse, Catherine had put out the snake whip's flickering tongue to within a half inch of the mule's ear. With a crack as loud as that from a severed forest tree the suddenness of the report shot the animal forwards.

Mathew walked with Mhlangana, nearside on to the span's middle pair, waiting for Bradfield's signal for him to turn the sixes across the chain. Now the team was level with the treetops and Catherine looked down upon the valley floor with trepidation. Balanced on the teamster's high seat it would prove almost impossible for her to jump clear if the wagon started tipping.

The lead pair reached the first bend, their freight bells jangling. The next ten mules, known as the swing team followed, taking the central chain closer in to the edge. Catherine's whip cracked like rifle fire and for a better reach she took an upright stance against her seat.

'Take them over!' Bradfield shouted to Mathew and when he bellowed the animal's names each of the pointers, sixes and eights, like soldiers changing step, swung away at right angles to the line – the left hand one of each pair cleared the chain and in unison, the animals dropped their heads and took the added pressure square across their shoulders.

With the chain arced back from the edge, inexorably the wagon ground into the bend, the wheels skidding as much as turning so that Catherine felt the plankings shudder against her feet. After what had seemed like a lifetime, the leaders and swingers straightened out and Bradfield shouted the valiant sixes back into line. Catherine slumped in her seat. There would be ten minutes more of easy driving before the leaders reached the second bend.

-74-

By late afternoon the first load had been stripped from the wagon and stacked in the lee of an ironstone ridge, the tempestuous haul from the valley floor to the mill site completed without mishap. With the transport free of weight, Bradfield turned the span as though the giant wagon with its team of twenty mules were a mere Cape cart rounding the head of some seaside promenade. Again the mules were led to where the track started, this time facing downhill to where already, Mathew's cooks had set their kitchen fires; the flames visible, flickering amongst the musasa trees. As part of the contract, Mathew was sworn to providing meat and fresh water for Bradfield's labour force; from experience, Mathew knew they would eat whatever they could lay their hands on. Along with his own, there would be forty men in total. By the time the fires had cooled, little more than half the ox he had supplied would be left to cover that next day.

Within the space of that next hour the wagon was back on level ground. Before the light faded, a second load was hoisted, balanced for fair weight distribution and lashed down.

'Three more trips should see you in the clear,' said Bradfield. 'By tomorrow night Mathew me boy I'll be knocking on your door fer me money.' He stood up from the fire, the half-jack bottle in his hand already three quarters emptied of brandy.

'As soon as we're done you'll be paid,' Mathew promised. 'Providing my machines are still in one piece and not at the bottom of a ravine.'

'Your mother – will she be back in the morning?'

'First light,' said Mathew. 'My question is, will you be sober enough to work the line, though?'

'Don't you worry about me laddie. By the time the sun comes up we'll be rolling into that first bend for another crack at your mountain.' He took a long pull on the bottle. 'Last to go will be that whore of a boiler. Make us top-heavy she will. Those lop-eared donkeys of mine will have their work cut out fer sure.' He slumped down next to the fire, with a drunk's eyes he stared deep into the embers. 'I knew them all y'know.'

'Who?' asked Mathew and recognised that slippery slope of a drunken man's morbidity. 'Who did you know Mister Bradfield?'

'All of them. Wilson, Robertson, yer father. A bloody crime it was. That bastard Forbes should have been locked up. Sent 'em across that river, laddie. Not a hope in hell did they have of getting back.' His eyes rolled in their sockets; the empty bottle slipped from his fingers. 'Not a hope in hell laddie.'

Mathew covered him with a blanket and walked to where the wagon stood out in the open. Starlight hung as glittering frost to the firmament. A light wind had come up; with it the day's dust and a dryness that comes with those months preceding the first rains. Mhlangana sat to his own fire, his face and fingers glistened with beef fat and he belched lugubriously.

'By tomorrow night our work here will be done,' said Mathew.

'That is true, we will be finished,' came the reply.

Mathew squatted against his heels and smiled through the firelight, his eyes already half closed from exhaustion.

'One more day and then we start to dig. Then we will see how well those Shona maidens of yours can tunnel inside a mountain.'

To be high enough for loading the boiler, the sheer-legs were set to their fullest extension. Slung to a steel beam between the gantries, the chains Bradfield had looped about the boiler's iron sides squealed and groaned, tormented by the slippage.

'*Isa pasi*! Bring her down!' Bradfield shouted to the men on the rope blocks. Like an iron whale the giant boiler settled against her wooden cradle. Shona labourers fell upon their adversary, releasing the shackles and chain before lashing the boiler down with heavy ropes.

'Pull her down tight or she'll roll,' warned Bradfield. 'Two bob bonus for every man when we get her up to the top.'

'*Yeh-bo*!' the acknowledgement came back at him and the labourers swarmed as a tide of black ants over the wagon.

Bradfield nodded his head to Mathew. 'Ten more minutes and we'll be ready.'

Mathew turned and looked protectively towards his mother.

'You do not have to do this. If the wagon rolls nothing will stop her from going over the edge.'

'Best we get on with it, Mathew.' Catherine ignored the opportunity to change her mind and climbed up to the teamster's seat. She looked behind, the boiler dwarfed her. Bradfield's oversized wagon with its massive wheels and team of twenty mules now seemed poorly equipped to cope with the gradient.

Mhlangana clung to the wagon's high side, ready to throw his weight to the break lever. Mathew walked as before, at the nearside of the mule team. The entire force

332

of black labourers stood behind the wagon; forty men, eager to follow on, charged with excitement and trepidation for the final ascent. Bradfield shouted out the names of the lead pair and for one last time the mules leant hard into their harness.

*

Three hundred yards from the mill site, Bradfield halted the mules. His men rolled heavy rocks behind the wagon's rear wheels and Mhlangana kept his full weight to the break arm.

Bradfield looked up at Catherine. 'I'll not be forcing you, Ma'am, but now would be the time to step down. Not that you've done a bad job mind, but this last bend is a bitch; the load's top heavy – if she rolls, our iron friend up there will kill you.'

'The last word lies with you, Mister Bradfield. I have just as big a stake in this as anyone.' She rested the whip stock across her legs. 'If it's my gender and not my ability that you hold in question, then let things lie as they are.'

Bradfield shrugged his shoulders, it was pointless to argue, Mathew's mother had the mindset of a bull buffalo.

Mathew stepped up to the wagon. 'Come on down, mother, let me take her through this last bend.'

'You forget so quickly my son.' She looked at him with hard eyes. 'When I asked your father not to go with Wilson's Volunteers, nothing I said nor prayed for was strong enough to keep either one of you at home.'

Mathew gave in. He felt a coldness come over his soul and he looked along the team to where Bradfield stood with his men.

'*Bvakacha!*' he shouted. 'Let's get them moving, Bradfield, and I'll be needing all of your labour and as much spare rope as we're carrying.'

*

Before the lead pair reached the last left hand sweep in the track, Mathew's men had double-looped a pair of thick manila ropes around the boiler and wagon bed. Twenty men to each rope walked steadfastly alongside, waiting for Mathew's order to take up the strain. Without regard for her own safety, Catherine focused on the job of driving the mules forwards, her eyes flicked from mule to mule, quickly followed by the lash if any were found to be slacking.

Only yards before that final bend, Bradfield barked out the names of six mules. Again, in turn, they swung at right angles to the rest of the team. They pulled with commitment, as though relishing the opportunity to perform the arduous task of walking sideways-on to the road.

Apart from the crunch of rock against iron tyres, the occasional whickering of a mule and the hiss and crack of Catherine's lash, the hillside was silent. No one spoke, but every man's eyes were as steel, riveted to the indomitable sway of Bradfield's wagon. Lashed to its wooden cradles, pitted with cankerous scars from past battles, the boiler clung as an old lion to the back of a shuddering wildebeest.

'The wheels!' Mhlangana called to Mathew. 'The earth breaks away from them!'

Ground by giant iron wheels the track edge had started to crumble; the downwards pressure, probing like the sculptor's slender chisel had searched out tiny fissures in the underlying rock formation. Eroded by millennia of lashing rains the ironstone had oxidised, turned soft and friable. Where it shouldered the harder sulphides, the fracture line had opened – close to the track's edge the ground had become unstable – wanting to slide away from the hillside.

'*Dhonza*!' Mathew shouted. 'Pull!'

Simultaneously, both ropes snapped taught and the dangerous, sideways pitch of Bradfield's wagon faltered.

'Jump!' Mathew heard his own voice screaming, but Catherine could not hear him. In her hands the whip had become the extension of her life. Where only hours ago there had been emptiness, now she had found the reason for her fighting on. Time after time the lash cannoned forward and unlike before, now the leather tongue flickered greedily for the animals' flanks, dancing about their legs and withers so that the mules lunged forwards in their harness to escape that vicious snap and sting of Catherine's anger.

The sixes and powerful wheelers stood firm into their harness. Braced against the drag from the heavy boiler, the muscle in their necks and shoulders was now more like rope than living flesh. Then, mere inches at a time, as a small child to the safety of its mother's knee, the mules clawed back their lost ground and inexorably drew the wagon away from the edge. Like an elephant to the wallow, the boiler settled down and steadied.

'Seeing is believing,' whispered Bradfield. 'Fifty strong men, but it takes a woman to stop my wagon from going over the edge.'

The team straightened out and for those last two hundred yards, Catherine slumped to the teamster's seat, her face ashen; from her hairline, a mixture of sweat and red dust had streaked her cheeks and run inside the collar of her shirt. Mathew reached out his arms and with buoyed spirit he helped his mother down from the wagon.

'Your efforts have got to warrant at least a week's holiday, mother.' He kissed her cheek and ruffled the dust from her hair. 'You're a bloody marvel! Without your nerve the boiler would've finished up at the bottom of a ravine.'

Bradfield joined them; the look on his face said it all. 'A miracle they never went over.' He held out a calloused hand, pumping Catherine's arm to the point that she thought it might break off at the shoulder. 'Anytime you want a teamster's job. Missus, it's yours. As it stands, there'll be a ten pound reduction in my price.' He nodded his head to Mathew. 'My thanks to the both of you, as God is my keeper I've never seen the likes of it before.'

-76-

Like a circus trick rider the boy flicked his feet clear of the stirrups and hit the ground at a run.

'They're coming in! No more than a mile behind me!' He threw the reins to his mother and bounced through the barroom doors. 'Mister Dickens, sir – you said for me to watch for the coach!' He stuck out his hand, palm up – his breathing quick with excitement. 'You'd best be hurrying outside or you'll be missin' it.'

John Dickens flicked the boy a silver sixpenny coin.

He crooked a finger at Mathew. 'Get yourself outside. Someone I want you to meet, been waiting nigh on a year for this.' Mathew followed him out. Dickens had dressed himself in freshly laundered breeches and shirt. His best boots shone like new saddle leather. When he stepped into Victoria's dusty street his beard caught well at the sunlight, a mass of springy whiskers pressed against his chest like bees to some rocky overhang; repeatedly, he sprung and latched the case on his gold Hunter.

'At least they got the day right, I'll give them that.' He grinned at Mathew. 'Keep an eye out for a pretty face, laddie and all shall be revealed.'

At first, the American-built stage coach seemed trapped inside the wriggling heat haze, its progress marked by a mere flickering of pale dust. Occasionally, when carried by a slight wind, the driver's voice and the crack of his whip would carry. People crowded around the hotel frontage, necks craned expectantly; a half dozen urchins and stray mongrels ran up the street, infected by the excitement.

'Here she comes!' someone shouted and the crowd parted.

'Do I look alright?'

'As you'll ever be.' Mathew smiled and saw Dickens' eyes widen with trepidation.

As mythical spirits the mules came out from the haze and though not as well-appointed as their equine cousins, still they were spectacular. At their best speed, a team of ten work-hardened hybrids dragged their Zeederberg mail coach rocking and lurching into the neck of Victoria's First Street. Grey with granite dust, Doel Zeederberg flexed his legs at the footboard and with his full weight against it, drew back the mules, easing the thrust from their harness.

A cloud of dust caught up with the coach, together they rolled towards the crowd. Magically, like the characterisation from some fantastical story, a woman's head and shoulders appeared at the coach's open window.

Her hair, freed by the wind, glowed the colour of midnight sea ripping the tide off Cape Agulhas.

With expertise, Doel Zeederberg coaxed his team in close to the hotel's frontage.

John was first to the coach and with his heart racing he opened the door.

'Welcome home.' Was all that he managed. Like a bear with its cub he lifted her out. Mathew held back, but already her eyes had found him.

'Elizabeth Anne.' She held out her hand. Deep cobalt blue, her eyes held him spellbound. Mathew rummaged desperately for the right words.

'Mathew Goddard.' He accepted the hand. 'You're John's...'

'Daughter.' Elizabeth helped him. 'You seem surprised?'

'I didn't know,' said Mathew.

'My father loves a secret,' Elizabeth admonished playfully. She looked around and with the sun directly overhead her hair sparkled with blue lights. Mathew wanted to touch it and though they had just met he felt his pulse quicken. Elizabeth's father watched him from the corner of his eye and he smiled like a man who had just that minute lucked to a winning streak at the crown and anchor table.

'Mathew has business out at the Dickens, he'll be coming back with us.' He nodded to Mathew. 'You can carry Elizabeth's luggage, young man. The carriage is round the back.'

Zeederberg's second teamster handed Elizabeth's luggage down.

'Will your daughter be staying on?' Mathew asked.

'Depends if living out in the wilds is to her liking, but hopefully, yes.'

They loaded the carriage and John climbed into the driver's seat. Elizabeth climbed up next to him and with a ribbon that matched her eyes, tied back her hair. John set the mule to a good pace and soon they were well clear of the town's dust and bustle. The cart was lightly sprung and comfortable, Elizabeth relaxed against the cushioned backrest and with tired eyes watched the countryside unfold.

'I hope there'll be plenty of hot water where we're going, father. For the past five days I've seen nothing but the cold dregs from some wagon barrel and there was little enough of that.'

'I left instructions for the boiler to be filled and kept hot, my sweetheart. Providing Rhodes hasn't commandeered the wash house there should be more than enough, even for you, Elizabeth.'

'I have no intention of going to bed smelling like Zeederberg's mules. What is Rhodes doing here?'

'On his way back to Bulawayo and then on to Kimberley.'

'Just Rhodes?' Elizabeth pushed, knowing from past experience that Cecil Rhodes seldom travelled with anything less than two companions. Always men; never had she heard him voice his preferences in favour of the female employee. 'The great Mister Rhodes is travelling alone, father? I would have expected at least his pet, Starr Jameson to be with him?'

'Jameson went on ahead.' John took up the whip and dropped the lash just inches from the mule's cheek. The act was borne of irritation; there was little room in his life for his daughter's negative regard for the most powerful man in the colony. 'Rhodes will leave with tomorrow's coach for Bulawayo. Take your bath and go to bed if you wish.'

'I might,' said Elizabeth and looked back over her shoulder at the lone rider. 'There again, father I might stay up for a while. Though I cannot say I like the man, your Mister Rhodes may think me ill-mannered if I abandoned his company too early on in the evening.' She looked away to the south; they had reached a place where the high plateau fell back amongst mopani forests. At the extremities of her view, granite hills, rounded and grey as sleeping elephants lined the far horizon.

'Your new home, up ahead.' John pointed out a gap in the trees. 'Over there on the right,' he added, 'our labour compound; half a mile or so beyond that we have put in the mill site. Listen carefully and you'll hear the stamps.'

The rhythm was unmistakable; the insidious clangour of cast iron to rock.

'Like iron drums,' remarked Elizabeth. 'Does it ever stop?'

'Only when there's trouble,' her father explained. 'We keep her running twenty four hours a day, seven days a week.'

-77-

John's household servants laid a fire between the musasa trees. Flames rose a yard up into the dark. Mesmerised, Elizabeth watched the fire shapes – imaginary beasts that since her early childhood made their nests and dens amongst the coals. Sleep, the offspring of exhaustion threatened to close her eyes, but determinedly she held it off. Rhodes walked with Mathew to where the firelight ended. A corridor of open veld ran almost arrow straight for some twelve miles over valleys and rocky defiles to where a dozen fires burned against a far-off hillside.

'Your Empress Deep?' said Rhodes and for the moment watched those eyes of light blink back at him. Mathew stood alongside him, the decision he made did not come lightly.

'I cannot accept your proposition.'

Rhodes sighed, that long exhalation of disappointment.

'You are sure of your decision?'

Mathew nodded. 'I would lose control.'

'To some that would be preferable,' said Rhodes. 'Starve a developing mine of finance and that in itself will take control, more often than not with disastrous results.'

'I would see my acceptance as a failure; my father's memory deserves better.'

'Then I must ask that you afford me a first option on investing in the Empress Deep, should you need the finance?'

Mathew relaxed. He had expected greater opposition from a man who seldom gave in to defeat.

'Without any hesitation,' said Mathew. 'As things stand, once the mill is up I'll need piping and the pumps to go with it.'

'Speak to Vigers. The Texas Mine, east of Victoria has fallen on hard times and will be selling off some of its assets. I have it on good authority that Slater's sale yard is expecting a fair influx of what you're after.' He turned his back on the view across the valley. 'Now if you will excuse me, Mister Goddard I have an early start if I'm to catch tomorrow's coach for Bulawayo.'

*

Elizabeth was alone at the fireside, she had fallen asleep, the heel of her hand supporting her chin. Gently, Mathew touched her shoulder.

'You should go to bed; you have a lot of catching up to do.'

She opened her eyes. 'Where's Rhodes?'

'Asleep, I should imagine.'

'And my father?'

'An hour ago; left us to it.'

In the firelight, Elizabeth's eyes glowed black as ebony heartwood. Once again, Mathew felt the need to reach out for her.

'I'll be away before you get up tomorrow.'

'If I wake up at all tomorrow, that in itself will be a miracle.' When she smiled, in the firelight her teeth were perfect. Her eyes, like a cat's, exquisitely shaped – black as the night behind her – flecked with golden sparks, reflecting the firelight. 'Where will you sleep?'

'Out here,' said Mathew. 'Next to the fire.'

'On the ground?'

He nodded and made light of her concern. 'Your father put out a pillow and blanket for me.'

Her smile softened, she stood in front of him.

'I forgot to bring a lamp,' she lied. 'Would you walk me to the house? There might be snakes.'

Elizabeth walked alongside him, the path between the trees barely wide enough to take the both of them. With every step their fingers touched and though he had known her for less than a day, still his breathing swirled as quick, exciting eddies about that moment of his life. She stopped with her hand on the door latch. On the window sill, John

342

had left her a lighted candle; the soft glow of its flame hardly strong enough to illuminate Mathew's face. Reluctant to talk, Elizabeth closed her eyes and lifted her mouth for him.

'Be sure to bar the door, Elizabeth. Goodnight Mathew.' John's voice crackled through an open window. 'Coffee in the kitchen at five sharp. Cook will have it ready for you.'

Mathew started guiltily.

'Goodnight, John. I'll see you in the morning.'

Elizabeth stood on tiptoe and gently brushed her lips over his cheek. 'I'll try to be awake before you go.' She lifted the latch and slipped quietly through the doorway.

# -78-

'Slept like a log.' John grinned at Mathew. 'What about you?'

'Like the dead,' Mathew concurred. The smell of smoked ham and frying eggs made his mouth water.

'So what do you think of Elizabeth?'

Mathew choked on his coffee. John watched him with lion's eyes. Above his beard his eyes glittered, a cat with a mouse, playfully tapping a response from its catch, though not so hard as to kill the conversation.

'I believe she teaches?'

'And what sort of answer would that be?' The grin hardened.

'I meant to say that your daughter is very bright.' Mathew floundered. 'I'm sure you must be very proud, John.'

The situation tightened and John let him squirm.

'That's the best you can do then?'

'Has Rhodes gone?'

'Yes. Now try again, laddie. What do you think of Elizabeth?'

'Very pretty.' Mathew nodded, unsure of what Elizabeth's father wanted to hear. Desperate for better words he righted the ship. 'Exceptionally beautiful is what I meant to say, not pretty – beautiful as well as being bright. I find that very attractive, John – I mean, from a man's point of view.'

'You approve, is what you're trying to say?'

'Very much, John, you must be very proud.'

'You've already said that.'

'Yes,' croaked Mathew, 'stupid of me. I like her, John. Truth is, I think she's stunning.'

'That's better.' He dropped his enamel mug in the sink. His beard stopped trembling; the bees had settled. 'Now let's have some breakfast and get us some mining talk in before Elizabeth puts the mockers on it.'

John's cook had covered the garden table with a cloth of white linen, in the midst of the household's best cutlery he had arranged his silver condiments and a bowl of fresh flowers cut from the garden whilst still covered in dew from that last night's watering. John took his place at the table's head and looked to the kitchen window for cook to bring out breakfast.

Though disappointed that Rhodes had left early, Mubiki was still dressed in his best whites, his smile, like the sunlight, spread across a face that only a mother would reflect upon with kindness. He stopped alongside Mathew's chair.

'Bacon eggs, sir?'

'Most definitely, thank you, Mubiki.' Mixed with the

aroma of flowers and open gardens, the sight and smell of hot bacon flooded his mouth.

'So, did you give in to our leader's demands?' John asked him.

Mathew shook his head and sliced off a square of bacon. 'Rhodes was after a fifty one percent share of the Empress.'

'Why am I not surprised, worst thing is, the egotistical old buzzard believes that everything under the ground is his by default.' He slashed his egg and stabbed a slice of warm bread at the yolk. 'Some sort of God-given right.'

Elizabeth came out from the kitchen and instantly, Mubiki was there at her side.

'How is little missy this morning?'

'Still tired but no doubt that will pass, thank you, Mubiki.'

'You will please sit here next to your father.' He drew out her chair and it was not impossible to see that Elizabeth had quickly become his favourite.

Mathew caught himself staring. Her skin was perfect; that same creamy hue as the flowers in front of him. At last he managed to speak.

'Good morning, Elizabeth.'

She nodded her head to him; her eyes sparkled. 'How was your night by the fire?'

'Comfortable enough.' Mathew smiled.

'When will you start tunnelling for the reef?' John cut in. Mathew was forced to divert his attentions away from Elizabeth.

'As soon as I get back. My hammer boys should have finished drilling the first set of holes by then.'

'What are they using?'

'Four-foot jumper steels.'

'You're timing the shots, of course?'

345

'Different lengths of fuse,' Mathew concurred. 'Cut out the middle first, then the easers and the lifters or she won't break cleanly.'

'Or she won't break at all,' John added.

Elizabeth drummed her fingertips at the table. John threw up his arms in mock surrender.

'Sorry, my sweetheart, no more talk of mines.' He swung the conversation on to a different tack. 'I was thinking last night, what do you say to us riding out to the Goddard place?'

Elizabeth looked to Mathew. 'Would you mind?'

'Not in the least, my mother would enjoy the change of company.'

'When?' Elizabeth asked and concentrated all of her persuasive powers on her father. John shrugged his shoulders, there would be nothing gained by his arguing.

'Makes no difference. Whenever its suits you, my sweetheart.'

'Today,' Elizabeth got in first, 'after lunch. I've rested long enough; we can make the journey on horseback, no more carriages and bumpy roads. I'll see more of my adopted countryside from the saddle.'

## -79-

By mid-afternoon, the Dickens Mine was little more than a smear on the skyline. Wherever possible, Mathew led them in a straight line for the homestead, ignoring tracks and wagon trails that criss-crossed valleys and open grasslands. He searched out things that more than once, Elizabeth was made to stand in awe of. Towering trees, as the masts of tall ships reached far above the forest canopy, rigged with leafy topsails. In their hundreds, colonies of weaver birds hung from gourd-shaped nests – the cock birds deeply masked in black, but yellow as native gold from throat to feet.

Where the valleys were more secluded, Mathew picked the interests out for her – the flash of kudu running for high ground, small family groups, kept apart from other species by a natural preference to stand with those of their own kind. At that distance the different herd colours blended naturally with their surroundings, overlapping forest hues with those dark, chocolate browns of the majestic sable antelope and softer fawns of the magnificent eland bull with his harem of sleek cows. They rode past hills and rocky defiles formed of quartz and banded ironstone, the soils around them deep lakes of red and orange, the colour of Indian spice and saffron from the market stalls of Port Natal.

'We had best be getting a move on,' said John. 'Another hour and we'll be riding in the dark.'

At last light, Mathew picked out the glow of hurricane lamps and that familiar, grey wisp of chimney smoke. Elizabeth stood tall in the stirrups and marvelled at the serenity of it all. As a woman, suddenly she yearned for the warmth of log fires, the thrill of hearing a child's voice and the aroma of her own kitchen – the strong chest of a man to lean against when the nights were cold.

Barred from Catherine's kitchen, John and Mathew leant against the paddock fence, the faint afterglow of sunset still that arc of paler sky above the horizon.

'Tomorrow morning,' said Mathew, 'Elizabeth has asked me to show her the ruins at Zimbabwe.'

'The ruins are ten miles out from here?' John frowned at what was being asked of him. 'You would have to stay the night?'

Mathew ignored the implication. 'Theodore Bent and his wife are still excavating part of the main enclosure. They were friends with my father; we would stay at their camp.'

John relaxed, Bent's wife was a diehard puritan, Elizabeth would be adequately watched over. Mathew got in quickly; still wielding the upper hand he dangled the carrot.

'I've arranged for Mhlangana to show you the mill site and proposed start of our first adit. Let me know what you think, John. I would welcome the opinion of an experienced mining man such as yourself.'

John still wasn't convinced. 'One night?'

'One night,' said Mathew.

'No funny business?' He scowled through the dark.

'You have my word on it.'

*

They left at first light. Elizabeth got up whilst it was still dark and with Catherine's help, packed a hamper with food and drink enough for her expedition. Dressed in breeches, shirt and soft *veldschoen*, Elizabeth was every inch the epitome of the frontierswoman. John came out from the homestead to see them off. The sky was clear, but in the east a skirt of pink cloud sat as snow to the hilltops. He gave Elizabeth a leg-up.

'Make sure you're back for tomorrow night. Watch for a change in the weather, the rains may well come early.'

Elizabeth leant from the saddle and kissed her father on the forehead.

'You worry too much, pater.' She patted her saddlebag. 'Taking my pencils and paints – I have it on good authority that now is a good time as any for capturing a likeness of the flowering aloe.'

'Give my love to Theodore and Mabel,' said Catherine. 'Tell them I insist on their calling in when they come back to Victoria.'

John insisted on watching them ride out, only when they were hidden by the forest did he follow Catherine inside.

Mathew glanced over his shoulder, half expecting to see John Dickens following on.

'You're father's convinced we're up to no good,' said Mathew.

'He means well,' replied Elizabeth. 'If Saint Peter himself were here I'm sure he would get the same treatment.'

She breathed in the fresh air, her smile perpetual and her artist's eye was quick to catch the shapes and colours of anything that flowered. The pathway led from thick forest to open parklands. In the low sunlight the grasses were tipped carnation pink and as the sun rose higher, the sky took on that deep, azure blue of a tropical ocean. Mathew let her ride in front, alongside his fascination with the Empress Deep, now there was a new and more exciting object of pursuit – more elusive, harder to tame than a mere place beneath the ground and yet to look upon Elizabeth as his conquest would not have rung true. The woman riding in front of him was much more.

# -81-

Mathew caught a first glimpse of the ruined city some two hours after leaving home. Those same walls he had looked down on whilst in the company of his father, again reared as fearsome stone sentinels from their cowl of ancient trees.

'Do you see them?' he asked Elizabeth, but she merely screwed her eyes at the sunlight and peered myopically about the horizon.

'Not sure what I'm supposed to be looking for, Mathew?'

'Stone walls, but look carefully, they're badly overgrown.'

Elizabeth cupped her hands against the glare.

'I'm not sure...'

'Use this,' said Mathew and extended the brass barrels of his telescope. His skin prickled with déjà vu, the moment seemingly identical to that of a year ago, almost to the day.

'My God, Mathew! They're enormous. How did they do that?'

'Don't know. If you're lucky enough, Bent and his wife may shed some light on what you're asking. From what my mother tells me, either one of them will quite willingly talk all night on the subject.'

In Africa, nature moves with swift determination, her twilights brief. Mathew and Elizabeth sat together at the fireside and watched the sun go down; fixed to the edge of the world for just a minute, then it was gone. No one spoke, for the moment they were content to watch the darkness fold about the firelight, black and thick with the scent of opening night flowers.

Theodore Bent broke the silence and smiled across the fire at Elizabeth.

'Mathew tells me you're an accomplished painter of fine pictures?'

'Pictures, yes,' said Elizabeth, 'though cataloguing my work as fine could by some be seen as fanciful, Mister Bent.'

'And what would be the subject of your brushwork?'

'Flowers, mainly; the odd landscape if I'm feeling adventurous.'

Theodore leant back in his chair. Dressed in breeches and open-neck shirt he struggled to cope with the weariness that often plagued him; his skin sallow from the debilitating effects of a recent fever. Yet above a well-trimmed beard his smile was pleasantly affable and his eyes sparkled from the firelight.

'Mabel dabbles a bit, don't you darling wife?'

'As and when the mood strikes, my darling husband, though if my brushes and pencils fail me, you know full well I am apt to take solace from other means.'

'My wife refers to her camera, and why not? The results of her efforts have astounded many a publishing house. Her pictures are all top drawer and don't let anyone try to convince you otherwise.'

Bent's wife stood up from the table, Elizabeth noted that she had adapted herself well to a life in the veld. Copying her husband's sensibility she had dressed herself in breeches and gaiters, topped by a rather long and robust looking tunic. About her neck she wore an eyeglass, on its length of braided twine, like the all-seeing eye it swung around and glinted at Mathew.

'You have been here before, Mathew?'

'A year ago, with my father,' said Mathew, 'but most of the ruins were choked with undergrowth.'

'And your commissioner for mines – a Mister Vigers? He related for us the unfortunate incident of your fracas with treasure hunters?'

Mathew nodded his head. Returning to the ruins had already brought back painful memories.

'A couple of wastrels, we took what gold they had and handed it over to Rhodes' Ancient Ruins Syndicate.'

'And the syndicate has indeed commented on your honesty,' Mabel commended.

Theodore Bent poured himself a small measure of brandy and then settled back in his camp chair before dipping back into the conversation.

'Forgive our intrusion, Mathew, but there are things I feel I must ask of you.'

'Then ask away,' Mathew invited.

'The black girl,' said Bent, 'what happened to her?'

'How do you know about the girl?'

'Stories, rumours,' Bent explained. 'There's many a man in Fort Victoria who, for the price of a drink, will spill up his life's history.'

'The fossickers raped her. We happened to be on hand at the time.'

'The word is you saved her life?' Bent persisted.

'I would say so,' said Mathew, 'but why the interest in a common native girl?'

Like those of a hunting spider caught in the lamplight, Bent's eyes glittered.

'Not so much the girl, Mathew, as in what she stands for.'

'I don't understand?' said Mathew, 'she's just a girl.'

Bent's wife shifted forwards in her chair, her interest obsessive.

'The girl is a seer, Mathew. The local people call her the *Muroyi*; the girl is a witch.'

'Mutiswa.' Mathew remembered the girl's name. 'She was young, perhaps a little strange though under the circumstances, understandable.'

Bent drained his glass and lit a small cheroot from the lamp glass. His demeanour had changed; his mood agitated by Mathew's failure to grasp the importance of their discussion.

'She had a child.'

'You have spoken to her?' said Mathew.

Bent shook his head. 'A small village, east of the ruins, the headman works for me. He swears she poisoned her own baby a few days after the infant was born.'

Mathew felt his gorge rise. 'Why in God's name would she poison her own child?'

'Apparently, one of your Irish fossicker friends was the father.'

Mathew looked away. 'Have you seen her?'

'I have not,' said Bent, 'but she's here. Mabel caught a glimpse of her, less than a week ago, no longer.'

'From the hill fortress.' Mabel related the event. 'I was sketching a view of the valley when I saw her, but only for a moment before she disappeared. She appeared to be naked. More like a wild animal than a girl.'

Bent excused himself from the table. 'Humour our reasoning, Mathew, there's more to this than you might suspect. I have something I would like you to see.'

They waited in silence for Bent's return to the fireside. Small sounds drifted out from the forest and at odds with them, men's laughter from a temporary labour compound further around the hillside.

'The headman brought this for me, only a few days ago.'

Composed of natural stone it had been broken away as a single piece. Mathew held it to the firelight. It was the size and thickness of a child's scribbling slate, one side rough and misshapen from it having been prised free of the rock face; the other, smooth, seemingly polished. Bent gave Mathew time to appreciate the importance of what he was holding.

'Throughout my travels in Africa and the Aegean Archipelago, I have never witnessed anything that has proven more fascinating,' Bent reached out, 'more so here, where the colours have been overlaid with gold.'

On Mathew examining the artefact, Bent's wife was quick to pick up on his agitation.

'You behave as if you have seen it before?'

'Similar,' Mathew lied, 'in books on ancient Egypt, but nothing like this.'

As part of an ancient mural, the colours were riotously interwoven; gold upon silver and deep-running tinctures of blue and emerald green. But it was the gold that demanded his attention. Laid to tiny grooves and eyelets in the granite the raw gold came alive in the firelight, as though it had within that very moment been let from the smelter's crucible. Bent took it back from him and set it down on the table.

'That is why,' Theodore emphasised his interest in the stone, 'we are keen to find out more about the girl. Neither Mabel nor myself are of any doubt as to where she acquired it.'

'Somewhere here, from amongst these ruins.' Elizabeth offered and as if on cue, eerie light from the full moon flooded across the valley.

## -83-

Whilst the Bents still slept, Elizabeth prepared a breakfast of bread and strawberry conserve for her and Mathew. They sat where the view was unobscured and looked down across a stretch of open grassland to the ruined city of Zimbabwe. The uneven feature, Theodore Bent had referred to as the Hill Fortress now stood out against the sunrise, a bastion fashioned of living rock, castellated ramparts built from hand-hewn granite which, by design, linked together boulders that were all of a thousand tons and more. As the sun rose, the entire surface of the granite citadel blistered with mauves and pinks.

'First, the temple as Theodore calls it.' Elizabeth bubbled over with excitement. 'Then the Fortress thingamajig on top of the kopje. We could take lunch up there, overlooking the valley?'

'What about Mabel's witch?' Mathew reminded her.

'Curses and spells,' mused Elizabeth, 'mumbo-jumbo my father calls it. Our Mister Bent has spent too much time in bed with the fever.'

By mid-morning they had reached the extremity of the ancient city. Mathew off-saddled both horses and left them haltered in the shadow of the temple wall. From his saddle bag he took out the Colt six-shooter and pushed it inside his belt.

Where the Bents had started their study of the inner temple, the ground had been partially cleared of undergrowth, the entrance to ancient walkways now opened to dark corridors, lined at either hand with thick walls of hewn stone. Multi-coloured lizards watched from high up on the parapets, crouched to patches of sunlight they waited for the natural warmth to raise their body temperature high enough for them to hunt. Elizabeth shivered from walking in perpetual shadow.

'It's so very cold in here, like an English graveyard.'

The granite blocks were cold to the touch, the air about them musty and dank; the smells of old cellar walls. Gradually, the passageway closed in on them, the vines and fallen trees now thick as tropical forest.

'That's as far as we go,' said Mathew, 'it would take ten men a week to clear it.'

They turned back. Mathew retraced his steps for the way out, once outside they soaked up the sunlight. Elizabeth studied the curvature and height of the outer wall.

'Who was it that found this place?'

'An explorer called Adam Renders,' Mathew told her, 'stumbled across the ruins whilst out hunting, some twenty or so years ago.'

'I will sketch the ruins as a whole from up there.' Elizabeth pointed out the hill fortress. 'Mable assured me that the way to the top has been well cleared of rubbish and there is definite access to the first enclosure.' She slung her satchel of artist's paraphernalia across her shoulders and nodded to Mathew. 'Lead the way, kind sir. Close to the stream is where Mabel said we will find the entrance to her witch's enclave.'

*

For almost an hour they scrambled upwards from the valley floor and though the ancient passageway had at some stage been opened up, still there were vines and tangled roots of wild fig; thickly woven together over the passing of many centuries. As the ancient builders had done with the temple walls, blocks of grey granite had been used to shield the way against the invader's spear and arrow. Built as thick redoubts between the boulders, the walls were stronger than any Mathew had ever seen.

'The stone has been shaped,' he pointed out for Elizabeth, 'the blocks sit perfectly, one upon the other – no space between them wide enough even to take the thickness of a knife blade.'

Some forty feet below the summit, as a glacier might shed its ice, so had the hillside relinquished its hold on granite the size and bulk of twenty fully laden wagons. Where the rock had split, the ancients had laid their granite steps. Keyed into the earth, the steps led upwards at a steep angle, the granite buttresses at either side only wide enough apart for those walking in single file to pass between them. Mathew imagined how a small force of men might for many days, have held their aggressors at bay.

Elizabeth was first to reach a gateway in the hilltop fortress wall, in the winking of an eye she was away between the stone portals.

Mathew caught up with her at the edge of a small

plateau-like enclosure and already, Elizabeth had taken out her sketching pad and box of graphite pencils. Mathew stood just slightly to the side and watched her select the tools she needed and then set them out in orderly formation, using blocks of tumbled stone as her tables. Elizabeth was keenly aware of his interest.

'Firstly, I shall make a light sketch of the valley's outline and natural features.' She selected a pencil from her rosewood box; the lid ornately decorated with delicate mother of pearl marquetry. 'You are more than welcome to stand closer, Mathew Goddard.'

Mathew stepped forward; perhaps a little closer to Elizabeth's side than was necessary for him to watch her work. With that natural skill of the gifted artist, Elizabeth's hand, small and slender-fingered, seemed to float above the paper.

'The shaded areas will prove the hardest to copy, the colours are more subtle.' Her pencil moved upwards. 'The skyline is always the easiest – less detail because of the greater distance.'

Mathew smelled her cologne, the fresh glow of her perspiration, warm and musky from the climb.

'The trees along the temple's east wall...'

'What of them?' Elizabeth interrupted. Not waiting for him to finish speaking she laid down her pencil and paper. She turned and faced him, her forehead barely reaching his chin. 'I have known you only three days, Mathew Goddard and yet the thought of not being with you fills me with trepidation.' Elizabeth closed her eyes and tilted her face for him to reach. 'I insist that you kiss me.' She parted her lips for him and to Mathew her breath was the morning's sweetened zephyr upon his mouth.

Her demands had caught him unawares; she poised there,

waiting for him. When nothing happened, Elizabeth opened one eye, glared up at his sunburned face and then broke away. Back with her pencils and sketch pad she made a hurried pretence of proportioning her copy of the landscape.

'That I obviously hold no attraction for you I find confusing as well as an embarrassment. I thought we both shared the same sentiment?'

Mathew reached out and touched her cheek.

'Why would I not want to kiss you?' He placed both hands on her shoulders; at first she stood rigid, still with her back to him. Gently he turned her around. Caught in direct sunlight his eyes were brilliant green, yet flecked with grey – moss and granite brought to life by recent rain. Lightly his mouth touched hers. Again her eyes closed and as those of a child's doll her arms hung limp at her sides. At the extreme edge of his vision, Mathew caught a first tiny glimmer of movement.

'Stay very still,' he whispered to Elizabeth, 'we're being spied upon.' Slowly, he dropped his hand to the Colt at his belt. 'Open your eyes.' Elizabeth obeyed him.

'Where are they?'

'To your right hand, but do not turn your head. Stay focused on my face.'

Elizabeth kept her composure.

'Don't be alarmed when I move,' said Mathew. She acknowledged him with her eyes.

Mathew cocked his pistol and turned swiftly on his heels, bringing the Colt to bear on the target as he did so.

Like a black leopard, Mutiswa had used thick intertwined limbs of a strangler fig to conceal her torso. Her face was unchanged, her gaze bright but challenging as if it were she not Mathew who had the upper hand. Mathew guessed that she had purposely moved to alert him of her presence.

'Once, I saved you,' he spoke candidly and in her own language, 'and yet now you hide from me? Step into the sunlight, or like the mouse that cowers behind the grain bin, does Mutiswa still not trust me with her life?'

Mutiswa stepped out from the shadows; naked, apart from rows of coloured beadwork about the hourglass of her waist. She stood fractionally taller than Elizabeth, sleek as the wild otter and in that full-on angle of sunlight she was the soft brown earth and darkest of winter nights. When she spoke her lips were supple, her teeth, unblemished and perfectly matched – startlingly white. She stopped in front of Mathew; her breasts full and rounded and at the juncture of her legs her body hair grew thick and black as a raven's wings. Above the arching moons of her cheeks her eyes were barely more than half open; the pupils staring and dilated, for she had been taking readily of the hemp pipe.

'Your father, why is he not with you?'

'My father is dead,' Mathew told her. 'He fought against the Matabele at Bembesi and Shangani.'

'Then he died as a warrior; a son cannot wish for a more fitting end.' She glanced at Elizabeth. 'Why are you here with your woman?'

'Like the Bushman,' said Mathew, 'she makes a shadow of what is real. My woman creates a likeness of your valley.'

'Does your woman speak the language of the Makalanga?' Again Mutiswa turned her gaze on Elizabeth, openly she studied the white woman's clothing, her pale skin and the way she had tied back her hair with blue ribbon. Unable to make sense of what was being said, Elizabeth stood defensively to Mathew's shoulder. There was a strange diffidence about the girl, an aura of mystery edged with danger; veiled threats that Elizabeth could not fathom.

Mathew shook his head. 'She does not understand.'

'Your woman is beautiful.' Mutiswa held up one finger. 'She will give you but one child, a son. He will be strong like his father.' Mathew tried to speak but she silenced him. 'There is another, an Induna – a warrior; kin to those your father fought against at the river you call Shangani. As a brother, he stands at your side.' Mutiswa moved to the edge of the outer wall and as lightly as the klipspringer she climbed to its highest point. 'You coming here to the ruins of Simbao was not through chance, white man. Tell your Induna all these things that I say. There is a child; a boy child, but not by his woman and not through the seed of his own doing. The boy will be the last born of a king. Your Induna has been chosen to take up the child's mother as his second wife, the boy shall be raised as the Induna's own son.' She saw confusion swirl as mist in Mathew's eyes. 'All these things are not for you to understand. Tell the Induna the spirit of his king; the one who drives like the wind, the stabber of skies has spoken this truth through me – I am the *Muroyi*.'

## -84-

Five miles out from the ruined city, Elizabeth kneed her horse alongside Mathew's and turned up her collar against a tailing wind. To the front the sky was still that powder blue of a hot afternoon, to the rear, black clouds were chasing westwards.

'My father was right. We aren't going to make it. The storm will be up with us before we reach the halfway mark.'

'About a mile up ahead,' said Mathew, 'a small kopje – there might well be shelter if we're lucky enough to reach it in time.'

They picked up the pace, but relentlessly the storm caught up. As a grey and heavy curtain it closed above them and shut out the sunlight. Within minutes, both of them were soaked through to the skin.

'Make for the rocks!' Mathew was forced to shout. Instead of easing, the storm strengthened, its intent now that of a full-blown tropical monsoon.

'Behind those trees.' Elizabeth pointed them out for Mathew. 'I think I see a place where we can shelter.'

The granite had formed as a natural overhang and stood side-on to the driving rain. They rode their horses beneath it and the storm with its spiteful wind was left alone outside.

They off-saddled and stood together to watch the rain; still it came out of the east, dark as ocean currents running before the wind. Mathew looked around him, water dripped from his nose and he shivered from the chill.

'I'll see if I can make us a fire, by the time this rain stops we could have our clothes dry.'

Elizabeth helped him gather wood and dry grass from where it had collected in windrows against the granite. Where roots had found a way though fissures in the roof there were tendrils of flimsy, bearded moss. They gathered enough to put to Elizabeth's kindling and from his saddlebag, Mathew took out a wallet of waxed Vestas. The first match fluttered weakly and then went out.

'One left,' he looked up at Elizabeth, mildly amused by their plight, then struck the last match against the sidewall and cupped his hand about the flame. Slowly, the flame strengthened and Mathew lifted open the tinder to form a tiny cavern at the heart of their woodpile. Gently, he inserted the match. Like some hesitant child the flame held back, then, as though inspired by a sudden change of heart, it started to feed.

Elizabeth held her breath; like Mathew she was shivering cold from the dank weight of her wet clothes.

'Please take,' she whispered, 'don't let it go out, Mathew. Oh please, please take.' She willed the flame to thrive on the tinder.

At first there was little more than wisps of smoke, but the tiny flame took hold and from the fire's heart it spread quickly, blooming as yellow petals amongst the kindling.

'Yes!' whooped Elizabeth and visibly shook with excitement. 'I'll bring some more wood. Keep it going, Mathew. Whatever happens, don't let it go out.'

They fed the fire until the flames reached waist high. Mathew stripped off his shirt and held it up for the heat to suck out the rain. Elizabeth stood as close as she dared – steam rose up from her shirt and breeches.

'Boots and stockings.' She realised. Without hesitation she unfastened her laces and pulled off her footwear, edging her boots in close to the flames. Mathew draped his shirt on the wood pile and crossed to where his horse grazed on the short grass near to the cave's entrance. Behind the saddle, rolled in an old oilskin he found his blanket.

'Raise your arms above your head,' he told Elizabeth. He wrapped the blanket around her and waited for her to take up the loose end. 'Tuck it in tight.' She folded in the

363

corner. 'Now take off your breeches and lay them in close to the fire'

'You want me to undress?'

'Either that or catch pneumonia,' Mathew countered.

'Turn your back.' Elizabeth glowered at him. 'Anything less than an honourable end to this next hour, Mathew Goddard and my father will shoot you.' She screwed her face at him. 'I said look away.'

He did as he was told. Outside, the storm lashed the forest with rain and hail stones, some were half the size of a man's fist and cracked like small- bore pistol shots when they burst against the hillside.

'You can turn around now, Mathew.'

Stroked by the sudden exposure to heat, her skin flushed with gooseflesh. Light from the fire wrapped about her nakedness.

'I thought...'

'I lied,' said Elizabeth, 'but I had to be sure.' She smiled at him then went on speaking quickly. 'And now I am. Since my first day in Victoria, deep inside I have known that I love you; that it is you I wish to live out my life with.' She was trembling; the dove looked upon by the eagle. There was fear in her eyes, that of a young woman unsure of what was happening.

'There's no need for this...'

'There is every need,' said Elizabeth and brushed aside her final chance of escape. She had laid the blanket on the ground, close enough to the fire for them to feel its warmth. 'What you see is what I am, Mathew. I have nothing to hide from you.' She held out her hand for him. 'Nor have I been with a man before, you shall be the first and God willing we both live for another twenty years, you shall be the last and only one, Mathew Goddard.'

364

They lay in each other's arms, with only the sound of thunder to cover their loving.

There was the moaning of the wind and the sharp crack of the lightning bolt; the tearing open of secret places and from the flooding of rain to the forest stream, the loud cry of the waterfall. There was a mingling of new life, a conjoining of sky and fertile earth, a brief shout to the wind and that final, desperate clinging together before begrudgingly, they let the tempest leave them.

They stayed together on the blanket until the storm ended. With the fury gone, the rain clouds shuffled away as old men, the occasional groan of thunder following them over the horizon.

## -85-

Mathew helped Elizabeth into the saddle. 'Friday,' he promised, 'I'll be there before midday.'

Elizabeth leant away from her horse and kissed him on the cheek.

'I'll be waiting, Mathew Goddard, don't you dare forget.' With radiance, she smiled down at him. 'Who can tell? Perhaps it will rain again.'

'With luck,' Mathew grinned and then looked to her father. 'Thank you for the advice, sir. We can discuss the rest of the mill's layout on Friday.' Again, Elizabeth leant down to him. 'Marry me,' she whispered, 'you have until Friday to work out your proposal.'

John Dickens tipped his hat to Catherine; 'Come on out to the mine whenever you feel like someone to talk to. Our guest cottage will be finished by the end of next week. It's there for as long as you want, Catherine.'

'Thank you, John,' she turned and smiled at Elizabeth, 'my thanks to the both of you for taking the time to visit. There's fresh lemonade in your bag, enough to see you home. Mathew would willingly ride part way with you, if you are unsure of the road'

John shook his head. 'No need.' He turned his attention to Mathew. 'Remember what I told you, young feller; once you've poured the concrete, keep her wet – she sets stronger under water.'

'I'll remember that,' said Mathew.

When Elizabeth reached the forest's edge, she turned and looked back. Mathew was still standing where she had left him; alongside Catherine he looked so tall. Elizabeth waved her hat above her head and then followed her father into the forest.

# -86-

With the overburden cleared, Mathew took his time examining what lay beneath. The underlying rock was banded ironstone, harder than the pillars of hell and when struck with a four pound hammer it would ring as solidly as the metal it had given its name to.

From the steep angle of the hillside, Mathew estimated the distance they would need to tunnel before hitting the reef.

'Twenty paces in, maybe thirty before we reach the gold.'

Mhlangana squared his shoulders and waved his gang of

miners up to the face. Each man carried with him a hammer and drill steel. With a piece of soapstone, Mhlangana marked the rock with a network of white crosses; the drill pattern for the Empress Deep's first blast.

Mathew threw off his shirt and took up the hammer and steel of the closest miner.

'I will drill the first hole.' He cocked his head at Mhlangana. 'If you were not already an old man, I would gladly have wagered your month's earnings against you finishing before me.'

'And were you strong enough, white man, I would gladly cover your wager - tenfold.' Mhlangana looked to one of his drilling crew and commandeered his tools. Theatrically he raised his hammer to the sky and he turned to Mathew. 'Let the boy step aside for the better man, *muRungu*.' He pushed his way through to the rock face; already the taste of victory was honey-sweet on his tongue. Both men picked a mark furthest from the centre.

'No changing of your drill steel before the halfway mark or your opponent wins,' warned Mathew.

Mhlangana nodded his head. 'When you are ready, white man.'

As tolling bells the hammer blows carried for five miles along the valley. Of the two men, neither paused to take in water, nor did they rest the arm that swung the hammer. Side by side they worked their steels deeper inside the rock, with each strike, bright halos of sweat leapt from their forehead. Still they took no respite and the drill steels sang their songs to the mountain. Each new blow was preceded by a sharp twist to the drill, setting the hardened tip at a fresh angle for it to break new rock.

At the same time, almost to the second, both hammers fell silent. Both men slumped down, their backs to the ironstone. Mathew dropped his hammer and openly marvelled at the ruined pads of his right hand.

'You must have lucked to a sharper drill,' Mathew chided.

'And yours was the bigger hammer,' Mhlangana countered playfully. '*Rova i nyundo*!' He shouted his crew forwards to the rock face. 'Use your steel, *murume*! I give you ten days to reach the lair of the snake.'

'And a bonus of ten shillings for nine,' Mathew promised, and like brothers they walked away from the rock, leaving behind space enough for the miners to swing their hammers.

*

# IV

# RHODESIA, 1979

# -1-

Moulded to the hillside, the farmhouse gardens were luxuriant emerald islands. Bougainvillea – scarlet, purple and brilliant white enclosed a sparkling swimming pool. Rainmaker sprays flicked yard-long crystal streams over perfect lawns – never missing a beat. A red ball and pedigree Doberman bounced between freshly laid out flowerbeds and from deep inside the house the nostalgic rhythm of sixties pop music found its way through open patio doors. The air smelled of wet grass, turned earth and sunshine.

Mike Rennie smiled at his luck. His wife, Julie, stretched out leopard-like in the late afternoon sun; fourteen years of marriage and two pregnancies had hardly touched her. Long legs, a midriff slim and flat as the back of his hand, two daughters blonde and pretty like their mother, lovingly precocious. Growing coffee in Rhodesia's eastern districts had left him contentedly wealthy. He had it all.

'How's your drink?'

Julie curled her toes against the bottom edge of her lounger and arched her back.

'Empty. But I think a swim first, I need to cool down.'

'Where are the kids?'

'In their room. More than likely fallen asleep listening to tapes.'

Mike went through to the kitchen, he could see Julie from the window; his mind raced. She knew he was watching. She rubbed herself with tanning oil – legs splayed either side of her lounger. Within reach, her 9mm Browning, loaded with Cor-Bon, Parabellum hollow points; cocked, but with the safety catch engaged.

'Gin and lime, Michael.' She capped the oil and dropped the bottle on the grass. 'Look in on the kids.'

'Ice, or without?'

'Ice,' said Julie, 'right to the top.'

Anticipation, not the ice made his hands tremble.

The fields were empty. Farm labourers had drawn their wages and gone back home to willing women and filled beer pots. The sky was Africa-blue from one side to the other. Saturday afternoon; the murmur of a swimming pool pump and Roy Orbison's falsetto the only sounds. Security fencing – twelve feet high diamond mesh surrounded the gardens. Powerful halogen lamps faced outwards, the dark would switch them on. Intruders would be caught in a fifty yard corridor of white light, gunned down before they reached the house perimeter.

Julie swung her legs clear of the lounger. Mike was still watching her and she smiled at his predictability. She cat-walked to the pool and at the deep end, dropped her bikini top into the water. It drifted towards the bottom – a fluorescent orange fish in the sunlight. The Doberman lost interest in the red ball and now sat with its ears pricked – distracted, watching the hillside. To the rear of the house long shadows leant through the fence. Two more hours and the sun would be gone – the hillside left as a black silhouette – extreme danger the unwanted bedfellow. Julie had learned to live alongside it. Guns, common accessories – claymore mines, powerful enough to cut a dozen men in half just beyond the perimeter fence – armed and ready to fire. The place was a fortress.

'Get on over here, Michael Rennie.'

He left their drinks on the grass. Julie stood with her hands on her hips, breathing in sunlit air – her eyes closed – heart racing – legs slightly apart.

'The kids?' Mike reminded her. His heart pounded. Her skin was porcelain white where the sun hadn't reached. 'They might wake up?'

'They won't. What about the gates?'

'Chained and locked.'

The water was warm. They clung to one another. Pretty Woman thumped in the background. Rainmaker spray rattled across the side of their Datsun pick-up. Julie fastened her legs around Mike's waist; guiding, pushing and as they both cried out from the violence of their love making a frenzied curtain of wild water ripped through the pool's surface.

# -2-

For two days Rex Khumalo held his men in check, the attack had to be initiated at exactly the right moment. Close to him, hidden by low scrub, five battle-hardened veterans looked down on the killing ground, their expressions dispassionate, the atrocities they were about to commit looked upon as little more than incidental – a process of cleansing. Killing the farmer and his family would send a clear message to every white settler in the area. The more violent and repulsive the attack, the more women would demand the safety of the city lights. The fertile valley would be left unused; laid open to control by droves of ZANLA insurgents. Pursuing soldiers would be driven almost to the point of insanity by the carnage. It would impair their judgement; blinded by rage, they would make mistakes.

Rex concentrated on the woman. What had taken her years to build was about to be destroyed in mere seconds. The awareness of her own mortality would be furthest from her thoughts, yet it was staring her in the face. The end of her man's life was so very close. For a brief moment Rex's mind flew back to a time before his life had changed. That fateful night. The father he had never known, dead in his arms – the dark walls of a ruined city – the diseased face of some ancient crone. '*Bayete*! *Son of Africa*.' Her voice still keened inside his head.

'Let the woman live.' Rex tapped the shoulder of the man next to him. A single burst from a Russian-built RPD tore into the pool's surface and threw it skywards. Close to the fence the Doberman yelped, but only once.

-3-

'Good evening, Mrs Rennie.'

'My babies?' Julie whimpered, but not in touch with what she was saying.

Rex smiled at her – the way a hyena would smile at a beleaguered buffalo calf, his eyes were cold merciless things in the shadow below his brow. For a moment, Rex saw the tiniest flicker of hope in her eyes. He found himself titillated and strangely aroused by her antics – a pathetic fluttering of wings before the final flimsy threads of her mind parted and left her floundering, somewhere between reason and insanity. He crouched at the pool's edge and raised her chin with the barrel of his rifle. Blood from her husband's corpse darkened the deep end. Julie stood up. The water barely reached to her waist. Slender as a girl, painted gold by late sunlight. Jewels of bright blood clung to her cheek.

'We will find them, Mrs Rennie, but first we must take care of you.'

He shook a cigarette from a packet in his breast pocket; a match spluttered, a bright spear in the half light and he lowered the flame to within inches of Julie's eyes. There was no reaction. Her pupils were dilated and unchanging. Rex had seen the phenomenon before in the field hospitals of Mapai and Kasala, it was the affliction of the dying and the severely traumatised. Men who had seen their comrades split in two by mortar fire or roasted alive by the ravaging flames of napalm dropped from Rhodesian Air Force strike aircraft.

Without looking up he dropped the match. On his signal, his men came forward and stood expectantly at the pool's edge.

'Do what you will with her,' Rex told them. 'Search the house for her litter.'

-4-

Captain Lee Goddard scanned the message pad.

'When did this come in?'

'A few minutes ago, sir. The Major told me to bring it straight to you.'

'No lights at the Rennies' place?'

He looked up at the Corporal. 'That's it, nothing more?'

'Nothing, sir. No response to our radio signal either, the phones are useless. All the landlines to that area have been down for weeks. Their neighbour came through on the radio, barely heard him before we lost comms.'

'Name?'

'Bowker, sir. Said he heard gunfire.'

Lee recalled his first visit to the Bowker's farmhouse. A traditional wood under corrugated iron homestead some six miles east of the Rennies' coffee plantation. The old man and his wife, Marietta, though still fit enough to manage their farm were both into their nineties; a pair of diehard Afrikaner settlers – both born out of lumbering trek wagons. Fighters – rifle in one hand and Bible in the other. Undeterred by the escalation of the war, the Bowkers had dug in their heels. Either way, live or die they were staying.

'Sir?'

'Try them again. Every five minutes for the next half hour then get back to me. Go through the relay station at Selinda. Tell my men to draw three days rations and be ready for uplifting at first light.' The Corporal left at the double.

Rhodesia had run out of time and Lee knew it. The Rennies, the Bowkers – to the rest of the world none of these people mattered. A year at the outside and the valley would be empty, save for shattered dreams and feral dogs. He looked at his watch; dawn was still six hours away, going in now would be suicidal. The Thrasher operational area had seen an upsurge of ZANLA fighters carrying SAM 7's. An Alouette helicopter flogging around in the moonlight would make for an easy target. He stepped outside the tent, his hands tied by the restrictive hours of darkness. The air was cool, the sky wide open and filled with stars. A hundred yards from where he was standing, the bulbous, Plexiglas canopies of ageing Alouette gunships caught at the moonlight; old guns on old aircraft deploying boy soldiers, barely old enough to shave.

## -5-

The screaming went on for a long time. One by one, Rex's men came out from the homestead; subdued and straight-faced – the atmosphere one of finality. The abuse had sprung from aggression; an act of war. Though left alive, the woman and what she stood for had been destroyed.

'We have finished, Comrade Commissar.'

'Her children?'

'We found nothing.'

Rex went back inside the house. The corridors were dark. Sun filter curtains halved the moonlight, furniture had been up-ended, the kitchen trashed and its fridges looted of food. It was their mark – the mark of a warrior – a destroyer. He listened for movement; sounds that would give sign to the children's hiding place. His weight shifted. Glass shards crunched between his boot and parquet flooring. A hall clock marked time with his heartbeat and from the back of the house a woman's mindless blubbering guided him to where his men had left her.

Julie was in the back bedroom. Her wrists and legs were bound with ski rope, secured to the heavy timber rail of the bed's headboard so that her arms were outstretched and her knees drawn up almost to her chest. In the moonlight, her face was pale and death-like; a clip from some bizarre horror film, the re-enactment of some demonic crucifixion. He watched her dispassionately, the way he would watch a fish struggle to breathe on the gutting table.

'Where are your children, Mrs Rennie?'

Her eyes were open, wide and unblinking – a mortally wounded antelope held by the throat. Her mind had almost slipped from bright lucidity to the furthest reaches of some dark forest. The door swung open and Rex sensed the urgency in his men – the soldiers would be there at first light, baying for his scent.

'Wait for me on the outside.' He angled his watch to the moonlight. Six hours of darkness at the most. He would let the woman live, her urgent need of medical attention would delay the soldiers. Killing her and firing the house would negate the impact of what he was leaving behind. A quirk of the white man's nature – they found the sexual abuse of their women by blacks even more abhorrent than the death of a loved one. Psychologically, the effects would be devastating.

He leant forward and turned her face to the window. For a moment, Julie's lids fluttered, her eyes searched him out in the moonlight. He saw in them a world of terror and those unfathomable depths of a mother's loathing.

'Where are the children?' he asked, but already she had returned to that safe and silent place where the reality of what had happened could never reach her.

## 6

Johannes Petrus Bowker cocked his head to the dark. Almost every night the sound of gunfire drifted across to him from the few remaining white-owned farms. Forced by circumstance, he had overcome the initial terrors of living deep inside a war zone, but still his nerves were flayed raw – the threat of attack by ZANLA fighters was ever present. Where once there twinkled lights from a dozen farmsteads, now only moonlight and that from the stars competed with the darkness. No car headlights. No music. No children's laughter, nor the vibrant throb of tribal drums. No yapping village dogs coveting the moon.

The veranda lamp had been trimmed to a slow flame and the old Afrikaner sat with a Rigby double rested across his knees. With expectant fingers he stroked the rifle's stock; satin smooth from a thousand hunts. His wife, Marietta sat alongside him, her hair more silvered than the moonlight, her eyes, though rheumy, blue as a winter sky.

Two cross-bred Rhodesian Ridgebacks lay stretched out at their feet. Wide across the jaw, muzzles deeply scarred by thorn and claw. Black obsidian eyes flecked in gold, the colour of wild honey, like those of the African lion.

Marietta reached out for her husband and though her fingers were arthritically disfigured, there was still that warmth and tenderness.

'We must be vigilant, my darling. Pray that God will stand at our side if the devils come for us tonight.'

'Read to me,' said Johannes. Looking at Marietta, his eyes filled with wonder for what the Lord had given him. 'Still as beautiful as the day I first saw you at the *kirksaal* in Umtali.'

Marietta squeezed his hand. She smiled through the lamplight though it was worry, not laughter that lined her face – her eyes were deep set and ringed with tell-tale blue shadows; evil, that permanent companion to the oppressed had come to live beside her. She drew the Great Book in front of her. She sprung the clasps; three hundred years of family worship had worn them almost to nothing. The covers were of full calf over bevelled boards, sombre and portentous – black as old blood.

'Our people's Covenant with God Almighty,' Johannes suggested. 'With a clear voice my darling.'

Marietta settled her reading glasses and gave her eyes time to adjust, though there was no need for she knew the words off by heart. The writing was that of the devout believer, put to a leaf of loose manila with a goose's feather and black ink – a handwritten commitment to God, still powerful and compelling. The words symbolised the very existence of the Afrikaner nation.

*Here we stand, before the Holy God of heaven and earth, to make to Him a vow that, if He will protect us and deliver our enemies into our hands, we will observe the day and date each year as a day of thanks, like a Sabbath, and that we will erect a Church in His honour, wherever He may choose and that we will also tell our children to join with us in commemorating this day, also for coming generations. For His name will be glorified by giving Him all the honour and glory of victory.*

'1838.' Johannes nodded gleefully. 'The Battle of Blood River, a fight to end all fights. It was the will of The Almighty.' His eyes glowed. 'My great-grandfather stood shoulder to shoulder with Andries Pretorius. Ten thousand Zulus defeated by a handful of Boers; a God-given victory, my darling'

The same thoughts he had voiced a thousand times, as

always and without complaint, Marietta listened avidly. The words instilled in her the will to fight and though neck and neck with fear, excitement tripped her breathing; a young woman's heart was beating the drum, she would stand at her husband's side and fight to the end. Somewhere out there in the night, in that darkest of African nights, the descendants of Dingaan and Dambuza were again honing their spears for war.

*

Rex halted his men at the top of a wooded ridge. The border with Mozambique was little more than twenty miles east of where they were standing. Again the cadre leader looked down on a white-owned homestead. As long as the dark lasted he had the edge – the upper hand. No one would follow, not before first light. By then he would be well out of reach. Up to that moment luck had been with them – the killing had been swift and without return fire, but now a strange and more powerful presence seemed to emanate from the low burn of a homestead hurricane lamp. Someone was there, in the shadows. With the eyes and ears of a hunter, another human being was casting for sound and movement. A woman's voice, soft though clear rose up to him.

Johannes Bowker slid his hand into the side pocket of his hunting jacket. Habitually, his fingers toyed with twenty, Speer African Grand Slam solids. Unlike those of the Mauser and the Lee Enfield, these were heavy, 400 grain metal jackets – each cartridge almost as thick as his index finger and only just short of four inches long from tips to the back of their rimless casings. At over two thousand feet per second, the solids would punch a hole through a brick wall and at fifty yards, would meet the charge of a bull buffalo with the head-on shock of an express train. He reached for the .416 side-lock Rigby. Not since he hunted elephant in The Valley had he fired it with intent. Light from the lamp enlivened the deep patina of both barrels; through shades of gunmetal blue to silver, the colour of raw steel. The stock was solid walnut – exquisitely patterned – dark as oiled iron.

Both dogs lifted their heads and stared at the night. Simultaneously, they stood up, backs almost matched to the height of the table. Something had moved. The smallest of sounds had spirited in from the forest.

'You must go inside,' Johannes whispered to Marietta.

Now the dogs, silent as arctic wolves were hunting the fence line.

'And do what, my heart?' Again, she reached for his hand and studied her husband's face in the lamplight, as if that moment would have to last for all of one eternity.

Rex locked onto the dogs. The animals were quartering, hunting – repeatedly crossing the gardens with their heads up and nostrils flared for scent, their leonine quarters powerfully muscled from a diet of raw meat and maize meal porridge. Their jaws were heavily armoured from Johannes' purposeful crossing of Mastiff with Ridgeback – the compression of their bite bettered only by that of the spotted hyena. The dogs left nothing to chance. They hunted instinctively and like denizens of Greek mythology floated silently from moonlight to shadow – from rockeries to garden sheds, ploughing through shrubs and islands of black cannas.

Rex scoured the fence for weaknesses; devoid of lights, but at four metres high and topped with vicious razor wire the galvanized pig-mesh barrier proved a formidable deterrent. They had to breach the gate – cutting a hole through the heavy fence would bring the dogs on to them. He whispered instructions to the man next to him.

'Go with your comrades and wait near the gates. On your life, do not cut the chains before I open fire or the dogs will be at your throats.'

He waited for their signal – the cry of the hunting owl. From a dead rest, with only the moon to light the rifle's foresight he squeezed the trigger.

As a beating of hellish wings, a hurricane of automatic fire echoed about the valleys. Marietta sat so very still. Johannes had seen the bullet strike; a sharp hammer blow to the centre of her sternum. The stinkwood chair held her upright – her hands so small, still resting on the table and though now her eyes were sightless, her physical presence instilled in him a fierceness of heart. A strange and almost godlike exhilaration rose up from inside of him – a final acceptance – a nearness to the Creator.

The hurricane lamp flew from its hanging. Fire, as gleeful yellow pools spread from the ruptured lamp bowl, but Johannes paid no heed to it. He fired into the shadows – down towards the gates – at the sound of slipping chains and that of running feet. Now the dogs were barking, frantic with fear and excitement and Johannes saw them break from shadow to moonlight – driving forwards like a hunting pack for the scent of lion.

One more time, Johannes bent and kissed Marietta's forehead. There was still the smell of jasmine in her hair.

'I will be with you soon, my sweet. But first there are matters here that I must attend to.' Without looking back, he reloaded the Rigby and stepped out into the night.

## 7

Rex broke cover and followed his men through the opening; the dogs, grey wolves in the moonlight. Now his men were firing from the hip, their rifles on semi-automatic. Fire lit up the homestead's frontage and the first shot from a heavy gun thundered over the chaos of small arms fire. Unperturbed by the gunfire the dogs came on, spirit-like they seemed to float above the earth.

'Kill them!' Rex heard himself screaming and fired from the shoulder. The male was driven backwards – flung lifeless amongst the cannas. Wide of its attackers, like a leopard the bitch came in low to the ground. For one fleeting moment, Rex saw her – sounds from her throat were those of a wild, demented beast – her eyes mere slits above the powerful arch of her muzzle – her mouth was a dark abyss lined with ivory fangs.

Gripped by supernatural dread, the man to Rex's right hand froze. Like a crocodile from the river's edge the cross-breed lunged for his throat and rolled him into the flowers. She held him fast, shaking her head with demonic strength until the vein in his neck ruptured and the life gushed out of him.

Johannes fed the Rigby's breech with his last two cartridges. Like the air around him, both barrels were smoking hot. Shapes stepped out from the smoke; those of men, dark silhouettes driven forwards by some deep fanaticism. Soon there would be nothing left. The fire would take it all. Closely bunched, the intruders were a black wave about to break at his feet.

Johannes fired with the Rigby pulled hard against his side. This time, both bullets found their mark and as though driven backwards by some unseen fist, two of his attackers were swept away. The others were close now – close enough for Johannes to see the hatred in their eyes, the fire, now a vengeful inferno behind him.

Wind came in from the north. The flames swung round and licked against his head and shoulders – his hair sparked as a halo of tiny lights. Spent casings rattled about his feet and only when the Rigby dropped from Johannes' fingers did Rex step out from the shadows.

For that smallest of moments the two men stared at each other. Between them flew a hundred years, a thousand reasons. Ancient prophecies, the creak of wagons over rough ground and a woman's yearning for infinite horizons, the strengthening of one man's belief and the imminent death of another.

Rex levelled the Kalashnikov and fired a single shot through Johannes Bowker's heart.

## -8-

First light had barely separated the night sky from Africa when two Fireforce Alouettes uplifted simultaneously and howled away from the tiny settlement of Chipinga. Within minutes, the whine of their Artouste engines had faded – the beat of their rotors barely audible. Urban smallholdings, gravel roads and the smoke from first fires were quickly left behind. To the east, hills covered with exotic hardwoods straddled the border with Mozambique, their summits capped with cloud, their crags and valleys threaded with silver streams – scarfed in blue mist.

Captain Lee Goddard crouched to the gunship's starboard Browning machine gun. Directly below, rows of burgeoning coffee bushes ranked in their hundreds. Against a hillside, the Rennies' garden stretched park-like between the trees. The house was in darkness. Close to the back fence, Julie's pedigree Doberman lay with its head twisted back at an awkward angle. Crows fled the growl of flogging rotors; a black cacophonous cloud from around the pool.

'Down there on the lawn!' Lee shouted, and as they went in low the worst of all his fears stared up at him.

Towels and T-shirts leapt from the downdraft. Loungers up-ended and a red ball spun across the surface of the swimming pool. The water looked dull – sullen. The sparkle had gone from it.

From ten feet, four men dropped from the Alouette and deployed as a defensive ring of firepower. The second Alouette circled low, above the homestead with its port side twinned Brownings angled and cocked.

'Confirm no movement?'

The pilot's voice hissed from the radio's handset.

'Nothing, Lee. They would have opened fire. They're long gone.'

Lee went forward. A strangeness – a morose feeling of emptiness hung about the Rennies' home; the heart torn out of it. Both Alouettes powered down – and silence, that of a sinister killing field screamed at him from open patio doors. Sergeant Lewis, Lee's number two, covered the barns and outbuildings.

# -9-

It was still too cold for flies; they would come later with the heat, swarming for the blood. Lee pushed the rate of fire selector on his FN rifle to semi-automatic then slipped silently through the open doorway. Apart from his breathing there was no sound. He crouched in the half-light of the corridor and waited for his eyes to adjust, then swung left to where he remembered Julie's kitchen. He pushed the door back against the wall. Ice-cream dripped from an open freezer box. Julie had taped a child's homemade calendar to the door of the refrigerator, 'Eleven today' had been felt-tipped across the 24th. They had insisted on him being at the party – the present was already bought and wrapped. He hawked the sickly scent of ice-cream from his throat and backed into the corridor.

Lewis came back through the gardens. Sunlight shone in patches under the trees, mildly warm. Dull shadows covered the pool's deep end. Mike Rennie's upper torso, buoyed by trapped air, showed above the surface. Crows had been at his face; perched on his chest they had enlarged the wound. Excited by a plethora of soft tissue they had gorged on ruined eyes and the soft innards of Mike Rennie's shattered skull. Lewis shook a cigarette free of its packet and lit it. The flame trembled.

*

Six doors lined the corridor walls; from memory, Lee recalled the guest room. Only a month ago, he had stayed for the weekend. Julie's kids, Helen and Carol had brought him breakfast. At night they all sat by the pool and watched the sky fill up with stars. Mike cooked steak over an open fire and Julie, stunningly beautiful, poured the drinks and put on the music.

He pushed back the first door, the girls' bedroom – pink curtains and pillows, pink carpet, pink-framed nursery rhyme pictures above the beds. No children. No blood. Clothes, toys and a trashed cassette recorder were strewn across the floor. The room had been destroyed, but there was no blood. When people died out here on their farms there was always blood.

Lewis stood next to him. The sun was higher now; broken yellow shapes filtered in from the garden. He touched Lee's shoulder.

'The swimming pool.'

'The kids?'

Lewis shook his head. 'Their old man.'

'Try the lights,' Lee told him.

Lewis found the corridor switch. Fluorescents flickered, struck and lit up the passage. A white kitten had been pulped against the parquet floor.

'To your left,' said Lee. 'The bathroom, check it out.'

Lewis flicked on the light and pushed back the door. It was empty. ZANLA FORCES had been scrawled across the tiled wall in bright red lipstick. Water pumped from a ruptured sink pipe. Toothbrushes and toiletries lay strewn across the bathroom floor. The toilet pan was full; the smell from it mixed with cologne and toothpaste.

'Clear.'

'Door on the right,' said Lee. 'The kids' playroom. Open it.' His heart raced. Julie wouldn't have left the children alone. Not the forward thinking Julie. There would have been contingency plans. Her and Mike would either have got the girls out or hidden them – inside the house –

388

somewhere guarded, ultra safe. He resisted the urge to call out.

'No one here,' said Lewis.

Again the room had been trashed; toys symbolically crushed and kicked against the wall. He sensed the children. Their smell was there in the room. Lee moved into the corridor and went straight to the furthest door – the master bedroom. Mike had shown him the bedroom's outlook across the farm; a clear view of the mountains and in the summer, in the earliest part of the morning, the sun was always there in the picture window. The door was slightly ajar. He could hear someone breathing; soft, shallow exhalations.

# -10-

Julie's eyes were wide open. Her face, once vibrantly alive now wan and expressionless. Silently, she followed changing patterns of sunlight and shadows on the ceiling. An army medic adjusted the drip flow.

'Talk if you want, she won't hear you.'

'What are her chances?' Lee asked.

'Sixty-forty, if we get her back in time. She's lost a lot of blood but without a full examination I would be guessing. Christ knows what those perverse bastards did to her.'

Julie's eyes closed. The drugs had shut her away. The medic swabbed away dried blood from her wrists, the ski rope had chafed through her skin – left her wrists and ankles with bloody bangles of raw flesh. Her lips, in places, were bitten clean through. Lewis appeared in the doorway.

'Get a stretcher down here, Sergeant and warn the pilot he'll be uplifting at least one casualty.' The medic finished taping the drip line to Julie's forearm. He looked sideways at Lee.

'Still no sign of the children?'

'Not yet. My men are combing the gardens and outbuildings.'

'You've obviously searched the house?'

'Twice. We've come up with nothing.'

'I need another ten minutes or so before we're ready to uplift. Check again, Lee. The kids are here. They're too frightened to come out. They wouldn't have left the house – not once the firing started.'

Lee went back through the rooms. Systematically, he checked each one for things that he may have overlooked. Helen and Carol would be out of their minds with fear. They had to be somewhere close. Mike would have made sure of a hiding place, the kids were his life. He searched for the less obvious: a hidden alcove, suitcase wells above built-in wardrobes, even the ceiling trapdoor was shoved open and with a powerful torch from Julie's kitchen. Lee probed to the furthest corners of the roof void, sweeping the torchlight back and forth through the darkness. There was no sign of anyone having been there. Desperate for time he called out. 'Helen! It's Lee. Your mother's safe. Talk to me, Helen, where are you?'

A bird flapped out through a hole in the gable end. Already the heat had started to build between the ceiling boards and corrugated iron roof sheets. No answer. He listened for movement – sounds that might filter up from the rooms below. Footsteps inside the corridor, but nothing else, no voices other than that of the medic barking instructions to the stretcher bearers.

Back inside the corridor, Lee increased the intensity of his search, anxiously sifting through the shattered household for something he might have missed. Nine o'clock. Sunlight streamed through open patio doors – glittered off broken glass – brought in the flies. Carol's favourite, tattered rag doll stared at him from the far side of the lounge.

## -11-

Mike Rennie had inlaid the lounge walls with natural stone quarried from the hillside; the locals called it glitter stone. With the iridescence of a peacock's feathers it reflected the incoming morning sunlight – blues and greens streaked with gold and silver, the colour of sunlit rain against the mountains.

In the dark, the insurgents had missed the family portrait. Hung high on the chimney breast, the picture, done in oils blended almost perfectly with the stonework. It would have been torn down – symbolically destroyed. Beneath it, caught between the fireplace wall and grate, the rag doll – red-haired and worn. Lee picked it up. The doll's arms were still moist, its face smeared with old fire soot.

'Helen, can you hear me?' With persuasive undertones, Lee called out to the children. He knew they were there, huddled inside some hidden alcove. 'Your mother needs you, Carol. It's safe to come out.' He could hear them; bare-footed, rustling against the stonework. Terrified, they clung to one another in the darkness. In the torchlight, Lee picked out the ladder; twist-bar rungs set to the back wall of the granite fireplace, big enough for tiny feet and fingers. Hidden above the grate, Mike had built a recess in the chimney breast – just enough space for his girls.

Helen's face materialised in the torchlight.

'You're lying,' her voice spat down at him. 'They killed her. I heard them do it, so you're lying I know you are.' She withdrew, back behind the dark veil of her hiding place

'She's alive, but she's hurt and needs a doctor. Your mother needs you with her. Believe me Helen, I'm not lying.'

Silence at first, then the face reappeared.

'Where is she?'

'In the helicopter. We're taking her to hospital.'

One at a time the girls came down from their hide. They stood in front of Lee, wide-eyed, unable to comprehend the destruction. Outside, stretcher bearers were loading Julie into the Alouette; the plasma drip bottle held high by the flight tech. Lewis came back through the patio doors. He kept his voice down and turned his back to the children – his expression grim.

'More trouble,' he told Lee. 'Smoke – looks like old man Bowker's place.'

Lee felt his stomach turn. The children stared up at him, blank faced – both covered in fire soot. Carol clutched her doll. Helen stood defensively close to her sister. Lee handed his rifle to Lewis and scooped up both little girls. He tried to smile, but inside, anger and revulsion had already taken charge.

'Have the second chopper stand by – yourself and two others. The rest stay here. Make sure we have spare batteries for the radio and two days rations – no more.'

The medic took charge of the children. Julie's eyes were

still closed; her breathing shallow. Strapped to the stretcher she looked so small. Helen and Carol covered their ears. Lee signalled the pilot to uplift and shielded his face from debris whipped away by the downdraft. Within minutes, the Alouette had disappeared.

\*

From the helicopter, what was left of the Bowker's homestead showed as little more than a black scar on the ground. Fanned by the rotors, rekindled fire sprang from the ashes. A mass of white, Barberton daisies leant away from the wind. Nothing else moved. The security gates had been flung wide open.

Lewis shouted above the noise.

'Just outside the smoke – down there between the gate and the house!'

Lee hung out from the open hatchway. A storm of white ash rolled through the gardens, then curled upwards from the perimeter of the downdraft. Again, revulsion rushed over him; bodies – one of them badly charred – another two lay sprawled in the flowers, thrown aside by the terrible hydrostatic impact of heavy calibre bullets. Dead insurgents, Lee realised with grim satisfaction. Old man Bowker had not gone down without a fight.

'Get us down there!' Lee shouted, and as the pilot edged towards a clearing the full horror of the attack unfolded. At twelve feet, troopers spilled from the Alouette and immediately secured the area, then in extended line, Lee took them through the devastation.

In direct sunlight, rampant decomposition had already blown the bodies with foul air; greenbottle flies had been quick to find the dead. Disturbed by the troopers, they rose as jewelled clouds, but settled again just as quickly – covering the wounds and other soft exposed body parts, laying their eggs in their tens of thousands whilst feeding on the putrefaction.

Johannes Bowker lay on his back, his arms thrown outwards. The Rigby double had been left where the old man dropped it, close to the steps. ZANLA had no use for the white man's obscure preferences in firearms. Lee picked up the Rigby and broke the barrels. Johannes' last two spent cartridges ejected onto the walkway.

Like a chill wind, a strange feeling of personal loss came over him, the urge to stay with the old man's corpse inexplicably strong, almost overwhelming. He forced himself to walk away.

'Look for survivors!' Lee ordered, but he knew they would not find any. Lewis beckoned to him from the burnt out frontage.

Marietta Bowker lay with her hands still clasped in front of her. Her blackened features were totally disfigured. The fire had cut her corpse to the bone, her charred limbs now shrivelled and stick-like. Prised away by extreme heat, her lower jaw was lost beneath the ash. The air about the ruined veranda reeked of fatty pork. It was the smell of roasting human flesh. Even upwind of the ash pit the smell followed and stuck in Lee's throat – he felt his stomach heave. In a single night, the Bowkers, along with their faith in God Almighty had been wiped from the hillside.

'The tracker has picked up their spoor, Captain, outgoing from the back fence.'

'How many?'

'Three sets of prints, heading east for the border.'

Lee glanced at his watch; seven hours since sunrise. The border with Mozambique was no more than twenty miles east of where he was standing, they could already have crossed over. He looked up at the mountains and deep forests – based on the terrain and remaining daylight, he made his decision.

'Sergeant Lewis. Get the men back inside the chopper, radio Sierra Bravo, tell the Major we're going after them.'

## -12-

Through pacing himself to the luminous sweep of his watch's second hand, Rex was able to calculate their rate of march. He followed streams that he knew had sourced in the high ravines of border hills, and always at a gruelling pace. The moon now behind and low to the western horizon – that first tentative hint of dawn drawing him eastwards.

'I give you one hour.' He slipped his pack. His comrades, plagued by exhaustion fell amongst the shadows and within seconds, both were asleep. The cadre had been culled to three men; the old man and his dogs had cost them dearly.

Where he halted, a stream ran cold and clear. His body ached and the strain of sleepless nights had settled as grit beneath his eyelids. One more day, that was all he asked for; one more day and they would be out of reach.

The sudden cold took his breath away, but then came the invigorating rush of well-being. Stripped naked he waded waist deep and let the stream wash over him.

# -13-

From the foothills, the high forests appeared impenetrable, a perpetually changing wall thick with Teak, Mahogany and the giant Leadwood, the sky above them now a vibrant wash of peach and eggshell blue. Rex picked out familiar points of bearing; a mirror image of his original ingress from the Mozambique border. He needed to reach a point in the hills where they had left a cache of heavier weaponry so that when the gunships came he would be ready for them, or face annihilation. Enraged by what they had found, the white soldiers would hunt him down, wheeling above the forest as vengeful birds of prey – surging ahead in Alouettes to drop their trackers. The hunt would prove relentless. There would be no let up.

He searched out ancient game trails, those barely wide enough to take his men in single file. Where the ground was soft, their spoor showed up as a damning pointer, but he had no choice; without the well-worn trails the forest would hold their speed to that of old men. For five miles they marched without stopping, higher into the forests with the Selinda Mountains, black as sleeping buffalo to their right hand.

'The trees.' Rex recognised the marker, an almost matched pair of ancient red mahogany – over sixty metres tall, their upper boughs were outstretched, spread above the forest canopy like the sails of giant windmills. 'Before dark,' he warned his men, 'we must reach the cache before the soldiers find us or we die in these mountains.'

They rested for twenty minutes and then Rex took the lead at a fast jog, the men behind at ten yard intervals, but always within sight of the man in front. Twice they went to ground; spooked by wild pig crashing through thick undergrowth. Once when a commercial airline's Dakota flew in close to the hills and they lay with bated breath, expectant of that tell-tale snap of opening silk from the aircraft's slipstream.

It was mid-afternoon when Rex found the cache; for an hour they dug with bare hands, pulling aside rock and branches. Inside the mound, protected by roots put out by the giant mahogany, the void was still intact. Warm air rose up from the hole and when Rex reached inside, his fingers found the pliant texture of waterproof wrapping. From their camp in Mozambique, each of his men had carried his own weight in armaments, an arsenal big enough to sustain two complete re-supplies of their original six man cadre. Beside a supply of small arms they had buried other, more lethal weaponry. It was this that Rex searched for now.

'Open the sides,' he ordered. 'On your lives do not move what is buried here.'

He had rigged the trap himself, A Russian made POMZ-2 anti-personnel mine – its spring-loaded striker linked to steel tripwire. A mere two kilogram draw on the wire was enough to fire the detonator. He followed their every move, urging them on, the threat of death now hovering vulture-like above the digging.

Satisfied that the hole was now large enough for him to work with, Rex brushed his men aside and went down on his stomach. He inched forward, into the jaws of the excavation. He worked blind, by touch alone. Inside the mound his fingers groped for the steel tripwire. He prayed that the mine's wooden mount still held firm – rotted through or eaten away by termites the mine could topple; covered by detritus, the device would be rendered unpredictable.

'I've found the tripwire,' he whispered to himself. The sound of his own voice focused his concentration. His fingers worked further along the wire. It was still taught – the way he had left it – stretched between the mine's striker release pin and the piled weaponry. 'I can feel the stake – still upright.' He gently raised his hand to where the tripwire met the grenade; six rows of preformed metal squares encased a core of TNT. A single mistake, a lapse in concentration – either one of them would end his life. With an effective killing radius of ten metres he would hear nothing; not even the metallic snap of the striker's mechanism before he died.

It took Rex the best part of twenty minutes to insert the striker-spring retaining pin. Twice the mine had threatened to topple over and only during a third attempt did he feel the pin engage with its locking hole. With the striker firmly secured he drew the mine clear of its hiding place and set it down at his feet. His men stared at the mine. The matt green canister was no bigger than a can of beans, though from the look in their eyes the devil himself might well have been sitting in front of them.

'The mine is safe,' Rex assured them.

Simultaneously, both men went at the cache with their bare hands. There was no need for Rex to drive them harder, for now a sense of self- preservation wielded the whip. The soldiers were coming. Three men against a possible ten; the odds were stacked against them – by nightfall, what now remained of the cadre might well be wiped out. The remaining miles to the border seemed inexhaustible – the dangers insurmountable. The carnage Rex had left behind, though it was what he had trained for, was now the vengeful lion snapping at his heels

Small arms were routinely set aside. Then, like a treasure exhumed from some ancient tomb, a Strela launcher still in its green, protective moulding was carefully lifted out from its hiding place.

'Now the missiles,' Rex instructed. One by one the protective tubes were drawn from the mound. 'Two is enough.' He looped the launcher's carrying strap across his chest and urged his men to close the digging. Once the hole was closed up they covered the mound with rotting vegetation, matching it to the forest floor as best they could. Rain would settle the earth, hide their digging. He prayed for rain.

# -14-

Again they marched in single file. Within the hour, Rex ordered his men to strip their packs to the bare minimum. They threw off everything but their weapons, ammunition and precious water bottles. The Strela's carrying strap chafed his shoulder raw, and still, Rex increased the pace, pushing himself and his comrades to the very brink of exhaustion. His own pack threatened to weigh him down – the dead weight of a Rhodesian military radio set he had taken from the Rennies' house sat hard against his spine. Once they reached high ground the radio would become his eyes and ears. For as long as the batteries held their charge, transmissions from within a radius of twenty miles would warn him of any follow-up operations; keeping him one step ahead of pursuing soldiers.

'Another hour,' Rex encouraged his men upwards. Where

the forest opened he checked the sky for movement. Fickle winds and the damping effects of thick forest would mute any sound of approaching turbines. Without his constant vigilance the Alouette pilots would quickly single him out – flies to an open wound.

They reached high ground just as the western skyline darkened with rain clouds. It was then, from the brink of a granite ridge that he had the first inklings of its approach. Insect-like, the Alouette G-car appeared as a tiny moth fluttering to a window of black sky; close to the forest canopy the matt grey livery rendered the hunter's presence almost undetectable.

# -15-

Rex took his men into deep cover just minutes before the Fireforce gunship howled overhead. Within that brief moment he recognised the soldier stood in the hatchway and his breathing checked. From behind the twin barrels of a .303 Browning machine gun the soldier's doleful stare swept the forest for sign. The pilot altered course; a low, sweeping arc to starboard. A mile out from Rex's position the helicopter turned on its axis and hovered there, like a dragonfly about to touch its tail to the surface of a lake. From both sides, soldiers dropped to the ground – light as sprinters straight from their starting blocks they disappeared inside the forest.

'Ready the launcher!' Rex ordered, and threw off the encumbrance of his own backpack. The soldiers had leapfrogged ahead, gambling on him not having reached the border. His ploy, if it worked, would give him back the advantage – shake the hounds from his scent.

One man stripped away the launcher's protective casing, whilst another drew out the first of two projectiles. Rex opened his pack and reached inside for the A63 military radio. He turned the channel selector to '4' and switched on the power. The battery indicator swung to full. For a moment, only a low sibilance from the handset's earpiece, then the carrier band hummed to life and a familiar voice confirmed Rex's recognition of the face behind the Browning. He let the incoming transmission end before pressing the transmit key on the telehand.

'You are a competent adversary, Captain.'

The carrier band froze; still active, but silent. Rex sensed the confusion.

'Who is this? What is your call sign?'

'No call sign, Captain.'

He instructed the man alongside to help him settle the launcher and then switched on the power supply. The launcher sat comfortably across his right shoulder, exactly to the weapon's point of balance. He transferred the radio's handset to his left hand then again, looked to his men.

'Load!'

The nine kilogram Strela 2 missile clunked against the ignition terminals in the launcher's tail section. For a moment the Alouette hung motionless above the drop zone and then, like an eagle leaving its young, swung towards the northwest.

'Time is running out, Captain. For the sake of your comrades, give me your word that you will open the way for us and I will let them live.'

'Identify yourself. I say again give me your call sign?'

Now, the Alouette was less than a half mile out from Rex's position – its flight path a high, climbing arc above the skyline.

'You know me well, Captain, yet in so many ways we are strangers.' Rex gauged the time he had left, paused for a few more seconds and again pressed the transmit key. 'Your indecision has let you down, Captain. The choice has been made for you.'

Rex dropped the handset, both hands were needed to steady and fire the missile. At three hundred metres above the forest, the target was perfectly suited to the SAM's capabilities. Through the iron eyepiece, Rex tracked the target and applied half trigger, uncaging the weapon's seeker electronics. A green target acquisition light came on and the audio warning buzzed as a swarm of angry bees. He fully depressed the trigger. A red 'locked-on' visual indicator glowed like a raptor's eye, urging him to use the launch window before the aircraft dropped out of range. Instinctively, like a hunter preparing himself for the recoil he leant into the shot.

Lee saw the missile rise from the forest canopy – a thread of silver vapour linked it to the earth. Compared to the speeding missile, the Alouette was a slow and cumbersome thing – floundering and awkward. In excess of four hundred metres a second the Strela missile appeared intuitive, an electronic predator with the committed mindset of a stooping falcon. Rex had been forced to wait for the Alouette to pass; a frontal attack would have stood little chance of success. The Strela 2 was a chaser, a revenge missile – needing powerful, infrared emissions from the hot throat of an aircraft's exhaust nozzle to excite its seeker. A storm sky formed a macabre backdrop, a wall of black rain. A feather of white light flicked from the

Alouette's engine and like a wild fowl struck by the hunter's shot the aircraft shuddered.

Rex discarded the launcher and recovered the radio handset.

'I know you are watching, Captain.' He held down the transmit key. The crippled Alouette was sucked beneath the forest canopy. Even at half a mile distant the sound of an aircraft tearing itself to pieces would have carried over the radio.

'I think you will agree, Captain – a dramatic finale? Perhaps – who knows? If you had taken up my offer your comrades might well have lived.' He released the transmit key. For long seconds there was silence; then the carrier band hummed angrily.

'You sick bastard!' Lee shouted into the handset. Like clearing mists, the realisation hit him. 'I will find you, Rex! You'll never get through!'

'At last, we have a name. Welcome back, Captain.' His smile showed up in his voice. 'I would say we are equidistant from the crash site, your comrades may well have survived. For their sakes, Captain, pray that you reach them first.'

*

Lee panned his binoculars slowly over the forest canopy. A plume of black smoke rose from the trees and he knew the Alouette's fuel had ignited. Angst, guilt and barely controllable rage were now conflicting emotions. His men sensed a growing pall of indecision and watched from the treeline. Sergeant Lewis stood alongside him.

'The bastard's sucking you in.'

'Mind games,' Lee agreed. 'He's using the chopper crew

403

as bait. They might be alive.'

Lewis shook out a cigarette. His eyes ringed with blue shadows. Already the day had taken its toll. His hand shook when he put up the lighter.

'He'll kill them and be long gone before we get anywhere near the crash site.'

Lee shook his head. 'It's a ruse. He's running out of time, he has to go for the border.'

The leading edge of the storm was almost over the valley. Again Lee put up the binoculars, this time he searched eastwards to where the valley narrowed; a natural breach in the hills. Short of Rex taking on a ten mile climb over steep terrain, the narrow rift in the granite was his only logical option.

'Get the men moving, Sergeant, before we lose the light.'

\*

An hour after dark the storm broke. To either side of the valley, lightning flew at the high hills and as restless lions, thunder growled. Lee looked up at the sky, deep cloud shut out the stars. If he were Rex, now would be the time he would choose to run for the border. First drops slapped at the granite. The air lit up, crackling with ozone and white fire.

'He has to come.' Lee told himself and stared at the dark. Doubt breathed inside his collar. Rex could have pre-empted his decision, taken his men deeper into the hills. The single, narrow escape route guarded by steep ground would lend to a swift and easy exit, but was it too obvious a lure? The luminous dial of his watch showed eight o'clock. Where he lay, already the ground was saturated. At his sides, Lewis and the others had burrowed in with the undergrowth; four men, flimsy defence against hardened guerrillas. Only the barrels of their FN rifles showed through the foliage. Lewis reached out and touched his arm. Lightning lit up the whites of his eyes and though he said nothing his sense of urgency cut through the silence.

At first, only the trees moved, lashed by the storm. Weird shapes jinked and ran with the rain – imaginary fighters. Then, as if spirited there by sleight of hand, three ghostly figures stood out from the chaos. Instinctively, Lee's finger curled inside the trigger guard.

## -16-

Not since that fateful night at Bella's house had Rex experienced the opulence of grand living, though many times with fanciful disregard for his commitment to the armed struggle, his mind had wandered. He had not meant it to be this way. Bella's vehement ending of their friendship had cut him deeply. The chance of a head-on confrontation with Lee had not for a single minute ever crossed his mind. However, they were soldiers and like bulls to the final thrust of the matador's sword, both would stand their ground and fight. Within those next few hours either one of them, or both, might well be dead. He prayed that Lee had gone in search of the Alouette; for fate to keep them apart.

*

In the space of two hours they reached the valley head, beyond it and masked by the night, Mozambique waited. From the front, Rex led what remained of his cadre down inside the storm.

At seventy metres out, the moving figures appeared grotesquely ethereal. Weakened by fatigue, Lee struggled to maintain concentration; his vision confused by intermittent lantern shows of light and dark. From the storm's black throat, rain fell as a solid wall to his front. Then, as suddenly as it had begun the rain eased. Snared by changing winds the storm faltered and sulked away to the south-east.

They came in single file, rifles at the high port. The RPD, supported by its carrying sling, balanced comfortably against the gunner's hip – all three men at a fast walk, using the softened ground to hide their footfalls. Then the cloud broke and from the eastern horizon silver light shot inside the valley.

Now, backlit by the moon, Lee's men were thrown into sharp contrast with the undergrowth, their cover stripped away. In that first devastating, ten second burst, two of them died, the life driven out of them by the RPD's hellish cyclic rate of fire; a full drum magazine of one hundred rounds. The return, intermittent firing of FN rifles stood for little against the RPD's blanketing firepower.

Robbed of the covering storm, Lee flattened against the earth, firing two-round bursts at an invisible aggressor. Again, gunfire raked the ground, mere feet in front of him. Lewis stopped firing. The bullet had struck precisely at the centre of his forehead. Reloaded, the RPD clattered incessantly, though now at a silent enemy.

Rex waited for the first showing of daylight before he broke cover. Both his men stood with him – unscathed. On the sodden field before them, nothing moved. Four bodies, those of white soldiers lay crumpled where they had fallen. He waved his men forwards. A quiet sky hung above the killing ground. The air was warm – fragranced with the smells of battle and wet earth.

'Comrade Commissar, one of them still lives.'

Rex kicked the soldier's rifle out of reach and crouched alongside him. The man's eyes were widely dilated; the bullet had found the highest point of his forehead – splitting the scalp at a steep angle whilst sparing the harder dome of his skull.

'On your life, Captain, do not try to fight me – raise your hand if you can hear me.'

Lee moved his fingers. He lay on his side; his hair thickly matted with blood.

'You will live,' Rex assured him. From his own pack Rex took out a waterproofed medipack and tore it open. From a smaller packet he selected gauze bandage and a padded dressing. 'This will hold back any bleeding until they find you.' He looped the bandage beneath Lee's chin; up and over his head, applying pressure to the wound. He unclipped the water bottle from Lee's belt and managed to pour a little water between his lips. Pulling Lee's radio clear of the grass, Rex unbuckled the waterproof flap and drew out a standard military ordinance map. A three digit call sign had been written across the back. Rex switched on the set and depressed the telehand's transmit key. The downed pilot would have sent out distress signals.

'All stations, all stations – this is call sign two-two alpha – do you read?'

The response was immediate. 'Strength five, two-two alpha - this is yellow-one. Confirm your call sign is still in vicinity of downed chopper?'

'That's affirmative, yellow-one. Three miles east of crash site. Request immediate assistance. Four men down. One in urgent need of a doctor.'

'Already in-bound to crash site. ETA figures ten minutes. Stay on this channel. Confirm you are in need of back-up?'

'Negative, yellow-one. They have already crossed into Mozambique. Will talk you in once I have you visual.'

An hour at the most and the incoming patrol would find him.

*

'If I could move I would kill you.'

'Your gratitude overwhelms me, Captain.' Rex pushed the telehand between Lee's fingers. 'Anger is good. It will keep you alive. Perhaps this time we have both won – if only a little.'

Rex stood up. The border was close; the time left for him to reach it was running out. Though still far off, he could hear the bass rumble of Alouette rotors.

'The war is almost over, Captain. Go back home and open your mines. Zimbabwe will need all the gold it can get its hands on.'

For a moment, Rex sensed a faint resurrection of old camaraderie, but he knew the feelings were fanciful. It would take time; months, if not years before a compromise of ideals could bridge the rift between them. They would meet again, but that day he knew was far into the future.

'I give you your life, Captain Goddard. Tell Isabella my debt to your family has at last been paid. What I have done, I do not expect you to understand.'

Rex shouldered the Kalashnikov and without looking back struck his fist at the sky.

'*Dzokera imusha*!' He looked to his men. 'We are going home!'

\*

# V

## Zimbabwe, April 18th 1980

# -1-

Two hours had passed since official confirmation of Zimbabwe's independence had been announced over the radio, yet to Captain Lee Goddard it was an eternity. The entire battalion headquarters had been cleared of personnel, only their discarded cigarette butts and empty bottles gave reason to think that anyone had been there at all. Within that short period of time, what had once been the headquarters of a proud anti-insurgent unit was now just a sullied shell, robbed of its soul by the ingress of one, final phone call from Joint Operations Command.

'Give me a couple of minutes,' he told Karen, and waited for her to close the door before cutting loose the pain that balled inside his chest. Through habit, he ran his fingers along the scar above his hairline – miraculously, he had been spared; the bullet had ridden just millimetres beneath his scalp.

'The proverbial wheel has turned full circle, Captain.'

The nuances of the accent were unmistakable. Lee recognised the deep baritone voice of Rex Jando Khumalo – a lion's growl from the shadows.

'How long have you been standing there?'

'Long enough to see how much it hurts to lose an empire.'

Lee turned around.

'You're looking prosperous, comrade. Your President must be paying you well for your efforts.'

Rex stepped out from the doorway; in the bright light his

413

face had that vibrant glow of a man in training. His shoes were Italian leather, his bespoke suit, Savile Row. Sleekly it hung from broad shoulders – a weave of fine, Cashmere, deep and dark as the African night.

'Isabella?' Rex queried. 'How is your grandmother?'

'She's good, considering the circumstances.'

Lee felt strangely out of place – detached from reality. His Rhodesian Army uniform just as out of touch with the present as the building he was standing in. Like the loss of a loved one, part of his life had been ripped out. The war was over, though to most Rhodesians their country's impotent fluttering to a standstill had been inconclusive. Smith's government had been strangled into submission, not by military superiority, but by nervous, western hands on its purse strings. Most of the military's top brass had already been spirited across the South African border.

'That day on the hillside,' Lee recalled and the images swirled inside the room – the fire, the smoke, the stench of roasted flesh. 'Were I given the chance, I would have killed you. The Bowkers were innocent – they were good people. You butchered them like dogs.'

'Innocence can be interpreted many ways, Captain. To use your terminology – how many of my own people were butchered? A hundred thousand perhaps?' He shook a cigarette from a pack of twenty. In the empty room his voice echoed. Already, the futile smell of abandonment had enveloped the building. 'An entire nation was decimated; its land divided amongst an army of white invaders.'

'You're talking about a hundred years ago, whatever your historical leanings, what you did to the Bowkers I find unforgivable.'

The discussion was pointless – going nowhere.

'I understand your angst, Captain. War is never the timid benefactor. The farmer died with respect, as a warrior. He expected nothing more.'

'Two old people?' Lee growled, his anger now mere millimetres beneath the surface. 'Both in their nineties? Must have been one hell of a battle, comrade.'

They stared at one another – each man true to his own beliefs and in the poignant confines of a once colonial army headquarters, there was a mental clashing of swords between the old and new orders. Rex flicked back the lid of his Zippo and spun the wheel. Blue smoke curled from between his lips.

'I knew you would be here.'

'So you came to gloat?'

'There would be nothing gained from doing so.' He reached inside his jacket. 'This number will get you in on my private line. When things have cooled down, perhaps we can talk again. And I suggest you leave the building, Fifth Brigade personnel will be here within the hour. Finding a white officer in their local HQ would not be taken lightly.' He paused in the doorway before leaving the room. 'Karen? Still resident archaeologist at Great Zimbabwe?'

'The best there is.'

'And I would never have expected otherwise, Captain. Please pass on my best to her, and to your grandmother – fond memories of her dinner parties.'

Within minutes of Rex leaving the room Lee saw a black, ministerial Mercedes Benz whisper past the window.

# -2-

Isabella Goddard stood with her back to the living room's open fire. Outside, the natural warmth of late sunlight had almost disappeared.

'Damn the man's audacity.' She slammed the tip of her ivory-handled stick at the floor. 'Delusional – sees himself as a reincarnation of his great-grandfather.'

'Lobengula would have been proud of him,' Lee mused. 'No mean achievement – from Mining Engineer to Minister of Mines in the space of a single year?'

Isabella's eyes narrowed at the fact and though her mind was still sharp her eyes had lost their sparkle. Deep-seated memories rallied in support of her abhorrence for political change.

'All those people dead, and for what? A pointless waste of life. All of it.' Again she slammed her stick at the wooden floorboards. The sudden report cracked through the house like a gun shot. 'Cecil Rhodes was too damned soft; that was his downfall. Should have chased the lot of them over the Zambezi and had done with it.'

'You're an indomitable, diehard colonial, Gran. Rhodesia's gone, life would be a lot easier for you if you got used to the fact.'

Bella shook her head, her eyes now fixed to a likeness of her husband hung on the wall in front of her. She had painted the portrait herself, copied from a photograph taken shortly before his death in a time when her hands were still untouched by the tremors of old age.

'Thank God your grandfather is not around to see it. His heart would have broken.' She juggled fantasy with memories. The painting flooded with life. Facing

416

westward, the rounded peaks of the Nyanda Mountains were bold and lush, the first storm of the season had just thundered past – aggressively quick; black with rain and lightning. Her eyes closed and for a moment she sensed the rain and the smell of it and she drew deeply at the air as though the storm were there in the room – raging all around her.

'Walk with me, Lee.'

'Gran, you're...'

'Wasting my time?' Bella interrupted. 'Perhaps I already know that.' She started for a side door; one that opened onto the more secluded parts of her walled garden. 'Humour an old woman,' she asked of him, 'something I want you to do for me.'

Late sunlight patched the lawns and crazy paving. The only sounds were the raucous cries of Swainson's francolin calling down from ravines on the hillside. Bella stopped amongst a grove of Jacaranda; the old trees were thick and rough-barked. Last year's seed pods lay where they had fallen. From her time as a little girl she remembered the flowers. *Like purple snow*, her mother had told her.

'There,' she used her stick as a pointer, 'alongside your grandfather. Promise me you will put me next to him.'

Lee kept his eyes on the gravestone; cursing the angst he knew must follow.

'I promise, Gran, but where is all this leading to?'

'To remembering things that matter, so don't look so damned morbid.'

Her countenance softened. She read from a granite headstone close to the wall. 'Mhlangana Khumalo. Not as a servant, but as a brother he came north with Mathew and Catherine.' Bella went on with the ritual. 'Catherine Goddard, nee Belingham. Now does she lie with those

417

who love her.'

She dropped her eyes from the writing. 'Nathan, her husband, never made it back from Forbes' blunder at the Shangani.'

'He was re-buried with the others at Matopos,' said Lee, they had gone through this a dozen times; his grandmother was quick to forget.

Bella nodded her head. 'Brave men. All of them gone. All their endeavours count for nothing.' She turned away from the tiny family graveyard, her eyes dry, but the pain was now the lion's claws inside her chest.

'Enough, I think. Take me back inside, Lee.'

Before Lee closed the door he caught the doleful wail of the mine hooter. The shifts were changing, miners were going home, others were drawing their lamps ready to go down inside the ground. Above the mine headgear an orange sky was heavily set with dark cloud. Somewhere it was raining.

\* \* \*

Made in the USA
San Bernardino, CA
26 November 2014